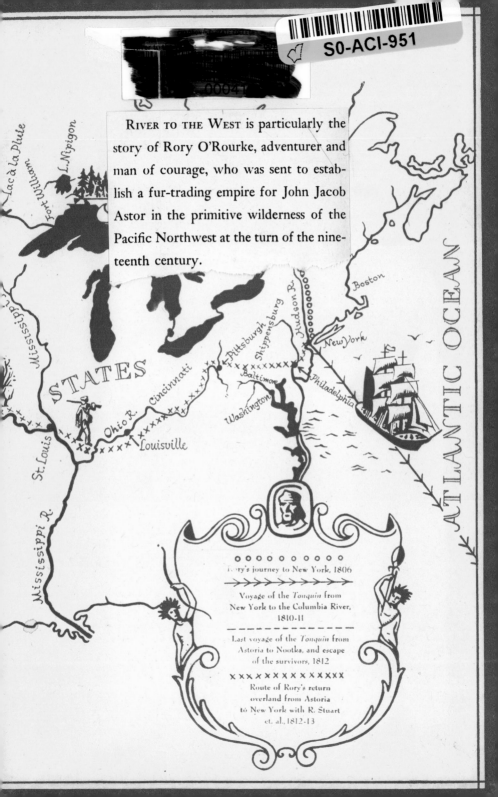

RIVER TO THE WEST is particularly the story of Rory O'Rourke, adventurer and man of courage, who was sent to establish a fur-trading empire for John Jacob Astor in the primitive wilderness of the Pacific Northwest at the turn of the nineteenth century.

Lac à la Pluie

L. Nipigon

Fort William

Mississippi

STATES

Pittsburgh

Shippensburg

Hudson R.

Boston

New York

Cincinnati

Baltimore

Philadelphia

Ohio R.

Washington

St. Louis

Louisville

Mississippi R.

ATLANTIC OCEAN

○ ○ ○ ○ ○ ○ ○ ○ ○ ○
Rory's journey to New York, 1806

〉〉〉〉〉〉〉〉〉
Voyage of the *Tonquin* from
New York to the Columbia River,
1810-11

— — — — — — — —
Last voyage of the *Tonquin* from
Astoria to Nootka, and escape
of the survivors, 1812

x x x x x x x x x x x x
Route of Rory's return
overland from Astoria
to New York with R. Stuart
et. al., 1812-13

River to the West

Books by John Jennings

~~~~~~

A Novel of the Astor Adventure

~~~~~~

RIVER
TO THE WEST

by

John Jennings

GARDEN CITY, N. Y.

Doubleday & Company, Inc.

1948

TO HAL

1938—1948

Ten years to me an agent;
But also Three thousand
Six hundred fifty three
Days to me a friend! In
Deep appreciation of a
Decade passed, and in the
Hope of decades more to come,
This book is affectionately

DEDICATED.

FOREWORD

MUCH time has passed since I stood at the gate of the log fort and looked out through the rain-drenched forest to the mist-ridden, steely rips of the river's mouth. Many of the things I might have said when I was younger have now to be reconsidered, and perhaps it is as well that I have been silent through these years, hoping that the man most concerned would, in his own good time, contrive to tell the tale.

But he is gone now, without speaking, and it seems to me that, in justice, his part in the shaping of those events, so full of consequence to the nation and so lately in the public eye, ought to be told.

There are only a few of us left who took part in the adventure. As I have said, John Jacob Astor is dead; the old warhorse is gone. Alan Fraser, our Cock-of-the-Woods, is an old man and keeps a tobacconist's shop in Toronto. Bob Westlake's straw-colored thatch has turned white. He has long since retired from the Navy, but he keeps to his quarterdeck, straight and tall as a stout pine stick, in the China trade. Gabriel Franchere, toothless and senile, leads a godly, sedentary life in Montreal. Little fox-faced Alec Ross, so I have been told, was last seen on the Red River. MacDougal and Old Concomly were drowned together, long since, in the rips at the Columbia's mouth; in their cups, so it is said, as befitted the sodden lives they led. Mike Shea and the Moose have gone to their maker, as has Robin Stuart, God rest them all! Ramsay Crooks has set up shop in New York. But what has become of all the others—of sullen, swarthy McClellan, or Fats Mackenzie, of the dour Wilson Hunt, of little Jones and grinning Vallee and gangling LeClerc and all the rest, I do not know.

But even if they survive, as I daresay some of them do; and even though they may be familiar with some detail unknown to me, yet I think there will be a few as familiar with the whole story of the venture as I. It may seem that I have included matter that is irrelevant. But I have thought it best to tell it all from my own experience, so that if one day it is pieced together with what others may have to say all of it will be there.

Each one of us who took a hand in the business, I daresay, did so for reasons of his own, quite removed and apart from the results. Some of these I have shown. Others I have not. In the case of our sponsor the outcome was personally disappointing perhaps; yet, as it has transpired, he builded better than he knew. Jonathan Thorn and some others dreamed of wealth and glory but found death and disaster. Most of the rest found quite other than they sought. Only a few—and I count myself among them—found far better than they dreamed.

But whatever may have been the personal aspirations and ambitions that impelled us, I think I am safe in saying that there was not a one of us who foresaw how far-reaching might be the sum of our small efforts. If we trod a stage, it was as unwitting actors. Mr. Astor, it is true, had a vision of power approximating empire; yet even he could only view the expected results through spectacles colored by his own personal desires. As for those who stepped but briefly on our boards, Mr. Jefferson's vision, though less personal, was not less faulty than was Astor's. And the same must be said of Mr. Gallatin and Mr. Madison; indeed, of all the great men of the time! If none of these could foresee what finally would come to be, surely lesser mortals are not to be blamed!

Of all it must be said that whatever ends they had in sight, by their combined strivings toward their own several and perhaps lesser goals, a greater result than any dared imagine has come about.

Today America spreads from ocean to ocean, from the Atlantic to the Pacific. I like to think that it was in small part through all our efforts—and by God's grace, my own—that this has come to be.

ROCHEBLAVE XAVIER O'ROURKE

New York, U.S.A.
December, 1848

Contents

IV
THE TONQUIN

V
ESCAPE

VI
ASTORIA

VII
OREGON TRAIL

VIII
HOME AGAIN

River to the West

I. John Jacob Astor

I. THE COMPANY'S EX-SERVANT

IT IS almost fifty years now since that grim November day when I was called upon to stand up before the Company's overlords and throw up ten years of my life and youth and all that I had then of hope and ambition. Yet I can remember that room as clearly as if it had been only yesterday.

It was a long room—long and somewhat narrow, yet not out of proportion to its enormous height. On one side there were tall, leaded windows looking out upon Vaudreuil Street, each set in a deep bay with a window seat. At the far end of the room there was a single similar window. On either side of the windows, and against the opposite walls, extending from floor to ceiling, was row upon row of books—Company books, books of exploration and travel and history and account, anything and everything that had to do with Canada and the fur trade, for the Company's servants were anything if not efficient. Against the left wall, as I stood, an immense fireplace with a stone mantel and trim of carved, black-stained native walnut, broke the expanse of musty-smelling leather backs, while behind me the only interval in the otherwise interminable shelves made way for the heavy oaken door that gave access to the room from the even longer counting rooms outside. Those counting rooms were alive with the scrape and scratch of quill pens and the murmurous drone of the clerks' whispers, comparing notes. But none of that penetrated here.

Down the center of the room there was a long, heavy oaken refectory table around which were scattered a number of black Windsor chairs, with a sort of heavy master throne at the upper end. There were men in those chairs—men with whom I had served and some of whom I knew intimately—but scarcely recognized at the moment. And there was a fire on the hearth—a blazing fire of stout quartered birch cord-

wood logs, for it was a cold, wet, raw, miserable day outside, and there
was no other heat.

I knew well enough why I was there, though I had not been told in
so many words. The summons to return with the annual brigade from
Fort William, a thousand miles to the west, without any other explanation than that my presence was required by the Partners in Montreal
had only one meaning. They were to sit in judgment upon me; to determine whether, after a decade of service, I had proved worthy of my
salt; whether I was to be summarily dismissed, or whether I was to be
offered the rank and privileges of partnership. Of the latter, I was
well enough aware, there was little chance. It was not that I had not
done my work well, for I was competent enough to be a judge of that.
But I had seen the same thing happen before, and apparently it was a
more or less cut-and-dried proceeding. If a man were to be named a
partner, he was given some hint of it before he left the Lakes. If he
were not, he was fetched home in an aura of synthetic mystery. That
was the way of it. In ten years I had seen younger lads—good boys, to
be sure, yet I doubted more competent than myself—moved forward
over my head. It was not that most of them wished it so, or even that
many of them did. But they were youngsters of good Scots fami-
lies with connections in the right places, and in the Company it was a
case of dog eat dog, a matter of *sauve-qui-peut* and devil take the
hindmost. If you had an advantage, you used it. I could not hold that
against them, for that was the way it went. What chance had I, an
Irishman among Scots, and a Yankee born, at that? Moreover, I knew
well enough that I had not been entirely complacent in those ten
years I had served the Company. I had done my work as I had been
told. But I had my own notions and morals and beliefs, and I had made
enemies—bitter enemies—some of whom were in this room with me
now.

It was, I gathered, not only a committee of notice but a sort of
informal court; a time and a place at which the Company might wash
its dirty linen in private and salve its own conscience without the embarrassment of having the world look on. And I was to be the victim.
Small wonder that the Irish chip I had inherited from my father was
plain to see upon my shoulder!

Sir Alec Mackenzie—he that had been north to the Frozen Ocean in
'89 and again had been the first to cross the continent to the Pacific
in '93—presided in the senior partner's seat, at the head of the long
table. I had seen him from a distance, but scarcely knew him well—
a tall man, shaggy, rawboned in his black broadcloth and spotless stock.

His face was almost round, weathered, his hair tousled. I had seen him good-humored in the field, where it came to me he was at his best. But here his eyes were bright and hard and sharp beneath his overhanging brows, and his mouth was straight and dour with his own self-importance. I could remember once, in the days of Simon MacTavish, when he had been the rebel. But that did not help me now. I knew something of the way in which he presided over Company affairs.

"Mr. O'Rourke," he said, evidently reading from a sheaf of papers on the table before him, "will you stand forward?"

I did so, saying nothing, but only rising from my chair like a prisoner in the dock and coming to stand at the lower corner of the table near the old clerk MacKinnon, whose quill I could hear scratching monotonously.

"You'll save us much bother and pother, Mr. O'Rourke," said Mackenzie, "if you'll give us a brief summary of yourself for the record. 'Twill save me reading through all of this."

He riffled the sheets before him, and I was half tempted to say I had no mind to save him trouble. But then, I reflected, that would do me no good and him little harm.

"My name is O'Rourke," I began.

"We are aware of that," put in the black Scot MacPherson, who sat upon Sir Alec's left.

I had good reason to hate his taunting, sour, sneering way. Yet I ignored him for the moment.

"Rocheblave Xavier O'Rourke," I went on tautly. "My father was Irish and served as an officer under the Young Pretender, in the '45. Later he came to Canada with Montcalm, as a captain in the regiment of La Sarre. After the fall of Canada to the British he settled in Quebec and became an attorney. My mother was Céleste Rocheblave, the daughter of a merchant of Quebec——"

"You may spare us the genealogical details, Mr. O'Rourke," put in Sir Alec dryly.

I am afraid I flushed.

"You are a Canadian?"

At his question, I fear, I did show my resentment. I had been long enough among them to know that these Scots of the Company did not use the word "Canadian" save in a derogatory, sneering sense. To them a gentleman was a Scot or an Englishman, or possibly French. A Canadian was a half-breed, in the main an Indian, for some curious reason a creature to be looked down upon, to be stigmatized.

"I am no Canuck, if that's what you mean," I retorted stiffly. "In fact, I am American born, though I was raised in Canada."

At the end of the room the stranger in the somewhat worn bottle-green coat stopped staring out the window and slewed about to stare, with somewhat phlegmatic interest, at me instead. Who he was I did not know at the time, save that he had come as the elder Henry's guest. He had been introduced to me at the outset of the meeting, but I had not caught his name. I rather resented his presence there at that moment, for, after all, it seemed to me, this was none of his affair. He would do better to keep his nose out of it.

"Indeed?" said Mackenzie softly, and I was abruptly recalled to my position by his tone. I had not, I could see, improved my standing with him by the admission.

"My father offered his services to the Americans during the War of the Rebellion," I explained. "I was born in Bennington, Vermont, in 1782."

"Yes," he said flatly; "that would have been twenty-four years ago. And then?"

I was no more anxious than he to prolong it.

"My parents died of the throat distemper in the winter of 1795–96," I told him. "They left me an orphan, in the care of my uncle Ross MacGillivray, of this city."

"So you came to Montreal," he put in dryly.

"My uncle had some acquaintance with Simon McTavish," I went on, ignoring his interruption, "and through that he obtained for me an apprenticeship with the North West Company in 1796."

"So?" he said. "McTavish? The old marquis?"

Too late I realized that for the second time during that interview I had given him grounds for disapproval. The feud between Mackenzie and McTavish had shaken more than Canada before the latter's death but two years since. Now Sir Alec sat in the marquis's place, and I did not doubt that he had a certain bitterness to all who had upheld or had been upheld by the older man. But there was no withdrawal at this point.

"The same," I told him.

"I daresay he promised you the world and all," he sneered.

"He promised me nothing," I retorted, "save that if I signed the articles I could serve my seven years' apprenticeship, like any other, and stand the same chance of being taken into partnership when that was done and a vacancy occurred. Whether I served my apprenticeship properly I will leave to Mr. MacDougal yonder who was my chief clerk and immediate superior at Grand Portage, before the Company moved to Fort William on the Kaministiquia."

Mackenzie looked at the man I mentioned. In the years since he had become partner Duncan MacDougal had not changed much, though I had seen but little of him. He was still round-bellied, round-headed, bald, rather pear-shaped. If the color of his nose and cheeks meant anything, he had not become less familiar with the bottle since his return to civilization, and I knew him to be pompous, supercilious; fawning toward those who were his superiors; rather domineering to those who were under him. Yet, I felt, he could not deny that I had done my work as well as any during the time I had been in his charge. Nor did he. He nodded, almost reluctantly, it seemed to me.

"Aye!" he growled dourly. "As apprentice clerk I know nae better. A tooch indeepeendent, ye micht say, but scruppelous an' thora an wi' a guid head for figgers. I haenae seen him ootside th' pust, so I would-nae be able tae tell ye mair."

"After Grand Portage," I put in quickly, to forestall any further discussion of that period, "I served as apprentice clerk at Fort Charlotte, as clerk at Fort Vermilion and Ile a la Crosse, and as senior clerk at Fort Chippewyan. The gentlemen here, I believe, will vouch for the quality of my services in these posts."

Mackenzie shrugged. He glanced at David Stuart, in his chair in the far corner. But for himself and the elder Henry and the stranger in the window, Stuart must have been the eldest among us; a quiet man, a mild man, and a great favorite with all of us, yet a man who had waited long years before he had obtained his partnership. I had no fear of what he might say. We had gotten on happily at Vermilion, on the Upper Peace. He nodded.

"I've never known a better clerk, at Fort Vermilion or anywhere else," Stuart said. "I think all this is a bit over-hasty."

" 'Tis not a matter of haste," growled Mackenzie.

He looked at McKay.

"You were in charge at Ile a la Crosse, Ellick," he said. "What have you to say?"

My own glance crossed with Alexander McKay's for an instant, and then he looked away. There was not a man in the Company whom I admired more or who, I felt, was more stoutly my friend. Yet in this one thing, I knew, he had his own convictions. We were agreed in essentials. He was as convinced as I. Yet he did not believe in butting his head against a stone wall. Perhaps I was stubborn. Or it may have been something else that drove me. He was a small man, almost birdlike in his appearance, but with a risibility, a laughing, devil-may-care attitude about him that in many ways reminded me of my father, though, of course, he was many years younger. That may have accounted for his attraction for me. It did not account for our friendship, which was based on years of association. I knew no man I would rather call friend. Yet on this point we differed.

He looked at Mackenzie, almost appealingly, perhaps remembering their journey together across a continent which no white man had hitherto spanned.

"I'll say with Davie Stuart," he answered, a little evasively I thought, "I know of no better."

Mackenzie opened his mouth to speak, but I forestalled him.

"Let us have this out in the open, gentlemen," I said. "We all know the facts of the case. Mr. McKay was chief clerk at Ile a la Crosse at the time, and there were three clerks under him: Derek MacPherson, who sits yonder"—I nodded toward Mackenzie's left—"Angus Mac-Bean, and myself. We were short of meat, for we had lost several canoe-loads on the way in. MacBean and MacPherson and a voyageur named Hamel went north to Lac a la Loche, to hunt. It was an early winter and a hard one, and they were caught there by the snow and forced to stay. Game was scarce. By rights all three would have starved. But MacPherson and Hamel came out in the spring, fat and healthy. MacBean did not come out!"

Dirk MacPherson clutched at the arms of his chair and half rose. I do not think he expected the accusation direct. His black hair, that grew low on his forehead, almost meeting his bushy black eyebrows, drew down in a scowl, and his dark face flushed. Mackenzie waved him down.

"You are saying, Mr. O'Rourke?" he demanded.

The stranger in the window seat leaned forward listening.

"I am saying," I retorted boldly, for it seemed to me that this was the crux of the matter, "that MacPherson and Hamel, between them, killed and ate MacBean, or they would not have survived!"

Mackenzie still held the other Scot back.

"Murder and cannibalism," he said. "Those are serious charges, Mr. O'Rourke! Have you any proof to back them up?"

"I would have," I retorted. "Hamel was ready to sign a confession when he was found hanged from a pine tree near the post."

"He hanged himself!" blurted MacPherson.

"You hanged him," I accused furiously, "to keep him from turning King's evidence, and made it look like suicide!"

There was silence for an instant in the long room—a silence in which the drip of the rain from the eaves outside and the crackle of the fire on the hearth within sounded loud.

"So you have no real evidence, Mr. O'Rourke," said Mackenzie at length.

I could hear MacPherson's breath whoosh out in a long sigh, and I could almost feel the others relax. I shrugged.

"No more than that," I replied.

Mackenzie shrugged and looked at McKay.

"What have you to say about that, Ellick?" he demanded.

McKay looked at me apologetically.

"I have nothing to add to what O'Rourke has said," he replied. "My personal convictions are not evidence, though I agree with O'Rourke."

Mackenzie shrugged.

"Loose charges of this nature are not idly to be flung about," he remarked. "If there is no evidence to support them, for the good of the Company they are best quashed here. Mr. MacPherson is a partner here. Mr. O'Rourke is a clerk."

He turned ominously to MacPherson.

"What have you to say to this?"

MacPherson scowled furiously.

"Bosh!" he growled. "They lie in their teeth!"

"Perhaps God will be the judge of that, MacPherson!" I retorted.

I glanced at the others about the room. The lean, gray Alexander Henry, standing before the fire warming the seat of his breeches, studied his fingernails, much as if to say that he thought well of my case but that the interests of the Company were best served if no more were said of it. Chubby MacLeod and the dullard Grant stared at the table before them woodenly. I could read no support for MacPherson in their expressions. But neither could I see sympathy for myself. Mackenzie looked coldly at the furious MacPherson.

"You were in charge at Chepewayan," he said. "What is your view of Mr. O'Rourke's commercial ability? I believe he was chief clerk under you."

"I found him insubordinate," McPherson flared. "He refused to divert an Indian train bound for the neighboring Hudson's Bay post."

"I do not believe in theft," I interrupted him. "Those Indians had contracted with the Bay people to deliver them their furs. To feed them whisky and induce them to do otherwise would have been no less!"

"He gave longer prices than were proper for the furs he did take in," MacPherson persisted.

"I offer a fair price in trade goods for what I receive," I retorted. Mackenzie waved a hand toward MacPherson.

"I'll keep the chair, Mr. MacPherson," he growled. To me he said: "The Company is in business to make as long a profit as possible for its participants. We are not missionaries, Mr. O'Rourke."

"So I have discovered!" I retorted caustically.

He pursed his lips.

"As you know, Mr. O'Rourke," he went on, "it requires a unanimous vote of all partners before a clerk who has served his time can be elevated to their rank."

"What about David Thompson?" I demanded cockily.

"An exception was made in his case," he replied a little wearily. "He had served his apprenticeship with the Hudson's Bay people, and he possessed knowledge of value to the Company."

"I daresay!" I commented dryly.

"A vote has been taken in your case," he went on, "and the result was not unanimously in your favor. It is the opinion of the board of directors that, while we feel you are an able man in the trade, the interests of the Company will be best served if we have your resignation."

"You have it!" I flared. "There's been no need for all this beating about the bush. I prefer not to serve with men who have no confidence in me——"

"I'm sorry——" He attempted to interrupt me.

"Save your stinking sorrow," I told him, "and put it where it will do the most good. If that's as much as you have to say, I'll give you good day, gentlemen. You may send the balance of my accrued pay to my lodgings. MacKinnon, here, has the address!"

I did not wait to hear more but turned and flung from the room, not hesitating to slam the door viciously behind me.

I daresay some word of what was forward in the inner room had been bruited about in the counting room outside, for as I appeared in the doorway a good number of the clerks I had known and called my friends in the ten years past climbed down from their high stools and came forward to offer me their sympathy and good wishes. There were the little birdlike Gabriel Franchere and the dapper De Montigny, both of whom had gone out with me on that first long voyage to the Lakes so many years ago. There were Robin Stuart, who was nephew to David, and Donald Mackenzie, who was no relative to Sir Alec, but rather one of the dozens of Mackenzies, as plentiful in those parts as Smiths in New York. And there must have been fifteen or twenty others, who were anxious to assure me of their good will. In addition there were added, in a moment or two, some of the partners from the room I had just left: Alexander McKay and David Stuart and dapper, good-natured Roddie McGill. But to these last, I am afraid, I gave but little in return, and for that I do not think I can be blamed. For the moment, at least, I felt that they had betrayed me, that they had let me down, and I fear I did not feel overfriendly toward them.

Yet they delayed me in my passage of the long, cold room, and it must have been twenty minutes or half an hour before I finally found my hat and coat and, jamming the one down about my ears and shrugging my way into the other, I passed out into the long, dank hall and found my way to the wide door that opened upon the muddy half-paved street.

I was balancing on the step, wondering which way I would turn now, my mind so bewildered by the abruptness of what had befallen me that I could not bring it to heel and form any sort of plan, when I became aware of a figure standing at my elbow, and turning, saw to my surprise the rotund, rather thick-set man in the bottle-green overcoat who had sat so quietly in the window bay all through the meeting in that long room. As I turned he smiled at me amiably.

"Miserable! Miserable weather, ya?" he demanded.

"It's always miserable in Montreal," I growled. "If it isn't raining it's snowing. If it isn't doing one of those, then it's too damned hot!"

He gave a low, rumbling chuckle.

"Ya!" he agreed. "With this I do not always agree. But today I cannot say I blame you. You excuse me, I hope, if I cannot help but overhear what happens?"

He jerked his head in the direction of the room we had just left.

"I couldn't stop you," I replied, no doubt a little ungraciously.

But he did not take offense. Instead, he smiled a little cryptically.

"Maybe it was a good thing, eh?" he demanded. "I wonder! Would you let me buy you a drink? A cup of tea, ya? I have somethings I would say to you."

I stared at him coldly.

"I don't know," I said stiffly. "I'm afraid you have the advantage of me. We were introduced, but I had a good deal on my mind. I didn't catch your name."

He smiled again.

"Astor," he said. "John Jacob Astor, of New York. Will you join with me?"

It was on the tip of my tongue to refuse him curtly, for the name meant nothing to me, and I was too miserable at that moment to have room in my mind for sociability. Perhaps something of the sort may have shown on my face, for his deep-set eyes narrowed slightly and he abruptly stopped smiling.

"Ya!" He nodded. "For your anger I do not blame you, but it is of this thing I would speak something. Maybe, it seems to me, we can for one another somethings do. Of course"—he shrugged—"if other plans you have, if already you have your mind made up what you are going to do, then I should nothing say but to wish you good luck."

I blinked, and all at once he was smiling again. Abruptly I held out my hand.

"I'd be pleased to join you, Mr. Astor," I said.

He nodded, grinned, and we shook hands, understanding each other as simply as that, I think. Without further discussion he led the way to a smoky, low-ceilinged taproom near by, where we took seats in the back and he ordered a brace of mulled ale to warm us as we talked. When the mugs sat steaming on the table before us and the hovering waiter had gone about his business, Astor took a sip of his drink and folded his hands on the table before him.

"What I heard at the conference back there," he said, moving his head in the direction of the Company's counting rooms, "does not much matter here, except that I learn that you are an honest, forthright, able young man; that you have by your own effort made yourself with the fur trade familiar; and that you are now, at this moment, at liberty. Bah! They are fools, these Northwestmen!"

"Not all of them," I retorted, a little on my guard. "Besides, what makes you think all that of me? I was fired, wasn't I?"

He chuckled.

"I have ears to hear. I have eyes to see," he replied, laying a finger, surprisingly long for one so square built, alongside his large nose. "What's more, I have already asked questions about you! It is not for nothing I am one of the richest men in North America! I tell you this not to brag, for I do not need to, but so that you should know I make no offers I cannot fulfill."

I nodded, but made no reply, waiting.

"Germany I left," he went on, "in the year you were born. Two years later I was at New York. In a little way I began, and never have I backward gone. First a little in furs and musical instruments I deal. Then I try a little speculation in land. Next I buy shares in shipping. In none of these things have I ceased to be interested, and now each pie in which I put my finger I find is too big for one man alone to be baker. Do I make myself clear? Always, when I am excited, I do not the English speak so good!"

I nodded, smiling.

"I understand," I said.

"Good!" he exclaimed. "Now, then! From the beginning with me it has been furs. More and more furs. Always furs, whatever else, growing bigger and bigger, until I can see I must have someone else to take charge of this part of my business for me, if other interests also I am to have. So, long ago, I have tried to prepare for this. A nephew I sent to Montreal to learn the trade. Perhaps you met him. Todd was his name, Will Todd."

I shook my head.

"No matter," he said. "What happens? Will Todd comes home. 'Uncle Jacob,' he says, 'I do not wish to be in the fur trade. To Providence I go to be in business for myself.' So I let him go. It is important who does this work should be enthusiastic, like me. Otherwise it fails!"

"So?" I said.

"So!" he chuckled. "You come straight to the point, I see! That I like! Ya! Many others have I tried, but none have been altogether enough to satisfy me. Now today I hear your past reviewed. I hear you recommended to each other by the best men in the business. Even this MacPherson, he recommends you, though he does not know it. And then they turn you away. To myself I am thinking, for me this is the man! What do you say? Will you come with me to New York and there with me work in the fur business? In six months, maybe a year, if you prove as I think you will, this end of things I turn over to you to manage for me as my agent under my sole direction. I tell you I have great dreams for this, which I will tell you after a while. You said you were an American?"

I nodded, rather taken aback by all this.

"I was born there," I said.

"Then you are an American!" he cried. "What do you say?"

I stared at him. New York! If I ever had an ambition that was stronger in me than had been my hope to become a Northwestman it was to return to the States. I had been too young, of course, to remember it when my father returned to Canada, and he had nursed a grudge against the new nation, perhaps because he was Irish, or for some fancied slight or other. But my mother had never forgotten her happiness there. It was she who had kept alive the spark of enthusiasm in my breast, and to me it was the land of opportunity and riches. Yet I was cautious.

"How much?" I demanded.

He laughed outright at that.

"That is good!" he cried. "It proves to me that you are not a man to be confused by pretty words. This I will make use of! For the kind of man I need I must pay. This I know well. I will give you eighteen hundred dollars a year, payable monthly, with an added annual bonus of 10 per cent of all business you personally do for me. Each year I will increase your annual salary six hundred dollars up to six thousand dollars. After that we talk about matters again, eh?"

I gulped. Even the initial salary he offered was more than I could hope to make as a partner in the North West Company, though to be sure I would have to find myself. Seeing me still hesitant, he put his hand in his pocket and drew forth a handful of gold coins, counting out a number of them onto the table before him. These he picked up and held out to me.

"Here!" he said. "A month's salary I will pay you in advance. Tomorrow make inquiry around town about me. If you do not find it true, all that I tell you, then you need not return the money!"

I shook my head.

"I couldn't do that, sir," I said.

He grinned.

"I'll risk it," he told me.

"Very well!" I said, deciding abruptly. "But I ask no questions. That you are a guest of Mr. Henry is enough for me. I'm your man if you'll have me after you've seen me at work."

"That I will risk also," he assured me. "Here is my hand on it!"

We shook hands as we rose.

"A bargain then?" he demanded.

"It's a bargain, sir," I assured him.

"Good, then!" he said, and dropped the coins into my hand. "That may be handy to help prepare yourself for the journey. I must leave day after tomorrow at the crack of dawn. Can you meet me at the ferry landing so we travel together? This way I can something of the business tell you."

"Day after tomorrow, sir," I assured him. "I will be ready."

"At dawn!" he prompted.

"At dawn, sir," I repeated.

And with a wave of his hand he was gone, walking heavily on his thick, stocky legs. It was only when the door had closed behind him with a thud that I realized I had not touched the ale he had bought me.

II. NEW YORK

AS I approached the landing place it was yet dark, and the light wind of the morning dragged dank streamers of ghostly gray mist across my cheeks with a fondly intimate touch. There was no one in sight. Only the smoky street lantern, mounted on a tall pole, cast its yellow glow, like a spattered egg yolk, upon the cobbles of the quayside, across the massive timbers of the stringpiece, and out upon the whirling black current of the river. There were a number of empty boats moored at the foot of the ladder by the landing stage, and up along the quay tall, thick bollards stood at intervals like distorted dummies in the dusk. Some distance below, a ship lay moored alongside, hulking black against the dim, starlit sky, and out in the stream one sensed rather than saw the other vessels that swung to their cables with the dark river gurgling and chuckling underneath their cutwaters.

As I came out of the alley and into the wide space by the landing, my heels rang hollowly on the cobbles, echoing off among the buildings mockingly. I felt a shiver of apprehension. Perhaps it was all a hoax! But as quickly as it came the fleeting sense of panic was dispelled by the clink of gold in my pocket. After all, a man did not go about handing out money to comparative strangers for his mere amusement!

I had little more than put down my *sac à commis* upon the string-piece and turned my collar up about my chin when I heard, far off, the clop of hooves and rumble of iron shod-wheels upon the pavement. As I listened the sound grew louder, and presently a *calèche* swung into the circle of light and halted. I saw my new employer drop down lightly for all his bulk, while his elderly host clambered rather more achingly after. At sight of me Mr. Astor waved his hand and smiled.

"You've not long been waiting, I hope it," he said.

"No, sir," I said. "I just got here myself."

Astor grinned at the elderly Scot.

"I told you," he remarked triumphantly.

Henry eyed me dourly.

"The mair fuil!" he growled. "If I had a yon money in my keek, I'd be quick oot o't!"

"And leave all the rest behind?" I grinned.

"Ha, there, you see?" Astor roared. "Already it is we understand one another!"

The old Scot cocked a beady eye at me.

"Aye!" he said. "Ye've a guid mon yon, Jacob. Hong ontae him!" He offered me his hand.

"Ye'll nae regret ye'r deceesion," he told me. "Guid luck, lod!"

With the arrival of the calèche a dozen or more dim, burly figures had abruptly materialized out of the dark and fell to transfering our luggage to the bateau below. As I handed my sac á commis to one of them, it gave me an eerie feeling to know that they must all have been somewhere, silent, near at hand when I arrived, quite aware of my presence, although I was unaware of theirs. In time I was to learn that it was characteristic of Mr. Astor to have everything in readiness for himself wherever he went; it saved time and, in the long run, expense. But I was not yet aware of this trait, and I am afraid I rather resented it. But there was no time then to brood upon it, for we were down the ladder and in our places in the boat before I had more than time to realize what I was about, and even then there was too much to occupy my attention. We were away almost before I knew it, threading our way among the anchored shipping, and behind us I could see the lank figure of the elder Henry clambering back into the carriage. Next I knew I was looking forward once more across the darkened waters toward the distant lights of La Prairie de la Madeleine, where we were to take up the road that would lead us ultimately to the Hudson and New York. It was Astor's voice that recalled me.

"It is a good thing to be starting out on a new life, ya?" he said. I turned and saw him looking at me as if he had read my thoughts, and I flushed.

"I didn't have a chance for coffee before I left," I said lamely. "To tell you the truth I was wondering——"

He chuckled that German laugh of his, deep in his throat, as much as to say he knew well enough that was not what I was thinking.

"Ach!" he said, with a wave of his hand. "We eat breakfast in La Prairie while they prepare the carriage. It is quicker this way."

He fell silent, studying the ships against the dawning light of the sky, and for the first time his absorption gave me an opportunity to study him with care.

He sat leaning on the gunnel, on the thwart facing me, so that his features were clear and distinct, and I was able to put them together in a way that was not possible before. Despite the chill of the morning he held his hat in his lap, letting the river wind ruffle his straight blond hair. His forehead, I saw, was not quite so highly domed as I had at first thought, but was rather prominent because of its bulge at the temples. The nose was jutting, a little curved and thin, with light nostrils, pinched a bit at the tip, so that while it had a hooked look it actually was not. The mouth was broad without being generous, well-shaped but not effeminate. The lips were thin and with an upward thrust in the middle and a slight petulance of the lower lip, which seemed to me to show considerable stubbornness and dominant insistence. In fact, it was that mouth that made me wonder a little if I had made such a fine bargain as I had thought. His chin was firm and well-pronounced, yet without being his outstanding feature. In its general lines it was a square, strong face, powerful, though not yet so powerful as it was to be in later years. Still, you could see in it the face it was to become.

I was surprised at the speed with which our bateau set us across. Accustomed as I was to the bark canoe, I tended to look upon the clumsy wooden craft with something of an aristocratic contempt. Despite myself I was *un homme du nord*—a Northwester, as they delighted to brag, and I could not bring myself to believe that such as these were a means of transport for other than hogs or hay. Yet under the steady stroke of our boatmen we made good time, despite the current. It was still dusk when we breakfasted at La Prairie and far short of midday when we alighted from our carriage at Saint Johns. Within an hour we were snug aboard a sloop, standing up the river, and before night we had passed out onto Lake Champlain, leaving Ile aux Noix, tree-rimmed, against the sky behind us.

I believe even the winds conspired to hasten Mr. Astor along, for in four days we were at Skenesboro, and in three more we had reached Albany. But from here contrary winds and tides took charge, and we were comparatively slow in our descent of the Hudson, for it required three full days more to drop down the broad river to the city at its mouth.

In the meantime, as I daresay he intended, I had opportunity to learn more of my new employer than what he looked like. In that first day, as we crossed the river and rode from La Prairie to Saint Johns and passed beyond into the land below the line, we had time to grow acquainted with each other. I told him a little of the line from which I had sprung and of my eagerness to see this new country where I had been born but of which I knew so little; while he spoke of the bitter voyage from England that fall and winter of '83 and '84 when he arrived in Baltimore and finally made his way to New York, only to find that his brother, a butcher and new married, could not keep him. They were small facets of men's lives, yet on either hand I think we learned something of each other. On the next day, as we swept up the Broad Lake toward the Narrows, with Grand Isle lying astern and the bright, wooded slopes of the Green Mountains rising on the one hand and the gloomy Adirondacks butting against the sky upon the other, he put me to work in earnest.

I turned from the sparkling blue lake and the fiery forest, all flame and green and gold in its bright autumn coat, with some reluctance. But as I took letters from his dictation and recorded in the traveling books he carried transcripts of the transactions he had completed on the journey, I found it not so terrible a task. There was time and to spare, and having the sloop to ourselves I could sit out on deck and do the work, while now and again he would pause to point out this or that passing landmark: Crown Point, Valcour Island—I do not trouble to mention them in order—Ticonderoga, or some spot where he himself had tramped and trapped or traded in his early days.

"Ach! Those Indians!" He would grin, and point off toward the wooded westward mountains. "You go back in the hills there and say that you know Jacob. That's all. Just Jacob say! And they will ask you can he still pretty musics play on the silver flute. That is a secret I never to anyone tell, ya! At night when I make my camp fire and the Indians come to smoke, out I take mine German flute and play for them musics. This they like and want to do themselves, so I cheaper wooden flutes bring out and show them that they play as well. I tell you, for one flute and three or four lessons they give fifty, sometimes a hundred, beavers! Enough to buy a dozen barrels of flutes! Ya! Flutes I have all over these mountains, and not an Indian is there that can play one! But always they remember Jacob with kindness, and when among them I go always beavers it is they have for me yet!"

I tell it merely to show something of the different sides of his character that he turned toward me. But it was not until we were nearly come to New York that he showed me that side of himself that was of greatest concern to me.

In the course of our journey he had told me much of his interest in the fur trade, and, indeed, even at our first interview he had let me understand something of the extent of his connection with the business. But now I was to look into his heart and learn something of his hopes and dreams and desires. I was to discover at least a measure of the position I was to hold in his general scheme of things.

We were a little below Anthony's Nose, just emerging from the

Highlands and entering the upper reaches of the Tappan Zee, when he evidently decided that it was time for him to speak. I was leaning on my elbows on the rail, having completed my work for that day, scanning the wooded shore with some wonder, for it was so different from our thorough utilization of every inhabited inch of neat French countryside in the Province of Quebec. He came beside me, and I suppose something of what I was thinking showed in my face, for I heard him chuckle.

"Ach! America!" he exclaimed. "It is an amazing country, no?"

"There seems to be so much of it," I said. "So much of it that is empty, I mean! Of course I am used to the great rivers and lakes and forests of the North, where there isn't even an Indian for a hundred miles. But here, so near to civilization! That I cannot understand. Why, we can't be more than a hundred miles from New York!"

He shook his head.

"Not so far," he told me soberly, "and this along the river is some of the oldest settled portion of the country. But this is a land of restless people, Rory, of people reaching out and spreading and dreaming great dreams. So they keep driving, driving, looking always beyond and not much behind. They leave big spaces behind them empty, not used. Someday all this will be filled. In the meantime America grows!"

"The land of opportunity," doubtless voicing my thoughts.

"Ach, ya!" he exclaimed. "Opportunity, that is it! Every man strives for it. Would you believe it, when first I came much of my best furs I bought from right about here? Even today the best rats I buy from the meadows of Jersey, directly over the river from New York! But the trade is expanding. Today it is Canada who controls the lion's share of it."

"They have the greatest territory to draw on," I replied.

"And have you thought of all that country to the west?" he demanded. "Have you thought of America beyond the Mississippi and below the Red?"

"I've never been there," I said—naïvely, I daresay. After a man has been to the Athabasca the rest of the continent seems scarcely unattainable. "The younger Henry, though, and some of the others, David Thompson and the like, have traded there and found it good."

He chuckled and rubbed his chin.

"Ya!" he agreed. "That is a thing I like about you, Rory! An idea does not frighten you because it is big. That is what I need, a man with the vision to see! Look you, today Canada controls the trade, and you and I for our best furs must go to London to buy what comes through Montreal—even if in the first place these furs might come from American territory beyond Michilimackinac!"

" 'Tis a ridiculous situation," I agreed, "but I don't just see what can be done about it. The laws of the Crown——"

"The laws of the Crown!" he scoffed. "Britain is greedy as always she has been! She wants everything for herself as she has always had! She is like an old man who lives in a changing world. She does not like the change, so she does not believe it. But the change goes on just the same!"

He paused and rested his own elbows on the rail, staring off at the darkening shore.

"Ya!" he said presently. "And so shall we change the trade ourselves. Who controls the fur trade of America and the West, of the Mississippi and the Missouri, ya, and even of the Columbia, he can control the fur trade of the world! And would you know who will be that man?"

"Astor?" I grinned.

But he did not chuckle in reply.

"Ya!" he said.

" 'Tis an ambitious scheme," I said, sobered.

"We get no place without ambition," he retorted. "Ya, it is ambitious, but we do it, you and me together, no?"

I swallowed.

"I'll do my best," I assured him.

"That is all I ask," he replied, and turning to me he smiled. "Together we furnish brains, ya? Then I tell you what to do and you do it, no? Me, I put up the money. You make it work! What do you say to that, eh?"

"I say," I said, "that it is a big job. But if you want to tackle it, I'm game to try!"

He punched me playfully on the shoulder.

"Ya! I thought you say that," he chuckled. "That is why I hire you. More of this I tell you later on, but first you must more of my business learn. Then you see it is not impossible what I dream!"

I may have had my own reservations about this but I kept them to myself. After all, if he wished to toy with such grandiose schemes, I thought, who was I to complain—so long as he carried out his bargain? If he did that on his part, he would find me ready enough to serve him and his interests.

As a matter of fact I had little opportunity to consider the matter. It was near dark then, and we lay the night off Spiking Devil with the wind sweeping up from the bay below, fresh and pleasant, for all it bore a nip to it, whistling in the rigging and giving us a smell of the wide salt sea. By early dawn we were away once more, and the fact is the passengers had not done rubbing the sleep out of their eyes when the cry, "Prepare to land!" fetched us running on deck.

I will confess to a certain sense of awe and apprehension, since I had never before clapped eyes on a city of sixty thousand; and well I might have felt so, for as I tumbled out upon the cold, windy deck, it seemed to me the grim, gray, low-lying city filled the whole expanse of the eastward world. We were running close-hauled, about six points off a southeasterly wind that blew across the city, keeping close under the shelter of the town to avoid the necessity of beating across from the Jersey side. The sun was not yet above the jumble of roofs, some of slate and some of shingle, and the windows showed like pale dead eyes in the blank façades of the buildings, while the wind that crossed the island at an angle fetched with it a depressing conglomeration of odors. Half-a-dozen wharves and docks thrust out long fingers into the river on this side, but this far upstream, at least, they were ill scattered. Here and there a lonely church spire thrust up out of the welter of chimney pots to catch the glint of the early morning. All in all it seemed to me a melancholy prospect.

Yet all this was changed as we stepped ashore, for there I had no time for thought of the weather, nor opportunity to indulge it if I had. Scarcely had we set foot to the pavement at the Albany Basin, at the foot of Cedar Street, before we were forced to leap for our lives before a careening, great wagon full of beer barrels with a wild-eyed driver, who flung curses at us as he passed—as far as I could see because we had been nimble enough to escape rather than for any other reason. Astor chuckled at my evident nervousness and amazement.

"That is New York!" he exclaimed. "Soon you grow used to it and begin to scramble yourself. Look out!"

He snatched me once more from the jaws of death as another dray went whirling by in the opposite direction amid a spatter of oaths.

"Better we take a carriage from here, I think," he said, grinning.

"By all means!" I agreed with him fervently, wondering if he had ever really meant to walk in that.

He hailed a hackney carriage, and we were whirled, it seemed to me, at breath-taking speed and at risk of our lives, up over Cedar Street to the Broad Way, where Mr. Astor pointed out his own house, as well as the little triangular patch of park, the Bridewell, the almshouse, the New Theater, and Saint Paul's Church. Then our carriage swung abruptly into Liberty Street and halted. We got down before a modestly imposing brick building that displayed a bright polished brass plate on which was inscribed the simple, but no less impressive, legend:

JOHN JACOB ASTOR
MERCHANT.

Inside the building we found a single long room running all across the front with a feature that was new to me. Down the center the room was divided by a low rail into two equal parts. In front of the rail, lighted well by windows on three sides, was a long space devoted to display of the goods Mr. Astor had for sale: samples of furs and silks and nankeens, of chinaware and Spanish fans, of English gloves and playing cards, and French goods of various descriptions. Mr. Astor evidently played no favorites. There were hats and gunpowder and lace and lutestrings, even a cannon and a rack of cutlasses! Often I had seen retail establishments where the goods offered for sale were displayed for purchase, but never before had I seen the same done by a wholesale merchant. Here was offered nearly everything that Mr. Astor dealt in, save land and ships, and I did not doubt but that if I looked diligently enough I might even find samples of those tucked away somewhere.

But this was only half the room. On the other side of the railing that divided the long chamber down the center there were a number of high, counting-house desks. Some of these were occupied by busy clerks in green eyeshades and paper cuffs, but the central desk, obviously that of the chief clerk, stood near the gate, at the center of the railing, where he could keep a sharp eye both upon those who worked under him and on those who entered the front door. At this desk, under the great lamp that hung from the ceiling and, even at this hour, spread its rays across the desk, sat, hunched on a tall stool, a long, thin man with thinning sandy hair and sharp, thin, freckled features, bitter, it seemed, in their concentration, and as puckered as the skin of a ripe butternut.

At first glance I thought I took a dislike to him, yet at the sight of us he unwound his legs from about his stool with an undulant, double-jointed movement and rose with a sort of small boy's grin to face us, and the way in which his lean face lighted up changed my first impression of him immediately. Here was a man I could like.

He came toward us smiling, drawing back the gate and holding out his hand easily to Mr. Astor. I saw his blue eyes were quizzical, politely curious as they brushed over me, yet not unfriendly.

"Welcome back, Mr. Astor." He smiled. "You take us a little by surprise. You see we're all here still!"

My phlegmatic companion looked at him without humor, and it occurred to me then that the jokes he saw best were those he made himself.

"Wouldn't you be?" he demanded.

"Well, I've always planned to elope with Betsy yonder," the sandy man grinned, nodding toward the tubby little cannon in the corner of the display room. "I rather thought I might run off with her before you got back."

Astor stared at him blankly for a moment. Then his face broke into a square, accusing smile.

"Ho! You are joking!" he said.

The lean man made no reply to that but winked quickly at me. Mr. Astor seemed to remember abruptly that I was there.

"Ach! I forget myself!" he cried, clapping a hand to his brow. "Will, this is Rory O'Rourke, who comes from Montreal from service with the North West Company to help us with the fur business. Rory, I would like to make you acquaint with our chief clerk, Will Sanders."

The other held out his hand.

"Welcome to New York, Mr. O'Rourke," he said. "We're glad to have you. God knows we need someone to take care of all the details of that business. Mr. Astor has so many irons in the fire now that he hasn't time to give it all the attention it needs, and I am just a poor pen-pusher and not quite certain what it is all about."

I shook his hand and smiled at him.

"I'll believe that when 'tis proved to me," I told him. "I have an idea you've forgotten more about the trade than I ever knew. Certainly you know about this end of it. Most of my experience has been in the *bois fort.*"

"The bois fort?" He looked puzzled.

"Forgive me," I apologized. "The term slips out through habit. It means the 'strong woods.' I was ten years on the Lakes or west and north of them, on the Saskatchewan and the Athabasca."

"You're the man for us then." Sanders nodded. " 'Tis just that knowledge we need here. We'll put you on to the market."

Mr. Astor broke in.

"I tell you, Willie, to the office I should go to see what is happening while I am away. The first thing we must do for Rory is to find him some place to live, for work we cannot expect from him while he is wondering where he is going to put his head."

Sanders glanced at me speculatively.

"To tell you the truth, there's plenty of room at our place," he said. "He's welcome to Jerry's room."

"I don't want to put anyone out," I said hastily. "After all, your family——"

Astor guffawed and Sanders grinned.

"He laughs because I'm a bachelor and mean to remain so," he explained. "As a matter of fact, you won't be putting anybody out. I share quarters with two other misogynists, but one of them was married about a month ago and moved to Brooklyn. We haven't seen him since."

"What about the other one?" I grinned.

"Brother Jonathan?" he asked. "That's Washington Irving. Quite a fellow. He doesn't like his name. He could live at home with his mother if he liked but says he's afraid to. He's been studying law for a long time, but he'll never make it. He thinks too much!"

"Thanks!" I laughed. "What I really meant was how would he feel about it? After all, I don't want to intrude——"

"Jonathan?" he interrupted me. "Good Lord, he'd welcome you as if you were the prodigal son! He's been groaning and growling about that empty room ever since Jerry left. It's the truth the place has been like a clubroom ever since he moved in. Come along. You're more than welcome."

Astor beamed, pushing me beyond the possibility of refusal.

"Ach, that is good!" he cried. "A solution it is I did not think about. With you two to look out for him, I will know he is in the best of hands. Take him along, Willie, and see him settled. When that you have done, back fetch him here and let him somethings of the business for himself see. Tonight, between you, you can the town show him. This Washington will like! When he has his way around learned, bring him to me back, and from there I show him the way. Eh?"

"You don't need to urge me to take a few hours off." Sanders grinned.

"I take it out of your pay," Astor growled.

"I bet you would too!" Sanders laughed.

Astor chuckled, but made no reply. He glanced at me.

"I leave you in good hands, Rory," he said. "If there is anything that troubles you, come to me, eh?"

Sanders and I left the office on Liberty Street toward midmorning, he carrying my bag over my protest as we went down over the hill, past Trinity Churchyard and across Wall Street, by Federal Hall, to

Pearl, where we came to a halt before a narrow, crazy-leaning little house tucked snugly in among its neighbors. There was a brass plate in front, with the numeral 362 picked out in black letters so that it was easy to read. Sanders took a big key out of his pocket and opened the door.

"Mind the steps," he warned.

He led the way up a flight of narrow, creaking stairs to an upper hall, where he threw open a door and ushered me into a comfortable apartment, made up of three small rooms overlooking a cluttered yard in the back and a fair-sized drawing room across the front. In the grate on the hearth a fire of sea coals glowed pleasantly, warming the place. Pipes, books, coats, papers, a bottle, and a pair of glasses on the mantel, ashes on the rug, and the mild, stale odor of tobacco smoke testified to the sex and nature of the occupants. As we entered, a stout young man in stockless shirt and trousers, with flopping slippers on his feet, appeared from one of the back rooms still diligently wielding a towel.

"Hullo, Will," he said. "What's wrong?"

At the sight of me he broke off abruptly. Will Sanders chuckled.

"You lazy dog!" he grinned. "So this is what you do all day? I thought you were working on something."

"I am! I am!" the stout young man protested. "Good God, a man might as well be married as nagged to death by his roommate! I can think just as well in bed, can't I? The only reason I'm getting up now is because I'm hungry. Besides, you ought to be at the office. What are you shouting about?"

"Ha! I've a better excuse than you have," Sanders retorted. "I want you to meet Mr. O'Rourke—Rory, isn't it? He's just in from Montreal, and I've offered him the hospitality of the house until he decides where he wants to live. O'Rourke, this is Washington Irving, of whom I spoke."

I shook hands with the stout young man, who gave me a quick quizzical nod, then turned upon his roommate.

"A pleasure, Mr. O'Rourke," he said. "What do you mean, Will, 'decides where he wants to live'? Are you mad, man? With all the other places he can go while we pay rent for an extra room? What's wrong with this? Nab him, quick, before he gets away!"

He grinned at me, and I grinned back.

"Wait a minute!" I put in. "I'd like nothing better, but how long would you gentlemen put up with me? It seems to me we can't know that until we've tried it awhile."

"Hark to him!" cried Irving. "A diplomat as well as a merchant! A rare combination, I promise you! Welcome, sir, to our modest household, and don't say I didn't warn you. Keep your eye on yonder Sanders. He'll drink the last of your best madeira and have the socks off your feet while you sleep if you don't watch him like a hawk."

"I'll chance him if you will," I replied. "After all, 'tis a solemn duty. I can see you're not safe with him alone!"

So began a friendship that was to last and ripen with the years. Sanders showed me the room I would occupy, and I dropped my *sac à commis* inside the door without troubling then to unpack. It was Sanders's suggestion that we three sup together, after which they promised to show me something of the town. To this Irving was more than agreeable, and so we left it for the time being.

My recollections of the office that day were no more than could be expected of a newcomer on his first afternoon. I daresay I learned something of the business, but, for the most part, when I try to pick it out, it remains in my memory only a vague, hazy jumble. I do recall, however, that when it came time to quit for the day I was more than ready to go home and take my ease.

But I was to discover, actually, my day was only beginning. We found Irving ready and waiting, and it did not take him and Sanders long to decide that the best beef and most succulent lobsters, the juiciest clams and oysters, the thickest soups and tenderest meat pies, the sweetest desserts and best coffee—to say nothing of the strongest drinks—in town were all to be found at the Bull's Head, in Chatham Row. Who was I to dispute them? Their discussion left nothing to the imagination, and long before they were done I was ravenous. I would have gone with them to Dirty Dick's by then had they suggested it.

As it was, I must say I found they had not exaggerated. Such food as I had set before me that night was as delicious as anything I had ever tasted before and most that I have eaten since. The drinks were all that they were claimed to be, and during the meal we were joined by four or five others, all evident cronies of my companions, whose names it would do no good to remember here even if I could—save that one of them was Harry Brevoort, dapper, handsome, suave, polished, a cousin of Mr. Astor's by marriage, so I understood, and a man with whom I was to work a good deal in the years to come. We were merry indeed by the time the dishes were cleared away and pipes and brandy fetched. I suspect there is a good chance I even may have boasted a little of my own adventures in the *bois fort*. If so, there were others who spoke for themselves. I do not know who it was that suggested the theater, only a few doors away, facing the Fields. But Irving caught the idea up with enthusiasm.

"There's an idea!" he cried, snatching at his watch and glancing at it. "We can still make it handily. What's on tonight? You have a box, haven't you, Harry?"

Brevoort smiled, as if he were hardly surprised.

"And by a curious coincidence," he said, "it isn't promised to anyone."

Irving scowled.

"Who has a bill?" he demanded.

Someone produced a printed advertisment.

"*The Maid's Tragedy*," he said, "with Mrs. Partington and the Beales, begins things."

"Then we've time for another," said Sanders. "I never could stomach Beaumont and Fletcher."

"I don't know," said Irving. "In general I'd agree with you, but the feud between Partington and Mrs. Beale ought to liven it up a bit."

"Well," said Sanders thoughtfully, "maybe you're right."

"What's the rest of it?" someone demanded.

Irving read on.

"After the opening," he said, "Mr. and Mrs. Placide will dance a hornpipe on the tightrope——"

"That's the girl with the big legs," someone commented.

"The one that always does at least one hornpipe," Irving agreed.

"She likes to display her talents," someone remarked.

There was a laugh in response to that.

"Afterwards they will play the violin and display the American flag in various attitudes," Irving went on. "The comedy follows, titled *The Suspicious Husband,* and this will be followed by a sketch called *The Antipodean Whirligig,* in which Mr. Robinson will stand upon his head and whirl around, without the aid of his hands, at the rate of sixty or a hundred times a minute!.The evening's entertainment will be concluded with a comic pantomine, in the course of which Mrs. Placide will dance a hornpipe for us again, this time, it is to be presumed, upon a more stable platform. To wind it all up Mr. Placide will render us a parting chorus of "Hail Columbia." Anyone interested?"

He looked directly at me, and I could do no more than nod. As a matter of fact, I could think of nothing more exciting at the moment. Never in my life before had I been inside a theater, and the prospect of doing so now, so spontaneously and without warning, filled me with anticipation.

Even in the ordinary course of events that first visit to the theater would have been for me an exciting moment. As it was there were developments far beyond anything I had dreamt of. In the end there were six of us who decided to go. Harry Brevoort, as owner of the box, was official host, though naturally we each insisted on paying his way. Kirke Paulding, a handsome lad about Irving's age, and Tony Bleecker, who was a little older than most of us, were the other two additions to the group, while Irving and Sanders and myself made up the remainder.

After we had been admitted and shown to our places in the first tier of boxes, stretched in a horseshoe curve around the first balcony, I saw why my companions had been swift to take advantage of our host's good nature, and I myself was glad that we had found someone with a box in which to sit. Below us spread the pit, in which those admitted found the likeliest seats they could. In the main, this was filled with men—gentlemen and otherwise—who were permitted to retain their hats on their heads, at least during the interval before the play and during the intermissions. If an obvious toff entered the area, however— and I am afraid we would have been included in the category, since we were all genteelly dressed—he was greeted by instant hoots and catcalls from the gallery above, followed by demands to doff his hat. If he refused, he was promptly showered with all manner of missiles, from rotten eggs and ancient vegetables to bottles and sticks of various descriptions. Since the throwers' aim was anything but good, the shower descended upon the righteous and the evil alike, until the offender either removed his hat or had it knocked from his head by some irate bystander. Since we were under the hang of the balcony, which separated us from the gallery at the top, we were able to retain our hats and at the same time escape this treatment. Upon the stage, however, it was a different story, for the actors in the full light of the candles which ringed the stage were favorite targets, and at the least word or glance or gesture which displeased them the lords of the gallery were likely to let fly with a shower of miscellaneous garbage, which would stop the performance until attendants with mops and brooms had been given an opportunity to clean up.

Apparently Mrs. Partington was a favorite of the "gallery gods," for her every appearance, every speech, was greeted with cheers and whistles and applause, and I must say she catered to them. Mrs. Beale, however, was evidently not popular, and every time she appeared upon the stage she was greeted by such a storm of vegetables and eggs and dead fish that ultimately the play had to be stopped and the show permitted to go on without her. The *Antipodean Whirligig* also seemed to enrage the crowd, though I must say I found his skill and balance wonderful to watch. On the other hand, Mrs. Placide, with her fat thighs and bouncing breasts, her buxom bottom and her coquettish, simpering airs, was, if anything, a greater favorite than Mrs. Partington, and coyly, I must say, she made the most of her popularity.

All of this was marvelous in the extreme to me who had never seen anything of this sort before, and I do not doubt but I would have worn my hands raw with clapping and suffered the next day from eyestrain had my attention not been distracted before ever it was done.

She sat in a box almost directly opposite to us, and I will admit that I did not immediately see her, for I was occupied with the scene before and below us. Nor did she take my eye during the first part of the performance, since my attention was centered on the stage. In the first intermission, however, I permitted my eyes to wander—I remember it distinctly even now—up along the columns which flanked the stage to the overhang of the gallery and along it, watching that crowd with some amusement. Then, when I could no longer see the faces of those above, I dropped my glance, first to an examination of the occupants of such of the balcony as I could see; and at last, growing weary of that, I viewed yet another tier—to meet her eyes looking directly at me, so abruptly that I almost started from my seat. Certainly I must have caught at Sanders's sleeve!

Long afterwards he told me that he thought for an instant that I had seen a ghost. Certainly if she was a ghost, she was such a lovely one that a man might almost wish himself dead. There were other people in the box with her. Of that I was vaguely conscious. But who they were or what they might look like, I know I could not then have told. My eyes were for her—and so evidently that she looked away, not actually smiling, not yet really uncomfortable, but only trying to act as if she were. Naturally, at that distance I could not tell the color of her eyes, but I had a feeling that they were of a sort of tawny, golden brown to match the red-gold of her hair. Her face from there was a small oval, but perfect in its outlines, and even across the theater I could mark the sweetness and invitation, the almost taunting flavor of her smile. The dress she wore was simple, white, high-waisted in the newest style of the day, leaving the figure untrammeled by artificiality. Yet plain and unostentatious as it was, it bore the unmistakable stamp of the skillful dressmaker. Even at a distance such as this I could appreciate the way it clung to her figure and was moulded upon her, almost as if it were something she were born in.

"Who?" I gulped, clutching my roommate's arm. "Who is that? Do you know?"

III. VALERIE

SANDERS did not need to follow my glance. He had already noted it and was waiting. It meant nothing to me then that he was not smiling.

"I was wondering," he said, "if you would see her. As a matter of fact, I rather hoped you wouldn't."

"What do you mean?" I demanded.

"Old Immunity himself," laughed Irving, who had missed none of this.

"You've got to admit, Will," Tony Bleecker offered, "that she makes an attractive picture."

Sanders did not answer any of us directly. Instead, he leaned over and tapped Brevoort upon the knee. As the latter looked up inquiringly, the sandy man nodded first toward me and then looked significantly out across the theater to the opposite box.

"Oh-oh!" said Brevoort. But I noticed that at the same time he bowed punctiliously and raised his hat and that the others, somewhat sheepishly, followed suit. Naturally, as a courtesy to all, I did the same, though I did not even know her name.

"Who is she?" I demanded. "You know, obviously—all of you! Tell me! What's all this mystery?"

Sanders smiled and shook his head, almost sadly, while Irving imitated him. It was plain they were making sport of me, but I scarcely cared. Fortunately Brevoort took pity on me.

"Don't mind them," he said. "It's possible they are just jealous because she smiles at you."

Sanders shied away from him in mock outrage. But I was in no mood for horseplay.

"Who is she?" I persisted.

"She's one of the belles of our little society here in New York," Brevoort replied gravely, "and rather a dangerous one, I might add.

She takes a sort of sadistic delight in breaking hearts. That's why your friends are so concerned."

"They needn't fear for my heart," I retorted, unable to tear my eyes away from hers. "Let the lady look to her own!"

"Hear that now!" cried Irving. "Our Lord of the Lakes and Forests doesn't mince matters when he speaks, at least!"

"No one ever stated their intention more plainly than that," agreed Kirke Paulding.

Tony Bleecker chuckled.

"If I were you, Will," he said dryly, "I'd make book on this. You and Jonathan are in a perfect position for it, and for my part I'd be inclined to back O'Rourke. 'Twill take a copper-headed Irishman to cut Goodwin down to size and trip her. You know she's been riding for a fall, and I think we've found the man to give it to her!"

"At least," said Sanders tartly, "he can never say we haven't let him see the worst from the beginning."

"Will you stop this chatter and tell me who she is?" I cried irritably.

"Her name," said Brevoort, "is Valerie Drake, and her father, Winthrop Drake, is—shall we say, quite prominent in commercial and financial circles here in town. In fact, I would say he stands among the first rank. I believe that he and Astor have been associated in some transactions. Is that right, Will?"

"She's a damned little flirt!" replied Sanders, which was a non sequitur if ever I heard one.

Brevoort glanced at me.

"Would you care to meet her?" he demanded.

I looked at him, not quite understanding the etiquette of such matters. He smiled, understanding.

"We'll go over," he told me. "It's more or less expected."

"Let's all go," grinned Irving.

But abruptly the lights were lowered and on the stage the curtain creaked up. My companions' attention swung in that direction, and Brevoort leaned toward me.

"We can't go now," he told me. "As soon as the final intermission begins I'll take you."

I fear I saw but little of the performance after that, for my eyes were always and again endeavoring to pierce the gloom of that box across the way. As my eyes grew accustomed to the dark and the whole scene lightened before me, I found I could make out the white outline of her face under the overhanging balcony, and I forgot the play and concentrated my thoughts on the task of re-creating around that nebulous form something of the beauty I had so briefly glimpsed across the theater while the lights were turned up. One thing I knew. I did not care what anyone said. Even at that distance I was convinced that there could be no other woman for me. The O'Rourkes are like that: impetuous! What did a little coquetry matter? That she had carried them off successfully and without harm to herself was, to my way of thinking, only an indication of her intelligence and her spirit, as well as her beauty. I dared say that at one time or another she had had all of these gallants dancing attendance upon her, else why would they be so vocal about her? As for this Goodwin, whoever he might be, I neither knew nor cared about him.

It seemed to me that that part of the performance would never end, but Mrs. Placide danced the hornpipe while her husband played the violin for us, and both displayed the American flag in various "attitudes." *The Suspicious Husband* was rendered for our edification and amusement, and at last the curtain rang down wheezily, and one by one the lights in the sconces were turned up. Brevoort turned about.

"Shall we go over?" he asked.

I could sense, rather than see, her eyes upon me, for now that it was light I suddenly felt too shy to look at her.

"By all means!" cried Irving, all but smacking his lips.

The others grinned their agreement. I nodded, and we rose and made our way around through the corridor behind the row of doors, nearly to the opposite end, where Brevoort paused before one and knocked.

"Come in! Come in! Henry?" a voice called cheerfully from the other side, giving no hint of surprise. Obviously, by our very departure from our own box, we were half-expected.

Brevoort thrust open the door and stood aside for the rest of us to enter.

"I've fetched over a newcomer to the city to meet you all, Mr. Drake," he said, and we all filed in.

The little booth was crowded with all of us inside, and I must say that I, at least, was confused. There was a tall, graying man, dignified, with a welcoming smile and direct gray eyes, whom I immediately took to be Winthrop Drake, standing against the forward rail of the box, the empty chair before him indicating where he had sat. Beside him was seated a rather buxum, carefully dressed and coifed, but rather vapid-seeming woman, who simpered her welcome somewhat superciliously. I gathered this was Mrs. Drake, and Brevoort's introductions confirmed both notions.

"Miss Deborah Drake," said Brevoort.

With an effort I turned and bowed to the third person there politely but perfunctorily. She was a pretty child of about fourteen or so, with dark-brown hair in which the lights shone prettily; dancing, mischievous eyes that I guess were brown, and a bridge of freckles across a turned-up nose. She smiled at me gaily, but I am afraid my thoughts were elsewhere. Who could blame me?

"Miss Valerie Drake," Brevoort went on.

I swung abruptly—so abruptly that I think I almost upset a chair—and caught my breath. Seen close to she was even more breath-taking than I had imagined. There was no flaw in her perfect skin, and her eyes and mouth, I saw, were even more lovely that I had dreamed, full of invitation and promise and with more than a hint of a smile. She held out her hand almost intimately, and I took it and thrilled to the pressure of her fingers.

"Mr. O'Rourke!" she said. "I am charmed! To tell you the truth, I've been simply fascinated watching you all evening! Harry! What do you mean not bringing him over before now?"

"Miss Valerie!" I managed to blurt. "You've sprung all the traps in my trapline! What can I oppose to such a greeting, except to say that I have been pestering Harry to introduce me ever since I clapped eyes on you!"

"That's only the truth!" Brevoort laughed. "We haven't had a minute's peace. In my own extenuation I must explain that Mr. O'Rourke has been in the great woods, beyond the Lakes, these ten years past, and has only just come down from Montreal with Mr. Astor today to accept a post in his business."

I admit I scarcely heard him, even when he completed the introductions.

"And Dick Goodwin, Mr. O'Rourke," he said.

For the fop he mentioned, disapproving this intrusion and all but indignant as he stood behind Valerie, I had no more than a glance and a brief nod. He was a man of about my own age, not much above middle height, and too stout for his years. He was soft, flabby, I thought at first glance, and his air was far too proprietory for my taste. His brown curls were brushed in carefully studied carelessness forward over his brow, and already, it seemed to me, there was a hint of jowls in his chubby cheeks, and the small, indignant eyes he turned on me were anything but steady. If this were my rival, I felt that I had little to fear. But Valerie's hand was still in mine, and I dismissed him with no more than a perfunctory nod and turned my attention back to her.

"I had not looked for such pleasure on my first day in New York," I told her. "I begin to think Mr. Astor did me a greater favor than either of us realized when he offered me the position he did!"

"Oh, is this the young man from the north woods?" Mrs. Drake cried, looking at me with new interest. "Mr. Astor was telling us about him only this evening. How intriguing! You must have a great many stories to tell, Mr. Burke."

"O'Rourke, Mother!" the younger girl corrected indignantly.

"Indeed he has," Sanders put in, grinning and winking at the child. "Some of 'em would make your hair stand on end!"

"Not really?" said Mrs. Drake.

"Oh, absolutely!" Sanders assured her.

Deborah clapped her hands excitedly.

"Oh, you must come and tell us some!" she cried.

I glared at Sanders and then looked at Mr. Drake.

"You mustn't mind Will, sir," I apologized. "He does exaggerate a bit at times."

I heard Sanders chuckle, but I ignored him and returned my attention to the older sister, who was eying me now with a rather speculative look. She may have forgotten that I still held her hand, but I must say that I was conscious of it.

"Still," I smiled, "far be it from me to refuse any suggestion that would allow me to see more of Miss Valerie!"

She had the grace to blush at that and gently withdrew her fingers. Abruptly she turned toward her father.

"I know!" she cried. "Why don't we invite the boys to join us at Cato's next Saturday night?"

Winthrop Drake blinked and then smiled almost wisely.

"I hadn't heard we were going, my dear," he said. "But if you say so——"

He glanced at my companions.

"What do you say, gentlemen?" he asked. "The invitation is general if the implication is not!"

I think Goodwin flushed, although I was scarcely in a mood to care.

"Sir, we didn't come fishing——" Brevoort protested.

"Nor did I mean to accuse you," Winthrop Drake interrupted him. "I think it a capital idea myself."

"By all means, then!" cried Irving. "You'll let us pay our share, of course?"

"If you insist," Drake conceded.

"Why, then, 'tis decided," Irving agreed. "What do you say, Rory?"

"Would I refuse?" I demanded.

The lights of the theater began to dim, and we bade a hasty farewell. Once again I felt the warm pressure of her fingers, and, as we returned to our own box, I must say I was walking, almost literally, on air.

I sat through the rest of the performance and felt my heart leap as we bowed to them in passing when we left the theater. It was only as we turned our steps homeward, along the wet, glistening cobbles, shining under the November rain, that Sanders ventured to protest.

"Look here!" he said. "You probably won't thank me for pushing my nose into your affairs, but at least I have no ax to grind. I've never looked twice at Valerie Drake, and I doubt if I ever will——"

"Hold on!" I broke in. "We've started off well together. I'd like to keep it that way. I don't know what your opinion of Miss Drake is, though I can suspect. Well, it's not my opinion. I appreciate the good will behind everything you say, but let's not interfere with each other's personal affairs. What do you say?"

"If that's the way you feel about it," he conceded somewhat grumpily.

"That's the way I feel about it," I assured him.

I think we were the better friends afterward for having fetched it into the open. Certainly, despite our differences of opinion, our relations could not then or after have been improved, and the discussion we had of it was maintained in a lighter vein.

We were early the next morning at the counting rooms, but not more than a moment or two ahead of Mr. Astor. He came stumping in, waving a copy of the *Commercial Advertiser* over his head, and shouting to me and to Sanders to come into his office.

"Rory! Will!" he cried. "Come in here with me! Have you read this?"

We followed him in and stared at each other and then at the paper blankly. We had seen it, of course, but nothing we had read had stirred us to such an extent.

"You mean you did not notice?" he demanded, and slapped it down on his desk before us, opened and folded to a notice on the second page.

As he stumped upon his sturdy legs up and down the big office, with its long desk and comfortable chairs, Sanders and I studied the notice he had indicated. It was an account of the return of Captains Lewis and Clark to St. Louis after more than two years' absence, with their expedition all in good health, and with amazing stories to tell.

They had, so the article said, followed the Missouri to its headwaters, crossed over the continental divide, and fallen down the Snake to the Columbia and so on down to the Pacific Ocean, where they had confirmed the claim of the United States to that territory already made through Captain Gray's right of discovery some years before. Lewis and Clark, the account went on to say, would return as promptly as possible to report in person to the President upon their journey.

When we had done reading, we looked up, still at a loss to account for Mr. Astor's excitement. He whirled upon us.

"You do not see?" he demanded. "You do not see the importance of this to us?"

I shook my head.

"You, Rory, of all people!" he exclaimed in a tone that was plain reproof. "You should see it."

"I'm afraid I don't, sir," I replied.

"Ach!" he exclaimed disgustedly. "Then I tell you. Sit down!"

We did as we were told, though he did not follow suit. Instead, he continued to pace the room as he talked.

"Already," he said, "I have told you somethings of my intentions. So we need not into that go now. But what I have told you is directly affected by this that you have read."

"I don't see——" I began.

"Hush!" he interrupted. "I tell you! By the purchase of Louisiana the basins of the Mississippi and the Missouri have become American. By this exploration the basin of the Columbia and a part of the Pacific coast of this continent becomes also American. At least a sound claim we have established to it. Now, then! Who controls the basins of the Mississippi, the Missouri, and the Columbia controls the fur trade of North America."

He held up his hand.

"Don't interrupt, Rory!" he forestalled me. "I am aware of what are doing those people in Canada. But if with this they are opposed, they cannot survive. Who controls the trade of the Columbia controls also the Pacific, and who controls the trade of the Pacific can control the Russian fur trade. Do you begin to see? With so much in their hands, they will control the fur trade of the world, and on this we will build!"

"What about the Mackinaws?" I put in. "They are already on the Mississippi and reaching southwest from Michilimackinac."

"Pooh!" he scoffed. "Them I will buy out—in due time! I know they are not of a match now with the North West Company. But perhaps we will make them so. They will be another lever for us to squeeze our rivals! Right now it is important that we take every advantage of this news! Rory, I want you and Will Sanders and young Irving to go to Washington——"

"Now?" I demanded.

It slipped out before I had opportunity to stop it, and at the sound of my voice he turned about and stared at me in surprise.

"Why not?" he demanded.

I think I must have flushed furiously. Sanders grinned and interposed dryly.

"It's our fault, I'm afraid, sir," he said. "He met Valerie Drake last night."

"Oh-ho!" Astor chuckled. "So soon it begins? Well, Rory, I do not blame you! If I were young again mineself——! But this will not interfere."

"We are invited to a party Saturday," Sanders told him. "I daresay that is what worries him."

Astor grinned.

"Still it will not interfere," he said. "About this we must not be hasty. After all, Captain Lewis and Captain Clark are yet on their way from St. Louis. There is time for us to prepare, and I would not have Rory go before he understands better our business and is ready to argue for it. What I wish to say now is this: Rory, you will prepare yourself carefully until the extent and the direction, the full scope of our business you understand. Study it, and make familiar with it yourself thoroughly. Do you understand?"

"Yes, sir," I replied.

"A fortnight, two weeks, it should take no more," he told me, "if you attend to no other business than this. Will Sanders, Irving, they are both already familiar enough with it, and maybe they can help you to see what I do. When you are ready, by the first of the new year, perhaps, I would have all three of you go and in Washington stay until you have accomplished as much as you can of what I will tell you. That is only this: a chain of posts I would build up the Missouri and across the mountains and down the Columbia to its mouth! And for this undertaking the interest and support of the government at Washington is—well, at least, infinitely to be desired. Do you understand?"

"I think I see, sir," Sanders replied. "Whatever official sanction such an undertaking may have cannot help but enhance its chances of success."

"Exactly!" Astor agreed. "What is more, in this country there is no individual who is better than I able to carry out the plan. Moreover, if it is not soon carried out by Americans, then quickly will the British or some other nation encroach upon that field! These are arguments that you must use. Do you follow me?"

We both nodded.

"Good, then," said Astor. "This is my plan: Irving, who knows that game, will use his every influence socially. It will not hurt us that the Russian Ambassador's wife is acquaint with our charming agent. You, Will, you know the commercial side of the scheme, and you will be able to point out to such people as Mr. Gallatin, to whom I will a letter give you, the advantages to this country of such a business. Rory, with the physical aspects of the trade, with the value of the furs, with the way it is done beyond the paths of men, with all of these you are familiar. You will point these out to the President, and, to him and to the other people to whom I will send you, you will explain how we will work and why it is best we should do it so!"

"You assume that we agree?" I commented.

"Don't you?" he demanded, pausing in mid-stride.

"Shall I say I do not disagree." I grinned. "If I should find that I do at any time, I will come to you first and tell you."

"Good!" He grinned back. "Then we understand one another. Go now and study this business as it affects me and my interests. As soon as you are ready, let me know and I will see that you have letters and yet more instructions. But do not too long be!"

The week that followed was one of as concentrated study and effort as I have ever before put into an undertaking. It was true Mr. Astor had asked me only to familiarize myself with his part in the fur trade of the world, but his own activities, both in that field and in others, were so ramified and so intermingled that I could not pick out the one without delving to a certain extent in the others. It was through this that I learned of his interest in the China trade, which was to play so large a part in things to come; of his land investments in upper New York; of his annual pilgrimages to Montreal and London and Leipzig; of the amazing amount of Indian trade goods alone— blankets and cloth and knick-knacks of manufactured wares that he bought cheaply abroad in all sorts and kinds of markets and imported to exchange for furs themselves. I came to realize how large an amount of West Indian cane was grown to be ground into muscovado, which would be turned into rum and sent out to the fur fields on Astor's account!

And this was only a sample of what I discovered. The more I studied it, the more feasible it seemed to me his plan became. To be sure it needed a man with capital and the organization to accomplish it, but from what I learned of Mr. Astor's interests and resources it seemed to me that he, if anyone, was the individual to carry it out.

But all this was in the way of business. I must admit a good deal of the time my heart and thoughts were elsewhere. It seemed to me that Saturday would never come. But even for Jacob Astor time did not stand still, and the week ended eventually to find me in a nervous fury of excitement.

My roommates managed, with some amusement, to hold me in check, at least until we were in the carriage and on our way gaily toward Cato's Inn, on the Boston Road, where it had been agreed we were all to meet. But at this point I fell into a twitch and pother that kept me beating at my fist and smoking one pipe after another, adjusting my stock, and otherwise exhibiting my restlessness in a thousand ways that kept them in roars of laughter and myself in a stew of embarrassment.

I had my reward, however, or at least so it seemed to me. When we came to the long, rambling building that was Cato's, with its gnarled vines creeping over it and the huge fires burning brightly on its hearth, it was to find the Drakes and a dozen others before us. Apparently, in the interval since she had proposed it, Valerie had decided to make an event of the affair. There was a bowl of steaming punch to begin with, followed by a sumptuous dinner with mulled wines and a flip to follow, accompanied by merry dancing to a special orchestra engaged for the occasion. But far more special than all this was the fact that Valerie, radiant and even lovelier than I remembered her in my dreams, took me for her partner and kept me at her right hand throughout the evening. What I said, in the main, I declare I do not know. Doubtless pretty inanities which she had heard from half-a-hundred other lips. Yet I am sure that if I said them, I meant them, and apparently she was not displeased.

Yet the ointment was not without its flies. For one thing it was almost winter. Outside the trees were bare and stark, and the wind in the naked branches was cold. I could imagine Cato's luxuriant gardens under the light of a summer moon, but this was a night when one hung close to the fire indoors, and there was no chance for us to slip away for a quiet, perhaps intimate, instant together. Another flaw was the younger sister who sat across the table from me, with Irving—full of amusement, curse him—sitting close at her elbow and prodding her onward, teasing me for stories of the bois fort, of the Indians I had seen and the scalps I had taken, and the number of toes I had left on my right foot because all the others had been frozen! Finally, in self-defense, I told her of the time three men had gone out to spend a winter and but two had come back, and of how those two had lived on the flesh of my friend, the third; of how one of them had confessed their crime to me, and of how I had found him hanging from a stout pine tree in the morning, in such a way that everyone except myself had thought it suicide.

After that she asked no more questions, and I noticed that neither she nor her sister seemed quite so interested in their dinner, while Irving appeared to be quite amused. I confess I was irritated with him. But afterwards, at least so far as Valerie was concerned, I think I made up for it. My father had been a gallant and a gay blade, and he had been at pains to set me familiar with the ways of the old French court, as well as of the dances of the Old World and the New. I held my own at that, as I had been confident I would, and whenever we came together, I made it a point to whisper something of my admiration to her. When the party ended and it came time to go home, I was not surprised that she agreed to ride with me or that Dick Goodwin went scowling and pouting in the carriage with her younger sister.

I had studied on this for some time, and I must say I was prepared for the moment when it came. Carefully I did not spoil it by slipping my arm about her shoulders. Certainly I had said enough so that she knew how I felt.

"Do you know," I said, as we whirled clear of the inn on the way homeward, "you have quite a reputation as a ruthless heart smasher?"

I did not think she would meet the challenge straight, nor did she. Indeed, if she had, I am not sure what I would have said next.

"Why!" she cried indignantly. "Whoever would have said such a thing?"

"It wouldn't help you any if I were to tell you," I said. "And it wouldn't do them any harm. It's been said by a number of people and hinted by more."

"Oh!" she cried. "And you believe them?"

"I didn't say that," I told her.

"You——" she began furiously, then, as she realized what I had said, "What?"

"I didn't say that," I repeated. "I only told you what I had heard. As far as I am concerned, Valerie, you are above reproach! I've never seen anything as lovely as you are, and I'll not believe what I've heard. I want you, Valerie! I love you, and I want to make you mine."

"Why, Rory!" she exclaimed. If she was not surprised, at least she gave an excellent imitation of it.

"I know this is sudden," I said. "I'm afraid I'm inclined to act abruptly. But that doesn't mean I am less sincere in the moves I do make. When I have made up my mind, I stay, and you will find I stick to this. Please, Valerie, tell me I'm not barking up a hollow tree! That's all I ask! Tell me I have a chance! Give me that, and I can be as patient as anyone; more patient than most. You'll see!"

"Why, Rory!" she breathed again, and swayed toward me.

I needed no more answer than that. I caught her in my arms and crushed her to me, nor did she resist. Instead, she melted against me. When I left her at home, with a tender good-night kiss, I had no longer any reason to doubt that my suit would be successful. Indeed, she had given me every reason to believe that it would.

As I rode homeward, with the soft pressure of her lips upon my own, it seemed to me that everything had turned out all right; that everything had turned out quite all right, indeed, and that I had most assuredly done well to take the course I had taken.

Will Sanders, I thought, would be surprised when I asked him to be best man!

IV. WASHINGTON INTERLUDE

I CANNOT say that I was highly impressed with my first view of the nation's capitol. For one thing, it seemed to me that it was harder to come at than Michilimackinac or Grande Portage. At least travel by bateau and canoe left a man's liver intact. But the road southward from Philadelphia was execrable, full of sloughs and mud holes, and between Baltimore and Washington it was little better than a trail. The city itself—this designation was sheer courtesy—was little more that a widely scattered village with few houses of appreciable size or grandeur.

The official residence was far from the most impressive. The plan was there, of course. A network of streets and avenues radiated from a pox of circles like the spokes of a clock full of wheels, all carefully laid out and cleared and marked with neat rows of stakes and, here and there, by board sidewalks. But in the main there was nothing in the streets but chuckholes and mud and an occasional boulder that had yet to be removed. Now and again there was a house or a tavern or an ordinary or two.

As for public buildings, they stood on an average one to the mile, and it was necessary to carry one's shoes between calls, official and otherwise. The circles, so we were wisely told, were for purposes of defense, but no one ever said whether from within or without.

But there was activity there, both social and official. Most of the congressmen and other officials lived in boardinghouses that stood scattered about within walking distance of the Capitol. A few of the wealthier or more solidly established rented residences of varying degrees of splendor, and a surprising number of foreign legations had been built.

Sanders, Irving, and I made the journey early in the new year 1807 and took up our quarters at Stelle's famous hotel. I must say that I was scarcely pleased at being thus forced to leave my heart behind me, but, after all, it was certainly no province of mine to protest.

Irving at once set himself to call upon Dr. Mitchill, who was our senator, Mr. Clinton, the Vice-President, and the amiable old Dr. Barlow, whose delightful daughters I must say I found as attractive as he did. Sanders went directly to the Attorney General, Robert Smith, but it seemed to me that we might make more speed with less haste, and accordingly it was a week before I presented my letter to Albert Gallatin, the Secretary of the Treasury, while the letter I had for Mr. Jefferson I decided to hold in reserve to play as a final trump card when the time seemed right.

Neither Lewis nor Clark had yet arrived from St. Louis, and I felt sure that, whatever proposals we might make, nothing certainly would be decided until those who had the nation's destiny in their hands could have a talk with them. As a result it was nearly a fortnight before I saw Mr. Gallatin, and in the meantime I made no move other than to familiarize myself with the city and as much as I could of its ways.

I don't know what I expected to find in Mr. Gallatin. Perhaps I looked for a bluff, hearty Teutonic type like my employer, of whom he was a close friend. I remember that I was somewhat surprised that he was a small man with delicate features, whose sensitivity was unmistakable. Nevertheless, the mettle of the man was evident.

He greeted me courteously, albeit with something of a challenge.

"Mr. O'Rourke," he said, "this is distinctly a pleasure. Mr. Astor tells me that you have been about the Lakes and beyond."

"That's true, sir," I admitted.

"Then you will know a good deal about Indians," he said.

"I believe I do," I told him.

"Excellent, excellent," he replied, rubbing his hands together.

It was only much later that I learned of his interest in Indian ethnology and realized that all of this had nothing whatever to do with the question at hand.

"Tell me," he asked, "what can I do for you?"

I saw no reason for evasion. It seemed to me that the direct approach would be the one more likely to have results such as we desired.

"Well, sir," I said, "I am here of course in Mr. Astor's interest. I think I hardly need describe to you his interest in the fur trade."

"Hardly," he conceded dryly.

"As you know," I went on, "at the moment that trade is largely concentrated in the hands of the British."

"So far as we in America are concerned, at any rate," he agreed, "that is true. The Russian fur trade is extensive, but it does not affect us."

I nodded.

"But the British trade does. Now that it is impossible for a merchant of Mr. Astor's stature, for instance, to obtain all the furs he needs in the American market. He can go to Montreal to buy, but often, as you are aware, the furs which he will purchase there were originally taken from American territory and sold to British traders in Canadian posts by Indians living south and west of the Lakes who go north to trade with them. But even though these furs may be American in their origin, we cannot ship them directly from Montreal to New York, for under British law they must come to us by way of London. So a skin taken south of the Lac des Bois is more than likely to be traded to the Canadians at Fort William and sent thence to Montreal, where it is purchased by Mr. Astor. From there it must go to London for reshipment to New York, where perhaps it is made into a hat and sold eventually to a gentleman in St. Louis, not so very far down the river from the point at which it was first taken."

He smiled faintly.

"It is stupid," he said, "but nevertheless true. You have described it quite accurately."

"And that is not all, sir," I said, "for every skin he buys in Montreal

Mr. Astor is forced to contribute a part or all of a tax dollar to the Crown Treasury."

"Precisely!" Mr. Gallatin nodded again. "That is the reason for it."

"That was one thing that Mr. Astor had in mind when he sent me to talk to you," I told him.

"There is something else?" he asked.

"There is," I assured him. "You are aware, of course, of the immense value of the trade in furs across the Pacific with China."

"I am aware of the profits of it." He smiled.

I grinned at him.

"We might put it that way," I said.

"Go on," he commanded.

"You know, of course," I said, "that there is a vast section of the Pacific coast, from the Spanish settlements in California to the Russian settlements in Alaska to the north, which is as yet but nebulously claimed but which now begins to grow interesting to various powers because of the wealth of its furs and the vast profits to be commanded in their trade across the Pacific. Each year sees an increasing number of ships trading on that coast, and each year sees some new movement to secure the territory. Already the English are moving in that direction from Fort William. Sir Alec Mackenzie has already reached the Pacific, and David Thompson, at this very moment, is somewhere in the Rockies establishing posts for the North West Company. Captains Lewis and Clark have reached the Pacific, according to the latest reports, and you expect them here momentarily. But it is one thing to explore and another to establish actual possession by means of posts, as David Thompson is doing for the English on the Kootenay and elsewhere, northward of the Missouri."

"I believe I begin to see your drift." He nodded. "I take it that Jacob has in mind establishment of one or more posts in the area to offset this British encroachment."

"That is true, sir," I said. "Mr. Astor proposes to form a company which will undertake to build a chain of posts up the Missouri and across the mountains and down the Columbia. Such posts would operate in much the same manner as those of the North West Company. Furs gathered upon this side of the mountains would be sent down the Missouri to St. Louis. Those taken beyond would be gathered at the mouth of the Columbia, to be used in the trade with China."

He looked at me wisely for an instant, without saying anything. Then, with almost a twinkle in his eye, he said dryly:

"And these posts you propose? The government's license to build them, I presume, would carry with it the exclusive privileges of trade in the area. No?"

I nodded. Since he put it so flatly, there was no point in denial.

"That is generally the idea, sir," I said. "After all, there should be some recompense for the risk involved, financially and otherwise, in establishing such a chain of posts."

"No doubt!" He smiled a little frostily. "But it would seem to me that this is a matter for the Superintendent of Indian Trade——"

"Who has not yet been appointed," I dared to interrupt him.

He shrugged.

"The office is newly created," he pointed out. "The President is weighing possible appointees. You see, Mr. O'Rourke, the government has considered this somewhat already. What you ask is essentially a monopoly, and it has been generally the feeling here that such a monopoly, if vested in private hands, is not good, for it will benefit only one privileged group. Indeed, we rather doubt if such a monopoly can legally be granted. The proposal has been made that the government build some such posts as you suggest and maintain them, retaining the exclusive right of trade to the government itself. The alternative to this is to throw the territory open to all under a system of licenses, and let who will build posts and trade in the area."

I shook my head.

"Sir," I said, "if the government builds and maintains the posts, it will be costly and inefficient. The government cannot trade with the Indians at a profit, and the whole undertaking will be an expense to the taxpayers and a drain upon the Treasury."

At the gleam of approval that showed in his eye I saw that I had struck a sound note there. My mention of the Treasury apparently came close to home. Perhaps I would have been wise to leave it so, but I did not.

"On the other hand," I said, "if the territory is thrown open to all, we will have what has happened wherever rival business interests have clashed in the North. We will have bloodshed and chaos, battle and murder between rival traders. We will have unscrupulous men who will debauch the savages with guns and rum to win them to their own purposes."

"That is what we fear." He nodded.

"But if you will grant the exclusive license," I said, "to a single company, the posts can be operated efficiently, at a profit to that company which will permit it to pay well for the privilege. The government would have the right to garrison the posts and would be saved the expense of building them. The fees which the company paid for the licenses and the taxes which were collected upon the furs themselves would go into the public treasury so that there would be no expense to the taxpayers; and the company, under government supervision, could regulate the trade with the Indians themselves in such a way as to be most beneficial to them. All this is to say nothing of the employment which such a company would give to persons throughout the country, for such a company would need large quantities of trade goods. It will require a vast system of transportation and men to operate it. It will employ clerks and traders, drovers, packers, voyageurs, warehouse-men——"

He held up his hand, laughing.

"Gently, gently," he cried. "All this is interesting. I am glad that you have told me, but you must know that I alone am not the man to decide."

"Such a company," I put in, determined to use every argument, "would open the country to later settlement."

He shook his head, smiling.

"Oh, no," he replied gently. "That country so remote! Ach! Never will it be settled by white people!"

Perhaps because I had something of the same feeling myself, I did not press the point.

"I have said I am not the man to decide it alone. There are others you should see. Have you talked with Mr. Madison? Or Tom?"

"No, sir," I said. "I have not. I came first to you, because I felt that you would be most interested."

"Well, well," he exclaimed, "they should know certainly what you propose, so that we may then all discuss it with intelligence, for it will be we three who make the decision. Let me make an appointment for you to see Little Jimmy, and after that, perhaps, we can discuss the business with Mr. Jefferson."

"I would be pleased and honored if you would, sir," I told him, and he made a brief note of it, then rose, smiling and rubbing his hands.

"Let us think no more about this for the evening. Come! You may leave it to me. Now you must have a cup of tea, then tell me something of the Indians that you have observed."

He took me by the arm and steered me toward the hall door.

"Tell me, with what tribes were you most familiar?" he asked earnestly.

It was not the next day nor yet the next but a full week later before he was able to arrange an appointment for me with the Secretary of State. We met at Mr. Madison's office, which was cold and bare and barnlike, and Little Jimmy's long nose was red at the end and rimmed with the rime of much blowing, while his long upper lip, which would easily have made four of Mr. Gallatin's, drooped and trembled like that of a tired horse after a long winter's canter. His bright blue eyes fixed themselves upon me almost balefully as we were introduced, and for a moment I thought from the cherry brightness of his cheeks that he was an ill man, although I was later to learn that this was no more than his normal color.

"Is this the young man?" he growled.

"This is Mr. O'Rourke of whom I spoke, Mr. Secretary," Gallatin assured him.

I noted both his manner and the "Mr. Secretary." Mr. Madison would be more difficult to talk to than the Swiss, I thought. He glowered at me and blew his nose loudly.

"Foul climate, gentlemen!" he exclaimed. "Foul! You have a proposal to make that may offer some advantage to the government?"

"I believe I have, Mr. Madison," I said.

"Why don't you make it then?" he demanded gruffly.

So invited, I did so.

Mr. Gallatin had heard me out in silence. So did Mr. Madison. But with what a difference! Where Mr. Gallatin's silence had been receptive, almost encouraging, Mr. Madison's was stony. I made as quick and precise a presentation of our plan as I was able.

When I had finished, Madison stared at me sourly.

"Ha!" he snorted. "Here's Lewis and Clark not yet back from their journey and they come flocking for concessions! Do you think, young man, the country beyond the Mississippi can ever be a part of this?"

"Why, sir, why——" I stammered. " 'Tis a part of it now."

"Mind you," he cut me short, "I'll go a long way with Tom Jefferson, but I tell you this is the worst thing that ever happened in this country. 'Tis not Tom's fault, after all, that Monroe and Livingston were such fools as to let themselves be trapped into buying the territory, though I did think better of Jimmy Monroe. In my opinion, 'twould be better if the west bank, aye, and all the land beyond the Mississippi were under a separate government, independent of ourselves. We'll grow top-heavy else."

"But," I gulped, "we already own the land."

"Much good will it do us," he scoffed. " 'Twill be a source of soreness and hostility for years unless some foreign power steps in to snatch it away. How are we to hold it without settling it? And how are we to settle it with so few of us to fill the older parts of the country? Eh? Tell me that! If we send settlers out along the Missouri, where are we to get them but to draw them from east of the river, which, I think you will agree with me, is already spread too thin. As I have said, 'twill be better if another nation comes to be upon that side of the stream."

I stared at him unbelievingly.

"You hold with Colonel Burr, then?"

"Not at all, not at all," he blared gruffly. "What Colonel Burr has sought to do is not to set up a new state on territory already belonging to us, but to seize territory belonging to a friendly power. Obviously we could not stand for that!"

I felt myself growing irritated at such an attitude.

"Quite obviously," I agreed. "And quite as obviously we could not sit by and let some other nation snatch territory we had already won!"

"What do you mean by that?" he demanded.

"I mean, Mr. Secretary," I said, "if we all took the attitude you seem to take, we would have put our pigs in an ill-stitched poke! Who speaks of settlement and colonization? Not I. Yet the territory is ours, and if we do not move to cement it to us, others will be there before us and we will surely lose it. What I propose will secure our influence at a minimum of cost to the government and maximum benefit to those who have the foresight to invest in it."

"Yes," he said slowly. "I see what you mean. But the profit is all to one pocket."

"Not as I see it, Mr. Secretary," I said. "The profit is to the pockets of the citizens of the United States, for we are prepared to pay for the concession, and what we pay as taxes may be reckoned as profit."

"Well, if I had my way," he growled, "no white man would set foot west of the Mississippi, but I see no way to prevent it."

"It has already been done," I interrupted him, "and with government sanction."

"Possibly something such as you suggest," he went on, ignoring my outburst, "will offer a solution."

He turned his baleful glare upon Mr. Gallatin.

"Have you talked about this to Tom?"

"Not yet," said the Secretary of the Treasury.

"Well, he should hear of it," Madison said, sniffing loudly. "After all, it is for him to decide. Do you want to arrange it or shall I?"

But obtaining an interview with the President of the United States was apparently a more difficult matter than seeing either the Secretary of the Treasury or the Secretary of State. I have no doubt that both myself and my plan were discussed thoroughly, and I was not surprised that it was months before anything further came of the matter.

In the meantime, we were not idle. Sanders, to be sure, feeling that he had accomplished as much as he could at Washington, returned to New York with Mr. Clinton's counsel and the advice of the Attorney General that the company be organized and incorporated in the state of New York, for it seemed to be the general consensus of opinion that the government could far more gracefully support an association of businessmen than it could a single individual. As a result of this, he wrote me from New York, soon after his arrival, that steps had been initiated for the incorporation of the American Fur Company under Mr. Astor's leadership.

In the meantime, Irving and I made the best of our social way about the Capital. Nor was the period an idle one. Captain Lewis and Mr. Clark, the one dark-eyed, moody, the other bluff, red-faced, red-haired, arrived from St. Louis, and the Capital was immediately thrown into a round of parties and receptions for them; and I do not blush to say that neither Irving nor myself was hesitant about scraping up an acquaintance with them. If we casually mentioned Mr. Astor's plan, it seemed to us it could do no harm. As is always the case in such circles, one reception led to another, and I found that there was a constantly expanding field in which to gambol.

It was a harsh winter and a harsher spring, and in consequence the Capital's gaiety was pursued with even greater abandon than usual. There was a scarcity of socially acceptable males under fifty, and perhaps because of my association with Irving, I met the somewhat rigid requirements, for suddenly we were both overwhelmed with more invitations that we could accept, and all at once the Capital turned lively and full of fun.

I thought it best to make the most of it. Certainly there was no point in making a recluse of myself simply because I could not see Valerie. I would have preferred to have her by me, and I daresay that her presence would have opened the doors of Washington's society even wider. But since she could not be there, there was naught to do but write to her daily, though I do not recall that in all the time I was in Washington I had so much as a line from her.

The day came at last when I had a note from Mr. Gallatin, warning me to be prepared at half after ten on the following morning to go with him to the White House for an interview with the President. I had called upon Mr. Gallatin and Mr. Madison without apprehension, for it had seemed to me that they were only men like myself, but in the case of Mr. Jefferson, I must confess to a somewhat different feeling. The thought that I was to come face to face with the President of the United States left me as skittish as a schoolgirl, and though I had been ready, dressed and shaved and groomed, with every hair in place, for a good hour before Mr. Gallatin arrived, yet I kept him waiting for another fifteen minutes after that while I went over my appearance, making sure that every stitch and hair was in order.

We took the North Drive and entered the presidential reservation over a rutted lane between bushes of scrub holly and majestic magnolias with broad shiny leaves and white blossoms. There we were saluted by a leather-stocked marine. My companion jogged my elbow and pointed to a high-pailed fence cutting off the end of the east wing and the ground beyond.

"You've heard of Jefferson's bear garden?" he asked. " 'Tis yonder he keeps the two Captain Lewis and Mr. Clark brought him."

"I've heard of that," I chuckled. "I take it they are as awkward as the Arabian nags that were sent to him a year or so ago."

He laughed, for everyone had heard not only of the horses but of the Moorish princes who had fetched them—as hard to keep in dancing girls as the beasts had been in grain.

But we were at the door before he could reply, and there we were greeted by a butler the color of an inkpot, with teeth the color of parchment in his dusky face. He ushered us into a large salon overlooking an inlet of the broad Potomac and what was evidently one day to be a lawn—but at present was little more than a litter of shavings and bits of lumber.

There we waited, Mr. Gallatin perfectly relaxed. It was evident that he had been here many times before, while I paced the floor in a literal sweat of nervous apprehension. In this I was interrupted by the entrance of the blackamoor who had ushered us thither. He came in with a great flourish, flinging open the wide doors.

"The Pres-ident o' the United States," he announced.

It seemed to me that a good bit of my life I had heard about Thomas Jefferson. Even in Canada his name had been on every tongue, either as anathema or in praise. He was the symbol and the leader of the Republicans, the "mad Tom" of the Federalists; he had been Minister to France and had fetched home the principles of the Revolution, so they said. It was he who had authored the Great Declaration. He had favored withdrawal from the slave trade, even though he had failed to emancipate his own two hundred slaves. It was he who was at the bottom of everything, who had begun negotiations for a city and ended by buying half a continent. I had heard him described in all manner of terms and tones; in praise; in acidulous criticism; satire; almost as everything from the anti-Christ to the Resurrection itself. I had seen portraits and caricatures of the man. Reports of his eccentricities and mannerisms were plentiful and unreliable. He was a rum pot; he took naught but a sip of light wine at meals; he lived like a recluse; his affairs were a blight upon the nation; he played whist; he did not know one card from another. Already he was part of the national lore.

But nothing I had heard prepared me for the man I met! As I turned from the tall window, he came in at the doorway, quietly, unassuming, but nonetheless striking for all that. Long, lean, lank, loose-jointed, six feet two, in run-over carpet slippers—for I declare that is what he had on his feet!

He seemed natural and perfectly well dressed to me. I had heard of those slippers, but I had to see them to believe them. The sight put me in mind of Mrs. Merry's famous description of him. But though I could see the threadbare coat and frayed shirt, I could see no hint of inground grime beneath the fingernails such as she had emphasized. On the contrary, he gave the impression of a well-scrubbed man who has on his favorite, comfortable old clothes and who feels that he has attained both the age and the position to indulge his whim.

His thin, rather spindling calves were encased in loose-fitting stockings of coarse white cotton yarn. These disappeared into a pair of old-fashioned plum-colored velvet knee breeches. His shirt he wore without a stock and open at the throat, and the red grosgrain waistcoat was his sole concession to propriety. The old green velvet lounging jacket that he wore was clearly a favorite garment, for it was almost yellow with age and hung upon his frame with nearly loving familiarity.

At sight of us he paused an instant in the doorway, inclining his head a little from force of habit.

"Gentlemen," he said, and his voice was mild, but deep and mellow, rich and conversationally at ease, as one who is accustomed to talking when no one else has aught to say. "I'm sorry to keep you waiting."

My companion bounded forward.

"Mr. President," he protested, " 'tis we who should apologize to you for taking your time."

"Stuff, Albert," Mr. Jefferson scoffed. "To be frank with you, I was doing nothing more serious than amusing myself with a translation of Juvenal, and I fear I had dozed off."

He glanced at me.

"This is the young man of whom you spoke?"

I bowed gravely, very much on my best behavior.

"Mr. President——" I began, but the lean man cut me short, moving forward with an outthrust hand.

" 'Tis a pleasure to make your acquaintance, Mr. O'Rourke," he said. "I knew an O'Rourke once in Paris, a colonel, I believe, of the Irish Brigade. Would there have been a connection, do you suppose?"

"As to that, sir," I said very seriously, "I could not say, for my father himself fled a number of years ago to France after serving The Pretender in '45."

"Indeed!" said Mr. Jefferson, much interested at once, or seemingly so. "Could it have been the same, perhaps?"

"I hardly think so, Mr. President," I replied. "My father never rose beyond the grade of captain in the Regiment of La Sarre. He was with Montcalm at Quebec. However, this may have been a brother or a cousin of whom I have not heard."

Mr. Jefferson nodded, smiling.

"Yes, yes, it could have been the same. You're not American, then?"

"Oh, yes, sir, I am," I replied. "I was born in Vermont."

He chuckled, putting me fully at my ease.

"That's good! It shows you are a man of sense! Mr. Gallatin tells me you've some thoughts on the Western fur trade and the opening of the Missouri."

"I have, sir," I told him, and went straightway into my story, explaining how I had been employed in this business practically from the time I was old enough to fend for myself and how it was my opinion as well as that of Mr. Astor that the trade of the Missouri would be best managed in private hands.

But here he cut me short impatiently, waggling a bony finger at me, then clasping his wrists behind his back. He began to pace up and down the long room and took to reciting my story for me. It was characteristic of the man, I was to learn, that he could not bear to be silent while others talked.

"Yes, yes," he exclaimed impatiently, but quite in such a way that it would have been impossible to take offense. "Yes, yes, all this I have heard from Mr. Gallatin and Mr. Madison. I tell you, Mr. O'Rourke, we have given considerable time to discussing you these few months past. I think your ears must have been ringing, eh?"

"Why, sir," I said, flushing, "they would had I suspected."

"I think you've fairly won Mr. Gallatin over with your argument in favor of economy," he went on. "There is soundness in it, I will admit. But the question of a monopoly is a vexing one. Aye, with me more than with him, even. Mr. Madison seems to favor your plan, too, though for somewhat different reasons."

"I——" I began, somewhat surprised, but he cut me short with his leveled forefinger.

"Don't interrupt," he commanded. "I must say I feel somewhat inclined to agree with Mr. Madison. The merit in your plan, it seems to me, is mainly that it will extend our influence in a way that governments cannot do."

"Exactly, sir," I broke in, unable to restrain myself longer, "and unless we do something of the sort, we will find ourselves in competition with the Northwesters and the Bay people. If our folk are not there first, then we will have the British or the Russians or possibly even the Spanish upon that side of us and our access to the Western seas will be cut off. But if we have established settlements at the mouth of the Columbia and along that river and across the mountains and down the Missouri, how, then, can they say that we were not there first?"

He smiled faintly and half-nodded.

"I see you are a visionary, Mr. O'Rourke," he said.

Visionary, indeed! I resented that. The thought was practical. I said as much, and I believe events have since proved it so.

"Wait." He smiled. "Wait! I think perhaps we have somewhat the same thought in mind."

I looked at him blankly. His blue eyes took on a look of almost studied mysticism.

"I know what you mean, Mr. O'Rourke," he said. "I honor you for it as I honor many another thorough patriot for what he believes. Yet I have told you that I agree with Mr. Madison to a great extent regarding the land beyond the Mississippi. In my opinion, it is scarcely likely to be a part of this country."

Before I could stop myself, I cried out.

"But, Your Excellency! Do you mean that you bought that land with no hope that it could ever be a part of the United States?"

He looked at me almost belligerently.

"If we people this continent with Americans, Mr. O'Rourke," he said, "will it matter whether or not they are all under the same government?"

"You go a bit too fast for me, sir," I said.

"Forgive me." He smiled. "I do not mean to confuse you, but I do feel that to bring that region under our government and into our union of sovereign states is rather more than we can expect. I tell you frankly, sir, that if this territory beyond the Mississippi, aye, and that beyond the mountains as well, as far as the Pacific, is set up as one nation or more, tied to us by the bonds of blood and language and cemented to our interest by the ties of commerce, I think that is as much as we could ask!"

"But the Missouri," I protested, "is already ours, and surely the Columbia must be ours by right of discovery."

"Technically, that is true," he said. "But should any seizure be projected or any breakaway planned, do you think we would be in any position to hold it?"

"We could at least try," I said.

"Hah!" he chuckled ruefully. "I could name a score of men who have their personal ambitions in that part of the world. Each seeks to pinch off an empire of one sort or another. Colonel Burr is but one, though he has cast his eyes farther south. To what does your Mr. Astor aspire?"

"To no more than the rights of trade," I said stoutly. "Let politics fall where they will, for if there is an American colony upon the Columbia and American posts up that river and along the Missouri, at least such claims as other powers may make will not be without opposition from us!"

"True," he said. "And there you put your finger on it. I tell you, Mr. O'Rourke, I am inclined to favor your scheme, not, mind you, to the extent of granting you the exclusive right of trade either upon the Missouri or the Columbia, for all Americans are entitled to the same privileges from their government. But I will say this: I will give you every opportunity to trade and every support in doing so in free competition with others. I have already decided upon my Superintendent of Indian Trade, and when his name is announced, I feel sure you will find he is a man of whom you will heartily approve and with whom you will be able to work. He will have instructions to forward the enterprise of every legitimate American trader in that region."

"Mr. President, sir!" I cried. "You can't do that!"

"Can I not?" he demanded. "And why?"

I saw at once that I had made a mistake.

"If you will pardon me, sir," I said, "I do not mean to dictate to you. But this is a thing of which I know. If competition arises we will have bloodshed."

"That will be our risk, Mr. O'Rourke," he said. "I honor you for your thought. It seems to me you have a greater interest in seeing this region brought under the influence of our country than others I have talked with. Now I tell you, it was many years ago I talked with John Ledyard, and it was his notion that America must one day spread from ocean to ocean. I see it is yours as well, and perhaps I am wrong to dispute you or to doubt that it can be so. I do not hope for so much. But I tell you that we are both of one mind when we say that we would see this continent, if not entirely in our hands, at least in hands like ours. They must be Americans, whether they be of one nation or of two or of many. They must be American nations, with no tie with the Old World. It seems to me it is for us, as the first independent nation on the continent, to encourage such others as may grow up beside us. I shall support your plan so far as I am able. Though I am sure you will understand why, I cannot offer more than my encouragement and the best wishes of this government. If you can squeeze more practical benefit out of that than I have stated, why then, more power to you, sir! And here's my hand on it!"

Fine words! Fine words, indeed, I thought!

"Will you give Mr. Astor my regards and assure him that I wish him every success?" he asked.

The interview was obviously at an end, and any further argument would be useless. I had not obtained what I had sought, but no one could say that I had failed entirely.

V. MASTER PEDLAR

WE WERE overtaken and passed in our return journey by the news of the *Leopard's* unprovoked attack on the *Chesapeake,* and we found the city in an uproar of indignation when we arrived.

Mr. Astor stared up at me, almost moodily, as I entered his office, and it seems to me significant that for the first time I thought of him as the "Old Gentleman." He had grown somewhat paunchy in my absence, and his jowels were more prominent, and I noticed that he breathed heavily as he spread his hands upon the desk top and pushed himself to his feet.

"Ach! Rory! Good it is to see you back again," he growled. "Sometimes the good God sends a ray of brightness through the clouds upon a stormy day! Is this not a miserable business?"

"Worse, Mr. Astor," I replied. " 'Tis the most damnable outrage that ever was committed!"

"Ya! Ya!" he agreed. "I am a man of peace, but to me it seems this is an act of war which men of honor only can resent! Yet what are we to do? Mr. Jefferson I like, but of our Navy it is true he has left but a skeleton and of our Army not even so much! How can we fight Britain? How can we and survive?"

"Exactly," I agreed.

"Eh, well!" he sighed. "It is no matter; that will be settled here today! What word do you bring from Washington?"

"None of the best, sir, I fear," I replied.

"You saw Mr. Jefferson?"

"I saw Mr. Jefferson and Mr. Gallatin and Mr. Madison," I told him. "I saw Mr. Clark and Mr. Lewis. Maybe I overstepped my instructions. I told the President rather more than you said I should. Yet I believe that alone gained us such enthusiasm as saved us from complete disapproval."

"So?" he said, scowling.

"Aye, sir." I assured him. "Mr. Clark has been appointed Superintendent of Indian Affairs. Mr. Lewis has been given the post of governor of Upper Louisiana—the Missouri Territory, I believe they call it now. Neither Mr. Madison nor Mr. Jefferson feels that this country should extend beyond the Mississippi; that is to say, as a part of this nation——"

"What do you say?" he demanded, interrupting.

"That is true, sir," I replied. "It is Mr. Madison's contention that to extend beyond the Mississippi will be to spread our population too thin over too great an area and will only have the effect of weakening us. Mr. Jefferson himself said with regard to the Pacific that he hopes to see nations established there whose only tie with us would be by blood and language!"

Mr. Astor stared at me, and it seemed to me his eyes went wide. "So?" he said thoughtfully. "So!"

"It seemed to me, sir," I said plaintively, "from all I had heard, that it was Mr. Jefferson's ambition that this nation should extend from the Atlantic to the Pacific. Now, by his own words, he has thrown that notion into the discard. He does not seem optimistic of any such eventuality. It may be true that it is not possible. If we stop to think about it, how would representatives from the Columbia attend sessions of the Congress at Washington? It would be necessary for them to leave their constituencies a year, or even two years, before the session!"

He continued to stare at me, tugging at his lower lip.

"Ya? Ya! Did he say that such a nation we would support? Would it have our friendship, our alliance?"

"Certainly that was his implication," I replied.

With his open hand he slapped the edge of his desk.

"Ha! Rory! Out of the mouths of politicians!"

"I'm afraid, sir, I don't understand." I said blankly.

"You will! You will." He chuckled. "I see. My judgment is confirmed. You have done well, Rory. One day you will be my Prime Minister!"

He laughed heartily, as at some private joke. I daresay I looked somewhat dubious, for I had a sense of having failed.

What he had in mind, I had no way of knowing then, and since he evidently did not care to tell me, I saw no reason to press the point. Certainly, it seemed to me, there were more important things that I might be doing in my own behalf at that moment.

I lost no time as soon as I was free in taking myself out to Greenwich Street to the big white house, in the midst of its spacious lawns and gardens, where Winthrop Drake lived. I had scarcely known it well enough before I went to Washington to be thoroughly familiar with it, but it seemed to me just as I remembered it.

Mr. Drake himself opened the door to my knock, and at sight of me he cried out in genuine enthusiasm.

"Rory O'Rourke! I hear you have been to Washington."

"I have, sir," I replied. "I only just returned."

"So?" He smiled. "And what's the news at the Capitol?"

"I daresay you know it as well as I, sir," I replied.

To that he made no answer but smiled again, so that I felt a little awkward.

There was a flurry of slippers in the hall behind him, and Deborah appeared from somewhere.

"Rory!" she cried. "Why, Rory, you're back at last!"

"*Look* who's here!" I grinned at her, seeing before me a handsome girl of fifteen. But for the older sister, I thought, I might be tempted to pay my court to her. But then, of course, I was so much older than she.

"Deborah, child, you grow more lovely——"

I was startled by the abrupt expression of exasperation that flashed across her face. She stamped her foot.

"Oh!" she cried. "You!"

"I—why——" I stumbled.

But she turned away furiously and went flying upstairs in a great flurry of petticoats without another word.

I stared at her father. He lifted his shoulders.

"Women!" he exclaimed.

"Aye, who can understand them?" I replied.

"Not I." He chuckled. "Every man must make up his own mind! But come in, come in. Valerie and Dick are in the drawing room."

"Dick?" I asked.

"Oh, yes, Dick Goodwin," he replied. "You remember him, no doubt."

"I don't want to intrude," I said.

"Nonsense!" he cried. "Come in. Come in. They'll both be glad to see you."

You may imagine that that was one of the dullest, most unhappy evenings of my life. I daresay it was for Goodwin and Valerie too. Not one of us said what he or she was actually thinking, and I for one was determined that, having stepped into it, I would not withdraw now to leave him a clear field.

We sat like a trio of marionettes before the empty fireplace and exchanged inanities, until at last Valerie herself could stand it no longer and rose to give us the signal for us both to be off. Thereupon we left, walking together only as far as the nearest corner, where we bade each other a surly good night and each took his own way.

I think I would have been scarcely human had I not resented the reception. Yet, when, after the first edge of my pique had dulled a little, I came to charge her with it, she stopped me and left me feeling dull and stupid simply by asking me why I should object? Surely, she pointed out, she had the right to entertain an old friend in her father's house without being censured for it. I had come calling unexpectedly. I had sent no word ahead. What did I expect? That she would sit demurely in the window watching for me?

Of course I had no answer to that, but she took the sting out of it by laughing and calling me a jealous, gruff old bear and kissing me so that I was mollified. But I noticed that that was the way it went all summer, and I could never pin her down to a definite promise to marry me.

In the meantime, the world of business did not come to a standstill. Despite the fear of war with Great Britain that hung over the city like a great cloud, Mr. Astor proceeded with his plans to incorporate the American Fur Company and even went so far as to send Harry Brevoort to St. Louis to appoint agents at that key center. He was six months on the journey, four of them spent in coming and going, and he returned to report that we would not be without serious competition, for several of the merchants of St. Louis, notably the Chouteaus and Manuel Lisa, had banded together to form their own fur companies with an eye to monopoly of the Missouri trade at least. This had made it difficult for him, but he had nevertheless been able to obtain trading licenses and the promise of franchises for several posts; and he had found two good men to act as company agents on the river. Ramsay Crooks, the first of these, was a trader and river man, once of Greenock in Scotland. The other, Wilson Price Hunt, he described as a quiet, shrewd, well-thought-of merchant, formerly a native of New Jersey.

Since we could see neither at the moment, we must necessarily accept his estimate of them without question—a risky proceeding, it occurred to me. Yet I noticed that Mr. Astor seemed to have faith in his good judgment, and I could ask no more than that.

During this time business in New York itself could hardly have been said to prosper. Owners of shipping were panic-stricken at the prospect of war or worse, and it may have been unchristian of me, but I could scarcely feel distressed at the knowledge that Richard Goodwin was one of those hardest hit. The business he had inherited was entirely dependent upon sea-borne trade. Indeed, the bulk of its capital was tied up in ships, and he and his associates seemed in a fair way to lose them all.

Mr. Astor, on the other hand, I soon discovered, had a sufficient diversity of interests so that he was little affected. If our shipping were to be forced off the seas by British encroachments and French insolence, he could lay up the vessels he owned and, provided it were not of too long duration and cataclysmic nature, perhaps weather the storm. Having a few thousand dollars to invest myself, I felt that I could do worse than follow his lead. As a result, I put my capital in real estate on the outskirts of the city, not far from Greenwich—land which I felt would increase in value, and later experience proved me correct.

Whether or not this could have had anything to do with it I do not know, but I felt that in spite of Goodwin's persistence Valerie generally inclined to me. Our disagreements, in the main, were minor. She teased me half-seriously for the interests Sally Livingston reported I had found in Washington.

"I told you I wanted no more than to be back here with you," I said.

"A likely story." She sniffed. "I've heard what fun you had!"

"See here," I cried. "I went there for a purpose."

"Of course," she jeered. "I know. Sally has told me how you courted the Barlow girls and were the life of the party at picnics."

"Did you expect me to be a hermit?" I protested. "I haven't heard that you had been one. I saw the President and the Secretary of State, the Secretary of the Treasury, our senator, and the Vice-President. If you'd go to Washington with me, I'm sure they'd bear witness I talked business."

"Business!" she snorted. "What do I care for business?"

"I'm sorry," I replied. "It takes business or some other way of making money for me to be able to support you."

"Who said you were ever going to support me?" she demanded.

I bowed as elegantly as I knew how and turned upon my heel.

"Please, Rory," she called after me. "Please let's not quarrel."

I stopped abruptly in the doorway and turned about, feeling suddenly very contrite.

"I don't want to quarrel," I said. "I only want you to know that I love you, Valerie. That's all I ask. If you don't want my love, I'll go and we—you at least—can forget it."

"Oh, Rory," she would cry. And all at once she would be in my arms again, and everything would be again as it had been.

But our tiffs, our quarrels, were not always so insignificant, and it needed but one actually to set everything back once more to a status of strained politeness. That one had to come, of course, in the late summer, at a time when I dared hope that at last she was actually approaching a mood to commit herself definitely, and it began, not at the Drake house, but curiously enough in the counting rooms of Mr. Astor.

I was there one morning in late August when he came in, crooking his finger at me as he passed on into his office. I followed him and found him pacing the long room, somberly tugging at his ear.

"Well, Rory," he said, "how soon can you go to Montreal?"

I blinked and gulped. If I had not completely forgotten that one of us made the annual journey, I had fatuously hoped that this year it might not be necessary.

"Montreal, sir?" I cried.

He smiled a little heavily, wisely.

"Ya," he said, "I did not wish your cart of apples to upset."

I must have blushed furiously, for he laughed.

"Is anything yet settled?" he demanded.

"No, sir," I admitted. "As a matter of fact 'tis not even officially admitted to ourselves."

"These women," he growled good-naturedly. "Hard it is sometimes for them to make up their minds."

"Yes, sir," I agreed. "So I have noticed."

"Ach!" he grinned. "You will notice it more as older you grow. But now about this business in Montreal. I think we have postponed it as long as we can. This year especially is it important that something we do to insure that our business there will continue in the event of war or any worse development. Perhaps, if suddenly you are sent away, it will help to make up the mind? Eh?"

"Possibly," I said a bit doubtfully.

I told Valerie about it very unhappily that evening when I saw her, and I cannot say that I found her reaction reassuring.

"Montreal?" she cried. "Good heavens! Now?"

"Within the week," I told her.

"But why?" she demanded petulantly.

"Business," I replied wearily. "Mr. Astor feels that we should not delay securing our Canadian trade in the event thàt our relations with Great Britain become more strained."

"Business," she scoffed. "Business! Business! That's all men ever think about. Daddy's the same way."

"That isn't so," I retorted defensively. "It takes a good deal of business to keep you in the things you like."

"Now you're criticizing me!" she flared.

"I am not," I retorted.

"If you had any gumption at all," she cried, "you'd tell Mr. Astor you're not going. Let him send somebody else."

"Don't be a fool, Valerie," I told her somewhat roughly. "Mr. Astor employs me for just this sort of thing and pays me handsomely to do it. I may be foolish in some respects, but I'm not such a fool that I don't recognize that what success I have enjoyed since I came to New York has been due to him."

"Oh!" She stamped her foot. "Cautious! You're always too careful to take a chance. It would be easy for you to set up in business for yourself, and then you could work when you felt like it."

"I'm afraid it's not like that," I told her. "Men who only work when they feel like it don't get very far. Besides, I can go a lot further if I follow Mr. Astor than if I strike out for myself at such a time. Look what's happened to Dick Goodwin."

"Don't you dare criticize Dick Goodwin!" she flared.

"I'm not criticizing him," I shot back.

She flounced and refused to meet my eyes.

"Maybe you prefer his company to mine," I growled foolishly.

"Maybe I do," she retorted; then, when I did not answer, "What will we do about the Hones' picnic?"

"Good lord!" I cried, "Philip Hone will understand. I'll explain. He's a businessman—he'll know I had no other choice."

"You may have no choice," she flared, "but I do. I'll go to that picnic without you if I have to. In fact, I'll get Dick Goodwin to take me."

"All right!" I roared, quite goaded beyond endurance and snatching up my hat. "If that's the way you feel about it, I hope you have a good time. But remember while I'm gone that I'm there in Montreal because I want to make a decent living for you and for me. Good night!"

I cannot say that that visit to Montreal was among the most pleasant. To be sure I was busy every moment of it. I had Astor's instructions to buy to the limit. I was also expected to make shipping and banking arrangements, independent of New York, so that in the event of hostilities Mr. Astor's business there would continue. But there was an air of tension about the city, as if war were expected at any instant; and if it were to come, there would be no question, a Yankee would be none too welcome in Canada! Moreover, I brooded about my parting from Valerie. I did not return to New York until December, and in all that time I heard not a word from her.

To tell the truth, I was not sure on my return to New York whether or not I dared to call. I passed the border with some difficulty, for you may be sure that all who traveled between Montreal and New York in those days were carefully scrutinized. I found the city restless with disquietude, for by now we had begun to have definite word of what was happening abroad. The Berlin decrees were outlined, and there was no question of the Emperor's intent. Nor was the word from Britain more reassuring. The rumor that new and even more drastic Orders in Council were to be promulgated showed that England was as determined as Napoleon to force us into the conflict upon one side or the other and that the King's proclamation recalling all British sailors in the service of neutral powers was intended as a warning, beyond the possibility of denial, that the right of search and seizure and of impressment would be insisted on.

In the face of this, it was clear enough that some measures would have to be adopted by our government. Plenty were indignant and clamored for war, but few appeared certain just which side we would take. To me it seemed a case of six of one and half a dozen of the other.

In my opinion we should have cried a plague on both their houses.

In this dilemma, all who were involved in shipping—and Dick Goodwin was foremost among them—seemed to me to be riding for a dreadful tumble. Nor, as it proved, was I wrong in that. Late in December, one cold and early dawning, the town was roused from its beds by the criers going about with copies of Mr. Jefferson's Proclamation of Embargo, closing our ports to all trade and calling back all American ships in foreign waters. Within half an hour of the first faint cries of the hawkers the darkened streets were ablaze with lanterns and torches, and every lane and way that led to the water front was a river of shouting, cursing, gesticulating humanity—seamen, sea captains, shipowners, and the like, all crying out to one another what were they to do? The most alert among them seized and signed what sailors they could lay their hands upon, threw on board what supplies and cargo they could find, and got their ships to sea, half-manned, and in many cases more than half-empty. Ports might be closed, but let the President enforce recall if he could seemed to be the general attitude. Better to have the ships at sea, plying between foreign ports forever, than to have them rotting away at our own wharves, they said, and, indeed, the Collector of the Port passively seemed to agree with the opinion, for it was nearly noon before he began to enforce the order that prevented further ships from leaving.

In the meantime, I think I never saw a man who looked so ill, so stricken in the pit of his stomach, as did Richard Goodwin.

Under the circumstances, perhaps, it was unfair of me to pursue my advantage. Yet I could not forget that he had not hesitated to press his when he thought my hands tied, and I remembered that all's fair when it must be. I had too squeamish a sense of delicacy to call at once on the Drakes, but on Christmas Day, when the season offered the excuse, I hurried around with my arms full of the presents I had picked up for the occasion at Montreal: a Murray Bay blanket for Mrs. Drake; a brace of pipes for Valerie's father; a grinning, habitant doll for the younger sister—for certainly I had no notion when a girl stopped playing with such things, and I was utterly at a loss in her case. For Valerie, I had fetched a sable cloak of the finest skins I could select, and these I hoped might be an adequate peace offering. Apparently they were.

Deborah greeted me with enthusiasm as I entered the door and to my confusion and embarrassment caught me under the mistletoe. Valerie, it seemed to me, was a little cool and openly chided me for not having come sooner to see them. Since both Mr. and Mrs. Drake were present, I did not feel I could reply as I wished. Instead, I gave them all a Merry Christmas and fetched out my gifts.

Mrs. Drake seemed restrainedly pleased with the blanket, while Mr. Drake was unquestionably touched by my thought of him. Deborah, I must say, acted almost insulted, and I felt really hurt that she should be so rude, for I had actually grown fond of the child. But Valerie's reaction to her present allowed me no instant to think about it. She opened the package and cried out in delight.

"Why, Rory, you shouldn't," she cried, yet obviously she was delighted, for she whipped the cloak out of its wrappings and flung it about her shoulders, draping it around her and admiring herself in the long mirrors at the end of the room, after which she turned and kissed me with enthusiasm.

Her mother gasped, and I must say Mr. Drake looked startled.

"Ahem!" he said, as confused as I was. "What's this? What's this? Isn't that rather sumptuous for a Chirstmas gift?"

I smiled.

"Hardly, sir," I said. "You forget I'm in the trade where I have opportunity at times to put hands upon such as this at a bargain. Besides," I added, seeing my opportunity and seizing it as it came, "I don't mean it altogether as a Christmas gift."

He blinked at me.

"The devil you say!"

"No, sir," I said, and caught Valerie to me—I daresay surprising her, so that she had no opportunity to protest.

"No, sir," I said, "you see, as a matter of fact I am in love with your daughter and I want her to marry me. She has given me to understand that she thought favorably of the idea, and it seemed to me that this might be a fitting way of announcing it."

He gaped at me and burst into a chuckle.

"I declare," he said. "If this is a proposal, it is the most extraordinary one I've ever heard."

"It is, sir," I assured him, taking a tight grip on Valerie's hand and feeling reassured by her return pressure.

"Well, then," he cried, "I'll be damned if I can understand, but you have my permission!"

Her mother cried on both our shoulders, and her father pumped my hand and insisted upon my taking a glass of brandy with him. Only when the congratulations were done did any of us notice that Deborah had quietly slipped away.

II. Dream of Empire

~~~~~~

I. THE PACIFIC FUR COMPANY

AND SO, somewhat contrary to my expectations, we went back to
something like the old status of the preceding summer, in which I never
knew from one day to the next whether or not our betrothal were
actually an accepted fact or when she would end the suspense and
name the day on which she would become my wife.

My roommates disapproved. There was no question of that. Sanders,
to be sure, was too diffident to say much about it, but Irving lost no
opportunity to twit me upon the situation. Still, so far as I was concerned, it was much that we were at least agreed, even if indefinitely
so. It may be that I became somewhat unduly complacent. Let her
take her own time, I thought. After all, it is not a thing that happens
every day. I admit that once, on my birthday, I grew a touch impatient.

"We grow no younger," I reminded her. "There are some who
would think a man of twenty-six aged."

"But, darling," she pouted, "I'm only a girl still. Don't hurry me,
please."

It occurred to me that there were folk who would not call a woman
of her age a girl, but I had learned enough of diplomacy by then to
keep the thought to myself.

"All right," I agreed, "but please, sweet, don't keep me waiting
always."

And she promised, leaving things, so far as I could see, exactly where
they had stood before.

To be sure, she did not lack some legitimate excuses. The business
situation was as bad, I think, as I have ever seen it. The nation's shipping lay rotting in the harbors up and down the coast; its commerce was
frozen in irons. How Goodwin managed to struggle along I hardly

knew, except that Mr. Drake, being already involved with him to such an extent that he could not afford to see him completely destroyed, tided him over. As a result, Mr. Drake's own situation was far from secure. In such circumstances, I could scarcely press for anything more definite, although it seemed to me that in marrying me she might be removing a rather heavy burden from her father's shoulders. At the same time, I was reasonable enough to appreciate her feelings, namely, that she could not leave him in such difficulties. I am afraid I was not so complacent about the other thought which she invariably added:

"Besides," she would say, "Daddy could never afford now to give me the kind of wedding I want to have."

That statement never failed to precipitate an explosion and lead to argument between us.

In April, Mr. Astor announced the final incorporation of the American Fur Company, and in May Brevoort again went to St. Louis, to return with word that matters were going forward satisfactorily in that quarter and that Hunt would presently be coming to New York, by way of New Orleans, with the furs that he had gathered.

It was while Brevoort was away at this time that one of those unlooked-for events, that come close to changing the whole course of our lives, occurred. As a matter of fact, it is possible that it did alter matters somewhat for me. Certainly, it is true that it came near to wrecking my romance with Valerie; yet, excepting a few letters I wrote, I declare I had nothing whatever to do with the famous "Mandarin Hoax" by which Mr. Astor was legitimately enabled to send out the only merchant vessel to leave an American port that year.

It was entirely Irving's idea to find a local Chinese and dress him up in silks and ribbons and send him with Sanders to Washington as the "Mandarin," Punqua Wingchong, to seek, respectfully, the government's license to charter a vessel in order to return to Canton, there to "bury his honorable ancestor, whom he had heard had died in his absence."

Certainly no one dreamed that the scheme would work. It was meant simply as a joke. Yet Sanders, alias "Palmer," a linguist, and Punqua Wingchong returned from Washington with the licenses, wrapped in high-sounding phrases about the sacred duties of international amity. And in August the *Beaver,* an Astor ship, sailed with Wingchong aboard and, under her hatches as ballast, a considerable cargo of furs and ginseng, specie, and other items in demand in China.

Naturally the whole story came out after she was gone. It was too good to remain secret. Yet many of our colleagues and competitors failed to see the humor of it. Indeed the incident stirred up the very devil of a tempest, and one of those who took most umbrage at it was Winthrop Drake. I must say, in a way, I could scarcely blame him, for it was hardly fair that one of the only merchants in the city who was still fully solvent should be permitted to send a vessel to sea, while those who had their ships laid up with barrels at their mastheads should be forced to lie by and continue to lose. As a matter of fact, but for Deborah, whose attitude toward me seemed to improve as the others' deteriorated, I became aware of a definite coolness toward me in the Drake household. Mr. Drake could scarcely speak. Mrs. Drake became subject to violent headaches whenever I called, and Valerie turned frosty, so that I was as well pleased when Mr. Astor suggested that I accompany him to Montreal in the fall. In the interval of my absence, I hoped, things would have a chance to quiet down somewhat.

We were accompanied on our journey by Astor's eldest daughter, Magdalen, who somewhat complicated matters for us by what seemed to me her excessively social attitude. We must dine with the governor; we must go here and there; and since she was a shrewish, sharp sort of creature, quite different from her father, I must say, I did not care much for her. Yet my employer and I did escape once or twice to the Beaver Club, where we sat on the floor with the members and their guests and played at being voyageurs, using canes, umbrellas, or swords in lieu of paddles, shouting the rollicking chansons of the canoemen at the top of our lungs, and tucking away quantities of good scotch whisky in place of the raw, rank rum which the company usually provided for such journeys.

On these occasions I presented Mr. Astor to some of my former colleagues. The wiry McKay he already knew; and bibulous, quaking, jellylike Duncan MacDougal. David Stuart he had met, but his younger nephew, Robert, was new to him. So was hulking "Fats" Mackenzie, who, as I think I have indicated, was no relative to Sir Alec.

It seemed to me he greeted them with rather more interest than I expected, and once, as we were waiting for Magdalen, he surprised me.

"These Northwesters," he asked casually, "they are all good men?"

"Every one of them, sir!" I replied, a little startled. "None better."

"So?" he said. "What would you think of combining our undertaking with the North West Company?"

I stared at him, finding it hard to believe my ears.

"Good God, sir!" I cried. "No!"

"Why not?" he demanded, watching me closely.

"To begin with," I said, "if you let them in, it would be no time at all before it would be all North West Company. In the second place, if you do fetch them in, you will be giving Britain a claim to territories we wish to keep exclusively American."

"Are not these Canadians also Americans?" he demanded. "Suppose Mr. Jefferson's fears proved founded and we thought it necessary to establish that independent state of which he spoke."

"I want no part of treason," I interrupted him.

"I do not suggest it," he retorted sharply. "I simply quote Mr. Jefferson as he was reported to me by yourself."

I shrugged.

"Do you not think that Britain would look more kindly yet upon such a nation as that, if it were established by both Yankees and Canadians together?" he persisted.

"No, sir!" I said positively. "As you say, Canadians may also be Americans, but you must remember they are at the same time Britons, and it is to Britain that their first loyalty lies. As for England looking with a kinder eye upon the independence of a state because some of its founders might also be British, I think to the contrary. Such a composition of our forces would be fatal, for it would bolster any British claim, and I for one have never known Britain to relinquish any claim she was not forced to."

He only shrugged, and since Magdalen appeared at that moment, we let the question drop.

That winter season offered no events worthy of recounting beyond the fact that it was the beginning of yet another year for me. Valerie still maintained herself against my siege for reasons of her own which I was certainly growing less and less able to understand.

Early in the spring the Embargo was lifted and trade immediately spurted, despite the mass of restrictions with which it was still hedged about. The next time I saw Goodwin, he had regained all of his old confidence and swagger, and it seemed to me there was trouble in the making. Any hope I may have had that Valerie and myself would be married that spring or summer was thoroughly dashed when Mrs. Drake fell ill of a common phthisic and Mr. Drake removed not only her to Newport to recover, but his entire family. So, from June until almost October, I saw nothing of them whatsoever.

As the end of September approached and I began to consider the possibilities of going to Montreal, I grew restless to be off, for I could obtain from the Drakes no definite word of when they might be returning. But when the time came, Mr. Astor announced that this year he would go alone while I remained in New York to attend to certain details of the business and to meet Wilson Hunt, who was expected momentarily from New Orleans. I must say I felt rather piqued at the decision.

It was December before Wilson Hunt, a dark, mild-seeming sort of man, arrived from St. Louis, and it was close to Christmas when Mr. Astor returned from Montreal. I wondered what could have kept him so long, but he did not enlighten me. Instead, he went at once into a series of lengthy conferences with Hunt to which I was not invited. My irritation at being left in New York in the fall rose almost to positive resentment at this, but if Mr. Astor was aware of it, he gave no hint. Not until we had turned well into 1810 and the winter was more than half over did he break his silence and take me again into his confidence. Then he summoned me to one of those precious conferences, and I admit I went with a chip on my shoulder.

"Ach, Rory!" he cried. "Of all the bargains I have tried, this seems to be the hardest yet to bring to a close! But now perhaps something we have that does the trick, eh?"

"What is that, sir?" I asked.

"The Pacific Fur Company!" he replied.

"I never heard of it," I said.

"Ya? I did not think you would have," he retorted. "Sit down, and I explain. An important part you have taken in our first moves toward the Missouri. Good! So! I think you will agree that all that can be there done has been done. Now we must wait until posts we can set up before more definite steps we can take. But the Pacific! This is something different! On the Missouri we did not begin fast enough, and from this we must a lesson learn! In the Pacific we will be first. On the Columbia we will have no rival."

"What of this Pacific Fur Company?" I asked.

Astor chuckled.

"We will be the Pacific Fur Company!" he announced. "To do what we have in mind, another company we must form—a company within a company, you understand? In other words, a part of the American Fur Company it will be, but where the American Company will have for its object control of all American fur trade, this company will only control the Pacific trade. You follow me? This we call the Pacific Fur Company, and it is necessary, because to obtain this control and such posts to maintain, new captal we must have!"

"I see." I grinned at him. "I can put in a thousand dollars."

"You have more than that!" he cried, pretending indignation.

"So I have," I retorted. "But you taught me never to put all my eggs in one basket."

"All right, that we talk about later," he chuckled. "Now, let us go on! This company will have a limited number of partners. As for capital, you need not worry! That I supply myself to the extent of four hundred thousand dollars for the first five years. If any loss is incurred—and I do not think that immediately at a profit we will operate—this I will bear. If profits there are, they will be distributed according to the shares. One hundred shares there will be, of which fifty I will hold. You understand?"

I nodded.

"The rest," he went on, "will be divided among the other partners. I suggest not more than eight or ten altogether, with none to have more than five shares or votes and some to have preferably less, so that new blood we may bring in, as have the Northwesters. This, also, we speak of later."

He looked to see if I had any comment, but I offered none.

"Now back to details! The company which we form will be at first limited to twenty years, with the right of extension and renewal by mutual consent of the majority, unless within five years the whole business so unprofitable seems that each, according to his own judgment, may withdraw and to the company there is an end."

"But, sir," I cried, "that doesn't seem to me fair to you! You put up all the capital. You shoulder all the risk."

"Not quite! Not quite!" He smiled. "In the first place, none are to be partners but who participate; who give services in return for shares. These partners, you see, will be *our* winterers. They will conduct the real operations in the field, and to their labors will be due any profits or loss. If they wish to earn, they must work; but if in spite of work it is no success, then all they will lost will be their labor and their time. So, you see, while I put up the money, it is for others to make it work. I think that is fair, and I think, too, you see it is not with me a new principle!"

"I recognize it, sir." I grinned at him.

"Besides," he added, "to myself I reserve the right to make over my shares at any time to the American Fur Company!"

"I see," I said.

"Now then!" he added. "Essential first a post we must build at the mouth of the Columbia to serve as a central depot, to which will be sent furs as they are collected at other posts high on the river; maybe even on the headwaters of the Missouri. To this will go our ships to collect the furs and carry them to markets."

I nodded.

"Ya," he said, with no false modesty. "Myself and Mr. Hunt we have worked out this plan."

"But it seems to me," I put in, "that you may be putting the cart before the horse. Aren't your feeder posts as important as your Pacific depot? Without them to send down furs from the upper river, the primary post will be confined to trade in the immediate neighborhood."

"Ya!" he agreed. "In the same channel go all our minds. That is true, and this is how we get around it. We could at the mouth of the river the post establish first and then send back parties from there, and this we will also do. But there is a way by which we can many such steps save ourselves."

I looked my inquiry.

"This year two expeditions we send to the Columbia," he said. "The first of these will be in charge of Mr. Hunt, here, and will go overland following up the Missouri and over the mountains into the Oregon. As they go, sites for upcountry posts they will mark, and if possible, even, some of those posts they will build, at least temporarily, as they pass."

I glanced at Wilson Hunt and wondered if he knew fully the immensity of the task to which he had agreed and which had been so glibly outlined in a few brief words. Yet, I thought, he must have more experience than I suspected, for he seemed perfectly assured.

"You spoke of two expeditions," I prompted.

"The other," he nodded, "will go by sea around Cape Horn. For this I fit out a stout ship, which every kind of supply and trade goods will carry, materials for building and so forth. In her will go most of the clerks and partners and enough woodsmen, voyageurs, and mechanics to build at the mouth of the river."

"That seems well planned," I said. "No time is lost. The primary post will be working by the time the overland group arrives. Then if upriver posts have not been established, their sites will have been chosen and they will be ready for building."

"Exactly! Exactly! So we pictured it! Now what do you say? Five shares I have in an envelope with your name on it. They are for you if you want them. If not——"

I swallowed. My thoughts ran swiftly. There was no question but it was a temptation. But he had said that upon those who shared as partners would fall the actual work in the field. If I accepted, might it not mean that I myself must go with one or the other of these expeditions?

"Thank you, sir." I grinned. "Somehow I find myself reluctant to go, quite so far afield at this time."

"Ach, ya!" He chuckled. "This I more than half-expected! In any case you lend us the benefit of your experience in the field."

"Whatever you say, sir," I assured him.

"First," he said, "I will go over with you a list of former North-westers——"

"Former Northwesters, sir?" I interrupted.

"Ya!" He nodded. "I have sounded those whom you presented to me, and all I list have said they will take part: McKay, Mackenzie, Stuart, MacDougal——"

I frowned. I must have looked a little doubtful.

"You do not approve?"

"They are good men," I replied. "I'll not deny that. But they are still Northwesters."

"Bah!" he snorted. "Northwesters they were, but each has expressed a grievance with the Company. When they have talked with you and Mr. Hunt they will be Northwesters no more. They will be partners in the Pacific Fur Company."

"That's very well to say, sir," I protested. "But it is not so easy. What will the North West Company do? We will have a fight on our hands."

"Pooey!" he exclaimed. "Already they are aware of it. When I was in Montreal I suggested that we pool our interests——"

I stared at him, aghast.

"You didn't, sir!"

"You oppose?" He scowled.

"If I were a partner," I told him, "I would. As it is, I only follow your orders. These men are all former Northwesters. They are all still Britons. I may be prejudiced——"

"May be!" he interrupted me dryly.

"What would you have me do?" I asked.

He glanced at Hunt.

"If Mr. Hunt is to leave St. Louis this summer," he said, "we must begin preparations at once. You and Mr. Hunt will go to Montreal. There you will talk to the partners and secure their signatures upon the agreement. To them you will explain the plan. Mr. Hunt will choose who is to accompany him. The rest you will bring to New York for transport by sea."

I glanced at Hunt. For my part I knew which I would pick for such a journey, but this did not seem to be the time to say it.

"Is that all, sir?" I asked.

"You will engage also clerks and voyageurs," he replied.

"When do we start?" I asked.

He cocked an eye at me.

"As soon as possible. Tomorrow maybe?"

I wondered. Could this be just the lever I needed?

"May I ask one favor, sir?" I said.

"As many as you like." He grinned. "You think me an ogre? Go and ask her!"

No grass could have grown under my feet as I left the office and hurried to Valerie's house. Even so, the long shadows of early winter dusk were darkening the house as I was ushered in and found her with a cup of tea at the fireside.

"Rory!" she cried at sight of me. "You're early! Why, darling, what is it?"

Her face showed a concern that must have reflected that in my own. Purposely I did not attempt to lighten my expression.

"What is it ever?" I growled, kissing her almost absently. "I'm away in the morning for Montreal!"

"Oh!" she cried. "Oh! Not now! You can't! There's the Livingstons' ball and Trudy Lyman's, and your own assembly."

"I'll have to put them off," I said.

"But tomorrow!" she wailed. "Can't you postpone it?"

That was what I had been waiting for. I stared at her.

"I might," I said. "One thing he'd scarcely refuse me!"

"One thing?" she cried almost eagerly, then abruptly realizing what I meant: "Oh!"

"Darling!" I blurted, unable to contain myself longer. "Darling! Marry me now! Tomorrow, the next day! Mr. Astor will postpone my leaving if I tell him 'tis for that. When 'tis done, we'll go to Montreal together. I didn't want to tell you, but I must. Mr. Astor is forming a company to trade in the Pacific, and he offered me a share. But I refused because it would take me away from you! Since I've done that for you, can't you do this for me? 'Tis only a short journey. I'll have only to recruit a few men, and most of the time I can give to you. We'll stay in luxury at the Mansion House, and when the business is attended to, we'll go on to Quebec, where I shan't have a thing to do but devote myself to you! Please, Valerie! Say you will!"

She had turned about as I talked and stood staring at me.

"I would never let my wedding journey be combined with business!" she said coldly.

I felt as if she had slapped me across my face.

"How are we ever to be married at this rate?" I flared.

She lifted her chin haughtily.

"I won't be spoken to in that tone!" she retorted. "When you can take the time from your precious business for me alone, perhaps I shall be able to find time for you!"

She turned and flounced from the room, and I gaped after her, wondering, almost at my wit's end. What could I do now? Absently I reached for my hat. As I did so, Deborah entered the far end of the room. I was blind not to see how lovely she had become at eighteen, but I have the excuse, at least, that I was preoccupied! At sight of me she stopped, smiling.

"Hello, Rory!" she exclaimed. "You're early! I'll tell Val you're here."

"Don't bother," I said harshly.

My tone, perhaps the expression on my face, my air of dejection, must have told her more than I realized. A moment she hesitated, then came toward me, bringing a faint, almost indefinable perfume that stirred me curiously, despite the fact that in my distress I was only half aware of it.

"What is it, Rory?" she asked. "Did she——? Oh, Rory!"

"Aye!" I gritted harshly. "Sometimes I wonder if the game is worth it!"

A shadow crossed her face.

"Are you going away again?" she asked.

"Only to Montreal," I said. "I asked her to go with me."

"And she refused?"

I started toward the door, walking slowly beside her, half-thinking aloud. Almost without realizing it, I told her of Astor's offer—of how I had refused just to be near her.

"What have I done, Deborah?" I cried out. "What do I lack? I'm well placed in business. All that I've done, I've accomplished for her!"

"That's nonsense!" she said sharply. "You've made your own way, and you could have done it as well if you'd never laid eyes on her! Sometimes I'm sorry you ever did."

"No, no!" I objected, not pausing to think why she would say that. "She inspired me. I came here unknown, almost a ragged Irish lad. Now, because I've wanted her, I can go where I please and see whom I will. I've made a place for myself."

"Is that so important?" she broke in. "Any girl who loved a man would want to help him do that, not wait till 'twas done!"

She took me by the shoulders and shook me angrily.

"Wake up! Wake up, Rory O'Rourke!" she scolded. "What is the matter with you anyway? Show her that you won't be used so! Stand up to her! Deliver your last decision! Don't you see what it's doing to you? You may be a very lion in the office, but you're no more than a mouse here!"

"What do you think I've been trying to do?" I retorted.

"Try it again!" she insisted. "Put your foot down hard and let her see you have made up your mind; that if she will not have you, then she may go find another. I know what I would do in your shoes! I wouldn't stay here piddling—yes, I said it, piddling!—if I could be out with men doing a man's work! Seeing history in the making! I wouldn't stay here for the sake of a woman who thinks she can walk all over me! Why, Mr. Astor's offer is the very thing you need! Tell her you'll snap at it unless she will have you! Tell her you'll go to the Pacific if she won't take you now! Tell her that, and I'll warrant she'll think twice before she says 'no'!"

"You don't mean that!" I cried.

"I do mean it!" she flared.

"Suppose she says go?" I demanded.

"Then go!" she told me vehemently. "You'd be accomplishing more there than here!"

"But, Deborah! Good God! Five years!" I protested.

"You've been blind as a bat and stupid as an old hen!" she stormed. "But if you'll only take the firm hand, she'll respect you the more for it."

"Are you truly sure?" I asked.

She looked down at the floor and swallowed, it seemed to me almost with an effort, drawing back from me a little.

"Don't worry," she said, in a voice that I could barely hear. "I'm sure she loves you!"

I looked at her a long moment in silence, the while she stared first at the floor, then lifted her eyes to mine.

"Well," I sighed at length. "Well, I can't pretend to be expert in these things. I certainly don't seem to have much to lose."

She made no reply to that.

"But I can't tell her now," I went on. "I've got to go to Montreal first."

"All right," she said. "But don't forget!"

I nodded slowly.

"I will," I promised. "You're probably quite right. I will, as soon as I get back! And thank you, child!"

I leaned forward and kissed her as fondly as any brother, at which she stamped her foot and cried out so furiously that I fell back a step. Before I could ask her what I had done now, she, too, turned and flung out of the room.

I did not go straight home but stopped at Mr. Astor's, where Mr. Hunt was a guest at supper. Mrs. Astor called to me to join them, but I excused myself, saying I had only a message to leave, at which Mr. Astor himself came out heavily.

"Come! Come in for coffee and segars!" he boomed.

"If you'll forgive me, sir," I said apologetically, "I'd rather not tonight. I only stopped by to say that, if Mr. Hunt will be ready, we'll leave for Montreal in the morning. Will you tell him?"

"So?" He blinked at me. "So! Well, I am sorry! But then I am also glad, for my sake. Ya! I will tell him, and better luck next time!"

II. MONTREAL

IN THE course of that journey to Montreal I came to know Wilson Hunt intimately. Although we had wined and dined and worked together in New York, I had always then seen him more or less on his company behavior. But there is not the man living who can keep up his civilized pretenses in the face of a month's overland journey in winter. On the whole, I found he wore well, though he was inclined to be opinionated. I found him sincere, hard-working, always willing to bear his share, capable of good conversation, although he had sometimes to be prodded, for he was quiet and somewhat given to introspection. As nearly as I could tell, his woods knowledge was largely that of a dilettante, and I must say this caused me some qualms, since what he was about to undertake seemed to me scarcely in the nature of a game.

We were fortunate to reach the Canadian metropolis when we did, for the ground was still frozen and the snow piled deep in the narrow streets, so that either by cariole or afoot it was possible to get about. That fact gave us an opportunity to set our business on its way with a minimum of delay. Within a fortnight the first spring thaws had set in. The snows melted and ran like rivers through the gutters. The hard frost came out of the ground, and the streets became like quagmires.

Winter gave way to that time of year peculiar to the Northland, known as the "mid season." At the same time, as so often happens in the spring of the year in these latitudes, the skies opened and let down their pent-up contents.

Only to set foot out of door was to find one's self soaked through and through. Still, there was business to be done.

For my part, that business consisted first in carrying Wilson Hunt about and presenting him at every office, bar, and tavern in which we might find some one or other who could help us forward our scheme. There was no difficulty in this, for if ever a man was genial, suave, it was he. He charmed everyone with his boyish smile, his dark and thoughtful eyes, his insouciant humor. Before the week was out he had half the ladies of Montreal hanging on his lips. Old Mr. Frobisher and Sir Alec Mackenzie, the McGills, the MacGillivrays, the Grants, the MacLeods, wined and dined and feted him—and by the same token myself—at least until they discovered something of what we were about, when, if they remained as cordial as ever to all outward appearances, it seemed to me that in private they grew cautious as only Scots can in the presence of a business rival.

It was, in the main, a happy time. I was far too busy to think of my own affairs for the moment, so that these gave me no trouble beyond an occasional sleepless hour in the dead of night. And there were bits of news and gossip that helped divert my thoughts. Archie MacLeod, whom I had hoped to interest in our plan, was on the Peace River. David Thompson, who had also seemed to me a bare possibility, was said to be west among the mountains, somewhere in the Kootenay, on the upper Columbia. Dirk MacPherson was said to be with him.

As Mr. Astor had ordered, we devoted our first efforts to the final selection of partners for our undertaking. Although I did not agree with him in some of this, yet I could not deny that in coming to Montreal and the North West Company he had gone to the heart of the trade. Better men he could not find anywhere in that field.

Apparently McKay felt himself slighted by the North West Company, and I suspected, though he never intimated as much to me, that he felt he had been shabbily treated by Sir Alec. While this may have been his motive for listening to us, it was his own vision and imagination that brought him so enthusiastically into our ranks and made him, in my opinion at least, far and away the most valuable of all.

My own second choice fell upon David Stuart. He was tall, lean, sober, older than most in the business. Though I admit he lacked a certain force, he had a friendly way about him that made him popular with all. When we approached him he, too, was enthusiastic and quick to sign the articles of agreement. He brought forward his nephew, Robert Stuart, whom I believe I have mentioned, and who had been for some years a clerk with the Company. He was about my own age and not without certain of his uncle's characteristics; though in time I was to realize he was possessed of far more judgment than his elder relative. In appearance, more like Wilson Hunt than anyone I had seen, he seemed to me one of the finds of our journey, and we signed him as clerk with first option of partnership, as such might be voted by the majority.

Donald Mackenzie, grown stout and heavy, showed no hesitation about signing. I could not quarrel with his ability, for I had seen how he could command a brigade, and whether I liked him or not, it was a fact that he had qualifications we needed. Still, I think I would not have chosen him for the task that eventually fell to him.

The last whom we approached, Duncan MacDougall, was able, thoroughly calculating, and so far as the business itself was concerned, so far as actual facts and figures and close preoccupation with profits and loss went, was undoubtedly far and away the most efficient of them all. The rest were adventurers. He was an exalted bookkeeper. But I could not forget his drill-sergeant tactics during the time I had been apprenticed clerk under him at Grand Portage. It seemed to me that he was a man to be kept close under a stern thumb, lest he be affected by the heady wine of authority; and, at the same time, as I observed him at the Beaver Club, I gathered that his natural addiction to the bottle had increased rather than otherwise.

By this much, at least, our task was comparatively simple. But it was more than a month before we had sufficiently completed this portion of our work so that I was able to turn my attention to other portions of the task. The problem of locating enough qualified clerks was more difficult, for such were far more apt to feel bound to the security of their present employ rather than to risk the possibility of uncertain gains elsewhere. It needed a good deal of persuasion to encourage them to risk all on a throw of Fortune's dice. Despite all this, however, I had good luck.

By the end of another six weeks I had ferreted out and signed on nine such.

It was by now drawing on toward the end of June, and clearly Hunt was growing impatient to be off. Consequently, I turned my attention to the enlistment of voyageurs and boatmen for him, intending to complete my own quota of clerks and other personnel when at last I had seen him on his way.

To my surprise, he did not appear partial to McKay but rather favored Mackenzie, and sooner than see him in a blundering error, I dared to express my apprehensions to him in the privacy of our own rooms in the Mansion House.

"D'you know," I said, "I have a feeling that your interests, as well as those of the Company, would be best served if you did not go on this expedition overland."

As I intended, I took him by surprise.

"What d'you mean by that?" he demanded.

"Naught to raise the hair on your back," I assured him. "You are a businessman—a dealer in furs and trade goods. You have no experience of the field."

"I believe I can do as well as the next," he said coldly.

"I am sure you can," I retorted, "though I'd feel better to see you with more practice. But apart from that, look at it in a practical light. If there is anything we need at this depot we propose to build at the mouth of the Columbia, it is a man with a sound head on his shoulders for business. By the same token, if two old hands are to make the passage across the country, the expedition will fare far better."

He picked up his fork and ate thoughtfully for a moment in silence, then lifted his eyes to mine, and I saw without any question that I had said too much.

"I believe Mr. MacDougal," he said, "is capable of commanding the depot at the mouth of the river, and I have small doubt I can make the journey with Mr. Mackenzie's assistance——"

"Mackenzie!" I cried. "At least take the best! Take McKay!"

"I have no doubt Mr. McKay is an excellent man," he said. "I prefer Mr. Mackenzie."

That seemed to me clear enough. There was no point in arguing. I shrugged and let it go at that. But it was the beginning of a coolness between us.

I had thought, and I think it hardly unnatural that I should, that the matter of securing voyageurs would be purely one of routine. Yet, to my surprise, this proved by far and away the most difficult task of all. For one thing, the brigades left about this time, so that there was a sudden dearth of crewmen in their usual river-front haunts. At the same time, I think the difficulty went somewhat deeper than that, for apparently the Company was taking steps best calculated to choke off our enterprise at the source. If we could not find man power, we could scarcely hope to operate. We might make our own arrangements with partners and clerks. But the simpler voyageurs, less capable of reasoning for themselves, were by nature far more inclined to listen to a whisper over a bottle or a judiciously planted dram. Even though McKay and Stuart helped, we found our hands full when it came to this.

It was only by dint of the hardest work that by the beginning of July we were able to assemble a crew to man a single large Montreal canoe. At that time we received a letter from Mr. Astor. All went well at his end, he assured us, and he hoped it did at ours. Mr. Hunt should be ready to set out, if indeed he were not already on his way. He had secured a ship and a captain, a naval officer on special leave of absence for the purpose, recommended by Mr. Hunt's brother. He had also secured three clerks, a carpenter, a cooper, a rigger and caulker, a blacksmith, an apprentice boy, and others. He urged us to make what haste we could and return to New York, and he asked that we send on the men we had already recruited.

I was disappointed that he gave no report of the Drakes, but I suppose that this was more than should be asked. In view of his urgency, it was decided that Hunt and Mackenzie should go on, selecting their clerks and taking such voyageurs as had been recruited, and leaving to me the problem of filling our quota at this end. Their own ranks, it was felt, could be built up at Michilimackinac or St. Louis. Accordingly, on July the fifth, following a moist celebration of our American independence, we gathered in the cool, wet dawn at the landing at Lachine to send the little party boisterously upon its way.

I will admit that it was a day or two before I brought myself back to the business in hand, and when I did, to my inexpressible chagrin I now found my task more difficult than ever. In accordance with Mr. Astor's requests, I sent all but a handful to New York, keeping only McKay and Franchère and De Montigny. But hard as we labored, we seemed to run at every side into a wall of frustration. One day our quota would seem to be nearly full. The next, the men would melt away like snow before the summer sun, for the Canadian boatman is nothing if not cute in his ability to sign a contract, accept his rum ration, and then forget the whole business. Twice over, I think, we had as many as were required and then, by morning, had none at all. I must say I was fair fit to tear my hair when the merest chance came to my rescue.

Following my habit, I had been combing all of the voyageurs' haunts between the Lachine Gate and the eastern end of the island, when, looking into one smoky tavern, a clap between my shoulders came near to oversetting me and a voice whooped in my ear.

"*Hola! Nom des p'tits balons! Toujours j'y pense! Et maintenant je le vois!* You aul'sonfabitch, goddamyou!"

I spun about and gaped at the stocky half-Indian before me. Years before he had accompanied me on the trail in the north woods, and to meet him here now was like being kicked by a ghost.

"Moose!" I cried. "*L'Orignal!* Charbonneau! Old friend! What are you doing here?"

"Eh? What do you here? I'm tol' you gone away!" he retorted.

"No, no!" I cried, submitting to his embrace. "I asked you first! A tot of rum to old times, and then let's have it! *Pardieu!* I think you are the very man I am looking for!"

We drank once, and once again, at his insistence, to days gone by, and it seemed to me that if he had changed by so much as a wrinkle, it was certainly not visible. The same leathery face was creased and crinkled in the same places and darkened by blood and weather almost to the color of fine moosehide. There was the same straight black hair, the same black beady eyes, searching and inquisitive. Even his build and carriage were the same. The years had not altered them by so much as the shadow of a paunch or the slightest stoop. He planted his feet solidly wide apart on stubby, bowed legs, sturdy as the gnarled trunks of rock maples, and his back was as straight as it had ever been. As I looked at him, it came to me that he was practically ageless, like a rock on a mountainside. I wondered if he had always looked the same; if he had ever been young, or if he would ever seem old.

"You're a long way down river for this time of year," I told him. "I'd expect you to be out with the brigade, at least halfway to the Lakes by now, if not somewhere beyond Fort William!"

"Ho!" he scoffed. "Dat brigade! Dat Nort'wester! I'm *voyageur-bout* now, me! 'Ow you say—steersman! *Ouai!* And for keep. Ees tam good, no? Me, I'm work for independent trader—wan beeg man! We're come an' go now w'en we's please! Ha! Goddam!"

I saw his glass filled again and posed my problem to him. He looked at me speculatively when I had done.

"To de Gran' h' Ocean, eh?" he growled. "So ees you, then? Of this I'm hear! W'at for we wait, hé? I know de man dat easy fin' you crew! W'at you say? I tak' you to heem?"

"If you don't, I'll break your neck!" I replied.

"Ho, ho-ho!" he laughed. "Look w'at gone brek ma neck now! Ha! You sign me on, too, no?"

"I'd already made up my mind to that!" I promised him. "Do you know fifteen or twenty like you that I can get?"

"Ho!" he roared. "Leave that to ol' Moose!"

"Done!" I retorted, clapping him on the shoulder and pulling out the articles of agreement and slapping them down before him.

When he had made his mark, we had yet another tot to celebrate, and he thumped me on the back with such force that I thought he must drive me through the bar.

"Now!" I said, wiping my eyes when I had done choking. "Where are these others?"

He laid a stubby forefinger alongside his crooked nose.

"Com' wit' me!" He grinned.

He led me away through the early summer evening to a place near the Bonsecours Market that seemed to me a cut above the dive where I had found him. I must say I was puzzled by this upward step in the social scale. I would not have looked for voyageurs here. The broad wooden sign that swung above the door proclaimed the place "L'Ours Hivernant." Inside I found myself in a long room, low and full of smoke and the smell of stale beer and whisky and the lees of sour wine. Apparently it was a place devoted to sergeants major and chief petty officers, petit-bourgeois, and farmers who owned more than two and less than six horses—gentry of the second rank, so to speak.

Holding me by the arm, the Moose drew me quickly down the long bar until we stood behind an enormous flame-haired fellow in light tanned buckskins elaborately decorated, whose bright mane brushed the rafters and whose back seemed broad as a barn as I looked up at it. Without hesitation the Moose smote him solidly between the shoulder blades. The stranger choked, spun round, and cocked back his fist belligerently.

"Sweet Jesus!" he cried.

His eye fell upon me and the Moose, and he paused with fist in mid-air, his scowl of belligerence replaced by a frown of puzzled interrogation.

"What do you want?" he demanded.

I glanced at the Moose.

"Is this the man?" I asked him.

He nodded.

"Dat's h'Alan Fraser, by tam!" he replied. "She's wan goddam good bourgeois!"

He used the hivernant's term for a woods boss, but looking at the clean-cut features, the arrogant eye, the obvious temper of him, I put him down for something better than that. Doubtless, I thought, he was the wild son of a sound old family in the trade, who could not stomach the restrictions and discipline of the Company and so had struck off for himself. I had seen dozens like him before, but somehow I felt drawn to this one. The others had only repelled me. He looked from one to the other of us, his handsome, cocky mouth drawn down at the corners, his fist still poised. But the Moose was still speaking, pointing to his fiery head of hair.

"He's call *Le-Coq-des-Bois*—Cock-of-the-Woods, him, on account part of de topknot, but mos' because all de tam he's so goddam noisy an' cocky an' ready for fight."

"Who are you?" the red-haired giant demanded.

"The name's O'Rourke, Mr. Fraser," I told him, "and I've a proposition to make to you. Will you take a glass with us?"

He looked somewhat mollified.

"A proposition?" he demanded. He glanced at the Moose. "You two are acquainted?"

"We were in the woods together," I told him, "a good many years ago, when we were both with the Company. The Moose will vouch for me. What are you having?"

At my reminder he seemed rebuked and dropped his fist, putting out his huge paw in some confusion.

"Glad to know you!" he said. "Any friend of the Moose——! But here, now! It ought to be for me! What are you taking?"

I shook my head and smiled.

"The first is on me," I told him, holding up three fingers to the barman. "Demerara—if that's all right with you?"

He grinned.

"What's better?" he demanded. "You have a proposition, you say?"

I nodded.

"I've already talked to the Moose, and he likes the idea," I said. "How about you? Would you like to sign up with a new company that plans a post at the mouth of the Columbia and turn at the Pacific trade?"

He blinked at me in surprise. Apparently Charbonneau could contain himself no longer.

"*Dits-donc, p'tit Coq!*" He blared, thumping the giant on the chest with his forefinger. "You remember, we 'ear of wan gran' fol w'at's think to 'ire men for mak' these voyage?"

The huge redheaded man stared at me.

"Is it you?" he demanded.

I nodded.

"It is," I told him. "And I've already signed on the Moose. How about yourself?"

He whirled on the half-breed.

"You what? What are you trying to do, you fool!" he cried. He spun toward me, belligerent again. "Aye! And you, you slick little pip-squirt, to take advantage of a poor devil that knows no better——"

"Hold on!" I snapped. "Why don't you wait until you know what you're talking about?"

Unequal as we were, we might have come to blows, for I had a temper of my own and I did not care for name-calling. But the Moose thrust between us.

"By Joe!" he roared. "I t'ink you both tam fools! Listen!"

Fraser glowered at me, then shrugged.

"All right!" he growled. "Talk, and see 'tis a good thing you offer, for you'll have small use for Charbonneau's articles if 'tis not!"

"That suits me," I retorted. "As for using the articles, I'll pleasure myself as to that!"

I nodded toward a table in the corner.

"Come over where we've not got half Montreal breathing down our necks," I said.

When we were seated I told them both, in more detail than I had to the Moose alone, of the project that was afoot. At the outset Fraser was skeptical, but as I went on I saw a gleam in his eye. When I spoke of the ship, he rubbed his chin with an apologetic grin.

"I've often thought to take a sea voyage," he said.

"Here's your chance," I retorted.

"Go on!" he prompted.

I did so, and when I mentioned that we must move swiftly, since Thompson was already upon the upper river, he chuckled.

"By God! I'd give a pretty to see Davy's face when he finds that for once someone's before him!" He grinned.

"Put your fist to the articles," I told him, "and you'll be paid for the privilege."

"Partnership?" He glanced at me speculatively.

"I can't promise you that, since I'm not one myself." I explained my own relation to the Company.

"I can sign you with the stipulation that next to Stuart you will be eligible for shares as they are distributed," I added. "One thing you can be sure of, those who come into it now will be soonest on shares."

"It seems reasonable." He nodded, musing. Then all at once he turned to me abruptly, the smoky light of the whale-oil lamps glinting on his fiery hair.

"By God!" he cried. "I'll do it!"

For answer I jerked out the articles.

"Sign there!" I said.

"Done!" he cried. "A drink on it to bind the bargain!"

I watched as he signed and added the postscript to the contract as to the shares. When it was done, we all three lifted our glasses and toasted a successful venture. Only when that was done did I venture to ask him about men.

"Men?" he boasted. "Voyageurs? How many d'you want? I'll have 'em for you by morning!"

I must say that I slept that night more soundly than I had for some time. When morning came he had turned up a half a dozen. Within three days our quota was full and we were turning away applicants. It was time, I thought, to be starting southward.

III. RETURN TO NEW YORK

IT WAS McKay's idea, enthusiastically seconded by Fraser and I must say by myself, that since New York had never looked on voyageurs in their native state, we should make the voyage by canoe, to arrive at the mouth of the Hudson with all the fanfare of a homecoming brigade. Accordingly I despatched a rider with a special letter for Mr. Astor, and after the great-granddaddy of all customary parting regales, we rounded up our various charges, and late on the twenty-sixth of July crossed to La Prairie, where we spent the night in preparation for an early start.

We left La Prairie long before dawn, loading our canoes and baggage upon wagons. At Saint John's, which we reached by midmorning, we took to the water again and, with paddles flashing and ribbons floating, swept out onto Lake Champlain and turned southward.

I must boast that I think that course has rarely been run by water in so brief a time. At Skenesboro our wild men of the woods, who took the whole thing as a huge lark, set citizens and tavern keepers by the ears. At Fort Edward we were on the river again, and from there, on down the length of the Hudson, we passed, shouting and carousing.

We were well received at Troy and Albany, often as not frightening respectable farmers, popeyed with our Indian whoops and rollicking passage. Many a stolid Dutch cow gave up its milk to us while its master slept, and many a henroost contributed eggs and poultry by way of tribute. I think our fine fellows had rarely lived so high off the land! Certainly we lacked nothing en route in the way of refreshments—both solid and liquid!

Within eight days of the time we left Montreal we came in sight of the lights of Manhattan, twinkling and winking at us across the black water. We were abreast of Spiking Devil and the mouth of the Haarlem when the lights of a small sloop showed and a voice hailed us out of the darkness.

"O'Rourke, ya?"

"Mr. Astor?"

The sloop altered course slightly and bore down gingerly toward us. Presently, by the yellow glow of a lantern, I could make out the vast form of my employer hanging on the rail. As we hove alongside, he grinned down through the murk.

"Since noon I have been out here looking for you."

"What's wrong?" I asked.

"Nothing! Nothing!" He chuckled. "Only was I giving up hope of seeing you ever again, so long you have been!"

"It took time," I admitted. "But for a bit of luck we'd not be here yet."

The other canoe swung in close to my own, and under the smoky light I directed his attention into it.

"Here's Mr. McKay," I said.

Mr. Astor lifted his heavy beaver hat and nodded.

"Happy I am to see you again, Mr. McKay," he said. "It was your idea, Rory tells me, to come so, in canoes."

"Good night to you, Mr. Astor," McKay replied dourly, cautious now that we were almost home. "It was."

"Excellent! Capital!" cried Astor. "An inspiration! Better I could not have planned it mineself!"

He waved his hand toward the shore, where a light glowed at the water's edge.

"Can you put in yonder, gentlemen?" he asked.

McKay lifted his hand and nodded.

"A small wharf you will find under Jumel's house," Astor called. "I meet you there."

As we came ashore, I saw that a camp had been set up with tents and cots and kegs on wooden horses, and, if my nose did not deceive me, somewhere near by a pit was filled with live coals, smothered in seaweed with lobsters broiling.

We disembarked and lifted our craft ashore, and a moment later the little sloop warped in to the landing. Mr. Astor leapt down, with an agility that surprised me for one so heavy, and I took it upon myself to make him acquainted with every man. His deep-set little eyes gleamed his satisfaction as he shook hands with each in turn.

"A fine body of men," he said when he was done.

Fraser sniffed.

"Do I smell food?"

"Ya!" Astor chuckled. "Supper for gods fit yet! For you is this camp and that feast! Tonight you camp here and tomorrow you come down. Put on the brightest of ribbons and sing the loudest you can! I will see that word goes around you are coming. At the Battery a company will be to greet you. There we show them how expert is the Canadian boatman, ya?"

I suppose I could have gone on in with him, but it did not, apparently, occur to him to ask me, nor did I think of it until after he had left. In consequence, I was privileged to take part the following day in one of the most extraordinary spectacles I think the city ever witnessed. Instinctive showoffs, our French-Indian voyageurs were as excited as children, and there was not one but was up before the crack of dawn, despite the fact that they had indulged in a gargantuan carouse the night before, feasting on lobsters—which were a new dish to them—and afterward putting away a good two-quarter casks of Jamaica rum and singing and dancing and rollicking till past two o'clock.

For all that, each one was out before the light of day, rooting through his *sac-á-tout-mettre* for his longest ribbands, his brightest plumes, and widest, most garish sash. I must say that Alan Fraser was not much behind them. Years in the forest seemed to have given him all the strut and swagger and bravado of a voyageur, and if ever I saw a very Gascon, it was he!

We could not have timed it better to attract attention. As we came abreast of Rhinelander's Wharf, we saw that even there a considerable crowd was gathered and a number of carriages were drawn up. As we passed, they began to keep pace with us, snowballing as they moved along the water's edge. I nodded to McKay, and at a signal from him our voyageurs broke into a rollicking, and quite unprintable, version of "Dans Mon Chemin," to which their paddles dipped and flashed in perfect unison, and our two great bark canoes seemed to skim across the ruffled surface of the Hudson with a flight as swift and graceful as any of the hundreds of gulls that also seemed to have gathered to greet us.

It was but ten minutes after noon when we came abreast of the Battery to find it black with crowds. As smartly as any brigade arriving at Fort William, we came about off the sea wall, and then went driving in, straight as a pair of arrows, for the landing where a little knot of figures indicated that Mr. Astor and his party were awaiting us.

With a great shout and a flourish of paddles, we drew up practically at their feet, tossed our caps in salute, then, neatly as any men-of-war's men, leapt out, in a flickering unloaded the baggage, and lifted the light canoes from the water.

Not Mr. Astor alone, but an official welcoming party was at the landing to greet us. Endless, it seemed to me, were the speeches, the thumps upon the back, and the congratulatory handshakes, the while our beribboned voyageurs strutted, swaggering and preening themselves, up and down upon the quay, bestowing their swarthy, flashing smiles upon the giggling housemaids who thronged the sea wall. I will confess it was gratifying to be so received. I daresay it was equally edifying to the citizens of the city to be thus privileged to look, with no charge whatsoever, upon such a swaggering crew. For a time, at least, our colorful voyageurs were the darlings of the town.

For myself there was an unexpected surprise. Almost the first thing I caught a sight of was a carriage drawn up near the landing stage, bright with parasols and gay with Sunday dresses. At first I took it to be Mr. Astor's, with some of the younger members of his household come to see the fun, and accordingly I did not look too closely in that direction, my attention being commanded at the instant by the committee of welcome. But all at once I heard my name called, and, glancing over, I noticed a small figure standing upright in the back, waving almost delightedly in my direction.

It was Deborah, and behind her, smiling and bowing, I must say, with far more restraint, but nonetheless so lovely as to stop the breath in my throat, was Valerie. Yet even as I saw her and made a quick gesture of greeting, astonishment rooted me to the spot, for on her left, there could be no mistaking it, sat Dick Goodwin, grinning, sardonic, almost triumphant. On the other side was a figure, somewhat indistinct at this juncture, I will admit, in naval uniform. And there seemed to be also another uniform upon the forward seat, beside the place that would have been Deborah's.

I do not doubt I must have gaped rudely, for Valerie flushed and cast down her eyes, and Goodwin's silly grin froze on his lips. Mr. Astor was saying something, and I did not hear it, until I was recalled by a tug at my sleeve.

"Ach!" he exclaimed. "You do not listen!"

"I—I beg your pardon, sir," I stammered.

"Ya! Ya!" he said dryly. "I know. Now first let me tell you. Then a moment you shall have to make your respects. That was excellent! Now listen! All together will be clerks and voyageurs quartered in Brooklyn. You will re-embark with the men. Will Sanders will with you come and show you where it is they are to be. Later, to the house you come and fetch all the clerks for supper. The partners I will take care of. For the men entertainments have been arranged. Ya?"

"Very good, sir," I replied, too impatient to express astonishment at the apparently awkward billeting arrangement.

He nodded and turned to McKay. I saw my opportunity and crossed swiftly to the waiting carriage.

"Valerie!" I began almost curtly, ignoring the others.

"Very pretty, Rory!" she interrupted me.

"Rory, it was magnificent!" cried Deborah breathlessly.

I scarcely heard either, for I was glaring at Goodwin.

"Hmmmph!" grunted the elder officer, eying me with something like distaste. "You should see a well-trained boat's crew in action, mem!"

"Oh, be fair, sir!" cried the other, the younger officer, beside Valerie. "For lubbers you must admit they did handily!"

I am sure it was not their intention to recall me to myself. I became suddenly aware of them.

"Rory! Forgive us," cried Deborah.

She turned to the elder officer.

"This is Lieutenant Thorn—Captain Thorn, that is, who will command the *Tonquin!* Captain Thorn, Mr. O'Rourke."

He was a gray man, lean, sharp-faced, with a pucker about his mouth even at rest, as if it were full of vinegar.

I bowed to him formally, even then thinking there was that about him I did not like.

"Your servant, sir," I said curtly.

"Howd'ye do?" He snarled, scarce even bothering to nod.

Deborah turned quickly to the other.

"And Mr. Westlake, Mr. O'Rourke," she said.

I glanced at the younger officer on Valerie's left and saw a man about my own age, broad of shoulder and slim of waist; as tall, I would have said, seeing him seated there, as Alan Fraser. Upon his shoulder he wore a lieutenant's single epaulette, and his blue coat, frogged and gold laced, was faultlessly cut, its brass-bound collar coming up close upon either side of his cheek to meet the classic golden side whiskers that grew down almost to meet it. His long legs, in immaculate white dress pantaloons, were carelessly crossed, so that the tip of a highly polished boot thrust out almost beneath my nose as I stood beside the carriage. His face was long, rectangular in its general outline, with heavy, dark eyebrows over a pair of cool blue eyes. He had a long, thin, aristocratic nose and a straight, flat mouth that evidently could smile when it was so minded but had been set by habit of military discipline in a harsh, tight line.

But it was none of these that made him appear outstanding. At the moment he held his officer's fore-and-aft hat in his lap, and the hair he thus revealed was in its own way as startling as that of Le-Coq-des-Bois. It was blond, the color of a golden spaniel's, but tight and curly. He had brushed it carefully and, with a flourish that indicated pride, in the latest classic fashion, back to front, so that it swirled above his ears and lay in studied confusion across the top of his brow in carelessly cocky style.

"Y'r humble and obedient, Mr. O'Rourke," he said in an accent that told me as plainly as if he had said so that he hailed from Boston.

"My honor to you, Mr. Westlake," I replied tautly.

"You know Dick Goodwin," Deborah added.

I glanced icily to Valerie's other side.

"I know Mr. Goodwin," I said.

I daresay it could have turned into an awkward moment. But a voice behind me reminded me that we were not alone.

"Noow!" it said, in much the broadest Scots burr I had ever heard, or anything the speaker habitually used. "I'd a better opeenion o' ye, Rory, than thot ye'd run awa' tae leave y'ur auld friends! Ha' ye nae monners? Present me!"

I whirled about to find Alan Fraser looming at my shoulder in a clean new suit of white bleached buckskin, with long fringes, bright ribbands at his shoulder, beaded moccasins on his feet, a scarlet sash about his waist, and a big, fur, coonskin cap with tail dangling down behind and eagle feathers and ostrich plumes—such a cap as only a man who has been west of the Lakes and north of the Height of Land is entitled to wear, tucked in his flaming curls. His feet were braced wide, and his hands were on his hips as his eyes raked almost insolently across the occupants of the carriage. For an instant his eyes met West-lake's, and it seemed to me that abruptly the air was charged with tension. Then in the next moment Fraser's eyes moved on and locked with Valerie's, until she glanced down at her hands in her lap, and there was no question that this time she flushed. I felt a surge of irritation.

"The great Scot," I told the folk in the carriage dryly, "is Alan Fraser, by birth of Montreal, but better known in the woods as Le-Coq-des-Bois—the Cock-o'-the-Woods, after a raucous, screaming, blatant sort of bird which he much resembles. He talks that way only to call attention to himself for the moment!"

If I thought to pique him, I failed.

"On the rear seat," I went on furiously, "Mistress Valerie Drake. Facing her, her younger sister, Mistress Deborah. Beside Mistress Deborah is Captain—ah—Thorn, I believe. To Mistress Valerie's left is Mr. Westlake. I've no notion what he is doing here. That on the other side is named Goodwin!"

My irritation, no doubt, somewhat carried me away, but I felt reckless and certainly by no means affrighted. I saw Westlake stiffen, but Goodwin only squirmed, and I saw contempt in the faces of both officers as they looked at him.

Quite as if the most ordinary courtesies had been exchanged, Alan Fraser made them all an elegant leg.

"Ladies! Your servant, indeed!" he said, and added, "Gentlemen!" in a tone which left no doubt in anyone's mind that he was not in the least interested in them.

He turned his glance back to Valerie's, and it seemed to me that she could not take her eyes from him.

"Ma'am!" he said, "I trust we'll both be seeing you later. For the moment I'll ask your pardon. We've work to do."

For the first time since I had known her, it seemed to me that Valerie was at a loss for words.

Fraser turned and caught me by the arm. I saw that the canoes were again in the water, each man in his place, waiting for me.

"Lead off!" he said, giving me a slap on the shoulder that all but sent me spinning.

I settled myself in something of a daze, and only when I had given the signal to cast off was I aware that we had a new passenger. He sat rigid in front of me in the middle, gripping the gunnel on either hand with a hold so tight that his knuckles showed white beneath the freckled skin.

"T—t—time you were coming," he said without moving.

"Relax, Sanders!" I replied. "Be easy!"

"Hah!" he snorted. "Relax! I mean to spend no more time in this infernal vehicle than I must! Relax and see myself overset? No, thank you!"

We drove around the point of Manhattan into the East River, and turned toward Wallebogt Bay.

"Who's the redheaded devil?" Sanders demanded.

I told him, and he groaned.

"There'll be hell to pay keeping him out of trouble, let alone the others, I'll warrant!" he said.

"Stop croaking!" I told him. "I've more important things to discuss with you."

"I thought you'd notice Goodwin's back in the running."

"Tell me about that," I demanded.

"There's little to tell," he replied. "Mr. Astor needed a ship. Goodwin needed the commission. Astor gave Goodwin the agency. Now he has been commissioned to victual her."

"I'd a better opinion of Mr. Astor," I growled.

"Don't blame him," Sanders retorted. "Drake owes Astor, and Goodwin owes Drake. Drake will never be able to pay the one until he can collect from t'other!"

"Who's Thorn? And who's Westlake?" I demanded.

"Stop jabbering down my neck!" he replied petulantly. "It makes me nervous."

"You're safe enough," I assured him. "What about them?"

"Thorn's to command the *Tonquin*——" he began.

"The *Tonquin?*" I interrupted. "What's that?"

"What's that?" he snorted. "Why, the ship that's to carry the expedition to the Columbia. What else?"

"Oh, for God's sake!" I swore.

"I thought you'd be pleased." He chuckled nervously. " 'Tis the first real sign of approval the government has shown that they grant leave to one of their best naval officers for the undertaking."

"One of their best!" I cried. "That I can't believe!"

"He served well at Tripoli under Decatur," he retorted, "and his shipmates think well of him! He's a very devil of a fellow, a true martinet!"

"What about Westlake?" I asked.

"Pretty! Pretty!" he replied. "But a good bit more human, or I miss my guess! Chauncy found him for us on the *President*. He goes second mate on the *Tonquin*—same arrangement."

"I'm just as well pleased I'm about through," I grumbled.

His chuckle was derisive.

"Oh, go to the devil!" I cried, and looked up abruptly. "Here! Where are you taking us?"

We were well abreast of the Brooklyn landing, and he began to wave his arms in excited gesticulation, forgetting.

"Hey! Here! Turn here!" he shouted.

"Sit still!" I admonished him, and abruptly he clutched the gunnels and sat rigid.

Within half an hour we had the men bedded down in the old barracks Mr. Astor had leased for the purpose. There we were permitted to store our canoes hard by the place where four gunboats lay drawn up on the shore in a row.

We found those who had preceded us already in quarters, awaiting our arrival with avid anticipation. With some misgiving I learned that a grand regale was in the making for the men, while the clerks and partners were to be at Astor's, and I began to scent Mr. Astor's method. In Brooklyn, at least, they would be out of the worst of harm's way.

Already things seemed fairly begun. A number of crewmen from the *Tonquin*, still lying at Eckford & Beebee's yard nearby, as well as some drifters from other vessels in the neighborhood, had dropped in, half out of curiosity to see these half-savage wildmen from the north woods and half to share their bottles.

In addition to those that I had myself recruited, there were some others engaged by Mr. Astor. James Lewis and William Matthews, of New York, had been employed previously as clerks, I understood, by small counting houses, but had been lured from them by prospects of adventure. A third, Russell Farnham, of Massachusetts, was a curious, stiff little fellow, trying very hard to be one of the lads and accepted as such, as much out of appreciation for his genuine efforts as for any real success he made of them. Johann Koaster was a ship carpenter, engaged to supervise assembly of the knocked-down schooner already stowed aboard the *Tonquin*. George Bell, the cooper, was from New York. Job Aitken, rigger and caulker, was a native of Scotland, while the blacksmith, Augustus Roussil, came from the Maritime Provinces.

Of the ship's people, I recall, at this moment, meeting only three, though there were undoubtedly more. These were Mr. Mumford, the *Tonquin's* third mate, an elderly man, to whom I took an instant liking. I expressed surprise that he was not to be at Mr. Astor's, it being my understanding that the ship's officers were also bidden. He only smiled benignly and scratched his nose.

"Well, sir, Mr. O'Rourke," he said, "somebody's got t' stay and keep an eye on 'em. Looks like I'm elected."

John Anderson, the bos'n, was a Scandinavian; an immense, fair-haired, blue-eyed giant of a man, mostly smiling and good-natured as he was tonight but, I was to learn, given on occasion to moods of black melancholia. But the crewman I remember most vividly was a bandy-legged little man, almost of a build with our own Moose. His body was thick as a barrel, and his arms were so long as to hang down almost to his knees. His hands were enormous and hairy, with stubby fingers, gnarled and calloused, with cracked nails half-hidden in flesh. His hair was coppery, not so bright as Fraser's, but unmistakably red, and his face was like a map of Ireland, with deep, darting blue eyes and a jaw like the side of a ham with the hair left on. It was he who whooped at the sight of us.

"Ho, hearties!" he roared. "Sure an' here they come all the way from Canady, an' that dry, I'm thinkin', as if they'd lived all th' way on wather, be God! Ha, ha!"

Will Sanders held up his arms for silence.

"Hush, Mike!" he commanded. "There's time enough for that and to spare, but first let me give you Mr. O'Rourke here, who's come down with these lads from Montreal to sing out their names to the rest of you. After that you can make yourselves acquainted in your own fashion!"

The bandy-legged little seaman tugged at his forelock.

"O'Rourke is it now?" he cried. "Why, then, sor, we've somethin' in common, for me own name is Michael Shea, plain Mike Shea, to you, sor, cap'n av th' maintop!"

Behind me I heard an ill-suppressed growl.

"*Quel salaud!*"

"*Ta geuele, Orignal!*" I growled.

To Mike Shea I smiled.

"Happy I am to make your acquaintance, Mr. Shea. I'll look to you for help if I say aught wrong."

"Ye shall have it," he growled. "Sure there be Irishmen an' Irishmen, but where Irishmen be set again' th' intire wurrld, they be all Irishmen together surely!"

"Thank you, Shea," I said.

"Th' name 'tis Mike!"

"Thank you, then, Mike," I told him.

"Think naught av it, Mr. O'Rourke," he replied.

"The name's Rocheblave." I grinned.

"Howly Mary!" he gasped, and I proceeded to name off those that had come with me.

To be honest, I found myself tempted to stay and watch what I felt certain would be fun. But we were bid to Mr. Astor's, and there was no gainsaying it; not, at any rate, for me. Alan Fraser was for taking the canoes to cross back to the city, but only at their mention I could see Will Sanders swallow and turn slightly green. Quickly I pointed out that they were fragile and might come to harm if left unguarded on the New York side. So it was agreed to go over by ferry and pay a visit first to our quarters, where we might offer a small taste of hospitality before going on to the principal affair.

So we set out in a body, a good dozen of company men, and at Pearl Street we stopped long enough to broach and empty a half-dozen of brandy and allow Sanders and myself time to change to our Sunday clothes. After that we pressed on to the big house in Broadway, a merry crew indeed, if I say so myself. Possibly I would not have been so conscious of our pause had not Fraser swaggered at one elbow, while Sanders tagged along upon the other. It seemed to me then that Le Coq had had, perhaps, a touch more than was good for him, though he walked steadily enough. Certainly his conversation did naught to reassure me.

"Ye de'il!" he rallied me. "Why did ye gie me no idea? I've been tryin' ma best tae catch ye aside!"

"You've been near enough to me most of the time," I said shortly, having an inkling of what was on his mind.

"Aye," he agreed, "but not where we could speak!"

He glowered at Sanders, but the latter only grinned.

"I know ye told me her name, but I didna catch 't."

"Who d'you mean?" I demanded, though I knew well enough.

"Why!" he cried, amazed that I should be so obtuse. "Th' lass wi' th' golden hair. Who else?"

I found myself irritated as much by his affected burr as by the question.

"Ye may tuck awa ye'r accent, Frraser!" I retorted, imitating him.

"All right! All right!" He grinned. "You can't blame a man for practicing. It may come in handy! Who was she?"

"Her name," I said coldly, "is Drake—Valerie Drake—and you may draw in your horns, my lad. She's already bespoke!"

"Poor devil!" he exclaimed. "Little does he realize! What chance has he against Alan Fraser?"

Beside me I heard Sanders chuckle, but diffidence silenced me, and next we knew we all were at Astor's gate.

As we entered the grand parlor, we were passed down a receiving line, much as Indian captives are forced to run the gauntlet. Indeed, I had often thought I would prefer the latter. It was done at last, and I finally stood free and entered the assembly to turn where I pleased. Perhaps it was unnatural, but I had thoughts for only one of all those who were guests. Deborah was there. I scarcely saw her conversing in a distant corner with Will Sanders. She caught my eye, and I waved absently and went on my way in search of her sister.

But the magnet that drew me seemed to exert its influence upon others also. I found Valerie beside an open window, through which the soft, mild air of the summer night drifted deliciously. She did not lack admirers. I am afraid my brow darkened when I saw that Dick Goodwin was among them. As for the others, there was Irving and Captain Thorn, neither of whom seemed to me serious competition either in intent or effect. Chauncy, for all that he was old enough to be her father, was more dangerous, but not dreadfully to be feared. But her own attention appeared to be divided between the handsome, carefully punctilious Westlake and the strutting, swaggering, blatant Cock-of-the-Woods Fraser, both of whom seemed to regard her as his own discovery.

I think, perhaps, had I not been deeply involved myself, I might have found the situation laughable. The way in which first one and then the other would push himself forward in the effort to impress her, each strutting his own importance to shoulder out the other, was actually comical. But it did not seem so to me then.

I must admit I plunged without hesitation into the game, though I fear I did not shine beside my new rivals, for apparently I had not yet learned patience. Possibly my attitude irritated her. At any rate, the opportunity I sought to draw her aside, to have her to myself for even the smallest moment, was utterly unsuccessful. When at last supper was announced, it was not upon my arm, as I felt I had a right to expect, that she entered the dining room, but rather with two escorts: the towering, glowering, red-haired Alan Fraser on her left hand and the imperious, I may say equally petulant, Westlake on her right. It was only then, in a sour fit of revenge, that I sought out Deborah. To my chagrin, I found her already bespoken by Will Sanders, who gave me a satiric wink that sent me off fuming. In the end I was forced to content myself with young Dorothea Astor, who did not question my motives but seemed altogether delighted. It was only after the supper, when the dancing began, that I had any opportunity to express myself to Valerie.

"Why, Rory!" she exclaimed chidingly, as she floated into my arms. "You're like a thundercloud!"

"Good God!" I cried. " 'Tis a fine thing indeed for me to come home and find you not content with gadding about with every fancy uniform. You even have Dick Goodwin in the same carriage with you! And you wonder why I am angry!"

"How dare you!" she flared.

"How dare I not?" I retorted. "Are we betrothed? If you think to treat me as a limp dishmop——"

"If you will dance me over past the door," she cut in, "I think I will withdraw to the ladies' parlor."

"I'll do nothing of the sort!" I retorted. "I've had no opportunity to speak to you tonight, and——"

"If this is all you have to say," she retorted, breaking in again, "I'd be as well pleased you did not speak to me at all! Ever!"

"Valerie!" I cried, instantly contrite. "Can't you see 'tis because I am distraught? I have been away a long time! When can I see you—without all these popinjays, I mean?"

It needed only her smile to tie my heart in knots again.

"There, now!" she said. "Tomorrow afternoon? But no! Wait! I've promised Mr. Westlake I'd have tea with him. And tomorrow evening there's supper and theater afterwards. Come Tuesday at teatime, and I'll see that we're not interrupted!"

It was on the tip of my tongue to say I would not, but I could not bring myself to it.

Until Tuesday evening was no more than forty-eight hours, yet I must admit even now that it seemed to me as many years. But when Tuesday came, Valerie appeared to have forgotten our engagement and had gone off to the hairdresser's to have herself made ready for the mayor's supper and the theater party that was being tendered our young gentlemen that evening. Indeed, it was the end of the week before I found the opportunity I sought.

In the meantime I had as much as I could do to look after our charges. They were a boisterous crew, and though at first they seemed a great novelty to the city, the canoemen especially, with their brawling and roistering and scant regard for property, they soon became as great a nuisance as they had been a curiosity before. New York was their oyster, and they meant to open it, setting about it as seriously as if they had but a few days to live. I spent most of my time in those days bailing them out of scrapes and packing them off again to Brooklyn and comparative safety. Consequently, not until Saturday afternoon, when I knew it was her custom to be resting for the evening, did I dare present myself at the Drakes' door and demand to see her.

The wench who admitted me was reluctant. But I handed her a gold piece, and she grinned and turned away.

"I'll be in the summerhouse in the garden," I said.

"Yassuh!" she replied, and went off up the stairs.

I must have waited nearly an hour before she came. When she did, she seemed uncertain whether to pout with annoyance or to appear anxious.

"Why, Rory!" she cried. "Whatever in the world———? You know I always rest at this hour!"

"Aye!" I said. "I know it. 'Tis why I came."

"What do you mean?" she demanded, as if she didn't know.

"I told you I'd a thing of importance to discuss with you," I retorted, "and you broke our appointment———"

"I don't like your tone," she interrupted me.

"Stop it!" I said roughly. "What I've got to say you must hear, for God knows, one way or another, this thing must be settled now!"

"What thing?" she asked.

"If you'll sit down and listen and not be forever interrupting me," I told her, "you'll learn!"

Primly, with eyes smoldering and tight-pursed mouth, she settled upon the bench and folded her hands in her lap.

"Very well!" she said.

I was forced to admit it seemed scarcely an auspicious beginning. I would not have had it so, yet I had demanded it. Now I had no choice.

"Valerie!" I pleaded, "let's not be foolish———"

She thrust out her lower lip sullenly.

"Can't you see?" I pleaded. " 'Tis because I love you that I am here!"

She made no answer to that but only gave a little sniff.

" 'Tis true!" I cried. "Valerie, I've come to ask you for the last time—will you marry me—now?"

She spun about to face me, startled, her mouth wide.

"For the last time?"

"For the last time in a long time," I amended weakly.

"Why—why, Rory! What do you mean?" she demanded.

"I mean," I told her, "that you must make up your mind. If you'll have me, I'll stay. If not, then I shall ask Mr. Astor to let me go in the *Tonquin*. It may be years before I return."

She stared at me as if she could not believe her ears.

"The worm has turned!" I said, no doubt rather stupidly.

"How can you say such a thing?" she demanded. "How can you ask me to decide at a time like this? You want me to spoil it all!"

"That's just it," I retorted. "It seems to me there's always something it would spoil! As I see it, getting married wouldn't spoil anything. It would make things perfect!"

"But now, Rory! Now, with so much going on!"

"We wouldn't have to plan it immediately," I said somberly. "Only promise me! We'll set a date for after the *Tonquin* sails and announce it. That's all!"

"Oh!" She beat a tattoo with her heel upon the summerhouse floor. "I couldn't announce it now!"

"No!" I snarled. "I understand! Believe me, I do! If we announced it now, Westlake and Fraser would lose interest!"

She looked up and faced me with her eyes blazing.

"How dare you imply such a thing!"

"My dear," I said, "the situation speaks for itself!"

"Well!" she cried. "You can't love me very much if that's the way you feel about it!"

"I wouldn't give a damn about it if I didn't love you very much," I retorted.

"Well, I don't love you!" she flared. "I think you're beastly and selfish and horrid and mean! If you think I'm going to say 'yes' to your proposal, you can guess again! I don't care if I never marry you! Go on your old *Tonquin*! I don't care!"

"Valerie!" I cried. "You don't know what you're saying!"

"I do know what I'm saying," she retorted.

"Very well!" I said. "If that's the way you feel about it!"

I bowed.

"Ma'am!" I said. "Your servant!"

I put on my hat and turned away and walked along the garden path to the gate, my head in a whirl, my thoughts in chaos, my heart in little pieces all down through my stomach. But though I walked as slowly as I could, even dragging my feet, she did not call me back!

IV. THE QUARREL

I DID not go straight to Mr. Astor when I left, although one might think that I should. The thought was in some vague way uppermost in my mind, for I went in that direction, and, indeed, I had already turned into Broadway before I realized that I should not broach the matter to him that day nor yet the next. The counting rooms were already closed for the week end, and it occurred to me that this was not a thing to bring into his home.

Instead, I turned glumly to our own quarters, where I found my roommates preparing for the banquet and ball being given that evening in honor of both officers and men by the city fathers at Federal Hall. This was to be the first such occasion, in which all hands, from partners to lowest voyageur, from captain to cabin boy, were to take part; and both Sanders and I anticipated it with no little apprehension, though Irving thought of it as a lark. Yet it was only when I chucked my hat disconsolately into the closet and poured myself a stiff drink that either cocked a quizzical eye at me.

"Better shake a leg," Sanders said.

"The hell with it!" I growled. "I don't think I'll go."

He turned about slowly, studying me with some concern.

"Oh," he said at length. "So that's it?"

"That's it," I told him.

"What happened?"

That I would once have resented the remark was in itself indication of a change in me. It seemed to me I was still the youngster who had come down from Canada. One way or another we are all entitled to a moment of self-pity.

"We quarreled, and there you have it," I told him.

He snorted. "If you ask me, 'tis the first sensible stand you've taken."

"Aye!" I said. "That's easy for you to say!"

"Come now!" he said soothingly. "Come now! 'Tis not so bad as that! She'll think the more of you for having stood up to her."

"Hummmmph!" I grunted. "It's a pretty theory, but it does not hold. She's already said her say and told me that she'll be as well pleased if she does not see me again, ever!"

"Have you never heard a woman fret?" Irving sneered. "D'you mean to stay away from the ball tonight on that score?"

"I'm in no mood to go," I retorted.

"Well, put yourself in a mood!" Sanders snorted. "I declare a man might as well be married as have to live with you! Go out where she can see you. Get out where you know she'll be. Show yourself whole and heart free! Take a look around you and let her know that you know there are other worms in the garden; that if she'll not make you happy, you'll make yourself so with one that will!"

"I don't want happiness with another!" I snarled.

"For Christ's sake!" he cried. "Do you need a primer?"

" 'Tis too late," I retorted. "I told her I meant to ask Mr. Astor to let me go in the *Tonquin*."

They both turned and stared at me.

"So?" Sanders said. "Have you talked with the Old Man about that?"

"No," I admitted.

"Well," he cried, "even if you had and you changed your mind, I daresay he'd release you. As it is, if you'll but give her a fright, I'll wager she'll come round! Go to the ball. Act as if nothing had happened. But pay her as little attention as you can. In fact, if you don't even speak to her 'twill be warning. Let her stew in it for a bit. They try her again."

I stared at him.

"That from you?"

"Don't misunderstand me," he retorted. " 'Tis not what I want to see, but I've no stomach to see you eating your heart out like a whipped puppy. If that's what you think you must have, I'll do my best to help you get it!"

"Thanks." I said sourly. "You're a help!"

I cannot say that I followed his advice with enthusiasm. Nevertheless, I followed it, at least to the extent of going. Valerie was there, of course, and when our eyes met it was to stare coldly at each other. I, at least, gave her the courtesy of a frigid bow, but there was not even the civility of a response on her part. Naturally I did not dance with her, and it seemed to me that she took obvious pleasure in keeping her two currently very worshipful servants prancing attendance upon her. Beyond any doubt it worked upon my temper and led me to precipitate the first of a series of small breaks and schisms which were to have reverberations aboard the *Tonquin*.

During the intermission the ladies, as was their habit, withdrew to their retiring room, while the gentlemen turned below to the bar in the basement for liquid refreshment and a pipe between dances. As I have said, the affair was offered to the honor of all members of the expedition indiscriminately; and while the great bulk of both foremast hands and wood rats, finding no doxies of the sort they preferred present, once they had paid their respects and done their duty, preferred to slip away to their own haunts, yet it remained a far more motley assemblage than heretofore. The result did not make for a spirit of general ease; not that this had a great deal to do with my own outburst, but I mention it as, perhaps, tinder to the sparks that flew.

So far as I was concerned, I think there was reason for my behavior, if small excuse. I am not so virtuous as to pretend that I did not try rather more assiduously than was either necessary or wise to drown my woe. Westlake and Fraser were at the bar, one at either end, each facing the other along its length, and neither speaking nor glancing in the other's direction. Had I been less concerned myself I might have found it amusing. Westlake's remark was probably perfectly innocent, but I think if he had said "Hail Mary!" I would have resented it.

"Whoever would have thought"—he grinned affably as he sipped at his punch—"that such a varied set of bedfellows would be found altogether at one time?"

I glowered at him.

"Is there something about us you don't like?" I demanded.

He looked utterly taken aback.

"Why, I—I meant no offense," he said. "But if the shoe fits, you may put it on!"

To my surprise, before I could reply, Alan Fraser rounded the bar belligerently.

"Others also find your remarks offensive, Westlake!" he bellowed. "If you want action, why not choose an opponent more nearly cut to your own dimensions!"

"Like yourself, for instance?" Westlake bristled.

"Like myself!" Fraser retorted. "Would you object to that?"

"Why don't you keep out of this, you backwoods jackanapes!" I cried.

The red-haired Scot blinked and then flushed.

"Backwoods jackanapes!" he roared, and reached for me.

God alone knows where all of this might have ended had not Mr. McKay and Captain Thorn interposed in the interests of peace and Will Sanders taken me by the elbow and led me away. It was only then that I noticed that the seafaring people upon the one hand had quietly ranged themselves to support Westlake if need be; while the woodsmen, just as imperceptibly, had drifted in the opposite direction.

After that, even though peace was nominally restored, I was yet sufficiently observant to notice that the two groups remained aloof during the rest of the evening.

A different sort of adventure also fell to me that evening, when once I came out of my sulks long enough to claim a dance with Deborah, not long before the party ended.

"What on earth has got into you tonight, Rory?" she demanded, as we whirled away across the crowded floor. "You look like a thundercloud, and I haven't seen you speak to Valerie once!"

"Has she noticed?" I asked eagerly.

"She hasn't mentioned it to me," said Deborah dryly.

My face must have fallen, for she smiled a little, though her eyes regarded me wide and seriously.

"I should have known without asking," she said.

"Aye!" I told her. "The same old thing!"

Her expression turned to one of impatience.

"What are you going to do about it?" she demanded.

"There's only one thing that can be done!" I growled. "That's to see Mr. Astor and go out with the *Tonquin.*"

She laughed.

"Oh, Rory! I think you mean that now, but you know you'll never do it. You've put all that behind you."

"We'll see about that!" I snarled.

In the next few days I found myself in something of a dilemma. Deborah's taunt rankled, and I knew I should not delay broaching Mr. Astor on the subject. On the other hand, I had no intention of cutting off my nose to spite my face. If there was any last hope, I felt the effort should be made.

Sunday was no problem, since I could not see Mr. Astor on that day. I presume I might have tried the occasion upon Valerie. But I was still resentful of her attitude the evening before, and I did not doubt but she was equally so toward me.

Monday was the day upon which I should, by all rights, have taken the bull by the horns. But I found myself reluctant, and I was secretly relieved that much of the day Mr. Astor was busy elsewhere and so might reasonably be considered not to have time for trivia. Tuesday and Wednesday it was the same. Thursday I had really no excuse but simply put it off. And so it went throughout the week and into the next, until it came to me that I was not being honest with anyone, including myself.

All of that time the festivities continued, and I drove myself to each event, hoping, but never admitting it, that somehow I would find an opportunity, just for one small moment, to speak to Valerie. During the interval my relations with Westlake and the Cock-of-the-Woods scarcely improved.

I did not find the opportunity I sought until Wednesday of the next week, and then I managed it only by chicanery.

Winthrop Drake gave a garden party that evening at Baker's Tavern, in Greenwich, at which thick steaks and juicy lobsters were served alfresco, followed by a recital of music, some entertainment, and dancing. Deborah was there, naturally, as was her sister. So also was Goodwin, looking as glum as I felt, while Fraser and Westlake glared at each other over Valerie's head when they thought she was not looking; and vied with each other in the extravagance of their courtesy when they thought she was. The rest of the party was about equally divided between partners, clerks, and ship's officers, with the ladies of their choice for the evening, and a scattering of ladies and gentlemen with no connection with the expedition.

Fundamentally, the party was not unlike others that had preceded it. The older folk gathered comfortably about the tables in the garden, mostly content to sip tall glasses of punch and talk, while a few indulged in whist. The younger group danced or watched the performers, who included a tightrope walker and a girl with big hips, who danced the usual hornpipe in skin-tight sailors' breeches, a juggler, who kept five Indian clubs whirling in the air at once, and a monologist, who commenced with Washington's Farewell Address, passed on through a most dramatic recitation of "Titans, Wist Ye Not The Hour?" ending with a fine barytone rendition of "Hail Columbia," which, I took it, was intended as a sort of complimentary pun upon our undertaking. I must say it fetched a roar of mighty applause.

It was getting on toward eleven o'clock, and the old folk were beginning to yawn. The entertainments had ended and the dancing was in full swing when I noticed a reddish glow against the sky a little to the south of east.

It was a fire, obviously, probably a barn or a haystack somewhere in the neighborhood of Corlear's Hook or Stuyvesant's Swamps. Perhaps a dozen others noticed it, too, and paused in their gaiety to admire the spectacle, but since the wind came from the southwest, so that it was impossible for the city to be threatened (which was ever our greatest terror), few paid more attention to it than that.

For my part, however, having little better to do, I watched it for some time, and all at once an idea occurred to me. The fire might as easily be in Brooklyn somewhere—say in the vicinity of Wallebogt Bay—so far as anyone here could tell. Without delay I slipped away from the party and looked into Mr. Baker's taproom, where, seated alone at a table with a pot of ale before him, obviously already well on his way, was the very man I sought—the monologist. My luck was in.

"Do you mind if I join you, sir?" I asked.

He blinked up at me owlishly.

"Notatall!" he replied. "Nodall! S'down 'n make 'self comf'ble! Always welc'm com'ny fa gelelm'n! How's come you notoutside withuther young p'ple, huh?"

I pulled out my handkerchief and mopped ostentatiously at my brow.

" 'Tis infernally hot," I said. "Will you join me?"

"Don' care 'f I do!" he cried with enthusiasm, and began thumping on the board and shouting for the landlord.

"To be honest with you, sir," I said, "I can't get a dance with a certain young lady out there, so I thought it better to come in here and drown my sorrow."

I sighed. " 'Tis better than standing and watching her dance with others!"

"Woman'sa fool!" he grumbled. "Likely-lookin' lad!"

Our landlord brought our mugs and set them down before us. I paid him, and he went away after a disapproving glance at my companion. The monologist stared into his ale as if he thought a tear or two would give it certain flavor.

"Did you see the fire?" I asked, when we had drunk.

"Fire?" he demanded excitedly. "No! Where?"

He half rose from his seat, but I caught him by the arm.

" 'Tis too far away to see more than the glow," I said. " 'Tis over toward Corlear's Hook, or that direction."

"Oh!" he grumbled disappointedly.

"Or it might be in Brooklyn," I added significantly.

At first he did not catch it. Then something in my tone must have penetrated his attention.

"Huh?" he said. "Huh, Broo'lyn? Whazza gotta do'th it?"

I looked at him severely.

"I don't think you could do it," I said slowly. "You'd have to go out on the stage and make it look real—very real!"

As I half expected, the words were like a dash of cold water in the face to him, exerting somewhat the same quick, momentarily sobering effect.

"Uh! What d'you mean, sir?" he demanded. "What'd'you mean?"

"You're drunk!" I told him.

"May be drunk now," he retorted. "Bu' for'y years man'n boy I've trod th' boards, 'n when I ge' out there, 're's not a man inna pit c'n say'f I'm drunk'r sob'r!"

He was probably right. At any rate, it was worth a chance.

"In that case," I said, "perhaps you *can* do it."

"Cer'any I can do it!" he retorted indignantly. "What?"

"Remember, I said yonder fire might be in Brooklyn?"

He nodded, blinking.

"Well," I went on, "could you get up on the stage and shout: 'The *Tonquin!* The *Tonquin's* afire, and half the yard about her."

"The *Tonquin!*" he yelped, leaping up. "Where? When?"

"Wait a minute!" I retorted, pushing him back in his seat. "There's nothing wrong with the *Tonquin* that I know of."

I drew a few golden eagles out of my pocket and held one up in my left hand. He watched me, quite sober now, running his thin tongue about his parched lips.

"What's this?" he half croaked. "I'll not be a party to any diddling rig! I want no hand in any raneygazoo!"

"There's nothing wrong with this," I told him. "You mind the girl I spoke about?"

He nodded, half suspiciously.

"I must have a word with her," I told him. "If you play your part, 'twill set up enough stir to accomplish it. 'Tis all about to break up anyway, and once you've made the announcement I'll warrant the sailors will scuttle for the ship and half the rednecks after them! They'll find out soon enough 'tis not so and come scurrying back. By then I'll have had my chance, and you'll have twenty dollars in gold and be miles away! There'll be naught they can do but make the best of it and enjoy a good laugh!"

His eye gleamed, and for an instant I could not tell if it was the sight of the gold in my hand or the thought of the prank. He soon set me right.

" 'Twill cost fifty!" he said.

I knew he took advantage of me, but it was worth it.

"Done!" I retorted impatiently.

I coached him carefully in the part I wanted him to play and gave him an eagle as an earnest. He was reluctant, for he wanted his pay beforehand, but on this I was adamant, and in the end he agreed to meet me at the corner of the garden in ten minutes after his announcement, so I went out. He gave me the allotted interval and then came running on the stage, waving his arms and shouting for silence.

Thinking it a joke, the orchestra gave him a fanfare, and as he held up his arms, stillness settled on the garden and all eyes turned in his direction.

"Quiet! Quiet, everybody!" he bawled, although already one could have heard a feather fall. "Ladies and gentlemen! D'ye see yonder glow? D'ye know what it is?"

Down near the platform someone laughed rudely.

"Aye, a fire to roast ye in!"

There was a roar of laughter, but the monologist drew himself up haughtily and held up his hands.

"Ye're right, friend, in one thing," he shouted. " 'Tis a fire. But not to roast me in. When I tell ye what 'tis, ye'll sing at t'other side o' yer face! Did ye know, friend, that 'tis the *Tonquin?* The ship and half the yard she lies in gone up with her! 'Tis said a dozen Frenchies have already roasted, and there're more that can't be got at——"

He might have said more, but the place fell into bedlam, and he had not finished speaking before some men were running for their rigs. Others dashed into the tavern for hats or cloaks. Westlake streaked for the stables, and Alan Fraser was hard on his heels, leaving Valerie standing in the middle of the lawn staring after them with fallen jaw. I moved toward her and became aware of Sanders at my elbow.

"We'd best get in and break the news to Mr. Astor!"

I looked aside at him and pulled free.

"Take Goodwin!" I commanded. "Go in his rig and leave ours!"

"Aren't you going?" he demanded.

"No!" I said, and winked.

He blinked about at the confusion, then followed my glance toward Valerie, and his face split in a knowing grin.

"Oh!" he said.

"Aye!" I replied. "Now be off before you spoil it!"

"Good luck!" He chuckled.

I crossed toward Valerie, whose bewilderment had had time now to give way to resentment at such precipitate abandonment, and it was clear that she was seething inside. She stood with fists clenched, staring in the direction her erstwhile swains had gone. As I approached her casually, I could not help but feel sorry for them when next they met! I was careful, however, not to overplay. I walked past her as if I did not see her, not hurrying, nor yet so slowly as to give her the impression that I came seeking her. I was almost past before she saw me.

"Rory!"

I turned abruptly and pretended surprise, bowing politely.

"You called, ma'am?" I asked. "May I help you?"

"Yes!" she snapped, then faltered and beat her hands together help-lessly. "I mean—I—— Oh, I'm sorry, Rory! Will you take me home?"

"I would be honored, ma'am!" I said punctiliously.

"Stop calling me 'ma'am'!" she cried. "Please!"

"Of course, ma'am!" I assured her. "You'd best go in and get your own wrap while I fetch the rig. Someone might borrow it if I don't get there first."

She nodded mutely.

"Meet me by the lower garden gate," I told her. " 'Twill be less confusion."

She hurried off, while I chuckled appreciatively at my own Machia-vellian attention to detail. It would also be more private at the garden gate, and unless I was much mistaken we would be able to slip away unseen.

I made a quick detour past the corner of the garden where I found the monologist somewhat nervously awaiting me.

"For a bit I feared they'd collar me," he said, licking his lips. "But I give 'em the slip. Where's th' money?"

"It was perfect!" I assured him as I counted out the coins. "Now I suggest you take the most inconspicuous route back to the city and lose yourself there!"

"That's what I mean to do!" He grinned. "Ye wouldn't have room in your rig to give me a lift, would ye, guv'nor?"

"No, I wouldn't," I snapped. "I've need for it myself."

He leered and winked at me knowingly.

"Aye!" he said. "I'd a notion! Wouldn't it be a shame now if the young gentlemen was to find out, eh?"

I saw what he was driving at.

"Why, you——!" I began.

"Sometimes," he grinned guilelessly, " 'tis amazin' what a touch o' the yellow metal'll do!"

He held up his thumb and first two fingers and rubbed them together under my nose.

"How much?" I said coldly.

"Say—forty dollars more?" he replied.

I paid him in silence, and he clinked the coins together.

"Not a bad night's work, if I do say so meself! Welp! I must be goin'! Me love to th' lady, and the best o' luck to yourself, sir!"

He gave me a broad wink in the moonlight and disappeared amid the bushes.

If the garden had been in an uproar, the scene at the stables was bedlam itself. Hostlers were sweating and swearing, horses snorting and rearing, gentlemen shouting, cursing, snatching whatever rig came handiest. Already there was a stream of chairs, carts, carryalls, and coaches streaming out of Minetta Lane to block the intersection with the cross-country road, and a number of the wiser and hastier were beginning to turn off along the backways, toward Mulberry Lane and McDougal Alley. It was as well I came when I did, for apparently there was little order in the choosing of vehicles. If a man picked some-one else's, he calculated to return it the following day.

Fortunately the chaise in which Sanders and myself had arrived had been stacked away behind several others, so that I was yet in time to rescue it. In due time I fetched the rig around to the lower garden gate, where I found it necessary to tie the horse and, with a prayer that he would be there when I returned, went in search of Valerie, whom I found waiting with tapping foot in the entry to the inn.

"I told you to meet me at the lower gate," I said quickly, before I realized that this was scarcely the way to open the conversation.

"I expect my escorts to come to me!" she retorted chillingly.

"All right!" I replied. "Here I am. But if we've lost the rig 'twill be your doing! We'll have to try to slip out quietly, this way! You've no idea what an uproar there is at the stables!"

She suffered me to lead her around the building and along the garden walk to the gate. Fortunately, no one had discovered the rig. I handed her up and then took the driver's seat and went round by Charleton's Lane to Perry Road and across Christopher into Varick and thus by back ways across Lispenard's Meadows and the canal.

It was a roundabout route, but it had the advantage of being clear of traffic, and we were able to follow it unobserved. Valerie questioned it, of course, as I expected, but I explained that the other roads were choked. For a time we rode in silence, I remaining very stiff and aloof, the self-righteous gentleman, who, having had his say, intends to say no more although his heart is breaking. And it appeared to me that before long my scheme began to have its hoped-for effect, for I was conscious that several times she darted quick little glances at me, and at length she sighed deeply and looked down at her hands in her lap.

I know a cue as well as the next man. I turned to her. In the moon-light it seemed to me that her lip trembled slightly, and certainly she let herself slump a little toward me; not enough to say that she deliberately leaned, yet unquestionably the pressure of her shoulder against my own increased, and she seemed to turn pliant.

"Rory!" she said in a very small voice.

"Ma'am?" I replied.

"Oh, Rory, stop it!" she begged.

"My dear!" I said. "What is it you would have me stop?"

She turned to me impulsively.

"Stop this coldness, Rory!" she begged. "Why are you so distant? You've not spoken to me in more than a week!"

"Isn't that the way you wanted it?" I asked.

She swallowed and bit her lips.

"Don't, Rory!" she half whispered. "I've been a little fool. I must admit it! First, Roger Westlake and then Alan Fraser! They swept me off my feet! I—I'm afraid I lost my head! Then, when they thought their horrid old boat was burning, they—they——! Even Dick didn't give me a thought! Only you, Rory! Can you forgive me?"

This time there was no question but that she leaned toward me. I took her hungrily in my arms and sought her lips with my own. For a long, ecstatic moment we clung, and at length had need to part if only for breath.

"Oh, my sweet! My Valerie!" I gasped. "What's to forgive? A misunderstanding that was as much mine as yours! My dear, only name a date now and I'll be your happiest slave from this on!"

Her fingers caressed my cheek; and the scent of her hair was sweet in my nostrils. It seemed to me that the warmth of her spread all through me.

"Give me only till tomorrow to consult my calendar, Rory!" she whispered. "We—we can't be offhand about it, you know."

It seemed reasonable. I gathered her again in my arms and searched hungrily for her lips.

"No longer!" I warned her.

"Not an instant!" she promised, and thereafter we clung together a long time while our nag ambled lazily homeward.

After a bit she thrust me away gently.

"Rory!" she exclaimed. "You're getting me all mussed! What will Papa and Mamma think?"

"Who cares?" I cried happily, reaching for her again.

"I do!" she exclaimed. "You won't have to explain to Mamma but I will!"

I gave her a quick kiss upon the lips and gathered up the reins, while she sat up and rearranged her dress. The nag broke into an ambling trot. The moon was bright, and the world, it seemed to me, was a very satisfactory one after all! I slipped an arm across her shoulders, and presently she settled against me with a little sigh of contentment.

"Wasn't it lucky the *Tonquin* should catch fire just then?"

"Ummmm!" I agreed noncommittally.

"I don't mean I'm glad it's burned," she explained. "But it was lucky for us. Don't you think?"

"Umm-hmmmm!" I nodded.

She was silent for a moment. Then she spoke indignantly.

"To think I ever let myself be carried away by those—those strutting peacocks!" she exclaimed. "Rory! I feel so ashamed!"

I'm afraid I all but simpered, and she looked up at me.

"Why didn't you go too?" she asked. "You have as great an interest in her as any."

"And leave you?" I demanded. "Certainly not! Let her burn. Then she cannot carry me away from you!"

"But, Rory!" she cried. "You know Mr. Astor will simply fit out another ship. He's so stubborn! And if you've agreed——"

"I haven't yet," I assured her, and some may think I was carried away by the impulse to boast, though I still believe I was prompted by common sense. After all, by tomorrow evening at the very latest she was bound to discover the hoax and put two and two together! It was better to speak now, while she was in a favorable mood. "Besides, the *Tonquin* is no more burning than this buggy!"

"What do you mean?" she demanded.

I grinned at her, riding my pride full tilt.

" 'Twas the glow of fire toward Corlear's that gave me the idea," I confessed to her. "I had to see you! So I bribed that actor to run on and make the announcement. The rest you saw!"

She blinked at me, unbelieving at first. Then, as realization dawned upon her, the change in her expression was almost frightening. Love, admiration, gave way to blind fury. Too late I saw what I had done. My heart sank. Had this been Deborah beside me, she would have been convulsed with laughter. But Valerie had never been known for her sense of humor.

"You—you——!"

"How else could I get to see you?" I bleated lamely.

"Oh, how could you!" she cried.

"I've just told you!" I cried. "Can't you see I couldn't do anything else?"

If she heard she gave no sign.

"Oh, you miserable, abominable, two-faced brute! You unspeakable beast! I've never been so humiliated! I—I'll be a laughingstock! Oh! I hate you! I hate you!"

"Oh, come now!" I protested. "It isn't as bad as that. What folk know it will think it funny! And certainly none of those who went off so fast are going to want to talk about it! It seems to me the joke's on them!"

I reached for her, hoping a few kisses and a word of love and apology might smooth matters, but she jerked away and moved as far from me as she could.

"Keep your hands off me!" she flared. "You Judas! You—you hound! Don't you dare touch me! Don't you dare to speak to me! To think I almost believed you a gentleman!"

In my own turn I began to grow angry with such unreason.

"You're talking like a fool!" I growled.

But she did not answer. Nor did she speak to me again throughout the rest of the ride, but rather sat primly jammed in her own corner, staring resolutely away from me.

I argued, I pleaded, and I explained all the way to the house in Greenwich Street, but if she listened to me, she gave no sign of it.

When I pulled up before the door, she did not wait for me to get down and hand her out, but instead she leapt out with most unladylike haste and scurried up the broad steps. There she turned about and fixed me with a blazing eye, while her lower lip trembled suspiciously.

"I hate you, Rory O'Rourke!" she cried. "I've always hated you! I don't care if I never see you again! I don't suppose I can keep you away from other people's houses or public places, but I'll do my best! And don't you ever dare to come to this house again! Do you hear? Because if you do, I'll—I'll—I'll—I—— I never want to see you again, and I won't! So there!"

V. CHOICE

OBVIOUSLY there was no point in postponing matters any longer.
Valerie had spoken in no uncertain terms, and it seemed to me that
only some such move as Deborah had suggested offered any hope at
all. I scarcely waited till the counting rooms were opened in the morning before I showed myself at Mr. Astor's door. He glanced up, his
heavy face lighting cheerfully at sight of me.

"Ach, Rory!" he cried. "The man I hoped to see! It comes to me I
have not properly told you what a fine job you have done!"

"Sir," I said glumly, entering and closing the door behind me, "I'm
pleased you think I have done well. I wonder if you'd grant me the
privilege of changing my mind?"

"Eh?" he said.

"I'd like to go out in the *Tonquin.*"

"So?" He stared at me as if he had not heard correctly.

"Yes, sir," I said. "I'd like to get away from New York—as far
away as I can!"

He put his elbow on the desk and tugged first at his ear and then
at his lower lip, frowning slightly.

"Well!" he said at length. "So that's the way of it?"

"Yes, sir," I said glumly.

"Hmmm!" He grunted.

He rose and began to pace the office, his hands clasped behind his
broad behind, scowling. Presently he turned to me.

"The shares," he said. "You are aware they are all bespoke now?"

"Aye, sir," I replied. "I hadn't hoped to go out as a partner. I'd be
satisfied to clerk."

"Don't be a fool, Rory!" he growled. "As a partner I would like
to see you! As a clerk—a failure? Pah! Phooey! Not worth two cents
would you be as such!"

I felt my heart sink into my boots. Was it possible that he was going
to refuse me? The thought had never occurred to me.

"But——" I began.

He interrupted me with a wave of his finger.

"I do not like," he said, "to see my best man go to a post that to him
is not fitting!"

"Sir!" I cried. "I don't care what you ask me to do! I'd rather be there than here!"

He stopped pacing and turned to face me.

"Very well! You say it so! But the post I am about to propose you accept first and agree that afterwards there is no changing of the mind. Otherwise we forget it!"

"I accept, sir!" I said recklessly.

"Good! Remember, then, beyond this room goes nothing!"

"You may trust me, sir," I assured him.

"I know that," he replied. "Listen! Since the beginning, rumors I hear! First, the North West Company will try to come before me. Then it is war—war with England. I hear the *Tonquin* by a British frigate will be stopped and all English subjects pressed. I have for convoy by an American frigate arranged, at least to sea! But it is not rumors that already one of our partners has called upon the British Consul to discuss this matter with him privately! It would surprise you if I said which one!"

I waited, wondering what could be in his mind.

"Someone has suggested that all be required to take an oath to the United States," he went on. "This is not sensible! An honest citizen you can make but from the heart!"

"I'll not quarrel with that, sir."

"So!" he exclaimed. "In this business, then, who is to be trusted? Perhaps all? Perhaps none? Some surely! But which?"

He paused. I began to see his drift.

"You trust me?" I said.

"Exactly!" he agreed. "You I trust! From you I know I have the truth! This, then, your duty will be. You are my confidential agent! No authority will you have beyond the duties of your office, which will be as clerk. For that the usual salary will be yours, so as anyone can see. But here in New York what pay you now receive I will set aside for you, and if you like also, I will invest it as if it were my own. In return, your eyes and your ears you will keep open. To me you will report, privately, the progress of the plan, the loyalties of those who command it, and any other thing you think I should know. It is clear, ya?"

He did not seem to see anything wrong with the proposal, and I had already pledged my acceptance.

"You will report to me at your first opportunity," he said, "in person, if possible, or, if not, by whatever other means themselves present!"

So it was done, and I was committed to it. Though I cannot say I was happy about it, yet I must admit it was a relief to have things settled at last. Not Valerie nor I could change our minds now.

When I told Sanders that evening, he nodded. For my part, my inclination was to draw into my shell and be seen no more in public. But at this he scoffed.

"Will you give her the satisfaction," he demanded, "of knowing she has driven you to ground? Don't be a fool, man! Let her see that your life has not ended. She'll think twice of it then and sing differently when you come home!"

It seemed to be good advice, and so, despite my reluctance, I dressed in my best and went with him to the concert and entertainment in the Gardens on the Battery.

There was no reason why I should have been surprised to see Valerie there with Westlake and Fraser. Indeed, she seemed gayer than ever—almost flauntingly so. Yet when our eyes met, her mouth drew down into a grim line and she turned abruptly to her companions, making some joke at which they all laughed uproariously. But it was in the intermission, when all the company was walking upon the sea wall and enjoying the cool breeze from the bay, that I saw Deborah.

"Why, Will and Rory!" she cried gaily, and looked at me almost mockingly. "When are you going to tell me that everything is settled?"

"Why, right now," I replied. " 'Tis all arranged at last. I saw Mr. Astor this morning, and I'm out in the *Tonquin*."

Despite my bantering tone, the smile froze on her lips.

"You don't mean that!" she exclaimed.

"Yes, I do!" I assured her.

For a long instant she stared at me, then turned abruptly and fled. I gaped at Sanders.

"Now what the devil?" I said.

He looked after her with a little frown.

"Excuse me!" he said abruptly, and stalked after her.

I did not see either of them again in the course of that concert, and, deprived of Will's somewhat lugubrious support, I felt it scarcely worth while to go on to the dance afterward. Instead, I went home, where I got into my dressing gown and slippers and settled myself with a pipe and a mug of ale and a book I could not read. I half had expected to find Will before me and to demand some explanation of all this mystery. But he was not there, and there was nothing I could do but wait.

It was after midnight when he came in, walking a bit slowly and wearing a frown of puzzled concern.

"What the devil happened to you?" I demanded.

He did not answer me at once but only stared at me over the rim of his mug of ale. Then, at last, when finally he had taken a long draft, he put down the pot and breathed a long sigh.

"Women!" he said, with a shake of his head. "If they're not the most unpredictable, exasperating, muddleheaded creatures God ever made, then my name's Nancy!"

Nor could I ever get him to explain what he meant by that!

It lacked but three weeks of our scheduled sailing when I signed the articles of agreement, yet there still remained a myriad of things to be done, a thousand problems to be settled.

My own personal problems and affairs would have required attention in any case. There was my will to make. My investments I placed in Will Sanders's hands, giving him power of attorney to act for me after consultation with Mr. Astor. I must outfit myself for the voyage and for the time I would be on shore in Oregon.

Since I was unfamiliar with the climate of the Coast, I took clothing for any emergency. I did not neglect hunting gear—my rifle gun and pistols, and a fine imported fowling piece with plenty of powder, shot, and ball. As a particular indulgence, I supplied myself with fishing tackle in enormous quantities—luxuries I had ample occasion to bless before I was done! I likewise invested in a few other practical luxuries: a folding lantern and a supply of stout candles to use in it, a collapsible bucket and washbasin of heavy sailmaker's canvas, and an invention of my own, designed for comfortable sleeping in all kinds of weather and under all conditions, consisting of several bags, one within another, fashioned from woolen blankets of varying weights, with an outer bag made of prime muskrat, both for warmth and protection.

But all of this was personal equipment. Since my return from Montreal I daresay I had been more deeply engrossed in my own affairs than I ought to have been. I had neglected much in connection with the expedition, thinking that someone else had been attending to this detail or that. Now I found that nearly everyone concerned had entertained a similar notion in one degree or another. The confusion that I discovered as a result appalled me!

In any case, my work was cut out for me. Unless someone took a co-ordinating hand, the whole business was likely to fly apart. It needed less than two days to discover this. Captain Thorn had taken it for granted that no more was required of him than command of the vessel: navigation, maintenance, and attention to discipline. The question of supplies he had left to Mr. Mumford, to whose duties as third mate were thereby added those of ship's husband. Mr. Mumford, like

Alan Fraser, taking advantage of the fact that Westlake must remain on board, had appropriated Valerie to himself for the day. And if I felt much as Westlake evidently did, at least I could also enjoy his discomfiture.

Naturally, however, I kept such thoughts to myself, and I was pleased to note that late in the afternoon Westlake was joined by Goodwin. That is to say, Dick Goodwin also came down to Whitehall Slip and strolled nervously up and down the quay. But it was not until near sundown, when it was all but time for us to be off to the final round of farewell ceremonies, that Valerie and the redheaded Scot appeared. When they did, it was with many a coy glance between them. Fraser smirked and swaggered and behaved in general like a triumphant rival, until the other two converged upon them, when, as I had suspected she might, she turned her smiles on Westlake, to the Cock's obvious and utter confusion! Standing near the bulwarks, I heard her ask the time, and when Westlake told her, reading proudly from his handsome chronometer, she gave a little squeal of dismay and declared that, Lawks! she must be off to prepare for the banquet, and away she went, scampering, on Goodwin's arm, leaving the other two gaping after her as nonplused as any country clods!

It was a full evening's entertainment that we were offered, beginning with a banquet at Fraunces' Tavern, followed by a theater party, for which Mr. Astor had taken the entire house, and winding up with a final grand ball at Federal Hall. Forewarned of the event, I had looked forward to it with some curiosity, since it was obvious that Fraser and Westlake could not both escort Valerie. She, however, neatly sidestepped that issue and came upon Dick Goodwin's arm, who, somehow, did not appear so pleased with her choice as I would have thought he should, possibly because of the black looks that came his way, not only from myself now, but from the other two as well. If Valerie was aware of it, she gave no sign. As for the other two, Westlake, having the larger degree of manners, I was pleased to note, found himself burdened with the escort of Valerie's mother, while Fraser bespoke Deborah, and I can scarcely say that any of the four appeared happy in the arrangement. Mrs. Drake seemed ill at ease, and Deborah seemed to me to be positively distressed for some reason. Several times in the course of the dinner I thought I felt her eyes upon me. Yet when I looked up, she was always looking somewhere else. The same was not true of Valerie. Our glances crossed frequently, and I believe had they been swords the sounds of their clashing would have interfered seriously with the general conversation. For my part, I squired young Dorothea Astor, grown now into an attractive little chit of fifteen, who appeared utterly enchanted at this opportunity to take part in a really, truly, genuine grown-up party; so much so, in fact, that I found it quite a happy solution to my own problem of the evening.

From Fraunces' we went on to the theater party, where it seemed as if all New York had turned out to wish us farewell, and from there to the ball, which was even more crowded. Now that it came to the point I was bold enough to claim a dance with Valerie. I think had she quite dared she might have refused me, but the risk of a possible stir in a public place called for a sort of courage I knew she did not have.

"Well, ma'am," I said as we whirled away, "I hope you are pleased."

She looked at me coolly.

"What do you mean by that, Mr. O'Rourke?" she demanded.

"You know what I mean," I replied. "But for you I'd not be sailing tomorrow."

"Really?" she said. "You flatter me!"

"Not at all!" I retorted. "Indeed, I am grateful to you for the opportunity. My one regret is that it will take me away from you for so long! Well! It shan't be forever. I hope you'll bear up well under the strain of absence."

"I'll try to do my best," she answered demurely.

"I'm sure you will," I replied, and she did have the grace to blush at my tone. "But never mind! I shall be back in five or six years. Perhaps by then you will have decided on a date. After all, you will be—let me see—will it be thirty-two or thirty-three?"

Naturally she made no reply to that but only gave an angry toss of her head, womanlike, and that was our farewell.

Quite different was my conversation with Deborah during our brief dance. She, it seemed to me, was close to tears.

"What's the matter?" I demanded.

"Rory!" she said in a low voice. "I—I feel so badly."

"You mean ill?" I said. "Shall I take you home?"

"Don't be a fool!" she retorted, eloquently demonstrating the difference between herself and her sister. "I—I mean I just feel terribly seeing you—you all—go off for so long and so far!"

"Why!" I cried. "What kind of talk is this? So far as I'm concerned, you should be happy. 'Twas your idea."

"Please!" she said. "Don't."

"Well, wasn't it?" I demanded.

"Oh, yes—yes, it was!" she snapped. "I—I still think it was the best thing. It's just that I—just that I—just——"

Her lip trembled and her eyes were suspiciously aswim. It seemed to me that she looked pretty that way, with all her freckles standing out sharp against the pallor of her face. I grinned at her in an effort to cheer her up.

"Come now!" I said. " 'Tisn't as bad as all that! Don't tell me you've fallen in love with one of our brave lads? Why, bless you! We'll none of us be gone so long but that by the time we come home you'll be just grown to size, ready and waiting! If you'll whisper me his name, I'll give you my promise to keep an eye on him for you and see that he's among the first to come home!"

It was nonsense, to be sure, but she did not laugh. Instead, there in the middle of the floor she stopped dancing abruptly and wrenched herself from me.

"Oh, you! You! Oh—— You!" she flared, and then, apparently unable to find words to describe me, she fled, thrusting her way blindly between whirling, startled couples, while I, utterly nonplused, pursued until she took refuge in the ladies' retiring room.

III. The Long Voyage

~~~~~~

I. DEPARTURE

I RECALL there was a brown taste in my mouth at dawn and a queasy feeling in my stomach. I don't remember putting on my trousers or my shirt and my coat. I have a vague recollection of making a slapdash pass at my hair and of feeling worse when I bent over to pull on my boots. Then the three of us were away, through streets that were gray and empty. Our boot heels rang hollowly on the cobbles, and the echoes of our passing crashed and bounced from one side to the other. The cool air braced me somewhat, and we came to Whitehall in time to find the longshoremen at the bollards and four of the crew standing by to heave in the gangplank.

I had no more than a moment to shake hands quickly and bid my roommates farewell before I streaked aboard. 'Twas not for me they were waiting, however, but for Mr. Astor, who was in the cabin giving last-minute instructions to Captain Thorn.

My foot had scarcely touched the deck before he came out and rolled ponderously toward the gangway. As he passed, he paused and clapped me on the shoulder.

"Well, Rory!" he said. "A fine voyage and a merry one! Ya?"

I fear the grin I returned him was a little wan, but it was the best I could muster.

"Aye, sir!" I said. "I'll do my best."

He thumped me on the shoulder again and gripped my arm, almost affectionately, I thought. In the next moment he was away over the side, and the plank was swinging in, the lines cast off. I found a corner where I would be out of the way and rested my forearms upon the high bulwarks, put my chin on my arms, and searched the dock below. Will Sanders was there yet, so was Irving, both standing a little forward, waving, and I waved back. I doubt if there were a score besides them, mostly relatives of our seamen or of the two clerks we had recruited in New York. It occurred to me that the city was not so anxious to wish us Godspeed now that the dancing and the feasting were over. The Astors were there, of course, all in a little group at the end of the wharf, waving and calling words of cheer.

A carriage came rattling down the cobbles, and I saw a flurry of petticoats leap from it. I recognized Deborah as she came running the length of the pier to stand beside Will and wave almost a little hesitantly. Behind her, at a more dignified pace, came Valerie on Dick Goodwin's arm, smiling, not waving. It seemed to me that Goodwin simpered almost triumphantly, and I never disliked the man so much as I did in that moment.

The strip of dark, oily water between us and the slip widened. Our head swung as we drifted gently out into the stream. I saw Deborah turn and say something sharp to her sister, and I knew by Valerie's expression that her own retort was equally sharp. Then Deborah turned away shortly and waved enthusiastically, and I waved back. At the same moment, in a sort of singsong hail from the quarterdeck, the commands went out.

From aloft came distant, modulated replies from the tops, the swish of bare feet upon the deck, and the rattle of rigging as the crewmen swarmed aloft like so many monkeys and the waisters fell to heaving on the sheets. I moved aft to join the little group of my companions that stood huddled upon the poop; the next time I glanced shoreward we were out in the stream and had come about and were standing down and across, on a reach toward the Jersey shore, tacking to take full advantage of the light air. Above our heads our sails spread like great white wings, and gently the canvas filled. We were gathering speed, and the figures ashore, on the slip, were all diminishing in size, rapidly, surprisingly, as if they had been sprinkled all at once with water of Lilliput. A few still waved with as much gusto as ever, but more lifted their handkerchiefs with obviously diminishing enthusiasm, and some were already drifting back to their waiting carriages. Overside the water began to hiss and gurgle. Somewhere under our feet the rudder chains clinked faintly. On the wharf I saw Valerie and Goodwin turn back toward the carriage. But Deborah and Will Sanders and Irving still stood, a little apart from Astor's group, waving and waving as long as I could make them out.

We did not go far that day. It was a sorry anticlimax to stand with the wind so fair away from Whitehall Slip, only to have it die to a whisper before we reached Staten Island, and there fall off entirely. As the tide was already beginning to turn by the time we had fought our way into the Narrows, there was naught to do but anchor and wait the evening ebb.

In the meantime, though passengers might fret, there was plenty for all hands to do; so much so, indeed, that it did not occur to us to dispose ourselves for the night we were to spend at anchor. Nor would it have done us much good if we had, for so cluttered with stores and baggage and ship's gear were the decks and the cabins, that we could not have climbed into our berths had they been assigned to us. Most of the day was spent in trying to bring some order out of this chaos; pulling and hauling, packing and carrying and stowing, a little at a time, each item handled carefully and stowed so as to be as accessible as its nature demanded, yet at the same time with an eye to possible rough weather and breakage once we were at sea.

It was a tedious business and fortunately one that occupied all hands. I say "fortunately," for had there been no such diversion, some of the storms which plagued us later might well have arisen before we were even away. As it was, the captain fussed and swore and threatened our "lubbers" in a way that grated upon the men and won him many a black and sour look. As a result, what should have been done completely by nightfall remained less than a quarter done by the time the sun dropped from sight behind the Staten Island hills. The tide turned toward evening, and although there was no wind, the *Tonquin* weighed anchor and rode through the narrows on the ebb, to anchor again in Gravesend Bay, in the shelter of the projecting hook of Coney Island.

Saturday dawned as still and breathless as Friday had ended. I think it was fortunate for us that Mr. Astor and Will Sanders came down to us in an eight-oared longboat about ten in the morning, for Captain Thorn was growing surlier than ever as it became clear that we were not to get to sea that day, and it seemed to me he had a tendency to take out his ill temper upon the defenseless voyageurs and mechanics. Even as between him and the clerks and partners, tempers were growing short. An idea had been growing in my mind which, because of his peppery humor, I had been reluctant to broach. But now I had an ally not to be denied. As soon as the opportunity presented itself I drew Mr. Astor aside. There was, I recalled to him, an excellent beach on the seaward side of Coney Island, upon which we had often picnicked and spent the day, and there was also a good little tavern at Gravesend which served the best of beer and ale, to say nothing of a delicious chowder and the most succulent steamed clams. If the landsmen, I hinted, might be allowed to sport ashore, they could relieve the galley of extra duty at suppertime and permit the crew to hasten the task of cleaning ship.

Mr. Astor fell in immediately with the scheme, but, to my surprise, the captain listened only sourly.

"I'll need the Canadians," he growled. "The seamen can't do't alone."

"They didn't sign for that," I said.

He glowered at me.

"Are you sea lawyer as well as clerk?"

I opened my mouth to answer, but Mr. Astor put his hand on my arm and chuckled in his throat.

"Ya!" he exclaimed. "With O'Rourke it is wise not to argue. He sticks to his point and more often than not he is right. As well it is perhaps I am here!"

Captain Thorn gave me a grim look.

"Now the orders I give, eh?" Astor beamed. "Rory! Clerks and partners will only be in the way in any case. Take them on shore and any way you can entertain them! Voyageurs and mechanics will stay on board to help."

"What if we get a breeze?" Thorn demanded.

"You can't sail until the tide changes in any case," I told him coldly, "by which time we'll be aboard if there is any sign of wind. If there's any other need for us, fire a gun and we'll be here as fast as a boat can fetch us."

The captain shrugged, as much to say that so long as the owner was present his hands were tied.

So partners and clerks, at least, spent the day on shore, sporting in the hot, late-summer sun on the broad beach. In the early evening, burned brick-red by the sun and caked with salt from the sea water in which we had been swimming, we returned as far as the village, where we washed our throats with quantities of cold beer and devoured gallons of clams, steamed, raw, and in thick chowder.

So occupied, we were scarcely conscious of the passage of time until the boom of a gun from the ship recalled us to the fact that we were not entirely our own masters. McKay jerked out his watch and glanced at it.

"By Holy!" he exclaimed. " 'Tis nigh eight o'clock!"

"Aye, and growing dark," someone put in.

Only when we were halfway to the ship did McKay notice what none of us had thought about.

"There's not a breath of wind," he said.

We all looked at the ship. She lay as still as if she were painted against the darkening sky, straining at her cables before the running tide. So far as we could see there was not a man aloft; no sign of preparation for sailing. Mr. Lewis voiced the thought that was in my mind.

"The tide must have set out two hours ago," he remarked. "D'you suppose he means to try to ride out on it?"

I shook my head.

"It would not carry her beyond the shoals," I replied. "I doubt he'd try it."

Clearly we had been summoned back for some reason, but none among us could guess why.

It was not long a mystery. I was not the first up, nor yet the last, but I was surprised when my feet touched the deck to find those who had gone before gathered in a little group, with the captain facing them belligerently. They stared at one another, the captain in evident temper, my mates in bewilderment. Nobody spoke, and naturally I joined my companions. Captain Thorn said nothing until the last of us had come over the side. Then for some reason he singled me out.

"Were you to spend half the night ashore?"

"We came at your first signal," I replied. Damned if I'd say "sir" to him! " 'Twas my understanding there'd be no need to come before unless there was a wind. Mr. Astor——"

"Mr. Astor has gone back to New York," he ripped out. "We'll see no more of him. I'm in command here, d'you hear?"

Somewhere behind me I heard MacDougal utter a choking sound, and I grinned inwardly. Mr. Astor had appointed him his proxy, and he had been strutting his airs somewhat pompously ever since. I could see there might well be some difference of opinion on that score. I ventured to suggest as much.

"You command the ship, Captain Thorn," I began.

But he cut me short with an oath.

"Goddam me, sir!" he roared. "I command the ship and everything and everyone aboard her! If you don't know it, you might as well learn now! Aboardship a captain's word is law and his whim is as God's. Let that be understood!"

"I'm sure we've no fault to find with your handling of the vessel or her crew, Captain," I heard David Stuart protest.

"The vessel and her crew be damned!" the captain roared. " 'Tis not the vessel and her crew I'm talking about. 'Tis the passengers—yourselves, gentlemen! I want it understood now that my commands are to be obeyed. Is that clear? The safety of the ship depends upon implicit obedience."

"You'll not find us inclined to endanger the ship by disobedience to the rules for her safety," McKay growled.

"Silence!" the captain thundered. "The habit of obedience to the rules of safety springs from the habit of obedience to all rules and commands issued by proper authority! In the Navy——"

"We're not in the Navy, Captain Thorn," I reminded him.

"I am!" he cut back at me with such vehemence that I fell back a pace. "And any vessel I command will adhere to naval procedure. Is that clear?"

There was no answer to that. If there were, I think we were all too taken aback by his choleric attitude to argue.

"Very good!" he snapped. "Then you'll remember my first rule: all lights below decks are dowsed at eight bells—eight o'clock by land-lubbers' time! Is that clear?"

We looked at one another in amazement. It was past that hour already. Did that mean we must find our bunks without lights?

"An' what's th' idea o' thot?" MacDougal demanded.

The captain glared at him.

"I order it so," he snapped.

MacDougal's hand moved, and a bit late I recalled he had taken his pistol on short to practice at marks. In the dusk I could scarcely see the weapon, but I could hear the click as it was cocked.

"Be domned t' thot!" he swore. "I gie ye fair warnin', th' mon thot poots hond tae my lomp'll fetch up wi' his boowells fu' o' lead, ye hear?"

I saw David Stuart stretch out his hand and calmly lift the pistol from MacDougal's hand, quickly, deftly, before the other could recover from his surprise.

"Na, na, Duncan!" he soothed. "Dinna ye be so hasty! I'm sure the captain has good reasons for his ruling."

I think there was scarcely a one of us but would rather have seen the thing out. But Stuart's move mollified Thorn.

"I'm pleased to see there's one of you at least has a penn'orth of sense!" he growled. "Aye! I have my reasons. Good ones! In the first place, the greatest hazard to any ship at sea is fire, and the less you use lights, the more 'tis reduced. If that's not enough, you'll remember this vessel is like to be fair game to both French and British cruisers. At night, at sea, a light shows to a great distance. Bear it in mind!"

I heard Stuart let down the hammer of the pistol gently.

"If you don't mind, Captain," he said reasonably, "we're not at sea yet."

The captain glared at him as if a puppy he had picked up in kindness had soiled his best new coat. With a kind of savage glee I heard the hammer of the pistol click again clear in the silent dark behind me. David Stuart might have shown himself reasonable, I thought. He was certainly not showing himself soft.

"Surely now, Captain!" I heard him say quietly.

Thorn turned on his heel.

"So long as we're yet in port," he flung over his shoulder, "I'll make an exception tonight. But once we're at sea, mind you——"

It scarcely seemed to me that the captain's attitude was reassuring. Nor, at the same time, did MacDougal's reaction promise harmony. But I was too full of sun and beer to be concerned about the matter that night. As much as I wanted was a berth in which to tumble and a chance to close my eyes in sleep. With only half my consciousness I made a note to remark the clash in my confidential journal in the morning and with no further thought sought my blankets.

When I woke it was morning. The sun was up and so were our sailors. I had heard none of it, but our anchor had long since been fetched aboard and catted home, and our sails had been loosed and filled, and we lay well over before a quartering breeze from the southwest, standing smartly out through the Ambrose Channel under a brilliant, cloudless sky, while away to the southward a speck of a hull under a cloud of canvas stood north and east on a course that must ultimately intercept our own. Apart from these, the sea stretched empty and unlimited before us, bright blue, laced with flecks of white, to the half-circle of the horizon. Behind, the white beaches of Long Island and Sandy Hook and the low, green hills of home were already shrouded in the blue haze of distance and would soon be lost to sight.

We dropped our pilot off Rockaway and stood off toward the southeast. Since most of the ship's people were still far too busy fetching order out of the clutter about the decks, there was little for most of us to do but lean upon the rail and speculate upon the identity of the vessel that stood north athwart our course. The sea was gentle, showing only the faintest lift and roll, so that none of us were yet troubled by it. By midmorning the ship was near enough to see her, a black-hulled frigate with a yellow streak painted about her gun ports and a cloud of spotless canvas above to put a bone in her teeth and leave no doubt among us as to her objective. I am afraid we were a shade apprehensive when Westlake came up behind us, grinning.

"Well?" he said. "What do you make of her?"

We glanced about at him.

"She's a man-of-war, obviously," he said, "but I see no colors yet."

I thought I knew the answer but held my tongue, for it seemed to me my duty to observe reactions, not to influence them.

Westlake glanced at us as if he had no great hopes for our intellects, then looked off over our heads.

"Why," he said, though she was yet so distant we could barely make out her outlines, "any fool can see she's American! As a matter of fact, 'tis the *Constitution*."

Perhaps something of my thoughts showed in my face, for he looked at me and grinned.

"When you've been awhile at sea," he said, "you'll learn . . ."

I never did know what he was about to say.

"Mr. Westlake!" said a harsh voice behind us.

The young officer whirled, and so did we all. Captain Thorn stood at the break of the poop and stared down at us.

"Aye, sir!" said Westlake.

"May I remind you of your duties?" Thorn demanded sarcastically.

Westlake flushed red as the gills of a trout.

"Aye, aye, sir!" he growled, and turned away from us abruptly.

"I'll thank you, gentlemen, not to interfere with my officers in the prosecution of their duty!" Thorn said, sweeping us with his icy glance.

Before we could answer, he had turned away from the break of the poop, and I think there was none among us that felt it important enough to follow and argue the point.

As Westlake had said, the frigate proved to be the U.S.S. *Constitution*, 44, Captain Hull. Like some vast-winged gull she came swiftly and gracefully across our track astern, then fetched about upon the weather side of us and brought us underneath her guns, at the same time summoning us to identify ourselves and requesting that we put a boat aboard her with our papers. Mr. Westlake was sent over, and for several hours we ran close alongside each other, until at length, late in the afternoon, she returned our boat and papers and, with a dip of her colors, sheered off and within an hour was gone from sight, leaving us at last alone upon the ocean.

Below decks matters had, by this time, been largely put to rights, and as the novelty of the first day at sea started to wear away, some of us began to feel that, in view of the voyage ahead, it was time we were assigned to the berths we were to occupy. I spoke to MacDougal about it but had little more than a growled retort for my answer. But

I do not doubt that several others did the same, for I noticed a spirit of impatience, and presently, after the *Constitution* had gone her way, the boy Perreault came about the decks, seeking out each one of us and summoning us to the great cabin.

One by one we obeyed his call. By the time I descended the companionway, being among the last eight or nine to appear, it was to find the place already well packed. Partners, clerks, bourgeois, mechanics, and canoemen were all wedged in together, some sitting on the deck, others leaning against the bulkhead, a few seated upon the transom or on the swing chairs that ringed the table. At the head of the table were MacDougal and McKay, with a sheet of the articles laid out before them and each man's name carefully listed. Apparently there was some disagreement between them.

"I tell ye there's nae room for them!" MacDougal half shouted, ruddy-faced.

"Room or no," I heard McKay's low retort, "I still say they're entitled to't!"

Captain Thorn's voice spoke abruptly behind me.

"Entitled to what, Mr. McKay?"

Everyone looked up, startled, and I must say I whirled, surprised. I had had no idea he was at my heels. McKay shot me a suspicious glance, then looked at MacDougal.

"I say the clerks are entitled to berths in the main cabin, Captain," he replied.

"Och!" MacDougal spat. "Entitled, aye! But how are we tae squeeze twelve pairsons intae space for six?"

"I'll handle this, Mr. MacDougal," said Thorn curtly.

"Wull ye?" said MacDougal sarcastically.

"Aye!" growled the captain, and their glances clashed.

"There are six berths in the cabin, besides my own and the first mate's," Thorn growled. "Mr. MacDougal, Mr. McKay, and the two Stuarts will occupy four. As my clerk, Mr. Lewis will occupy one of the others, and as a concession to you, Mr. McKay, your nephew will occupy the sixth."

"I ask no concessions for him," McKay growled.

"I concede it anyway!" snarled Thorn. "The rest of you clerks to the steerage, with the junior officers. If there are not enough berths, sling hammocks!"

He glanced at MacDougal.

"That accounts for fifteen of you, right?" he demanded.

MacDougal meticulously counted the names on his list.

"Aye!" he replied laconically.

"Then you'll have eighteen or twenty more?" Thorn demanded.

"Fifteen canoemen and a boy," MacDougal replied dryly, "and five mechanics—bourgeois they rank as."

"I care naught for their rank," Thorn flung back at him. "I must lodge them where I have room! Let the canoemen sling their hammocks on the gun deck——"

"The gun deck?" demanded McKay.

"The main deck if you prefer," said Thorn impatiently. "The same as this, but forward of the steerage. Mechanics and the boy will lodge in the fo'c'sle with the crew!"

McKay leaped to his feet.

"That's hardly just!" he cried. "These mechanics rank above the cut of crewmen!"

I saw Captain Thorn stiffen, although I knew what McKay meant. Our mechanics were lads of special skill, who had some training and who stood in line for clerkships when vacancies occurred, just as most of the clerks expected to become partners in due time. The crewmen to McKay were like voyageurs who could scarcely aspire to be bourgeois by the very nature of their work. To see the mechanics and bourgeois placed among the crew and below the voyageurs must have its effect upon their authority. Yet it was true that the captain must use what space he had.

"I have not asked you if 'twas just," Thorn said coldly.

"Would ye order officers to the fo'c'sle?" McKay demanded.

"Aye! For a matter of space or discipline!"

From the far side of the cabin a voice interrupted.

"If 'tis a matter of space, why not find another place—sick bay, perhaps, rather than upset the ranks. Would you move forward of the mast with the crew yourself, Captain?"

Thorn's head jerked up.

"Who is that man?" he demanded.

"The name is Fraser," the Cock himself replied, smiling and faintly derisive.

"He's named for a partnership," MacDougal growled.

The captain's lips drew tight and his jaw thrust forward.

"Do you say so?" he demanded. "I care not what he is to be. He will go forward with the mechanics for his insolence and share quarters with the seamen!"

"Now, by God!" Fraser barked, and I could not but grin.

Thorn glowered at him. Even if he had overreached himself, for such a man there was no drawing back.

"I have naught to do with your petty ranks!" he thundered. "I'll remind you all, gentlemen, that I command here!"

MacDougal was on his feet in an instant. But Fraser cut in before him.

"You may command the seamen," he cried. "But the rest of us are contracted to Mr. Astor. Mr. MacDougal represents him! I'll hear what he has to say!"

"He has naught to say!" Thorn roared. "I've told you the law of the sea. I *am* in command here. You are insolent, sir! Aboard ship we have ways to manage such as you! Get forward with the mechanics and lodge in the fo'c'sle. If I hear another word from any of you, you'll join watches with the seamen!"

"Are we to suffer such treatment!" William Wallace cried in his curious accent, half-French, half-Scots.

"Aye!" I put in. "This seems hardly fair!"

"Fair!" snorted Thorn. "Am I to consider that now?"

He set his foot to the lower step of the ladder.

"You've heard my orders," he growled.

McKay stood forward.

"By the Lord!" he cried. "We have papers to show our positions."

Captain Thorn whirled, and whence it came I could not say, but he held a pistol in his hand.

"Is it so?" he demanded. "You have heard me! If you would dispute me, try! I'll blow out the brains of the first to argue! Understand, gentlemen! The law gives me that power over mutineers, even if they be passengers!"

There was no reply to be made to that. Thorn half smiled.

"Since you've seen fit to dispute me," he growled, "let it be understood. Those in the fo'c'sle will take watches with the seamen and work ship as part of the crew. The bos'n will assign you."

"Now, by God——" Fraser swore again.

The pistol swung grimly in his direction.

"Were you praying, Mr. Fraser?" Captain Thorn asked.

Fraser broke off abruptly.

"That's all!" said Thorn, after an instant's pause.

He thrust his pistol in his belt and turned to the ladder.

"See to it!" he growled, and in the next instant was gone.

It seemed to me scarcely an auspicious beginning for so long a voyage.

II. JONATHAN THORN

THE business might have boded far more ill than actually came of it had not the gods that rule the waves taken a hand and fetched winds to whip the seas into a thundering welter of spray and brine that kept us tossing for more than a fortnight like drowned flies in a leftover rum pot. In an endless procession the great gray-backed rollers, laced with plumes of yellow foam and spindrift, rushed upon us like mobile mountains, lifting us sickeningly with belly-weighting speed to the crest, where we trembled, shuddering an instant, then dropping us, dipping, swooping, careening down into the trough between. There, before we could catch at our stomachs in our throats, we would be climbing again. All the while, night and day, the interminable wind howled and shrieked and moaned in the rigging. The masts and cordage creaked and groaned and whistled, and the ship's timbers protested each racking shudder, as if she had rheumatism in all her joints.

Even those of us who had been to sea before felt it, and I know that I, for one, was several days indifferent to where I slept or what I did. As for what I was served—my feeling amounted to more than mere indifference. It became a definite aversion to food in any form.

I was not alone. By far the great bulk of my companions were suddenly too miserable to care for so small a matter as injustice. A few of the more spirited, to be sure, allowed themselves the luxury of moaning, wondering what folly had induced them to agree to such a journey. But for the most, they took to their hammocks, once the seamen had condescendingly deigned to teach them the trick of getting in and staying there. There the voyageurs, especially, stuck like burrs, only coming infrequently above decks to attend a call of nature or to offer tribute to Neptune. Invariably they would cast up their accounts to windward, to the fury of the captain and the despair of the mates. Thorn damned them all roundly for a pack of filthy lubbers, with no more human decency or notion of decent cleanliness than the hogs we carried in the pens amidships.

But they were too miserable to pay him any heed. Having accomplished their ends, they would turn from the rail, retching and groaning, their eyes hollow and listless, like burnt-out coals in their head;

cheeks sunken, ghastly gray, their hair matted and beards unkempt and tangled, grizzled with the vomit that had dried upon them, their dirty blanket *capots* sticky with grime accumulated through days and nights of wear. Without pausing to retort or even to look about, they would plunge once more into the dark scuttle that led to their quarters, like so many groundhogs, there to creep back into their hammocks in the gloom and wrap themselves once more in their misery.

The lot of the mechanics and dwellers in the fo'c'sle was more Spartan. I think I never saw a man so galled and at the same time so sick and helpless as Alan Fraser. Yet there was no resisting Thorn's command. Neither he nor his fellows had the strength to fight against it, and daily, with the seamen, they were kicked from their hammocks and set to scrubbing decks and hauling at the lines and halyards that controlled the trim of spars and sails. I think the captain would have delighted to send them aloft, where they might well have been tossed from the catapulting spars into the raging seas. But some shred of discretion seemed to restrain him, and he left their assignment to the mates in whose watches they served.

Even that work was not without dangers. At the height of the gale we were taken several times aback, shipping heavy seas, and once we were driven so far down by the head that it seemed that the ship must founder. When this occurred, several men were on the forepeak with Westlake. From where I clug to a stanchion amidships I saw them all swept like so many chips against the rail, where most of them held on by the very skin of their fingernails, like so many drowning rats. Fraser was among them, and I saw his feet and legs wash over the railing, but in the same flashing instant, Roger Westlake, no doubt acting entirely by instinct, the while he clung with one hand to a stay, reached out with the other and caught the red-haired woodsman by the slack of his collar and by sheer strength of muscle hauled him back to safety. There was no question but that by main strength and quick thinking the sailor saved the Cock-of-the-Woods' life that time. Yet, so far as I could see, no word passed between them.

Better than a fortnight the weather held so. Then, imperceptibly, we came into calmer seas and sunnier, warmer days, and it seemed to me the captain reaped the seed of his own sowing. First, the mechanics before the mast, the very vigor of whose labor forced them to respect the normal needs of their appetites, then partners and clerks, whose somewhat easier lot allowed them to recover more quickly, and, last, the voyageurs found their sea legs and their appetites and looked with interest at their plates. When this happened, we were not slow to discover the low quality of the slop that was put before us. Despite the fact that we, of the clerks' mess, had provided ourselves with stores of delicacies, fresh and preserved meats, as well as wines and spirits, we were strictly forbidden to broach them. To my irritation and chagrin, we were placed strictly upon ship's stores; rationed a quart of water a day per man, fourteen ounces of hard bread or biscuit, a pound and a quarter of salt beef or a pound of pork, a half pint of Souchong tea with sugar, rice one day and beans the next, and once a week a corn pudding with molasses. On Sundays, in the steerage, there was a bottle of sour Teneriffe wine served out to each. Aft, in the main cabin, where the partners and senior officers lodged, there was some variation: fresh pork and hams, smoked beef and tongues and daily puddings and wine being the usual thing there. But forward, among the hands and the voyageurs and petty officers, the ration was even simpler than ours!

It was MacDougal, I believe, who growled that it was a "damned shame that men upon their own vessel could not fare as they willed," a remark that put the captain into a towering rage, and one for which, I must say, I could scarcely blame him. Yet in the end the clerks, at least, did win some concessions from him, for we were granted the privilege of pooling our stores and broaching them once each week, on Sundays, when we might withdraw a strictly limited amount for the use of our entire mess. Humanlike, I will say we were scarcely satisfied with that, for we saw no reason why we should not each be allowed free access to what we ourselves had bought out of our own pocket. But the captain was adamant.

"By God!" he would cry. "If I'd but let them, they'd eat up everything in a week and then come sniveling to me to know why 'twas permitted and where they were to get more."

But the voyageurs were his pet anathema. Since he could scarcely reduce their rations beyond their present miserable level without the excuse of necessity, he would descend into their quarters unannounced, storming and shouting and holding his handkerchief to his nose, declaring them stinking lubber nests. Then he would turn out every man with his gear and drive them on deck, where he would command the officers to see that they aired their bedding and scrubbed their belongings with soap and salt water, so that the ship looked like a floating laundry with lines strung all about the deck and dingy shirts and underwear fluttering in the breeze. Gradually, however, this first fine frenzy of scrubbing shook down to routine, and the men began to appear in groups upon the deck, to sit for hours in idleness and play; for God knows there is little enough to do aboard ship once the essential chores are finished.

To the captain such idleness was not only a nuisance but an abomination. Nothing was more maddening to him. And when they would be joined in their circle by David Stuart, he turned purple with fury. To see a man who pretended to the name of gentleman settle himself among these half-breeds and pass the pipe from mouth to mouth, laugh at their jokes and lead their outlandish songs, swap stories with them for hours on end, seemed to him beyond all comprehension, and though I believe at the outset David Stuart enjoyed his respect and confidence if any among us did, by this he forfeited both and fell as low in Captain Thorn's autocratic estimation as the lowest seaman on board.

We had been perhaps a month at sea when the scent of the land came to us, strong and nostalgic, and next morning we fetched the Cape de Verds up out of the brassy ocean. They lay upon our larboard beam, with over beyond them and below, some leagues faint in the distance, the nebulous outline of the African coast.

Our partners made excuse that, since our water ration had by now been reduced to a pint and a half a day, we should go ashore and fill our casks. But at the suggestion Captain Thorn flew into a towering rage and swore that we had no thought for our business but were interested only in sight-seeing. Nor would anything stir him. We bore down past the islands, cracking on all sail, and stood along the African shore only so far as to catch the trades when we hauled off in all haste to the southwestward.

We stood down the back of the northeast trades and presently crossed the Equator, where initiations into the Order of Shellbacks and a welcome to the realm of Neptune, reminiscent of the ceremonies at the passage of the Sault, were held. In those days of steady driving we came to know one another better upon both sides.

Mr. Mumford, our third mate, was mild-mannered, though perhaps a little inclined to think more highly than he should of his own abilities and authority. Mr. Fox, the first mate, was pleasant, with genuine capacity of mind and the courage to use it, but so self-effacing we were scarcely aware of him. Indeed, apart from Thorn himself and his nephew, who seemed cut of the same timber, we were singularly fortunate in our officers.

The men themselves seemed average enough; salt-soaked counterparts, in the main, of our own voyageurs. They shared the same tastes and enthusiasms, apart from their duties; wenches and the rum pot being the primary preoccupation of both. In fact, it seemed to me that Mike Shea and the rocklike Charbonneau, between them, typified the relationship.

At New York, Charbonneau, like his fellows, had been all bluff and bluster. If fists flew and noses were bloodied, there was never a question but that somewhere in the middle of it would be Mike Shea and the Moose.

"Aaarrrh! Th' great bloody booger!" Shea would growl.

To this the Moose would reply simply by spitting upon the palms of his hands and opening his arms wide.

"*Eh, bien, salaud!*" he would snarl. "Com' see who is bettair man, eh?"

Once aboard, however, it seemed to me much of Charbonneau's spirit fled through his teeth, at least for the first few days. He took on a sort of moldy cast, almost a fuzz, like mildew, beneath the stubble of his grizzled beard, and though I have seen many a sick Indian, I have never seen one so fearful that death might not pass him by.

In this condition, Shea taunted him unmercifully. It was the Irishman's delight at the height of the gale to carry up his plate with the utmost ostentation and offer it to the half-breed in his hammock with the tenderest of mock concern, then roll in the scuppers and howl with glee as the bandy-legged voyageur would retch and clutch at his mouth and scramble for the companionway. On other occasions Shea was not above emptying a bucket of icy sea water over the sleeping Moose as the most effective means of turning him out.

As he gradually recovered life and the will to survive, however, Charbonneau began to seek revenge. It became a rough and hazardous game, all played in the spirit of utmost good nature. Once during a night watch, when Shea was late aloft, the Moose stealthily slipped up into the rigging and cut the ratlines all the way to the rail, so that when the little Irishman came down in the darkness he all but tumbled through, full thirty feet to the deck below, and only his native sailor's agility saved him, while L'Orignal clutched at his sides, gurgling, and danced a lumbering caper on the deck.

It was a grim prank, indeed, and one for which it was necessary to reprimand him severely, but he took the censure in good part and promised—no doubt with tongue in cheek—to behave. Yet only a day or two later he gathered up all the flying fish that fell upon the decks and, without disturbing a hitch, stuffed Mike Shea's hammock full of them where it hung amid the others on the clews along the forward rail, so that when Shea came to sling his bag that night, a cascade of slimy, stinking, half-spoiled remnants poured out upon the deck to the delight and glee of Charbonneau and all his fellows.

In retaliation Shea somehow or other inveigled the Moose into the chain locker at the moment when the captain was inspecting cable and having it restowed. Anyone who has seen the great links of an anchor chain, almost as big as a man's skull and of far harder iron, come crashing in through the hawse hole will appreciate the dance of death the Indian was compelled to perform, leaping from this side to that to avoid the flailing, whipping lengths as they clattered in. One brush of them could have crushed his skull or cracked his legs like broomstraws and left him lying helpless to be ground into a bloody pulp.

I would have thought the Moose had reason to be angry, yet he was not. He merely grinned and promised to get even. Not so Captain Thorn. It was he who reprimanded Shea, and I was shocked at the shipboard discipline that saw him triced up to a grating at the gangway, bared to the waist, and his back striped to bleeding with a dozen of the cat, laid on with a will by the captain's nephew.

Yet even as I had been astonished at Charbonneau's reaction to the prank, so was I amazed at Shea's reception of the flogging. It was all in the day's work so far as he was concerned, and I heard him later saying to his mates that it was not a breeze in a bucket compared to a flogging round the fleet, such as was often ordered in His Majesty's Navy!

Before the trades, we ran down under the snout of South America, and by the first of November we found ourselves across the Tropic of Capricorn. There, not long afterwards, we ran out of the trades altogether and fell in with foul weather, somewhere off the mouth of the River Plate, and here we began to feel the shortage of water. By December we were down to a gill a man a day, and some were offering a gallon of brandy to the voyageurs for a man's day's ration but finding few takers.

By this time, however, we were well down in the southern latitudes and no great distance off the coast of South America. The partners dared hope that the captain would put ashore in Patagonia, where he might fill the casks, and the rest of us would have a chance to see the giant natives, of whom we had heard so much from the sailors: folk with web feet and spinach-green hair, the men eight and a half feet tall and the women only slightly under. But the captain scoffed and said there were none such. Secretly, I think he was afraid of the creatures! At any rate, he flatly refused the suggestion and, instead, bore off again to the eastward. There was an air of tension, it seemed to me; almost a mood of mutiny aboard when at mid-morning, on the fifth of December, we all were brought standing by a hail from the masthead lookout.

"Land ho!"

Mr. Fox, who had the deck, gazed aloft.

"Where away?"

I don't think any of us were aware that the captain had come on deck.

"That will be the Jasons, Mister Fox." He spoke from the quarterdeck behind us in a chill voice that made us all jump and glance about. "We'll look for water there."

I think some might accuse me of exaggeration in referring to the bits of rock we first put into as land. I would scarcely blame them, for the Jason Islands, lying just northwestward of the Falklands, are little more than dry reefs; jagged spires of barren, forbidding, black rock, thrusting above the surging seas that break white about their feet.

We had some difficulty finding a place at which to land, for the rocks rose precipitously and the seas broke so savagely among them that in many places it seemed dangerous even to approach. However, we were fortunate at length to find a narrow strip of stony shingle, sufficiently sheltered in a cove to permit us to beach our boat.

The island upon which we landed was not large, but it was extremely rugged. Though we searched it from end to end, we found no living streams or even springs among the rocks but only here and there a pool of rain water in the crevices of the ledge. However, if we did not find the water that we sought, there were compensations. Myriads of birds swarmed upon the rocks and rose before us like clouds of mosquitoes kicked out of the sedge: gulls and terns, albatrosses, ducks, shags, white and gray geese, eagles, hawks, and vultures. I never saw so many or such a variety. Among them were vast flocks of penguins, whose short, stubby wings would not permit them to fly, but who could only waddle before us like so many dignified old men wrathfully started from their privacy and hurrying with clacking beaks and breeches dragging, so to speak, out of our path, while all around the shore the ledges were black with seals and sea lions and sea wolves, so that we had no trouble bagging all the meat we could carry.

We spent the greater part of the afternoon at this, and I, for one, heard no signal from the ship. Yet, at last, when it came time to return, what was our amazement on gathering at the landing place to see that she had weighed her anchor and was standing off and on, the very way in which she carried her sails bespeaking the captain's irritation.

When we came on board, Thorn greeted us with the most unbridled fury, cursing us for a pack of knaves and ne'er-do-wells, despite the fact that we fetched with us enough fresh meat for several meals. Sarcastically he referred to our sport ashore as a "wild-goose chase" and declared that, by God, he had been half a mind to sail without us.

Since we had found no running water that day, we sent out another party the next morning upon the neighboring island to resume the search. I did not go, perhaps fortunately, although McKay and Stuart took a number of the clerks. Toward midafternoon a gun was fired to signal them off, but they did not come. After an hour or so, watching through the glasses, we could see them, searching along the shore, and presently we saw a smoke and a flame running through the dry grass. Something was obviously amiss, yet Captain Thorn would have none of it. He signaled again impatiently, then ordered the anchors up, and swore he would sail away without them. Fortunately, we were able to persuade him to delay yet a little longer, and in about a quarter of an hour the longboat returned to report that one of the seamen had been missing and had been found asleep in a hollow not far offshore. Naturally, they could not come off and leave him.

Any reasonable man would have accepted without cavil so legitimate an explanation. Not Captain Thorn, however. The partners, he declared, had deliberately sought to prolong their "wild-goose chasing" —and this, despite the fact that they had again fetched out as much fresh meat as the boat could carry. Roundly he abused the poor seaman, Johnson, who had fallen asleep, and in his fury even threatened the man's life. After that he turned upon those who had taken part in the search and berated them for delaying our sailing! No one troubled to reply. It was clear enough to all that there was nothing to be said. The man was almost insane with temper and jealousy of his authority.

A little before nightfall we stood out again to sea, hauling clear of the vicious fangs of the Jasons, and, the wind rising in the night, we fought all the next day against it. But on the seventh we were able to come about again and run down to the larger islands, where it seemed more likely we would find the water we needed to fill our casks. Late in the morning we came to anchor in the sheltered, almost landlocked harbor of Port Egmont, where occasionally, Mr. Fox said, whaling vessels put in to careen and water. There was no settlement, but we found a clear, flowing spring and the remains of some fishermen's huts, to say nothing of immense herds of seals and sea lions and incredible flights of seafowl.

We lay several days here while the crew, the voyageurs, and all the mechanics, under the supervision of the mates and the cooper, were set to cleaning and refilling our casks. For the use of partners and clerks, a tent was set up ashore, not far from the spring, and all who felt inclined were permitted to move ashore with guns and bedding.

I must say it was a welcome change from shipboard life. Several of the more pious among us, Franchere, Thomas McKay, and sharp-faced little Alec Ross, discovered a pair of ancient graves upon the hill above—the resting place of two long-forgotten seamen. Wooden head-boards leaned crazily above the somber mounds, half-rotted away and all but illegible, and these they set out to renew, while the rest of us turned to the more earthy pursuit of meat for the living.

Despite his remarks about "wild-goose chasing" Captain Thorn now proved himself not altogether without sporting blood, for on the second day he came ashore himself with a tremendous long fowling piece, with a bore like that of a six-pounder, to try his hand at fetching down a few ducks and geese and Cape pigeons. I observed that it was his invariable habit to wait until his game was well settled on the ground, and never once did I see him waste shot and powder on a bird that had taken wing. But evidently he enjoyed himself.

I daresay this was as much as any of us could ask. He joined us first on the eighth. On the ninth and again on the tenth he came on shore to hunt, afterward joining us at our campfire and showing himself gracious enough to growl that the gray geese we had roasted on spits over the coals were "tolerable tasty."

On the tenth the last of the water casks was filled and stowed, and that night MacDougal and McKay accompanied the captain once again on board, where they stayed the night. In the morning—which was the eleventh—they came off to us and assured us that the vessel would not sail until the following day. When we ventured to express surprise, McKay grinned.

"He's enjoying himself, that's why!" he remarked.

It happened that our stiff little Russell Farnham had had the fortune, the evening before, to catch a gray goose, high among the rocks, and fetch it in, and we had tied it up at a little distance from the tent, thinking to make a mascot of it. Now a puckish sort of humor prompted Farnham to move the bird a little distance down the hill toward the landing place, where he drove a stake and tethered it by the leg, a little off the path, yet where it must be easily seen.

McKay gave him a puzzled look when he returned and joined us by the pale morning fire.

"What's that for?" he demanded.

The little New Englander grinned.

"Stay around a bit," he replied. "You'll see!"

"Not I!" said McKay, and went off with his nephew and Ross and Franchere to finish the work on the graves.

"I'm for a bit mair shootin'," said MacDougal. "David?"

He glanced at the rest of us.

"I want to cut some grass," I excused myself. "We'll be running low of feed before 'tis time to slaughter the last of the hogs if 'tis not done."

Farnham gave him an impish look.

"You ought to stay around a bit. There's plenty of time."

"Aye! Time tae rot in yon stinkin' vessel!" MacDougal growled. "Not me! I'm for stretchin' ma legs th' whiles I can!"

He and Stuart picked up their guns and went off over the hill among the rocks, where the clouds of sea birds that rose before them marked their passing.

The rest of us sat some moments wondering, each studying Farnham, who kept his own gaze on the fire in the main but now and again would shoot a quick glance down toward the landing. Obviously he had something afoot, and some of us were curious enough to wait about and see what it might be. MacLennan and Matthews busied themselves upon the remains of a cold goose we had had the evening before, while McGillis and De Montigny and I went down into a little swale near by and fell to cutting the grass I wanted. From there we could see both the landing and the path that led upward from it.

We had not been working above half an hour when the captain's gig came ashore, with the captain in it, but no sign of Robert Stuart. They beached where the ship's boats had drawn up to water, and the captain took his immense fowling piece and started up the path. Halfway up he caught sight of the tethered goose by the trailside, sitting calmly on the ground. Before any of us could cry out, he flung up his piece and fired.

The goose, of course, scarcely moved, for even were it not dead already, it could not. The captain, evidently thinking he had no more than winged it, made haste to reload and fired again, when, seeing it flutter a little under the force of the charge, he became sure of his game and went over to pick it up.

His expression as he bent down to pick it up was one of triumph. But as he discovered the prank that had been played upon him, the look, first of surprise, then bafflement, that crossed his face was a delight to behold. I tried my best to contain myself, but I did not succeed. Like my companions, I burst out into hoots of laughter, falling down amid the fresh-cut hay and rolling over and over in it while I held my sides with glee.

It was not politic, it is true. Yet God knows it was no more than any voyageur would take in good part. But Captain Thorn had not their humor. The sound of our laughter grated on his ears. His face clouded. He scowled first down into the little swale at me and my companions, then glared up toward the tent where Farnham and the other two clerks had buried their mouths in their hands. His face turned nearly black with rage. Without a word he turned abruptly on his heel, flinging the dead, inoffensive goose, still tethered, to the ground, so violently that the feathers flew, and strode back to the waiting gig, where he re-embarked and an instant later disappeared around the rocky point that blocked the ship from view.

The laughter died in my throat. I sat up and glanced at McGillis and saw him looking where the gig had disappeared, as serious as myself.

"That was not good," he said.

Quietly we finished cutting the grass and carried it down by the armload to the boat. From there we returned to the camp above, where we found Farnham and his comrades still chuckling.

"You shouldn't have done that," I said. "He'll have someone's blood for it. You'll see!"

"Bah!" snorted MacLennan. "Who gives a fig for him?"

"Nevertheless," I replied, "I don't trust him. I think 'twould be as well to sleep aboard tonight. Come on! Give me a hand! Let's get this gear together."

"Stuff!" he snorted. "Leave it where it is. We can carry it down later if the others agree. I'm off to shoot!"

He went off with Farnham and De Montigny, while Matthews and McGillis stayed with me. Between us we knocked down the tent and rolled it and the rest of the gear into packs. Only when all was ready to be carried down to the boat did we take up our own pieces and set out.

It was as well we troubled ourselves. Such was the noise of the surf among the rocks upon the jagged shores, the screams and cries of the sea birds, as they rose in clouds about us, the beating and whistling of their wings, and the barking of the seals among the ledges, that no other sound could reach our ears above them, not even the booming of a single gun. It was only when we came out upon the crest of a low ridge above the camp that our eyes could show us what we had not heard. McGillis caught wordlessly at my arm.

I looked where he pointed and saw the *Tonquin,* standing out from the harbor, the white spray curling before her bows and every rag of sail set.

"The devil!" I cried. "The old bastard's gone and left us!"

McGillis spat.

"D'ye not mind, he's threatened as much before?"

"Aye," I told him, "but 'twas understood we'd not be sailing till tomorrow. I heard no gun."

"No more did I," retorted the Scot. "I'd wager there was none."

"I'd not put it past him," Matthews growled.

"Nor I!" I agreed. "But we do no good standing here! Mac, cut across and pick up Stuart and MacDougal. Fetch them back to the landing as quickly as you can. Matt! Do the same for Farnham and the others. I'll fetch McKay and the lads at the graveyard."

They were away almost before I had finished, firing their guns as they went to try to draw the others' attention. Among the graves, on the ridge, I found McKay and his comrades already aware of the ship's departure. They must have just seen it, for they were standing in a little knot staring after her in bewildered disbelief.

I will say for McKay that he wasted no time in recrimination. Between us we got the gear stowed and the boat afloat and ready by the time the others appeared, and we all clambered aboard, disposing ourselves as best we could in our tiny cockleshell, for when we left the ship we had had no thought that it would be necessary to take her outside the bay. I doubt our freeboard was more than eight or nine inches, and the seas that ran outside the harbor were not small.

By the time we gained the harbor mouth, the ship was a good two leagues offshore and gaining steadily, though we tried frantically to overtake her. We rowed with all the strength that was in us, six of us at the oars through all the time, for we could not shift places for fear of oversetting our crazy little craft. As we rowed, the wind increased in strength and the seas turned into literal mountains of water that rushed upon us without mercy, showing their fangs, and ever and again lifting us up for a quick glimpse of the ship standing off to the northwest.

While we rowed, the others took turns at bailing, no child's play, for we had only a single scoop, and it was as much as a man could do, working steadily, to keep abreast of the water that sloshed in over the gunnels. More than once it seemed to me we must surely founder. Toward five o'clock, after we had been rowing close on to three hours steadily and without respite, and those of us who were at the oars were nigh dead with the strain of it, David Stuart, whose turn it was, inadvertently let the bailing scoop slip from his fingers into the sea. In despair we angled for it with an oar, but only succeeded in breaking that. I must say at that moment it seemed to me that all hope was lost. Alone in a cockleshell of a boat in a freezing ocean, with a gale making and the ship all but hull down on the horizon, we might as well give up and let the sea take her way of us. But at that moment someone forward cried out that the ship was coming about, and, sure enough, it was true!

At that we fell to laughing and joking among ourselves in relief. Captain Thorn, we were at first inclined to agree, had taken thorough vengeance for Farnham's prank and played one of his own upon us. But a little later the wind came about, blowing from the ship to us, and we wondered, though we did not say what we were thinking to one another, if perhaps the *Tonquin* had not turned because the wind fell foul rather than because of the captain's conscience.

Fortunately, in these latitudes, especially at that time of the year, it stays light far into the night. Had it grown dark, I doubt he would have found us in that tossing sea. As it was, as she came alongside, we experienced the greatest difficulty fending off and, at the same time, letting our people up one by one upon the heaving, jerking, jumping Jacob's ladder that was all that was let down to us. At one moment we would be almost level with the ship's rail, so that we could look across her decks and see the captain, looking black and angry as a thundercloud, leaning on the quarterdeck rail, with Robert Stuart standing close at his shoulder with his thumbs hooked in his belt and an ominous expression upon his young face. In the next, before I could be sure of what I thought I saw, we would be down in the hollow between the great green combers and the ship would be towering above us like the side of a cliff, the tumble home of her side threatening to crush us like an eggshell as she rolled.

Three—four times we rose so and dropped, dizzyingly, before it came my turn. Only when I stood at last upon the relatively solid planking did I dare take time again to look and confirm what I had thought I saw. There was no question of it then. There was a pistol in Robert Stuart's belt, close by his open hand, and the expression of his face said plain enough he meant to use it if the need arose. Only when the last man was on board and the seamen had expertly grappled the longboat with tackles fore and aft and swung her up into her empty chocks, did he turn away and leave the captain to the lone enjoyment of his own deck.

What he said as he did so I could not catch, but there was little doubt as to the nature of it, for I saw Thorn's face twist into a snarl. For an instant he stood staring at the youngest partner's back, and then abruptly he turned upon his heel and flung away down the companion ladder to his own cabin.

Only afterwards did I learn that Stuart had ordered him at his weapon's point to put about for us. And even then—it was Mr. Fox who told me—Thorn might have refused through stubbornness had not the wind, at that instant, come about foul and left him no choice.

During the night the storm increased almost to a hurricane, so that two of our sails were shredded by the wind and the larboard bulwarks were smashed in by the sea. We were forced to lie to under bare poles for six hours before we could resume our course, and any man of reason may judge what must have happened to us in our little cockleshell of a boat had it been necessary for us to lie out in it.

We had no worse weather as we came around the Horn. It was rough, aye! It snowed and blew, and the tremendous combers pitched us about like a chip in a rough sault. The tremendous seas were green and clear and cold as icebergs laced with white. There were times when we wondered if we would weather them. But we did. On the fifteenth of December we saw Staten Land with her forked peaks and barren flank, her snow and glittering glaciers; and not long afterward we passed Tierra del Fuego, with its mysterious flickering lights, coming and going, glowing and fading, like will-o'-the-wisp. Next day we found ourselves under the cape itself. But here we were forced to beat back and forth, unable to make headway against wind and current, until Christmas morning, when the wind came round a point and gave us just enough, with nothing off, to double the jagged jut of it. New Year's Day found us well into the southern seas and the weather growing warmer almost by the hour.

The voyage north was comparatively calm and peaceful. We had brought our sea legs with us from the Atlantic, and all the Pacific had to offer us in that season and at those latitudes seemed to us mere child's play. Thorn sulked, to be sure, while the partners spoke among themselves in Gaelic and the voyageurs talked in French and Ojibway, so that I am sure he was convinced they were both plotting against him. The feud between Westlake and Fraser and myself had nothing to thrive on; for Fraser was by now accustomed to sailoring, and I suspect secretly enjoyed it, while I could feel no hostility toward either of them when Valerie was not in sight!

By mid-January we were past Valparaiso, and the seas were calm enough for MacDougal and McKay to set to drawing plans for the new fort—plans over which they fell out bitterly among themselves. In all that long run we touched at no port, but scuttled northward as if all the Spanish devils in hell were at our heels, sighting land only once when we slipped past Juan Fernandez. On the twenty-fourth we slid back across the Equator, and at last, on the tenth of February, we fetched in sight of the Sandwich group, where we put in to provision and water and sport and recruit our ranks. I daresay I could fill a book with all that happened there, but none of it is properly within the province of this account!

III. WHERE ROLLS THE OREGON

WE WEIGHED anchor on the last day of February, 1811, and stood off to the southeast, around the tip of Woahoo, and bore away on a due course northeast for the Columbia.

Our decks were as lumbered as ever they had been when we left New York, for we had taken on a considerable quantity of live-stock. These we had placed in sizable pens at the gangways, with the tops boarded over to make runways from which the ship might be worked. In addition there were, all about, vast piles of fruits and vegetables for provisions for ourselves, fetched on at the last moment. A veritable hennery had been rudely thrown up at the break of the fo'c'sle, and a vast mountain of sugar cane for fodder for the animals was stacked like cordwood between the pens and the mast. In addition to all this above decks we were well-nigh doubly crowded below, for every available corner had been stacked with foodstuffs, and even the actual living space had been cut down by two dozen or so of the recruited islanders, some to act as boatmen and voyageurs attached to the new post, the rest to serve as seamen aboard the Tonquin.

In the course of the first few days we managed to fetch a degree of order to our decks, and with our recruits shaken down at length into something like the norm of shipboard routine, we managed to live together without untoward event for as much as a fortnight. Until the second day of March we had contrary winds, but on that day, being finally clear of the islands and standing on our new course, they blew more to our advantage and sent us steadily, if not merrily, upon our way. From that day until the twelfth of the month, nothing out of the ordinary occurred, and I think more than one of us dared hope, as a consequence, that our internal conflicts, at least, were ended.

But evidently this was more than we ought to expect, for on that day we sailed abruptly out of the tropic climate into snow and freezing sleet, whipped out of the north by bitter gales that blew between leaden seas and sullen skies.

In the best of circumstances, with a tight ship and warm clothing, plenty of rum to warm our bellies and a certain amount of cheer and good fellowship to warm our hearts, I think we would have been cold. As it was, laboring in a tubful of drafts, wearing only the clothes we had worn through the heat of the tropics—a torn shirt and a pair of tattered trousers—it seems to me little wonder we came nigh to freezing! At the islands the nights were balmy and mild, the days warm and bright and sometimes even uncomfortably hot. The seamen and our voyageurs had put on a minimum of clothing, and what they had had remaining of their old gear was often as not traded for female favors before sailing. Colder weather we were certain to have, even the dullest was aware. Yet until we met it, apparently, it occurred to none to do anything about it.

Within a few hours of the first blow, however, the thermometer had tumbled below freezing, falling more than forty degrees in an hour's time, and each of us was shivering and clutching at his ribs in an effort to find a little bodily warmth in the pressure of his arms. So far as partners and clerks, the captain and the ship's officers were concerned, the situation was not serious, for all of us had provided our own gear and were in some measure prepared to cope with the change. The men, however, were in a different fix. Few of the poor devils had so much as a pair of boots, and only a couple of them were able to find a pair of socks in which to climb the rigging.

I think it was scarcely extraordinary in such circumstances that MacDougal and McKay should propose to broach some of the warm clothing which had been stored in the hold, partly for trade and partly for just such a purpose as they now had in mind. To our astonishment Captain Thorn positively refused to permit the breaking out of a single box or bale. To propose it, he ranted, was an encroachment on his authority and in violation of the laws of the sea. Mr. Astor, he declared, had given no such power except to him during the time we were at sea, and he did not intend to violate his trust. In vain the partners argued that Mr. Astor himself would certainly approve. Captain Thorn was adamant. Let the men freeze. If they lacked the foresight to anticipate their needs, it was not his fault! The partners, he swore, would broach the cargo only over his dead body!

At the suggestion MacDougal flared.

"Aye? Well!" he raged, drawing his pistol and cocking it. "If yon's the way ye feel aboout it, we maun be takin' matters in our ain han's. I'm partner o' this venture an' proxy here for Mr. Astor himsel'. I say these supplies belong tae th' Coompany, not tae ye, sir, nor yet tae th' vessel. If sae be ye insust, then ower yer dead budy it shall be."

This took place on the quarterdeck, in sight and hearing of all. Within a twinkling, it seemed, the ship was split in two unequal camps. The voyageurs and most of the seamen took the part of MacDougal. Westlake, young Thorn, Mr. Mumford, Shea, who was now bos'n by virtue of Anderson's desertion at Owyhee, and perhaps three or four others—I suspect because mutiny was as unthinkable to them as murder or highway robbery—took the side of the captain. It was by far and away the most serious outbreak we had seen, and I, for one, was sure it must end in civil war and bloodshed. But as had happened on other occasions, the two Stuarts and Mr. Fox intervened.

So effectively did they reason, that, as usual, the crisis was averted for the moment. Indeed, it might have been counted a victory for Captain Thorn. The bales and boxes remained unopened, and the men were allowed to shiver and warm themselves as best they could. But many were forced to take to their hammocks; so many, in fact, that I think had it not been for our native recruits we might have had difficulty in handling the ship. One would expect that Captain Thorn would feel a certain degree of gratitude to Mr. Fox. Yet apparently it was not in the man's make-up. Though I could scarcely credit it, there were words between them when Captain Thorn actually accused the mate of pusillanimity in having endeavored to restore peace rather than militantly adopting his part in the controversy.

At best, I felt the truce was temporary, and the next few days were to me like living in a powder magazine. The partners had evidently made a compact to talk among themselves only in Gaelic and would address no word to Thorn. Indeed at his approach they would fall silent. While in like fashion the voyageurs and Canadians employed their French-Indian patois. Mr. Fox refused all communication with his commander save in response to orders.

It seemed to me a situation which any least spark might touch off, for Thorn was convinced that these conversations in French and Indian and Gaelic were directed against him and concerned some deep-eyed plot to seize the vessel. As a consequence it was almost more fortunate than otherwise that on the sixteenth we were overtaken by a sudden storm from the S.S.W. which shredded our sails and plucked at our rigging, opened some of the seams so that the ship leaked, if not badly, enough to cause her to labor. By the force of the blow, everything above decks—bulwarks, hogpens, chicken coops, supplies—were either smashed to splinters or swept overboard, and only the boats, secured in their lashings, remained, somewhat the worse for wear.

By this we lost a great part of our supplies and livestock, only managing to rescue a handful of hogs and chickens and a few bushels of provisions which we snatched and stowed, willy-nilly, below in the few moments when we saw it coming and before the fury of the storm struck us and we were forced to batten down our hatches and shiver below in the subterranean darkness, while a handful of men and officers fought the ship to safety through the blow. When at last it had spent itself and we could return on deck to survey the damage, we realized the extent of the catastrophe that had struck us, and I think there was no room for any thought in any mind but to reach our destination as quickly as we could.

In this, at least, the storm produced one good effect, for it drove us at a rate beyond computing, despite the laboring of the vessel, the icy rigging, the slippery decks, and the snow and sleet that alternated with the rain. On the morning of the twenty-second we were tumbled out on deck by the lookout's cry: "Land-ho! Breakers!"

Sure enough, it was there, three or four leagues distant, stretching away north and south, an undulating coast line, inhospitable at the water's edge, yet rolling and folding into high hills covered with the dark green of fir and pine behind the cliffs. Bluffs and rocky headlands tumbled abruptly from the higher hills into the sea, and here and there between we could discern bits of shingle; sometimes sandy strips, but more often narrow, stony beaches between ledgy outcroppings, upon which the tremendous seas crashed and spouted in an endless procession.

It was difficult to see much in detail, the skies were so lowering. Even some of the tops of these low hills were covered, and of course we could not see the towering snow-capped range of mountains that marched parallel behind them. Midway of the quadrant we could see very nearly broad on our beam, a flattening of the hills and gradual lowering of the land and a gap, four or five miles wide, with an immense field of breakers all across the mouth of it, not always visible for the fog and squalls that blew between us and the shore two and a half to three miles deep and a good four miles wide. The heaviest of the seas, great, thundering graybeards, piling up row upon row, mile after mile, seemed to cut through the center of the field, barring all access to the shore, and, indeed, the whole was such a sea of frothing foam that I wondered any ship would dare approach so near as we had, let alone attempt an entrance through them to the bay beyond.

The bulk of us, clerks and partners, voyageurs, mechanics, seamen, and mates, gathered on the deck at the lookout's hail, leaning upon the remnants of the rail, drinking in this first unpromising view of our land of promise, wrapped in blankets, capots, tarpaulins, whatever came handiest to shelter us against the raw, wet wind, the steady drizzle that fell.

"Here's one piece of luck at least!" Mr. Fox remarked.

David Stuart looked glumly at the shore.

"How so?" he demanded. His tone told his ready disappointment with what he saw.

"Yonder lies the Columbia," Fox replied, pointing.

"Ye mean yon's our river?" McKay asked.

"Aye," Fox grinned, "we've hit it square on the nose!"

"I see no river," Stuart said.

" 'Tis there nonetheless." Fox chuckled. "Mark the line of breakers yon? 'Tis where the river current meets the sea, aye, and a treacherous, evil bar it is! We'll have trouble crossing. The headland just to north'ard, yonder, is Cape Disappointment."

He pointed to a rocky promontory, barely visible in the mists, like a huge paw curved down from the north. He swung to southward to show us a long, low spit of sand below the opening; little more than a strip of beach grass, scrub, and sand dunes half-hidden in the sea wrack that blew across it.

"Yonder's Point Adams," he told us. "Between's the mouth of the Columbia."

"Mister Fox!"

We all turned, though there was no need for it.

"Aye, sir?" said Fox.

"I have taken exception to your freedom with the passengers before, mister," Thorn growled, drumming with his fingers upon the quarter rail. "I'll not speak of it again!"

The mate made no reply, but it was obvious he was irritated.

"Go forward and put the leadsman in the chains," Thorn ordered.

"Ye'll not try to take her through that!" Fox said, nodding toward the foaming river mouth, where the huge breakers, white-crested like the fangs of a rabid wolf, reared, held all but motionless by the thrusting force of the outrushing tide. At the mouth of the gap they seemed fully as high as our tops, and whipped by the stiff northwest wind, it seemed obvious that no ship could hope to live in them for an instant.

"God damn ye, do as I say!" Thorn thundered. "I'll navigate, mister! You follow orders!"

"Aye, aye, sir!" replied Fox dutifully, and turned away.

Behind him, upon the quarterdeck, the captain resumed his stomping up and down, shooting occasional glances ashore.

Yet it must have been evident to him that this was obviously not a thing to be rushed at. If the bar, or series of bars, were as bad as they were reputed, it would be folly to attempt to cross save on an incoming tide, and that with time allowed to be within the mouth of the river at the crest of the flood. It would require exact timing and a careful study of the tide's stages at the channel's outer edge; something to be accomplished only by comparative soundings. But we were only too well acquainted with the captain's impatience. Inwardly, we each of us braced ourselves for anything.

For all our apprehensions, however, he seemed to respect those ugly seas. Most of the morning we lay off and on, taking a series of soundings from the ship, between two and three leagues offshore, feeling for a channel from a point opposite the beetling crags of Cape Disappointment to about a league southward, opposite the wind-swept dunes of Point Adams.

As I leaned upon the rail and studied the fir-clad hills through the misty drizzle, it seemed to me incredible that this was, after all, the distance we had come, actually the back door to my own homeland; that this land I saw before me stretched unbroken, over forest and plain and prairie, to the other ocean. A man might walk dry-shod to Boston if he could keep his hair on!

Yet impatient as we were to be ashore, we were sensible that it might be some time before we could set foot to ground and sense the fresh odor of the firs in our nostrils. It would scarcely profit us to be cast lifeless upon that inhospitable shore. Accordingly, we were content to sit and look and wait until the seas might turn gentle enough to permit our passage.

But we reckoned still without our captain. I have never understood why he should have been so precipitate. We had scarcely finished our noonday meal and come once more above when he appeared on the quarterdeck, stamping and glaring about him like a thunderhead upon a mountain peak.

"Mister Fox!" he barked.

From his place at the forepeak, for he had not even been relieved to eat, the first mate responded.

"Aye, sir?"

"Take those four men." Thorn glanced down into the waist and singled out three of our Canadians, Basile and Ignace Lapensee and Jules Nadeau, and a French sailmaker, John Martin.

"Aye, sir?"

"Take the gig," the captain ordered, "and those four men to assist you and sound the channel!"

For an instant there was no sound but the whistle of the wind in the rigging and the creak of the ship as she labored, the distant thunder of the surf upon the bar. I doubt one of us could believe he had heard the man correctly. Fox himself at length ventured the question.

"Pardon me, Captain, I must have misheard—the wind makes such a clamor! Did ye say the gig?"

Thorn stared down at him coldly.

"You heard me, mister!" he replied harshly. "Take the gig and sound the channel! Have done with questions and get about your work, if you're man enough!"

"My God, sir!" Fox cried. "The gig!"

"You have my orders, Mister Fox!" retorted Thorn coldly.

"You damned murderer!" cried Fox.

The captain, who had been turning away, spun back.

"Mister Fox! If you are afraid of water, you should have remained at Boston!" he snarled.

Fox looked bitterly at us.

"My uncle," he said, "died on this bar. Now I am going to lay my bones alongside his!"

He glanced up defiantly at the captain.

"At least give me seamen," he demanded.

"There are no seamen to spare," Thorn replied curtly. "I've given you experienced watermen—so they say!"

He tossed the last in our direction with a sneer.

"Watermen, aye!" MacDougal growled. "Rivermen, canoemen, mon! They knaw nowt o'tides an' surrf!"

Thorn's hand slipped under his wide-skirted coat and came out with an immense pistol.

"I'll sail the ship, sirrah!" he thundered.

MacDougal merely shrugged and glanced at us.

"See to your orders, Mister Fox!" the captain snapped.

"Aye, sir," replied the first mate dully, and started away.

Roger Westlake, I noticed for the first time, stood near the back of our little group, and I never saw such horror and disbelief upon any man's face. He opened his mouth to speak as Fox drew abreast of him, but the first mate clamped his hand quickly upon his arm.

"Quiet, Mister Westlake!" he admonished.

In silence we watched the preparation for that perilous voyage. A breaker of water was put into the little craft and someone fetched a gallon of brandy and a small cask of biscuit and quietly stowed them on board. Oars and thole pins were carefully examined and some small repairs were made upon the strakes which had been damaged by the storm. After the battering it had been subjected to, the little craft was scarcely seaworthy.

"I haven't even a sail!" remarked Mr. Fox.

"Sails are not part of the equipment of the gig," Captain Thorn reminded him peremptorily.

With an oath David Stuart turned away and plunged into the main cabin. His nephew turned toward the captain.

"In God's name, sir," he cried, "reconsider this order. Surely there's no need for such a sweat! You can see for yourself how the seas are running! Wait till they're calmed."

But there was no reasoning with the man. At the words, he flew into a tantrum, jumping up and down upon the deck, stamping his feet, cursing, and making hideous grimaces, such as convinced me that he was mad as a March Hare.

"I God! I Jesus!" he cried. "There is a combination against me to frustrate every effort I make. I do believe ye all are traitors! Turncoats, every one! If ye can, ye will destroy the expedition, but I will not let ye! No, by God, not I! Be still, or by the living Christ I'll have the swivels turned into the waist and blow you all to hell as quick as a pack of savages!"

" 'Tis no good arguing, Mr. Stuart," said Fox openly. "The man's infatuated o' himself. We'll put the best face on it we can!"

He began then shaking hands with each one of us.

"We'll not meet again," he said; "not in this world!"

He spoke firmly and in a tone that was loud enough to carry to the captain, and if ever a man was challenged it was Thorn then. Yet he merely hung upon the rail and leered, sneering, never deigning to reply.

David Stuart reappeared with a pair of bedsheets.

"They are not sails," he said, "and they are not much. But you may find them of some service."

There were tears in the mate's eyes.

"I thank ye, Mr. Stuart," he said, "but 'twould only be a waste o' property to take them."

"Don't be a fool, man!" Stuart cried. "Here! If they will not serve for sails, perhaps they can be made to do as a sea anchor!"

The mate swallowed, thanked him, and ordered the boat lowered away. As it touched the water, he ordered the men over the side and they all took their places.

"Good-by!" he called again. "Good-by, gentlemen!"

He waved his hand.

"Get on with it!" Thorn bellowed. "What d'ye hope to gain by delay? Get on and find the channel!"

"I'll find the channel straight to hell, Captain Thorn," Fox retorted, "and we'll be waiting there to meet ye!"

The little cockleshell gig sheered off and stood out from the lee of the sheltering ship, and we held our breaths and watched. No human sound broke in upon the creak of the rigging and the hissing of the waves.

Before the boat had gone fifty feet, we could see her only occasionally as she was lifted, teetering perilously, to the crest of one tremendous comber after another, and as each wave passed, we would lose her again as she was flung down into the trough between. Before she was a hundred yards away, she appeared to become entirely unmanageable. Twice she broached broadside to the seas and only by a gnat's eyelash missed being rolled over and swamped. But miraculously she righted, only to spin like a top at the crest of the next wave and then plunge dizzily from sight like a toboggan that raced at the brow of a precipice. Within fifteen minutes she was little more than a spot on the face of the tumbling sea, with a few tiny, antlike creatures gesticulating wildly in her, and when we found her in the glass, we could see that she had run up her flag at the jackstaff, with ensign down, in unmistakable signal of distress.

Both Westlake and MacDougal turned upon the captain.

"I' th' name o' God, mon!" cried MacDougal. "What for a twa-legged ghoul air ye thot ye stond yon an' willna lift yer finger t' aid? Wull ye see them drooned li' rats beneath yer nose? Run alangside an' fetch them aboord! It could be done in ten minutes wi'oot danger tae th' shup!"

The captain only glowered at him.

"I will not remind ye again, Mister MacDougal," he growled, "that I command this ship!"

"Will ye quit hawkin' yer rank aboot and stir yersel' tae save th' lives o' dyin' men?" MacDougal retorted. "'Twould be na mair than th' wurrk o' an instant!"

"You don't know what you're talking about!" Thorn retorted. "I'd not take the ship in yonder breakers for all the gigs in hell! 'Tis too great a risk. They'll have to fend for themselves!"

"Aye!" growled McKay bitterly. "We see ye now for a coward as well as a fool, that ye dare not take yer vessel into seas ye never hesitated to send them among!"

"Aye!" Westlake echoed him unexpectedly. "'Tis a risk, but of your own making. If you lack the guts, give me the order then! I'll take the vessel in after them! Aye, and fetch her out again with them safe on board!"

"You are mutinous, sir!" thundered Thorn, purple with rage.

"But at least I am no murderer!" retorted the younger officer.

"I'll remind you that your conduct is unbecoming an officer of this vessel!" Thorn roared.

Westlake sneered bitterly.

"Of this vessel!" he agreed. "But I tell you your own is unbecoming a human being, Captain Thorn!"

"By the gods, I'll break ye at court-martial!"

Westlake laughed wildly.

"Men drown and you prate of courts-martial!" he taunted.

"Now, by God!" cried Thorn, and once again fetched up his pistol, leveling at Westlake. We saw his finger tighten on the trigger. But someone who was standing near by—in the excitement I could not see who—knocked up the gun, so that it exploded in the air. Only later I learned it was Alan Fraser.

Wildly the captain whirled away and snatched a second pistol from his belt, pointing it ominously at the lot of us.

"Mr. Mumford! Mr. Thorn!" he cried. "Seize that man and have him confined below in irons!"

For an instant no one moved, then Westlake turned abruptly.

"Never mind!" he said. "Are you coming, Mr. Mumford?" Without a backward glance, he disappeared down the companionway with Mumford at his heels.

I think one or another of us might have protested, but at that very instant someone cried out: "She's gone! The boat! She's gone!"

We whirled about as one again to scan the seas where last we had seen her. But there was not a rag or stick to be seen, only the wild, tumbling waters where she had been.

All afternoon we stood to and fro before the mouth of the river, just out of the reach of the line of breakers. An hour or so before dusk we took to firing signal guns in the forlorn hope that they might yet survive somewhere and give us a sign to prove it. But the only answer we had was the wild, angry shrieking of the gulls we frightened with our cannon, and as it began to fall dark, for the safety of the vessel and the rest of us left on board, it was necessary to haul away and stand out to sea again.

We were back at dawn, and it seemed to us that the wind had dropped and the breakers appeared less angry. Ashore, the clouds were higher, and, for the moment, at least, the rain had stopped. Behind the rolling fir-clad coastal hills we could see quite clearly, for the moment, a tremendous snow-capped mountain. There was no sign of the gig or the people in her.

But if the captain's conscience troubled him, he gave no sign of it. We ran down the long line of breakers and came about and turned north again, coasting to within a league or two of Cape Disappointment, where we anchored in fourteen fathoms. But, so far as we could see, the waves, where the surf passed over the riffled sands and met head-on the foaming current of the river, seemed as impassable as ever. By noon, however, the weather appeared to have cleared still more, although the wind was still fresh, and the seas to have abated somewhat, and the captain's impatience took hold of him once more. He summoned Mr. Mumford and ordered him off in the longboat to search for a channel.

The possibility of some such second attempt had already been considered among us, and we had agreed that, rather than see our men sent off to sacrifice, we would insist that a number of us be sent with it. Accordingly, hoping such a gesture might have a calming and salutary effect upon the captain, Mr. McKay stepped forward. To our surprise and, for himself, at least, dismay—the captain assented readily, and Mr. McKay, Mr. Stuart, the elder, Mr. Ross, and myself, were assigned places in the boat.

If the seas appeared appreciably lower than they had been on the day before from the deck of the *Tonquin,* I shudder to think how they must have looked from the gig. For from the longboat, which was considerably larger, they seemed enormous as mountains! We struggled through the first chain of breakers at the northern side, all but turning turtle in the process, and came into slightly clearer water, yet a great distance from the channel. From there we stood in toward the cape, and, without being aware of it, ventured perhaps closer than we ought to have done, for before we knew it we were gripped in a vortex of whirling waters that sucked us toward the river's maw, where the thrusting spate must mangle us and spew the remnants forth again to be swallowed up forever by the ocean deeps.

Mr. Mumford saw it first. Frantically he threw over his helm and shouted at us.

"Pull! Pull, lads! Put your backs in it!"

At the desperate note in his voice we needed no spur, but realized, whether we saw it or not, that dreadful danger threatened. In turning, the boat broached broadside to the surf, and for a few long moments it seemed to us she was unmanageable. For all our combined efforts, we were near ten minutes struggling in this dangerous position before we could break clear and the boat began to answer her oars and helm.

Yet we were still full two miles from the shore and had found no sign of a channel. I daresay, had it not been for Mr. Mumford's quick action, we would have been fairly trapped, our boat swamped, and ourselves sent to Davy Jones's locker to join our bones with those of the five who had drowned the day before. As it was, we moved along and three times attempted to approach the channel. Three times we were driven back. Yet when we returned exhausted to the *Tonquin,* it was only to meet black looks from the captain and the implication that had we made a respectable effort we might have done better!

We lay that night at our anchorage, and early the next morning, before the rest of us were on deck, the captain ordered Mr. Mumford out again, this time sending with him a crew of good seamen, sound hands all, and far more experienced in such matters than any we had yet put overside. Though they tried their best, still they could not approach, and three times they, too, fell foul of the currents. At noon they returned, tired and wet and crestfallen, to the same spite and vilification. Only once, Mumford reported, were they able to break through and that to find no more than two and a half fathoms. The captain listened with a stony face, and when Mr. Mumford was finished speaking, he offered his only comment.

"I see ye've not the stomach for the task, Mister Mumford! What have I done that God should punish me by sending me to sea with such a parcel of nincompoops and cowards?"

"Why don't ye try it yourself, Captain?" Mumford demanded stiffly, and turned about on his heel and stalked forward to the fo'c'sle where he ate with the men. Nor could all the captain's raging fetch him forth again until we had weighed anchor. He would rather serve as an ordinary seaman before the mast, he declared, than as an officer under such a shitepoke!

So matters stood until near three in the afternoon and the tide turned, standing out at the ebb for more than an hour before any further move was made. What was our surprise, then, when Thorn came on deck roaring that he would not lie another night at sea with such a pack of lubbers, and summoning Mr. Aiken—the rigger and caulker, forsooth!—ordered him to have over the pinnace, which was the largest of our small boats, and take the armorer, Stephen Weeks, and John Coles, the only remaining sailmaker, and two of the Kanakas, and sound somewhat to the northward of Mr. Mumford's last efforts. There, if they found three and a half fathoms, they were to signal and we would get under way at once.

I will say for Mr. Aiken that he was a thorough sailor, if anything, better versed at handling a small boat than Mr. Fox had been. Immediately the pinnace cleared the ship's side, she ran up the sail with which this craft, at least, was equipped. For nearly an hour, or perhaps an hour and a half, we watched as she fought her way up into and through the breakers to within half a mile of the river mouth, and there we saw that she hoisted the agreed-upon signal. Accordingly we promptly weighed anchor and stood in, feeling our way carefully along as we nosed through the channel. Every heart was tense, and whether it was by the captain's orders or not, I saw that someone had seen fit to release Mr. Westlake; that he had come on deck and was standing in the shadow of the mainmast, watching.

The small boat fetched about and came down to meet us, so that by the time we came up with her she was in comparatively calm water, perhaps half a mile outside the core of the breakers, in some eight fathoms, while the ship's rate, going in against the tide, could not have been greater than three knots. As we converged, it almost seemed that we must run her down, and accordingly Aiken sheered off a point or two to our starboard, while the *Tonquin* held steady as she went. The pinnace, sails furled now, pulled just away from our track and then came about in smooth water, and the men lay on their oars waiting to be picked up.

To our amazement the ship glided straight on past, within a dozen yards of them, in utter silence. I think on deck, every man, stricken dumb, was waiting for the order from the captain that would send the throwing line snaking out across the water. It could easily have been done by any of our landlubbers. Westlake, who alone among us could have appreciated what must be happening, for Mr. Mumford was still below, evidently assumed the order had been given, for whatever I might have thought of him, I knew that inhumanity was not one of his faults.

Only when the gap between us began to widen was it evident that the captain had no more intention of picking her up then he had of rescuing the gig two days before. One by one our faces turned toward him in consternation, for it was obvious the little craft could not survive the breakers that lay before us.

"The boat!" someone cried.

"The boat! The boat! Quick!" Others took up the protest.

The gap widened.

The captain did not even turn his head to look back.

"I can give her no assistance," he growled.

Westlake stood clear of the mast.

"Back your mains'l," he cried, "and throw them a rope!"

The captain glared at him.

"Who fetched you on deck?" he demanded. "I will not endanger the ship for a whim of yours!"

In all this time not so much as a hail had been offered to the boat. Indeed, it is almost beyond human capabilities to describe the expressions of amazement and horror with which the five men in the little craft watched us sweep past.

All the while Captain Thorn stood braced upon his quarterdeck, his feet wide and his eyes fixed steadfastly ahead. Never once did he look back, though the rest of us watched and hoped, until the curl of the waves blotted her from our sight and the first plunge of the ship turned our attention to our own plight.

Mr. Mumford came on deck and needed only a glance to see what had happened. I never saw a man with brow so black, and I had a feeling that he and Westlake might have seized the command and put about at that moment and had the support of all. But all at once it was too late. The sun, already low when we nosed in, chose that instant to dip behind the bank of clouds upon the western horizon, painting their rim and the skies above our heads blood-red, while at the same moment the ship bucked and dipped her bows, taking her first plunge in the terrific breakers.

She buried her nose to the hawse pipes, plunging even her figurehead under, and at the same time she yawed to the great surf lashing up astern of her, swinging to larboard, rolled sickeningly, then lifted her bows in the air, straight up, and danced along on her stern like a skittish mare. Those of us who had been standing by the rail could think no more for an instant of the pinnace behind but must clutch at anything handy to keep from being washed overboard.

Even so, some went down in a tangle of arms and legs in the scuppers, then fought and clawed their way to their feet. I did not hear the order that sent Mr. Mumford to the foremasthead to con the channel ahead, but I became abruptly aware that the seaman in the chains who swung our lead must have lashed himself securely to stay at his post. Between the intervals of wiping the brine from my eyes and shaking my hair away from my face I could hear his steady, droning voice:

"By the deep three—and a half three!"

"Shoals ahead!" sang out Mumford from aloft. " 'Ware shoals!

"And a half two!" moaned the leadmen. "Shoaling! Hold hard!"

We needed no orders to claw our way into the rigging, as high as we dared, and there hang by main strength, securing ourselves if we could with coats or belts, no simple task with the masts whipping like catapults.

Yet even as we raced upward it seemed to me she struck with a grinding crunch upon the sand of the first bar, shuddered, and lay over, so that for an instant I thought that she must have been dashed all to little bits below, and I wondered if she could ever right herself. Yet apparently she was not done. For with a heave and a groan that was almost human she slid on over the bar and slowly came back upright.

'Tis curious how flashes of memory sometimes stand out, as clear as pictures painted on a canvas, of a man's moments of terror. Much of a sequence of events may be forgot or telescoped into a single horrifying experience. But in almost every case one or two or three incidents stand out sharp and vivid in the mind's eye, almost as if at that instant time stood still to etch it clearly on the consciousness.

'Twas so with me. As I clung in the mizzen shrouds, high above the quarterdeck, something fetched my head around so that for a moment I stared aft over the tumbled water, and for that instant I had a brief glimpse of the pinnace, standing nearly end to end on the crest of a tremendous comber, her sail in tatters, half over on her side, obviously filled with water that cascaded from her thwarts. I could see but three figures clinging. And then the mast whipped and I lost sight of her. Beneath me the ship shuddered on the second bar and lay far over once more. It seemed to me every timber in her groaned. But as the wind astern thrust and the seas lifted her across in the bar, she righted once again. On deck I could see Roger Westlake with the two seamen, clinging to the great wheel, fighting it, while the seas washed round their hips, straining, struggling to keep her stern to the seas and at the same time guide her through the winding channel.

Captain Thorn, I observed, like all the rest of us, save those three and the poor, half-drowned devil in the chains, was clinging to the ratlines, a good six feet above my head upon the opposite side of the mast. From far forward we heard the leadsman's chant.

"By the mark, three!"

For an instant the ship righted again. I started down. But as I did so, the water shoaled abruptly from eight to two and a half fathoms, and again she struck a spine-cracking blow upon the bar that ran, like a vast, solid, underwater wave, from the tip of Point Adams out and across the river mouth. It seemed to me that it was harder yet than any she had touched, and I expected her to split. When she did not, it was as if a miracle had happened, and I clung where I was, praying, if ever I had, that we might break through, but at the same time not very hopeful of it.

Now darkness added to our dangers, while to make matters worse, with the falling of the sun, the wind dropped, and, the tide still ebbing, it seemed we must be racked to pieces among the rocks close under the cape. Desperately the crew struggled forward under Mr. Westlake's direction and let go the anchors. But to our dismay the heavy hooks dragged and we could find no safe holding. Inevitably we drove, almost inexorably, toward the booming, spouting rocks.

But whether it was the mingling of our prayers or whether someone among us sent up an extra mighty plea to heaven, Providence for once appeared to favor us, for we were not a quarter of a mile from complete destruction when the tide turned, and the flood setting in, we rode along with it, sounding as we went. Thrice more we shuddered sickeningly on sand bars. Yet each time we squeaked over with a squeal of protest that was enough to set my teeth on edge. In the end we stumbled through and came to quieter water, dropping our anchor in the shelter of Baker's Bay, six hours from the time we had weighed anchor outside and stood up into the breakers. There, in utter exhaustion, we tumbled at last between our wet blankets in our soggy hammocks.

IV. The Tonquin

I. COLUMBIA

THE twenty-fifth of March came in gray and blustery and stormy, and
we who remained aboard the *Tonquin* were reminded of our good
fortune by the cloud rack that scudded in shreds through the tall
pines that crowned the hills ashore. We were safe, at least for the
moment, inside the protecting arm of Cape Disappointment. Outside,
the wind had risen through the night until it was blowing a small
hurricane, and the Pacific, whipped to an angry lather, heaped its
wrath upon the series of bars across which we had driven the previous
evening, until the entire river mouth became literally a seething,
foaming hell.

All hands were spent. We were wrapped in a cloud of deepest
gloom, but natural in the circumstances, and oppressed by the loss of
so many of our comrades. To be sure, most of us had been comparative
strangers when we left New York, but men cannot live together
cramped in the confines of a small ship for seven months and more
without developing some feeling for one another. We, as individuals,
comprised the entire population of one another's little world, the
only living objects now with which, by habit, any one of us felt any
degree of familiarity. In a world so circumscribed no individual can
be removed, however meanly he may be regarded, without each one
of the others being conscious of it, The ruthless, reckless, wasteful
criminal way in which these men had been sent to sacrifice their
lives could not but increase our horror at their loss. And the fact
that Mr. Fox and Coles and Weeks had been almost universally
loved and respected, while Nadeau and the brothers Lapensee had
been bright and gay and popular, did nothing to lessen our depression.

We came from our damp blankets, cold and shivering and still wet, to contemplate the day's duties scarcely with enthusiasm. But life must yet go on, and the demands of men's bodies cannot be denied, for all that a deaf ear may be turned sometimes to their souls. With some effort the galley fires were lighted once more and steaming tea and pork and porridge prepared. An extra dram was passed out all around, and warmed by food and drink, we were, at length, able to collect our wits sufficiently to consider what our next move must be.

To some extent, at least, the problem brought its own solution. Even Captain Thorn could not deny the first things that must be done. Miraculously the ship itself appeared to have suffered no major damage in its buffeting passage of the bars. As nearly as we could make out, the keel had not been sprung, nor had any other vital part been injured. A seam or two had been started and we were taking some water, so that it was necessary to man the pumps at intervals to keep the cargo dry. But this was nothing that could not be repaired from within. The masts were racked in their steps and the footling and partners weakened from their whipping. These should be reseated and reinforced, while the main yard, which had been sprung, had to be set down, the trestletrees upon the foremast repaired, and all the standing rigging, which had worked slack, taken up. At the same time, so long as there remained any hope at all, the neighboring coasts must be scoured for traces of our comrades.

Mr. Westlake and Mr. Mumford, who, by default of others, had been reinstated in their duties—if not in the captain's good graces— were assigned the task of turning out the carpenter's crew and of overseeing repairs aloft and alow. At the same time it was decided the holds must be checked and cargo inspected, damage noted, and goods readied for landing. This duty fell to me, not because I sought it, but rather because I was the one most thoroughly familiar with both stowage and the articles of lading. Captain Thorn himself, whose conscience I think secretly troubled him, announced that he would accompany some of our gentlemen ashore to the northward, where they would scour Cape Disappointment and as much of the coast as they could reach.

With so much determined upon, we started: Mr. Mumford and the bos'n, Shea, forward to sound the bilges; Mr. Westlake aloft with the carpenter; I with Mr. Lewis, the captain's clerk, a sandy-haired, freckle-faced, somewhat morose man of my own age, for the cuddy that served as ship's office for the manifests. Captain Thorn himself turned out the boat's crew and prepared to lower away. But we were scarce about these chores—indeed Lewis and I had not left the deck—when Westlake hailed from the rigging:

"Ahoy, the deck! Here comes company!"

I could almost feel Captain Thorn bristle.

"Let me hear your report in proper fashion," he snarled.

"Canoes," retorted Westlake, no whit abashed, "putting about the point to east'ard."

"How many?" called Thorn.

"Ten or a dozen."

"Are they armed?"

"Can't say," was the reply. "They don't appear to be."

"Very good!" snapped Thorn.

He looked where Westlake pointed, and the rest of us followed his glance and saw the first of the strange craft just appearing about the tip of a wooded, rock-studded point. They were long, as long as a Montreal canoe, perhaps even longer. Apparently they were dugouts of some sort, hollowed from a single trunk of a great tree, probably the huge firs or great white cedars that forested the hills above us. Their bows and gunnels were flaring to turn away the seas and fling them evenly to either side. By way of ornament each carried a curious sort of figurehead, jutting at an acute angle, in some cases as much as five or six feet; a grotesque carving meant to represent some bird or animal of fact or Indian fancy; an eagle, a great beaked bird or flat-faced beast or grinning windigo, or whatever its equivalent among these people might be. They each were manned by a double row of expert paddlers.

We watched their approach with some curiosity and, indeed, with a degree of apprehension, for as these folk received us, so, we felt, might we expect friendship or hostility. Captain Thorn, it seemed to me, watched them with an air of distaste.

"Scurvy-looking crew," he growled.

MacDougal said nothing.

As the canoes drew near, exclamations of surprise and ribald wonder rose along the rail where the seamen and voyagers crowded.

"Be Jasus!" cried Shea. "The half of 'em is women!"

"A good sign," I heard Wallace growl. "It means they come in peace."

"I've been a long time in the trade," Mr. Stuart remarked, "but these are the strangest Indians I ever clapped eyes upon!"

One of the seamen laughed.

"They look more like Chinee to me," he scoffed. "Look at the hats! I've seen the like at Canton, only flatter."

" 'Tis the first time," said someone, "that ever I saw a grass roof with legs on it!"

"Take a look at the shape o' their heads, man!" another replied. "I'll warrant if ye'd a noggin like that on ye, ye'd carry a roof to hide it under yer ownself! Look yonder in the first canoe at the lad with his hat slung at his back!"

I, for one, could scarcely blame the men for their amusement, for more curious people I admit I never clapped eyes upon. Indians they were, to be sure: Chinooks, I learned later. But Indians of a far different sort from any I had ever known before. They tended to be short, stocky, thickset, with barrel bodies and great chests, long from hip to shoulder and short from thigh to foot, with very crooked legs, twisted and gnarled, thick ankles, and great splay feet. But where the northeastern canoe-Indian's legs were crooked and gnarled and sturdy, like the warped trunk of an ancient oak or rock maple, these folks' limbs had the spindling twistedness of an old, red-barked madroña, so that when they grew old and portly, as they were inclined to do, one wondered that such rickety shanks could support their weight.

These people were lighter than the Indians I had known, more of a tawny, yellowish cast. Their faces were flatter, their cheekbones wider, and their eyes almond-shaped, almost slanted, so that they had a sort of oriental look, not nearly so pronounced among those I had hitherto encountered. The hats which caused so much comment were wide, conical contrivances, so broad as to cover the wearer's neck and shoulders, and were obviously designed as protection against the chill, misty rain that fell so much of the time.

Since the rain, for the moment, had all but ceased, some of the Indians had pushed their hats back so that they hung against their backs, with results that took us utterly by surprise. We could scarcely believe our eyes. Yet it was true that those heads we could see were flattened from a point just above the brows, backward, at an acute angle, to a spot just above the ears. Similarly the back of the head was inclined forward, though less noticeably, so that the two planes met in a ridge that ran across the top of the skull from ear to ear, giving them a most curious and at the same time ludicrous appearance. Only when we grew more closely acquainted with them did we discover that this was a form of mutilation achieved in babyhood by pressing the skull for a year or more in a contrivance of boards. In the eyes of the Chinooks, and indeed of all the coast Indians from the Columbia at least as far north as Nootka, it was a mark of aristocracy and distinction.

Their hair, we could see even from the deck of the *Tonquin,* was in many cases not the straight black of eastern tribes, but brown, shading even in some toward chestnut. And later, when we were able to approach them more closely ashore, I observed that in a great number their eyes were hazel or even of a greenish cast. And, as one of our men had remarked, nearly half of those who came out where women, taking their place at the paddles with the men. Indeed, so far as I could see all but one of the steersmen were of that sex.

With one single exception, apart from the great conical hats, both men and women wore a sort of short crude jacket made of common skins—the wood rat's, I learned later—sewn neatly together and curiously painted. These covered them from shoulder to hip, while the women wore only a sort of skirt contrived of the inner fibers of cedar bark suspended from a belt about their waist as far as the knees. For the space of perhaps three or four inches about the belly, this was woven into a single piece, but below that it hung loose in the breeze like thrums of rope yarn, affording some privacy when the wearer stood still or the wind was quiet but scarcely serving to screen nature under ordinary circumstances; not that this was a matter of concern to them, for they were more remarkable for their complete absence of morals than for any value they placed upon chastity or virtue. It was an exceptionally convenient garment in certain circumstances, and, indeed, when the weather permitted it, both men and women preferred to go stark naked about their daily chores.

The exception to the rule I have described was a stout savage who occupied what obviously was a place of honor in the first canoe; a lowering, glowering, evil-visaged, crafty-seeming individual, perhaps fifty or so years old, who studied us speculatively out of a single eye, the other having been eaten away by some disease or other or perhaps gouged out in some fight. This Indian was wrapped in a fur cloak extending from shoulder to ankle, as fine in texture, as nearly as I could see, as the best beaver. Later I learned that it was made of the much-prized sea otter, but it was new to me at that time. In his case, and I found it frequently so, it was worn as a badge of office, denoting him the chief of his village. His hair had been thoroughly buttered with fish oil, to make it greasy and gleaming, and sprinkled freely with down, so that one thought immediately of tar and feathers at sight of him.

But his expression of haughty dignity warned us to choke back our laughter. As they drew near, the canoe in which he sat hove to within speaking distance of us, while the others ceased paddling and drifted left and right. The one-eyed chieftain rose and faced us and began a long speech in a series of guttural grunts and half-swallowed clucks accompanied by gestures, pointing to himself, to his canoes, to us, and to the river, finally reaching down to a bundle at his feet and holding up a beaver pelt of extraordinary quality.

Undoubtedly it was a speech of welcome and an indication that they were prepared to trade. Thorn looked expectantly at the partners, who in their turn eyed one another. Down the rail I heard Shea chuckle.

"What was that ye were sayin'? Sure I didn't catch a word av it!"

For my part I could scarcely repress a smile.

"Try him in Ojibway, Davie," said MacDougal.

Stuart spoke to the big savage in that tongue. The latter looked blank and waited still. McKay tried him in Knisteneaux and Assiniboin and at length in Athapascan, but he only shook his head at each. English and French both failed as well, whereupon the partners endeavored to make themselves clear in sign language, such as the northern Indians used, and with this he appeared a bit familiar, so that at last they were able to convey a little of their meaning to him. They pointed to one another and repeated their names, and for the first time the old savage broke into a smile and smote himself on the chest.

"Con-Comly!" he announced. "Con-Comly. Tye-yea!"

"Connolly, is it?" I heard Shea hoot. "Sure an' be Jasus ye meet these Irishmen everywhere!"

There is no need to detail all the rest of that visit. It was trade, to be sure, that they sought. On our side, by signs and grunts we let it be understood that we were not yet ready; that we had to repair our vessel after the buffeting of the storm and fetch up our trade goods in preparation to receive them. Though they seemed disappointed, yet they seemed also to understand, and we tried to tell them that we hoped to set up a permanent establishment among them. Whether they grasped this at this time or whether they came to realize our purpose later on, I could not say. At length they went away, giving us to understand that they would be back the next day.

"*Winnipiè nica chicko!*" they called. If they knew anything about our comrades, we could not learn it.

In view of this, my own duties for the day were somewhat altered, and I was ordered to prepare access to such trade goods as I could;

orders, incidentally, that Captain Thorn found distasteful, for it
was his opinion that we should first locate the site of our proposed
establishment and begin construction of it. In principal, none disagreed
with him, though for somewhat different reasons. So far as he was
concerned he was impatient to be off about his own business. He
longed to be rid of his contumaceous passengers; to unload such of
the cargo as was necessary, and then turn to the northward trading
voyage to which Mr. Astor's instructions assigned him. There he would
have none to dispute his authority. We, on the other hand, would
certainly have found it more convenient to build our post first and
then in orderly fashion proceed to trade. But, unfortunately, the
Indians themselves left us no choice. To refuse to trade with them from
the outset might belittle us in their eyes. We would be off to a bad
start. As a result we could not choose, and the savages, quite unwitting,
drove home another wedge between us and the captain.

It was by now moving on toward midmorning and clearly time to
turn our attention to our various duties. I became quickly absorbed
in my work and was scarcely aware of the passage of time, so that I
was in the hold, deep amid the cargo, when some time, long before
noon, a startled hail from the deck above fetched me tumbling out to
see what the excitement might be. To my surprise and delight it proved
to be the captain and some of the party returning with the shivering,
bedraggled, stark-naked form of Stephen Weeks. They had found him
dazed and half-frozen, wandering ashore on the back side of the cape,
and they fetched him on board, where he was immediately bundled in
blankets and carried off to the galley, which was the warmest spot in
the ship. There he was plied with scalding tea, laced with generous
quantities of rum, and questioned until even I felt like crying out "Have
done! Have done!"

At the outset he appeared to be in a state of shock and mildly
hysterical, for he could not control his weeping, and he looked with
special accusation at Westlake and Mumford.

"You did it purposely!" he cried in great agitation. " 'Twould not
have cost ye ten minutes to stop and pick us up, but ye left us there
to die as if we were no more than savages and never your own shipmates!"

Despite all assurances to the contrary, he persisted and demanded
why some one of us had not tossed them a rope at least, a demand, to
be sure, there was none could answer.

At length, however, the rum and the tea calmed him, and we were
able to draw his story from him. On board the pinnace, he told us,

they had not for an instant doubted that we would pick them up as we bore down toward them. Consequently not one of them had thought to hail us until it was too late and we had swept majestically by, quite calmly leaning upon the rail and staring down at them as if they were no more than some strange new sea bird.

So as soon as it was evident to them that we had no intention of stopping, they bent their backs to their oars and hoisted their sail and pulled after us with all their might and main, making every effort to overtake us, calling out to us at the same time to take them on board in God's name. Yet we distanced them, and within the space of a few moments they found themselves caught in the raging maelstrom of the breakers.

To be brutally brief the little cockleshell craft was swamped and overset and all hands were thrown violently into the sea, where each was forced to struggle to save himself. Coles and Aiken, Weeks told us, he did not see again, but the rest managed to regain and right the craft. Toward morning the two Kanakas, losing hope, lay down in the bottom of the boat to die. Weeks fought to keep out of the tremendous waves, but when the tide turned, he, being near the point of exhaustion, they began to be drawn helplessly toward the river mouth. Deeming death preferable to the continuance of such an unequal struggle, he made up his mind desperately to brave the surf that thundered on the beach. Apparently the gods favored the bold course, for at length both boat and survivors were flung high upon the shore.

Weak, half-drowned, faint from hunger and exhaustion and the cold, Weeks staggered from the boat and lay some time upon the sand. But presently recovering a little, he remembered his companions and returned to find one of them dead and the other but barely alive. With some effort he half-dragged, half-carried the living man up on the beach and into the shelter of some bushes. After that he pulled the dead man above the tide mark and partially covered him with sand and driftwood. Then, seeking help, he found and followed a beaten path that fetched him over the shoulder of the cape and into the place, on the shore of Baker's Bay, where our people had found him.

This was our introduction to this new land. Weeks was put to bed in warmed blankets, where he soon fell into a deep sleep that lasted well nigh twenty-four hours, while a party went to seek out his companions. The living islander, however, was not found until the following day. He, too, was fetched immediately on board and put to bed, where, under careful nursing, he eventually recovered.

There were other activities, of course. After nearly eight months of idleness there was scarcely a man of us who could find enough to do, and for once the captain had little need to drive us. We were as anxious to be ashore as he was to be rid of us, and the bulk of our energies was bent to this end. Some, under pretext of clearing the gangways, took time to erect crude pens on the bay shore, in which they placed such of the livestock as we had been able to rescue from the storm, and thereafter took turns at guarding them. As for the partners, they searched constantly for a likely place for the new post.

It was on this quest that the captain, with David Stuart and McKay, went off for a look at the north shore. In the meantime it fell to Mac-Dougal and me to see to the trade with the Indians, who came down as they had promised, fetching with them a quantity of furs, though nothing as extraordinary as Concomly had shown us. I found them as canny traders as any I had ever dealt with and possessed of an excellent notion of the value of their pelts, as well as of the worth of what we had to offer. They did not seem unduly interested in alcoholic liquors, though in lewdness and laxity of morals they easily surpassed any I had ever before encountered. Strangely enough, once one became accustomed to the curious shape of their heads, their women were not unhandsome, so that our men could scarcely be kept within bounds. So far as I was concerned, I may say, without smugness, I was not tempted.

On the first of the month Mr. Ross and his people came in from the south, where they had sought in vain some trace of the gig's people, and on the same day the captain with Mr. McKay and Mr. Stuart returned, all looking like thunderclouds, by which I gathered it had been neither a pleasant nor a successful journey. Although I had no report in so many words—since as a clerk I was forbidden the great cabin, something I believe Mr. Astor had not foreseen when he assigned me my peculiar mission—I gathered it had been a quarrelsome expedition. Mr. McKay hinted that the captain was more than merely disgruntled that their survey of that shore had produced no results. He felt their time worse than wasted. It was his feeling that the partners were more interested in sporting excursions and puffing themselves up in the Indians' eyes with endless powwows, sitting about and smoking from the same pipe and sucking the same spittle. The captain found the savages disgusting and their habits worse. Nor was he impressed with the argument that if we meant to dwell among them, we must make friends with them and respect their ways. The partners, so Thorn maintained, were dilatory and neglectful of their duties. A dozen sites, he maintained, would have been suitable, yet for silly and stupid reasons both Stuart and McKay persisted in continuing the search, and he did not propose to stand for it.

When I asked McKay the truth of that, he admitted that Thorn had suggested as many as a dozen spots a day, but these he had picked by seaman's eye and without regard either to convenience or safety or accessibility. One had been a good fifty feet above the river, up an almost sheer bluff. Another had been dominated by surrounding hills, so that raiding bands might easily shoot us in our beds and would certainly make the inner compound uninhabitable. We might hope to live in peace with our red neighbors, but we would be fools if we were so naïve as to neglect the most elementary precautions. Yet another site had no water, while a fourth had too much, standing on low-lying, swampy ground that would unquestionably be inundated in the annual freshets.

So it had gone. Yet at each refusal the captain, instead of seeing reason upon their side, had argued quarrelsomely or had fallen into a fit of the sulks. He now threatened to set everything ashore here in Baker's Bay and be off about his own business, leaving us to shift for ourselves since we did not appear to be able to make up our minds. It was this that infuriated MacDougal.

"Be domned t' ye for a stubborn, batter-brained fool, mon!" he flared. "I've a better regard for th' lives o' me mun, aye, an' for yon sovages, as wull, than ye hae for yer ain! I'd lik' tae remind ye thot 'tis tae see th' coomp'ny well established in a soond an' secure poseetion i' this place that we are a' here."

"I pointed out a dozen sites to Mr. Stuart and Mr. McKay," the captain protested.

"I have told ye, Captain, why none of them would do," Stuart interrupted.

"Aye!" growled Thorn. "And a sillier set o' reasons I never heard. I have told ye gentlemen what I intend. Tomorrow I shall go ashore here, for I see no likelier spot. I shall select a site and order sheds built. As soon as this is done, I shall set ye ashore with the things ye'll need until I return. Then I'll leave ye to your own bickering and cockle-deedee, and joy may ye have of it!"

"Now haud on!" roared MacDougal. "Mr. Thorn, we are i' th' reever. I am i' commond th' noo."

"No one commands aboard this vessel but———"

"Gentlemen! Gentlemen!" cut in Mr. Stuart. "We get nowhere! Captain Thorn, I am sure that none of us will object to your going ashore and looking for a site for your sheds, but I think it would be wise to survey the south side before we come to any final decision. At this juncture it is important that the right place be chosen and surely a day or two will not matter!"

Captain Thorn glowered.

"A day or two," he agreed grimly. "But no more. I cannot waste the entire summer!"

Stuart looked at MacDougal.

"If you'll go with me tomorrow, Mac," he proposed, "we can look at the southern shore and be back by the seventh."

"The seventh!" Captain Thorn literally yelped.

MacDougal nodded, grinning without humor.

"Thot wull suit me if Captain Thorn can wait sae lang!"

The captain controlled himself with an effort.

"I will wait," he said, "until the seventh. But, mind! If ye're not back by then, I will set about putting things on shore and sail as soon as I may."

"An' guid riddance I'll ca' 't!" MacDougal growled.

So it was left, and on the next morning the two partners set out. During their absence the trading operations begun by MacDougal and myself were carried on by McKay, to Thorn's vast disgust. On the sixth the captain himself went on shore, for a look around, he said, but I rather gathered it was to select a spot for the sheds as he had threatened. The seventh came wet and rainy and blustery, and the Indians did not appear, for the weather was too bad for anyone who did not have to be out in it to be abroad.

Mr. McKay and I were at first as well pleased that this was so, for our partners did not appear, and for all the captain fussed and fumed he could no nothing. Even in Baker's Bay it was too rough to risk putting out a boat, and the rain came down in such sheets that it was out of the question to set men to work on shore. But by evening McKay and I at least were alarmed, while the captain, with his usual unreason, was beside himself with rage, as if he believed the others had deliberately stayed away to anger him. It made no difference that no boat could come off in such weather. He declared loudly and for all to hear that if we did not hear from them by morning he meant to start work.

We spent an uneasy night, much of it on the lookout for our comrades, who, we felt sure, would try to come off if they could. But there was no sign of them, and in the morning I think even the captain was somewhat alarmed. Despite the heavy fog that held the river in irons, two Indians came down from above and by means of signs reported to us that the longboat had been overturned the evening before, and though we could not determine whether it was the equipment or the passengers or the boat itself, they made it clear that something had been totally lost.

This was scarcely reassuring. The Indians either could not or would not reveal more, and so we had nothing to do but wait for further developments. The ninth fortunately dawned clear, with the wind shifted about to the southwest and considerably abated, and we were putting off a boat to go up to the Chinook village and make inquiries when two large canoes appeared about the point and bore directly for us.

They came from the village we had been preparing to visit, it proved, and carried, in addition to the old chief, Concomly, and his crew, all ten members of MacDougal's party. They had, it appeared, after examining the south coast, stood across to pay a visit, and on the evening of the seventh, in accord with their promise, they had embarked to return to the ship, despite the fact that the weather was such that even Concomly had urged them against it. They had pledged their word, and they were determined to risk it.

Accordingly they had set out but had got scarcely a mile from shore when a huge wave broke over the boat and capsized it. Fortunately, Concomly, well aware of the danger, had despatched two canoes to follow them and had sent out four more the instant he saw their predicament. But for this they must all have been drowned, for MacDougal could not swim a stroke and the others could never have covered the distance to shore. Thus, by the Indians' foresight, they had been rescued and taken to the village, where Concomly had made them welcome, large fires had been built, and their clothing dried. The boat had been recovered, but everything in it—tools, guns, supplies, compasses, axes, powder, and shot—all had been totally lost, and I truly believe that this irritated the captain far more than the rescue pleased him.

But when morning came, we found ourselves no better off than before. Stuart and MacDougal reported that they had not found the ideal spot for which they had sought and that they hoped that they might be able to persuade Thorn to wait while they made one more longer expedition up the river. But the captain would have none of this. He even implied that they had not crossed to the south shore but had gone directly to the Chinook village, probably throwing their guns and supplies overboard on the way, or, perhaps, even more likely, giving them to the savages so that they might have excuse for staying and carousing with their dusky doxies.

II. NOOTKA

SO INSULTED were the partners by the captain's attitude that they determined, at all costs, to leave the vessel. Though the site was not ideal for our purposes, Point George, fifteen miles across the Columbia, at the mouth of Young's River, was the best spot they had so far found. Accordingly they pitched upon it and the very next day began the movement to it by despatching the longboat with sixteen men to establish camp there. The rest of us followed a day or two later, and on the twelfth of April, in the steady rain, the *Tonquin* dropped anchor in the little cove off the river mouth and returned the salute of the campers with four guns. So, at last, we came to *Astoria*, as all, by common consent, were agreed the new post should be called.

The site chosen was well wooded, covered with immense firs and tall cedars, but commanded by no high hills. At the same time it was high enough to be beyond the reach of the spring floods. There was a good spring and a flowing stream and fairly deep water close in shore, so that vessels of as much as two hundred and fifty tons might lie close in; while the little cove inside the point offered safe anchorage for small craft and shelter from the boisterousness of the wide, wind-swept bay outside.

The building of the fort and the establishment of the post is a story I should like to dwell upon if I had both time and space, yet it is a fact that my own part in it was slight. We went on shore with high hopes and great optimism, and almost miraculously, it seemed, the weather turned suddenly better. The sun came out. Spring, which generally comes much later in these parts, seemed suddenly well advanced. Buds burst upon the trees. Flowers bloomed in the moist woods, and all the world seemed verdant, gay, and happy.

The shoulder of a knoll, perhaps fifteen or twenty feet above the river and fifty or seventy-five yards back from shore, was our choice. Here the ground was comparatively level and would afford room for a spacious palisaded fort and leave space over for kitchen gardens. All of us, except possibly Ross, had had some experience with an ax. But none of us had ever encountered such trees as these. They were often as much as fifty feet in circumference, and they posed a serious problem in felling. We pitched our camp well down toward the shore of the bay and set to work, first building a scaffold about the tree we meant to fell, some ten feet from the ground, then setting a team of two men to work, whittling away at the enormous trunk, a task that often took as much as three or four days to a single tree before the giant would come crashing down and send us all scurrying this way and that, like so many ants, to places of safety, until the immense trunk had settled through the intervening branches and all the bits of bark and flying needles and dust and twigs it had stirred up in its fall had come to rest once more. At the same time some of the men set to work building a short wharf at which to land our supplies, while others cleared a space and began work on a rude shipways in which to lay the keel and put together the knocked-down schooner that we carried in our hold.

So we toiled from dawn to dark, day in and day out, for more than a month, until we had our space cleared and enough timber gathered, I thought, for a dozen forts. It made me laugh all that while to see the way the captain cursed and stomped and threatened in his impatience to be off. Ultimately he arrived at the point where the only communication between him on the ship and MacDougal on shore was by letter. Yet even he was forced to admit that he could not leave us until we had at least finished one warehouse.

The good weather in which we landed did not last, and we suffered intervals of drizzling rain and chilling fog and mist, which seemed to penetrate the thickest clothing and set the men to coughing, even sending a number of them to their blankets with fever and dysentery. At the same time our ration, to my way of thinking, at least, and to that of many of the men, was not all it should be. This, of course, was Mac-Dougal's fault, for instead of seeing to such matters himself, as he should have done, he left them to others, and himself became a bashaw, with as much pomp and ostentation ashore as Captain Thorn had shown aboard ship. His table was constantly supplied with every sort of delicacy, while the rest of us might scrimp along upon rations as meager as on board the *Tonquin,* eked out by such salmon and sturgeon as we might take from the river. Indeed, he seemed to spend the greater part of his time at the Indian camp that had sprung up near us, in the company of the one-eyed chief, Concomly, and it was only later that I learned that all the while he was assiduously courting the old savage's daughter.

As April ended and May brought brighter, milder days, some signs of progress could be seen. The ground, at least, was cleared, stumps blasted away—at a tremendous cost in gunpowder!—the first sheds built, supplies stored. Many of the great logs we cut, far too large to use in construction, we had rolled to the water's edge and, floating them, had formed them into a crude landing stage that rose and fell with the tide and was connected with the shore by a railed plank gangway. It was big enough to float nearly a shipload of gear and greatly facilitated the landing of equipment and goods.

To be sure we lacked fortifications, even of the simplest. None of our guns were mounted, and had our neighbors chosen to attack, we must have been forced to flee to the ship. But the timber was largely gathered not only for the palisades, but for the buildings we proposed to build within as well. Work upon a number of these structures was already well advanced, and one of our great warehouses was nearly completed.

In the meantime a growing restlessness began to show itself among us. The delays which we encountered because of the weather, the size of the forest trees, and the like seemed to the captain evidence of procrastination on our part. To the bourgeois and the voyageurs it seemed as if we had fetched them out with no intention of making use of their peculiar talents. They were, they complained, neither lumbermen nor carpenters. We transgressed our rights when we demanded that they do work fit only for such! They were *Hommes du Nord!* Canoemen! Lords of the green forest and the white water! And when did we mean to make use of them as such, rather than keep them forever building privies in order that fat-bottomed ex-clerks and sailors might relieve themselves in comfort?

Even I, who surely had much less to complain about than most, was conscious of increasing disillusion. Each one of us, I think, felt it, and no doubt it was due to as many various causes as there were individuals among us. In myself, I suppose it was not unnatural that I should in one way or other find Fraser and Westlake at fault. Yet there I fell into the sin of inconsistency, for in blaming them I surely put the cart before the horse. Certainly it was not because of them primarily that I had elected to come upon this expedition. By day I could direct my anger at Captain Thorn or Duncan MacDougal with good reason. But often at night, when I lay rolled in my blanket bags, I would spend the last moments before sleep brooding upon events; wondering what Valerie might be doing at the moment. Often it occurred to me that I had acted with witless precipitation in allowing myself to be persuaded to such an undertaking. Had I stayed at home, by now I might have been securely married to Valerie!

Curiously enough, it never occurred to me to think of Deborah.

All of this came out in various ways. An example was the rivalry that flared between McKay and MacDougal. The two Stuarts alone continued their way unruffled and with sound good sense. Indeed, the more I saw of Rob Stuart, the more I came to admire him. He was quiet, sober, sensible, and always practical, for all he was my junior. Among the clerks I think only Franchere remained totally unchanged, while both Charbonneau and Alan Fraser complained that they so far found all their labors anything but those for which they had signed.

"By damn!" grumbled the Moose one evening by the campfire. "I'm voyageur, canoeman, me! Not squaw!"

"The hell ye're sayin', Frenchy," retorted Shea across the crackling logs, for the sailors often came ashore despite the captain's orders and sought human company among us. "Sure ye're cart horse an' navvy combined an' not so good at it at that, be Jesus! I could fell a tree better meself wid me eyes shut!"

It was a small taunt, yet it started a great brawl that it took partners, clerks, and officers combined to stop.

Later Alan Fraser spoke more to the point to me.

"I've been sailor," he growled, "though you promised me 'twould not be necessary. And now that we are here I see no prospect of the partnership you hinted at. Did you cheat me, O'Rourke? For if you did, I warn you, you have picked the wrong man!"

"Have patience, will you?" I snarled at him. "It will all even out in the end."

Not far away I heard Roger Westlake chuckle tauntingly.

"Now mind the man, Fraser, you redheaded dog," he grinned. "Stay to your last like a good fellow. When I get back to New York before you, I'll remind the lady of you—after she's told me that 'twas myself all along she was waiting for!"

"The hell you say!" the Cock-of-the-Woods retorted. "You may come home before me, but little good will that do you!"

He spoke with his usual confidence, but I could see he was troubled. It occurred to me that this thing might be more serious than I had imagined. Yet I saw no sense in revealing my own place in it then.

By the end of the month the first warehouse was completed, some sixty-two feet long by twenty wide, and in this we fell to stowing the goods that had been put ashore. Captain Thorn had unloaded about a third of what was destined for the fort, yet all at once, to our amazement, he made abrupt announcement that nothing further would be landed until his return from the north.

That was an argument I chanced to overhear, for I was checking the last of a boatload of baled trade goods on the landing, while Mac-Dougal was talking to Stuart at the head of the gangway. The captain landed from the jolly boat and without further greeting addressed himself directly to the senior partner.

"Ye have enough," he said flatly, "to see ye through the summer, aye, and most of the winter. I sail at the first opportunity."

MacDougal turned fiery red in the face.

"Be damned to that!" he cried. "Ye've the best part o' our guids and provisions yet aboord. Set them ashore first, an' then ye may sail tae hell if ye like!"

"I've lost too much time already," said Thorn. "I'll take them with me and land them when I get back."

"Ye're mod, mon!" swore MacDougal. "Take th' guids thot's consigned tae ye but set on shore th' things that are mine. Cannae ye see ye'll ha'e mair place for ye'r pelts sae doin'?"

"I've no fear of that," the captain sneered. "I'll carry as much as I can find, I'll warrant."

So they wrangled and played at cross-purposes for the week that remained of the month, MacDougal perforce yielding little by little, though it galled him hideously to do so. Truth was he had no choice, for even if the goods were set on shore, there would be no place to store them, and the captain would never wait until we had built other warehouses.

When this had at last been recognized and the decision taken, it became necessary to determine which of our traders and people should go with the ship, for Captain Thorn himself declared that he was now short-handed and must have assistance. Accordingly Mr. Lewis was left in his duties as captain's clerk, while Mr. McKay volunteered to go as trader.

Having had no part in any of the explorations until now, I suggested that McKay take me along as his assistant. Alan Fraser, however, had more cogent reasons. To my amazement he volunteered as an additional assistant, and when I taxed him with it, thinking that surely he must have had his belly full of shipboard life, he snorted knowingly.

"Hah!" he cried. "Let Westlake out of my sight? If I did, he'd be back in New York before ever I saw him again to cut me out. No, sir! I mean to keep him under my eye!"

I almost told him that he flattered himself, to say nothing of according Westlake much more than his due, if he thought Valerie attached to either of them. But I held my tongue, and he, misunderstanding my silence, smiled.

"Ah!" he grinned. "I'll admit the man's a sailor. But it needs more than seamanship to win a woman's heart!"

Where Fraser went the Moose was never far behind, and it was probably because he made such a hoorah about it that MacDougal finally consented to his attachment to our party.

So the group was determined, and once again we sent our gear on board, and that last evening was celebrated among us landsmen quietly, by way of farewell, and without a word to the captain or his people, for we had it in mind that our parting from our comrades would carry us long enough among the ship folk. But we were scarcely begun the feasting when the door to our long cabin burst open and in came Mr. Mumford with his sea bag on his shoulder and a scowl as black as any thundercloud up on his face.

"Forgive me for intruding, gentlemen," he apologized, kicking the door shut behind him and flinging his bag into a corner. "I must ask your indulgence till I can find passage home."

"What's that?" cried MacDougal.

Mr. Mumford looked apologetic.

"I'm sorry, sir," he said. "Captain Thorn and myself have parted company——"

"Ye mean he's——" began Mr. Stuart.

"Aye, sir," Mumford assured him. "Handed me my papers, lock, stock, and barrel, you might say, and thrown me off the ship. I've been discharged, gentlemen. If perchance ye need a skipper now for that schooner you're building——?"

MacDougal rose with a roar of laughter.

"By all means! By all means!" he cried. "Sit ye doon. Thraw ye'r gear on McKay's boonk yon. He'll be awa' frae us for a wee bit, I'm thinkin'."

We made a great joke of it. Yet a few moments later I noticed McKay staring glumly at his plate.

"What's the matter?" I asked.

He looked up with a start.

"Eh? Matter? Why, I don't know as to yourself, but if I could escape this cruise, I'd do it in an instant."

"What's got into you?" I demanded.

"Just this," he growled. "Having killed off two of his officers, the man now turns out of his ship one of the only three remaining! I tell you he's mad. I'm sorry I ever agreed to sail with him!"

He looked across the table at Ross.

"Hark to me, Alec!" he said. "You'll be left behind. I've a premonition——"

"Premonition, pooh!" I snorted.

He paid no heed to me.

"I'll not be back," he said. "I have the feeling. And if 'tis true, man, will you take it on yourself to see to my nevvy yon? Aye, and I've one or two other requests I'll leave with you in a writing. I cannot trust it to MacDougal!"

For myself I was amazed at this sudden, and, for him, quite unnatural burst of pessimism, and I believe Ross was too. Yet he pledged his word, and in a moment we had both forgotten.

But apparently McKay did not forget, for in the morning at the landing I saw him hand a packet of papers to the small clerk and wring his hand in farewell.

A moment later we were bouncing across the waves in the jolly boat, and even before we had set foot upon her decks, the *Tonquin* was heaving in her anchor and shaking out her sails.

The *Tonquin* dropped down from Astoria on the first of June with a leadsman in the chains, picking her way leisurely through the twisting channels to Baker's Bay. The day was clear and dry, the wind a shade west, and one might have thought that we would put directly to sea. Captain Thorn, however, had learned respect for the Columbia bars, and in consequence we lay in the shelter of the cape for four full days, until the wind came round to the east and we were able to take advantage of both it and the tide. Then we rode out of the river mouth without once touching, or even for an instant feeling the slightest discomfort.

We turned our bows to the northward immediately upon clearing the river and coasted along, two or three leagues offshore, intending to make a number of stops along the way, in the hope of finding suitable trading sites within easy reach of Astoria, where subsidiary posts might be established. Our spirits rose as we did so, for it was a beautiful day. The water was blue in the sunlight, lightly capped with white where the breakers rolled between us and the shore, and behind the stony beaches and the craggy heads the hills rose green-furred against the mistier slopes of the distant mountains, while these in turn climbed in a series of hazy ridges and massive buttresses to the far-off line of snowcapped heights that flung like fleecy, nebulous, half-seen clouds against the pale blue of the sky.

On the evening flood we looked into Willapa Bay but found nothing there of interest, the natives having sent their furs overland to the fort already. In the morning we stood out again and once more turned northward.

But the fine weather was done for the moment, as is so often the case with the brief springtime flashes of sunlight that brighten these latitudes. We crept to sea in a thick fog, standing well offshore and feeling our way through it all day. The next day proved wet and stormy, with the rain sluicing down in sheets and the wind howling out of the north upon its heels, so that we clawed off and rode it out through the night. Next day it was still raining and misty, so that the low points at the entrance to Gray's Harbor were wraithlike and difficult to distinguish against the grim background. But the wind had pulled round to the southwest and we rode it in.

Here we found the Chehalis Indians, not too rich in skins, the great bulk of their crop having already been traded to the Chinooks for trade to us at the Columbia. But when they learned that we were prepared to offer them the same prices we had to the lower Indians, they were not only angry with the Chinooks at having cheated them but were eager to deal directly with us in the future.

Our business here, as in Willapa Bay, was quickly done, and, as might be expected, we had scarcely come to anchor when the rain stopped, the mist cleared, and the sun smiled warmly down upon us. The wind, however, still held for several days from the west and southwest, and we were wind bound in the harbor with little to do but pow-wow with the natives and enjoy, to the full, the superb fishing.

We must have been four or five days at this place when there came aboard an Indian from the coast to northward; a shifty-eyed, rather sullen individual, he seemed to me, with too many of the earmarks of the renegade for my taste. He was, he told us, one of a tribe that lived to the northward of Puget Sound and that, being of a rather more roving temperament than most of his people, he had traveled widely in this area. His true name, he said, was Kasciascall, though the Chehalis called him Lamazu and the whites dubbed him simply "Jack." According to his story he had crossed the mountains to the eastward and visited white men's posts high up on the river and beyond, where the waters all flowed to the eastward. There he had learned a smattering of English, French, and Ojibway. Also, he said, he had served up and down the coast as guide and interpreter to a number of ships, and he now offered his services to us. Since he claimed to understand most of the tongues that were spoken between this place and the Russian post at Chitka, both the captain and Mr. McKay welcomed his offer. For my part, I could as well have done without, for I felt there was something sinister about the fellow, and more than once, in the days that followed, I thought I caught him watching me with a covertly speculative look, as if for some reason he found me of particular and not very reassuring interest. Several times, abovedecks at night, going from my quarters to the head, or perhaps just catching a breath of air before retiring, I came about suddenly to find him close behind, and it seemed to me that on such occasions he was singularly unconvincing in his pretense of innocence.

The weather remained bright and clear for two or three days after our departure from Gray's Harbor, and we stood along the coast, enjoying almost breath-taking beauty with each fresh point we rounded. The mountains themselves appeared to have drawn closer to the shore by now, so that they stood out more plainly to our view, rising steeply to a single, massive, snowcapped peak whose gullied flanks were thick-clothed in the somber green of pine and fir and whose bright summit caught the golden rays of the evening sun in such a way that it seemed a sort of symbol of a land of dreams that rose beyond a man's far-off horizon.

Such dazzling weather, however, could scarcely be expected to hold. On the fourth day it turned off hot, sultry, all but breathless. A thick blue haze closed us off from the shore and left us alone upon a sleekly heaving sea with sails slatting hollowly against the masts, and the only sound above the creak of the cordage and the groaning of the ship's timbers was the occasional bark of the seals that played about us.

It must have been about this time that we passed the mouth of the Strait of Juan de Fuca, but we saw no sign of it, nor would it have made a difference to our commander if we had, for he had no intention of entering.

Toward the twentieth of the month we came abreast of Vancouver Island, with its craggy dark shores, rock-fanged and rugged, dense clad in cedar, spruce, and fir and the low, black bluffs wearing the appearance of scowling brows, the ragged rocks like gnashing teeth amid the boiling seas. There we coasted along, standing well offshore out of respect for submerged shoals and ledges, seeking the entrance to Clayoquot Sound.

But evening had scarcely fallen when we were struck suddenly by one of the most furious gales out of the southwest that I have ever experienced, and we but barely fought free of the rocks, for safety's sake standing out to sea. It was as well we did so. For two days it stormed so that we could not even try to regain our landfall, and only on the twenty-fifth were we once again able to fetch in close to shore, and seeing the narrow entrance to Nootka Sound, fled for it like a frightened rabbit, with the wind at our heels, desperate to come within the shelter of the land before the wind might shift again and drive us off once more.

We could not have had a more perfect time to find it, for the wind had pushed aside the rain wrack and the entrance stood up sharp and clear, just as Captain Cook had described it, with the low wooded tip of Point Breakers thrusting up from the southeast and some distance off the arm of Woody Point, rising high against the horizon, and in between the bay, the island, and the sound, all gashed and serried and indented with fingers and inlets of the sea. Behind them, the dark, tall forest rose straight against the water's edge, with the snowy mountains forming a backdrop for them all.

No doubt we should have recalled the great English navigator's warning note of sunken rocks that lay a league or more from the shore at the entrance, but doubtless all on board were too thoroughly engrossed in the approaching land, and for an instant our attention must have wandered, for it was only when the leadsman in the chains cried out frantically, in unmistakable alarm, that we came back abruptly, quite literally with a rude thump.

"Breakers! Dead ahead! In God's name, sir! 'Ware shoals!"

At his tone I thought Captain Thorn turned gray.

"Where away?" he managed to squeak.

But the words were no more than out of his mouth before we struck, smashing full tilt upon the sunken rocks with a rending crash and such force that our teeth were shaken in our heads. I doubt there was a man of us but was flung to the deck. It seemed to me she must have torn her bottom out, for I could scarce imagine bolts and copper and timber that would withstand such a shock. For an instant she reared upon her stern like a sharply curbed horse pawing at the air. Then she lay over on her side with a groan and a shudder, so far upon her beam ends that I swear she dipped her yardarms in the water, and I thought she must surely capsize. Then, with the wind to help her, she seemed to give a final, desperate heave and shuddered her way across the reef, slipped into deeper water, and slowly righted and went wallowing on.

I never saw a man so white-faced as Captain Thorn as he picked himself up and sent Mr. Weeks scuttling below to see what damage she had taken. It seemed to me an age before the old man was back with his report, though it could scarcely have been ten minutes. When he did return, what he had to say was scarcely reassuring. The ship, he said, was taking water rapidly forward and larboard amidship. A few of the timbers appeared to be sprung, but he thought that if we could manage to keep her moderately dry for a day or two he would be able to make temporary repairs upon them. Real danger, however, lay along the keel, which was badly sprung. As soon as possible the ship must be fetched into a likely beach or shingle, and careened. In the meantime, any such weather as we had but just passed through would drive her to the bottom like a stone.

In this condition we crept in through the narrow passage to the broader, deeper waters of the sound, where here and there our dipsey lead, even, could find no bottom at eighty-five to ninety fathoms, while at others we found thirty to sixty fathoms so close inshore that a man might almost have leapt to the bank from the deck had he been so minded. The sound itself was cross-shaped, but with so many little side arms and fiords, inlets, and coves and fingers as to be vastly confusing. Everywhere the tremendous dark forests of pine and fir came down close to the water, and great boulders strewed the shore amid their roots, half above the shore line and covered with moss and lichens, their lower part submerged in the emerald waters. On this we gazed, quite at a loss to know which way to turn, for as yet no canoes came out to meet us and we could only look to our interpreter for guidance.

"Where away, Kas?" the captain asked.

The Indian pointed up the center main arm of the sound, stretching away past a small island to northeastward.

"Captain Cook go 'long him canal," he grunted. "Up along by'n by at end you find main village name Eyuck Whoola."

"Sounds good enough to me," growled Thorn. "What about it? Will I be able to careen there?"

"Careen?" The Indian looked puzzled for an instant, then brightened. "Careen! Oh, yes, Cap-tan, very good place for careen! Very pretty woman! Fine flat-head! All very nice too!"

The captain turned scarlet at the snicker that went up.

"Shut up, all hands!" he snarled.

After that we slipped along in silence, only the water rippling under our forefoot, the wind soughing in the pines, while our clanking pumps kept up a sort of melancholy accompaniment.

Under Kasciascall's piloting we came at length into the bay he had described to us, where we were able to lie within a hundred yards of the shore, sheltered on two sides by low-ridged, pine-covered points, with the village, a place of some considerable size, upon its eastern end. There we dropped anchor in some thirty fathoms, at a point from which, despite our almost landlocked berth, we could look directly back between the wooded points, down the channel to where the breakers of the open sea marched in an endless procession.

There, for the first time, we saw signs of life. A number of Indians came off to us in canoes, not greatly differing from those with which we had become familiar at the Columbia, save the greater number of them carried no more than six or eight and were slender in proportion. The one exception had a more erect and higher figurehead in the shape of some hideous but beautifully carved mythological creature. This belonged to the chief, Maquinna, and it being late in the day with little time left for trading, he alone, with a few retainers, came aboard and bade us welcome in a long, rambling speech full of clucking and gulping. He was a handsome man, of medium height but solidly built, with a hawklike face and a scent of fish oil about him that made me think involuntarily of an osprey. His hair was generously sprinkled with down and was drawn back over his ears, in which were fixed rows of small shells. His eyes were slanted, his brows finely plucked, and he wore both a mustache that curled about his mouth and a tiny black goatee—both remarkable, indeed, almost unheard of in an Indian. Covering him from shoulder to ankle, he wore a robe of the most magnificent sea-otter skins I have ever seen; undoubtedly a badge of his office.

For all his cordiality there was a cold craftiness about him that made me uneasy. But as far as I was able to tell, few of my companions felt the same. Only Alan Fraser expressed anything like what was in my mind.

"Brrr!" he whispered. "These folk are too much like heathen for me. Give me a good north-country Cree or Assiniboin! A man knows where he stands with them!"

In view of that feeling it was ironic that I should be asked to accompany McKay and the interpreter on shore, to spend the night in his lodge, in place of the captain, who begged the needs of the ship as an excuse. I think he had in mind the memory of some other feasts to which he had been bidden on the coast, at which he had been served raw fish, well-aged, and a kind of small dog, raised for the purpose and roasted upon a spit, to say nothing of Captain Cook's mention of signs of cannibalistic practices among these folk.

III. MASSACRE

I THINK, for once, I would have been inclined to take the captain's view. McKay, however, seemed to feel it important to conciliate the man, and before I could protest had accepted for me. Poor Ellick! I wonder if he would have been so ready had he been gifted with second sight!

As I have said we were accompanied by Kasciascall, who seemed secretly amused by the whole thing, and while the meal which we were served proved to be as civilized and as edible and as well cooked as any I have ever eaten under a savage roof, I cannot say I was comfortable eating it. Nor was I anything but enormously sleepy all through the gambling that served as entertainment afterward, so that I lost and thereby inadvertently proved a thorough diplomat. When it came time to retire, we firmly declined the services of the flat-headed virgins—or near virgins—that were offered us and lay down upon the most enormous and comfortable beds of sea-otter skins to sleep. Yet I was restless and wakeful, thinking always, for some reason, of the Indian Kasciascall.

I must have slept, for I suddenly opened my eyes to find it morning. Yet the fact remains I spent an indifferent night. What took place on board the ship during that absence I have no means of knowing, nor, I must say, did McKay appear to be in any hurry to return. I gathered he slept well, for he appeared in fine fettle. Toward midmorning, when the Indians came with bowls of boiled salmon and camas root, which was a wild vegetable a little like the spring onion but lacking its flavor, he stretched and yawned and scratched himself at the crotch and under the arms where the Indian lice were bound to settle.

"Eh, Rory!" he smiled. "I hope ye'd a good night of it?"

"Good enough," I growled, lying.

"Ah!" he chuckled. "Ye grow nervous in your old age. What's eatin' at ye?"

"I wish I knew," I told him. " 'Tis that Indian for one."

"Kas?" He lifted his eyebrows. "There's no harm in him."

"No doubt," I admitted. "But the notion is there. I find it hard to escape."

We breakfasted well, and toward the end of the morning went out with the Indians to the ship, where we could still hear the clank of the pumps, accompanied as a chorus by the thump of the carpenters' hammers. As we left the village, I noticed that, though we had seen quantities of skins of the first value ashore, most of the bundles which our comrades now carried out were of an inferior grade, and what was our surprise when, on coming aboard, we found fifty or more of the savages already before us, with bundles unrolled and laid out upon the deck, and hard at the business of bargaining with the captain.

I think I may be excused if I expressed a degree of surprise at this. Before we had left the Columbia it had been understood that the captain was to navigate the ship and that McKay was to act as chief trader. And this was at Thorn's own suggestion and insistence. Accordingly, now to come on board and find him dickering with Indians, far shrewder than himself at this sort of thing, was disconcerting to say the least. I think McKay looked as startled as I felt, and his long face fell.

"What the devil's this?" he demanded.

"Surprise to ye, eh?" Thorn leered. "The savages wanted to trade, and, since ye dawdled, I led 'em on. We're getting on famously."

He grinned triumphantly. McKay glanced quickly at me and then shot a look at the furs spread out upon the deck.

"Have ye bought much of this?" he demanded.

"Oh, I've done well enough," replied Thorn smugly, smiling, well pleased with himself.

"Well, then, I hope ye've had good advisers to guide ye," replied McKay, "and've not paid more for them than they're worth, for, I tell ye, man, they're worth little! Ye may ask Mr. O'Rourke yonder. Even the skins they fetched out with us canna hold candle to the best they have."

The captain bristled, as I was afraid he would.

"I've had need of no advice," he growled. "The redheaded one there—" he pointed where Alan Fraser scowled by the rail, looking off at the forest and pretending not to hear—"the redheaded dog that they call Cock-of-the-Woods tried to object, but I set him in his place! Look!"

He held up a dozen of the mangiest pelts I ever looked at.

"I had these at a bargain!" he boasted.

McKay stared at them.

"I hope the bargain was on the right side!" he replied. "We talk at cross-purposes, Captain. Will you step down to the cabin with me for a moment? There's a word I should pass on to ye!"

What McKay had to say to him below is something that I can only guess at. Yet it would call for no especial shrewdness to see the captain's surly reaction and to form a fairly accurate opinion. I think he must have said that Thorn had been diddled, and fetched up evidence to prove it, for if ever I saw a man with gall in his mouth, it was Thorn.

Whether it was a good idea for McKay to have told him he had made a fool of himself and us and was in a way to ruining our dealings with these people, I am still uncertain. Rather, let me say, in view of what resulted, it was a very poor idea. Yet none of us are gifted with clairvoyance, and I am sure that under the same circumstances I would be inclined to do the same. In the light of what followed it would have been far better to let him carry on as he had: to give away our trade goods for these inferior pelts, accept the loss, and draw away at the earliest opportunity. Beyond question we would have profited more, however great the loss! But, as I say, all that is clear enough now. It lay in darkness then.

Evidently McKay did not forbid the captain to trade. Indeed, how could he on the man's own deck? But apparently he had urged caution, for Thorn's manner was quite changed. He scrutinized each pelt carefully, then flung it aside with a bark of derision.

"*Pishak!*" he would snort. "Bad! *Wake mackouk!* No trade! *Mika capshewalla!* You steal!"

Obviously this was not the way to trade. The Indians, it seemed to me, showed infinite patience, for they would only smile and pick up the skin and return it to the pile in front of them. Yet they offered nothing of value. Mr. McKay did not even trouble to offer goods. Through Kasciascall he told them firmly that their furs were worthless and that we would deal only in such skins as we had seen on shore, yet they patiently persisted in the game, stolidly waiting, hoping perhaps that they might break the captain down again to something like their demands.

"*Makouke patlach?*" they would ask. "Make present?"

The suggestion sent Thorn into a towering rage.

"Wake patlach! Wake patlach! No present!"

And he would launch into a torrent of abuse in English, the tone of which was obvious to the dullest savage, even if the words themselves were the sheerest mumbo-jumbo.

In the circumstances it seems to me scarcely surprising that as the afternoon wore on tempers grew strained and angry bile began to rise. The Indians, as always, grew quieter, seeming meeker, as the day passed, for that is their way. I think a more observing, more experienced man than Thorn would have been alarmed. But upon him the most obvious signs were lost. So far as he was concerned, all these people were but dirty, ignorant savages, little better than dogs, and that they defied him on his own deck—as he conceived it—was more than his temper could abide. Maquinna, I noticed, though he said nothing, missed little. He sat in silence, watching, listening, with his bundle of furs before him and his patience worn as evident as a hat. To be sure, Lewis and McKay and Fraser and myself did our best to offset the captain's rantings, conciliating, offering a present of tobacco here, a brass bracelet there.

It came late in the afternoon, and it was apparent, by this time, that matters were drawing to a head. McKay was quietly and as diplomatically as possible trying to clear the ship, without much success, while obviously Maquinna, our bosom companion of the night before, who seemed by now a complete stranger, was just as quietly urging his fellows to demand even greater and more outrageous prices for their wares, and telling them to stand their ground. Moreover, he was entering the rounds of conversation now gently, quietly, putting in a word to goad, to flick the captain on the raw. One of the elder chiefs, to precipitate it, had the temerity to bring forth for the third time a thin pelt of summer beaver, which he held up for Thorn's inspection. The captain snatched it from his hands and flung it back in his lap furiously.

"Why show me these?" he demanded angrily. "All these I have seen! I have told you that such are worthless."

His eye fell upon Maquinna's sea-otter robe, and he went across to the chief, arrogantly lifting a corner, so that it tugged at the wearer's neck, and shook it.

"This!" he fairly screamed. "This is what I came to buy! For this will I trade!"

Kasciascall raised his eyebrows languidly and spoke to Maquinna, who settled himself stolidly, after quietly pulling back the corner of his robe. The chief replied briefly. The interpreter turned to Thorn.

"He say this robe belong him chief people. He say not trade, but maybe give *patlach* [gift] to white man that come as brother. Never make *kaltash-wa-wa* [idle talk], but now is tired to hear *Hias-tye-yea* [great chief] speak all day like *tlutchemen* [woman]."

Thorn turned almost savage with fury. For an instant I thought he would fly at the chief, but with considerable effort he controlled himself.

"Clear the decks!" he bawled. "Get off the ship! Every last one! On shore! Ye blasted ragamuffins!"

Kasciascall translated, obviously judiciously, but Thorn's meaning was evident enough. One by one the other Indians began gathering up their furs, rolling them in bundles. A few laughed and made a joke of it. So far as I could see they were not yet unfriendly. They were simply ready to cry quits to the day's business and let such matters be forgotten for the moment.

But Maquinna made no move to join them. Hitherto, slightly smiling, mildly, easily affable, his face now seemed turned to stone, waiting. And his little eyes were cold and glittering.

The captain did not at first appear to notice as he stamped away, but when he turned and saw the chief still squatting on his hams, he uttered a roar of rage.

"Did ye hear me, ye dirty red dog?" he bawled.

Before any of us could stop him, he crossed the deck in three bounds and seized the still-sitting chief by the scalp lock, jerking him to his feet.

"You insolent scoundrel!" he roared.

"Captain Thorn!" McKay called out, aghast.

But the captain evidently was beyond hearing. Stooping, he snatched up the roll of furs that still lay at the Indian's feet and with it slapped the chief solidly across the face, then thrust it into his unresisting hands.

"Take your damned trash and get off my vessel," he fumed. "Jonathan Thorn will accept no insolence from any savage! When ye've a mind to trade for proper pelts, ye may fetch them out and take what price I give ye for them. Until then stay on shore, and be damned to ye!"

With an angry shove he thrust the unresisting savage toward the gangway. I was startled to see that already the decks were cleared. Captain Thorn had scarcely reached for the chief before the rest of the Indians had vanished over the side, and the chief himself slipped swiftly down into his waiting canoe without so much as a backward glance. By the time I could look out over the rail, the canoes were scattering away from us in evident haste, as if we had been suddenly discovered to harbor the plague. McKay glared at the captain.

"Are ye gone mad, man?" he cried. "What have ye done? Do ye know no better than to raise your hand to their chief?"

"Pooh!" cried Thorn. "Ye think I'm afraid? A touch of discipline'll teach 'em we're not to be trifled with! They'll be back in the morning as meek as lambs."

"They'll be back with weapons in their hands and knives for our throats, unless I miss my guess." McKay spat. "If ye've the sense of a jack rabbit, Captain, ye'll up anchor and put to sea! Leave these people be. There are others on the coast!"

"And leave them laughing in their sleeves at all white men? A bloody pox to that, Mr. McKay! Ye may be a coward, but I'm not! No! Not so long as I've a knife or a handspike to fight with! Besides, the vessel is not fit for sea."

McKay turned away with a shrug.

"I see it is no good to argue with a fool!" he retorted. "Suit yourself, Captain, but I hope ye'll not call me 'coward' if I suggest ye put up the boarding nets and double the watch!"

That was an end to it for the moment and, indeed, for the night, though I noticed that neither was the watch doubled nor the boarding nets raised. Neither were any arms served out to the men. Unquestionably Captain Thorn had his back up and was bound he would show his disdain for such a pack of red ragamuffins. Fortunately, though I slept little, and I am sure McKay did less, no one came near us that night. The next morning, however, there were already a dozen canoes about us when I came on deck, their crews calling out *"Makoke! Makoke!"* and holding bundles of furs above their heads as an indication that they wished to trade.

The watch would let none of them on board, however, until the captain himself or one of the traders appeared, and as Mr. Lewis and myself came up from our early breakfast, Kasciascall turned from the rail with what looked to me to be genuine surprise.

"They wish trade, sar!" he assured me. "Not understand, me! But is true. You look, see woman in canoe."

It was true. The usual squaws were among them, and what was more I could not see that one of them was armed.

I looked at Lewis, still cautious, I don't know why.

"You better let the captain know," I told him. "I'll not accept the responsibility of asking them on board."

He turned away, and a moment later Thorn himself appeared, still clutching his napkin and wiping his mouth with an air of satisfaction. At his heels came McKay, looking puzzled and uneasy.

"I don't like this," he growled. " 'Tis not in nature!"

"Pah!" snorted the captain, grinning triumph from ear to ear. "I told ye, if ye'd but listen. D'ye see how it works? Treat the rogues gingerly and they ride over ye!"

He glanced at the interpreter.

"Well, Kas," he said, "are they in a good humor?"

"Never see him better," Kasciascall assured him, and indeed I could scarcely disagree in the face of appearances.

"Well, let them come on board then," Thorn ordered.

"I don't like this!" said McKay again, frowning.

"Stuff!" Thorn growled. "They'll not be so insolent, now I've humbled the damned dogs a little. We'll get on better!"

"I still say I don't like it," McKay retorted.

"I daresay ye don't," the captain shot back. "But 'tis fortunate I am in command here. Ye pretend to know a great deal about Indian character, McKay, but the truth is ye know nothing at all!"

Obviously there was no arguing with him. It was perfectly and unaccountably true that the Indians did appear chastened. So far as I could see they held no grudge. Nor did they offer us shoddy, valueless pelts. Instead, they fetched out several bundles of first-grade skins and seemed willing to part with them for a reasonable price.

The savages were allowed on board without restriction, since there appeared to be no more than a handful of them. These fetched up their furs and each one of them spread one of his bundles on the deck, keeping the other roll close beside him, a circumstance that aroused no suspicion at the moment, for it was quite customary. The women remained in the canoes below, not one venturing on board. Yet here again we saw nothing to alarm us, for, after all, someone had to stay in the craft, and it was not unusual, while the serious business of trade was in progress, that it should be the menial sex.

No sooner were the first Indians on board, however, than two or three more canoes put out from shore to send a few more men with bundles of furs on board us. These settled down beside the rest and spread out a part of their wares. One or two of the firstcomers rose from their places and wandered smiling about the decks, examining this and that, as if they had never before seen a ship. Even as they did so, still more came off to us.

All of this was most gradually accomplished, so that the morning was well advanced before even Mr. McKay and myself, who were half on the lookout, were actually aware of it. As for the captain, he neither saw nor cared, and when McKay attempted to warn him, he shook him off impatiently.

"Leave be, old woman!" he cried. "Must ye be forever starting at shadows? Look at the furs I am getting and the prices I pay! Are ye jealous, man? Leave be!"

"If ye'll swallow your greed long enough to look about," returned

McKay coldly, "ye'll see there are already nigh two savages to every one of us. Not one of us is armed. For the sake of your own skin, if not for the rest of us, let me pass out the arms quietly to the men one at a time, and in the meantime do ye keep other Indians off the vessel until ye have dealt with these!"

The captain turned upon him impatiently.

"I have not time to stand arguing with ye, Mr. McKay!" he flared. "If ye're afraid to stay above deck, ye're welcome to hide in the cabin. But leave me to my trading."

McKay turned away with a shrug, and, to my surprise, I saw him disappear below. For a moment I wondered if the captain were right. But presently I saw him return and take up a stance against the larboard quarter rail, where he watched with an air of indifference I knew he was far from feeling.

By this time the deck was aswarm with savages, who wandered about, some trading, some looking, yet all carrying at least one bundle of furs. I judged there must have been nearly a hundred of them, while we, at the outside, could have mustered only thirty-three, counting the boy. Nor, as I began to realize, were McKay and myself the only ones who had become uneasy. Charbonneau sidled up to me.

"W'at dey keep in dem bundles?" he demanded.

"Why, furs," I told him.

"Ha-yah!" he scoffed under his breath. "You watch 'um! She don' trade dis bundle bot keep h'always by de han! I bet you me he's got knife in dat bundle. You no can buy! I bat you!"

It was an idea. I lost no time arguing. But though I offered several of them as much as twice what the best skins they had fetched aboard would bring in the New York market, I could not persuade them to part with the rolls. Once was curious, but might indicate that the bearer had some particular prize he was saving till later. Twice was suspicious, and too much a coincidence. But three times was confirmation of what Charbonneau had suggested. I became definitely alarmed and edged over toward where McKay leaned upon the rail. Out of the corner of my eye I noticed that Kasciascall sat perched upon the poop rail, with his feet dangling over, watching the scene with lively animation. More sinister, it seemed to me, three or four of our visitors moved almost unconcernedly after me, drifting, yet definitely within reach. Beside McKay, I leaned my forearms on the rail and stared down into the canoe that lay below. The three squaws in it leered up at me invitingly.

"I think they have weapons in those bundles," I said.

I did not think Kasciascall, above us, could hear. I hoped he could not. Yet it was a risk I must run.

McKay turned toward me and lifted the corner of his coat a trifle, as if reaching for his kerchief. I saw the butt of a pistol stuck in his waistband.

"I have armed myself," he replied. "Ye'd best do the same."

"I mean to," I replied.

"Ye, too, Mr. Lewis," he said to the clerk who had come up.

"Aye!" Lewis agreed. "Have ye noticed how each of us is covered? Mark the four about the captain now, for instance!"

McKay glowered.

" 'Tis unfortunate we must waste our strength trying to save him. If I am not wrong, there'll be other blood than his shed this day and through his doing. But there's no help for it! Can we get men aloft and others to the capstan? If we are swift and have only a few guns, we may yet intimidate them."

"We can try," I replied, and made a signal to Fraser, who stood not far off.

It seemed to me the Indians about us tensed for an instant as I did so, and I wondered if it were coming now. But when I did not move and Fraser only drifted over, smiling, they seemed to ease.

"Are you thinking the same as myself?" Fraser asked.

"I am!" I assured him. "These seagoing loons have plucked our goose and spitted it for the roasting!"

He spat over the side, never troubling to look if there were a canoe below.

"Let it come if it must," he said grimly.

"Are you armed?" I demanded.

"I've my *skean dhu*. I'd not sleep without it!"

I nodded.

"You've been in the rigging. See if you can get five or six of the men aloft. Be ready to loose the sails when we call."

He flushed.

"Now, by God, I'm not used to taking orders from——"

"In Christ's name!" I cried softly. "Can you not see that the lives of us all may depend upon it? I am not ordering you, man! I am but pointing out how best we can do this together!"

"Well, in that case——" He shrugged. "But we'll not get far with the hook down!"

"I'll try to see Westlake about that," I told him. "You look to your end and the rest of us will take care of ours!"

"Him!" He spat again and turned away, hitching up his belt.

"I'll get my guns," Lewis said.

"Go ahead," I told him. " 'Tis best if we don't leave the deck together. I'll speak to Westlake and then come for mine."

I watched him drift over to the companionway and drop quickly below, then crossed over myself to where Westlake was bartering with a savage for a sea-otter pelt. He held it up for my inspection as I came near, and I eyed it critically. I was glad none of the Indians understood English.

"They have weapons in those bundles," I told him, examining the pelt carefully and speaking as if I were remarking upon it. "At least that's what we think. Fraser is going aloft with five or six. Can you see to the anchor?"

"Why not?" he demanded. "I've been wondering if they weren't up to something. Too many of 'em. Has anyone told the captain?"

"You know what he thinks—if he thinks," I replied.

"Aye!" he growled. "We can't move without him, nonetheless. If you won't tell him, I'll have to."

"I'll get word to him," I promised. "You take the anchor."

He glared at the Indian.

"*Ight enna!*" he snapped. "One beaver!"

The price was ridiculously low; so low, indeed, that the Indian owner, before he could catch himself, looked insulted.

"*Wake!*" he snapped. "No! *Kaltash-wa-wa!*"

"*Winnipiè!*" Westlake shrugged. "By and by!"

He turned away, and I followed as if arguing. Midships we parted, and I moved over toward the captain, repeating the byplay. He looked alarmed, and I saw at once it was a mistake. It would have been better to leave him in ignorance until the last moment. But the cat was out of the bag. He glanced about the deck, for the first time seeming to realize that all was not as it should be.

"What will we do?" he demanded characteristically.

"Keep on with your bargaining," I ordered him, and it did not even occur to me to chuckle. "Fraser's aloft with a crew now. Westlake's rounding up men for the capstan as quietly as possible. We need only move to rid ourselves of them for the moment, and once they're ashore we can hold them off at least until we're ready for sea. This fur is worth four beaver, but you'd best bargain with him. I'm going below to get my guns."

"I'd best clear the decks!" he said, panicked.

"Bargain!" I ordered. "You started this. If we can arm ourselves one at a time, we may yet be able to come to the point before them. If not, we are lost. Bargain, man!"

I turned on my heel and walked to the companion, never daring to look back, though I felt sure he was staring after me. If I looked back, even to give him encouragement, he might break and precipitate the crisis I feared.

It would scarcely have mattered. I dropped below and found Lewis, trembling with excitement, his foot on the ladder.

"Wait," I told him. " 'Twill be better if we go up together."

For a few moments apparently he did as I asked, while I ran to my cabin and fetched out my rifle-barreled pistols from the sack. A glance verified the primings, but when I returned to the foot of the ladder, he was already on his way up and only his legs and the seat of his breeches were visible in the square patch of light. Vaguely, it seemed to me that all at once there was a good deal of shouting and uproar from the deck above. I heard someone cry out "anchor!" and then a shot, followed by the blood-curdling whoop that is the same whether uttered by Chinook or Chippewa. I leapt for the ladder and thrust up behind Lewis, snatching at the pistols in my belt as I went.

But I had little opportunity to take part in the melee that swirled upon the deck. What could have precipitated the storm, I never knew, but there was no doubt that something had touched it off. As I lifted my face above the coaming, grasping the edge to give myself support upon the steep steps, I saw, out of the corner of one eye, Mr. McKay's body go overboard, upturned at the rail by a trio of savages who yelped as they turned him, and his pistol went skidding across the deck, leaving a little trail of blue smoke behind it, so that I guessed it was his shot I had heard. There was a savage sprawled grotesquely, with head and neck and shoulder crumpled under him, near where McKay had stood, and a little bright trickle of blood rolled crazily across the deck from him, zigzagging this way and that with the slight movement of the ship. The captain I glimpsed for an instant, but for an instant only, over against the mainmast, defending himself with a clasp knife. I saw two of the savages double in pain before the whooping horde swept over him; and even as I saw that, I caught sight of the long body of John Weeks, turning slowly in the ratlines where he had leapt, to slip sickeningly and then plunge headforemost to the deck below. Somehow, through the corner of my eye, my brain registered the fact that Kasciascall was no longer in his place upon the after rail. Overside I could hear the women in the canoes shrieking with blood lust.

But even as I noted all this, half-consciously, something toppled upon me, thrusting me down and away from the steep ladder by which I was mounting. I could not see what it was, save that it struck with force and a well-nigh crushing weight. Frantically I snatched for my balance, and my head seemed torn from my shoulders, while the fingers, with which I had been holding to the coaming at the top of the hatchway, were suddenly without strength, indeed without being, as if they had been severed, and all at once I had nothing left to grip with. For a moment I seemed to float in space, in a tangle of arms and legs. Something warm and wet sprayed across my face. Then I could feel myself falling—falling, down—down, still struggling, to land abruptly with a deafening crash and a stab of blinding pain. All the lights in heaven seemed to whirl and flash and flare before my eyes, and I could hear in my ears a roaring, as of some giant waterfall near by. Yet before I could shake my head and look about me all this was followed by a crash of utter, silent darkness, into which I seemed to whirl and from which I came back only painfully and slowly and with an immense effort.

I could not have been unconscious more than a few seconds, for when I opened my eyes the body of James Lewis still lay across my legs as it had fallen, and the blood was still spurting in a pulsing stream from the stump of his arm. The section that had been shorn from his head, from the part of his hair, diagonally down to the middle of his ear, gaped up at me like an opened coconut, not yet shrouded by the screening fluid, so that the gray matter lay all exposed and I could see his brain, like a mass of white worms with little threads of crimson in between. Apparently he had been struck down as he emerged from the hatchway, probably by the blow of a hatchet, swung as a tomahawk in such a way that it sheered down at an angle, slicing away the corner of his skull, and then flashing on across his shoulder to sever the arm that had been raised to a level with his face, just a little above the biceps.

It came to me that the same blow could have struck me, and involuntarily I looked down at my hand, half-frightened of what I might see. But I still had my fingers, although there was a deep gash across the back of my fist, from the base knuckle of the little finger almost to that of the thumb. I could feel no pain from it even yet. Undoubtedly it had been Lewis's body, hurtling down upon me as I mounted the ladder, that had torn me loose and sent me tumbling back into the cabin below. Beyond question, too, that fall, with him on top of me, as jarring and as painful as it had been, had saved my life, at least for the moment.

With something of a start I suddenly became aware that it was ominously quiet on the deck above. I glanced up cautiously from where I lay upon my back, but for the instant, at least, there was nothing to be seen but a little square patch of blue sky that brightened the out- lines of the open hatch. What could be happening up there, I won- dered. Had the savages taken the vessel in so brief a coup? Was every- one dead but me?

Gingerly I tried to roll clear of Lewis's dead weight across my legs, and as I did so, he slumped off my thighs onto the deck with a gusty, sighing groan that froze the blood in my veins. For an instant I could feel the pulse inside my stomach come to a definite halt, and I stared at him with a sense of horrified fright that was far more real than any I had felt as I had looked out that flashing instant from the hatchway. It was as if the fleshless, dead, and buried body of someone I had seen tucked long ago away had risen from the well-sealed grave to speak. I can recall thinking that he could not be alive with such a wound as that, then almost crying with relief as I assured myself that of course he was not! That sigh had been only the wind squeezed from his lungs through his unresisting throat by the movement of his body.

But I had little opportunity to make certain, for at that moment a hideously evil, savage face thrust over the coaming above, limned in the opening against the sky, and peered down at me. For the briefest instant our eyes met, and I could not say now which of us was the more surprised. But I have no thought of boasting when I say that I was first to recover. My life depended upon it! Instinctively I snatched at the other pistol in my belt and fired.

The head flopped back, but whether it had been knocked so or abruptly withdrawn I had no way of knowing. Only later I found his body sprawled out beside the hatch with a neat round hole by the side of his nose, underneath the eye, and the back of his skull all blown to splinters.

At the instant I fired I wondered if I had not been foolish. If they did not know where I was before, they certainly would now. Still, it seemed to me I had had no choice as to that. At least they knew I was armed.

Still a little dizzy and unable to think what I ought to do next, I began, instinctively, to reload my weapon. But I had no more than begun to pour in the powder when I was startled fairly out of my wits by the figure on the deck beside me, for this time it definitely moved, shuddering and scrabbling at the planking with the tensed figures of its one hand. At the same time it uttered a sort of sobbing, bleating moan that raised the hair upon the back of my neck, I jumped, so that my hand shook, scattering grains of powder all across the deck, and shied away like a skittish horse. Only when I was at the far side of the cabin did I glance back, and to my horror saw that the man's eyes were open in his gray face and he was watching me with cheek pressed to the flooring, helplessly, almost pleadingly. As our eyes met, his lips moved, his jaw worked a little in grizzly, gasping motions.

"I—I'm—h—hurt," he managed.

I swallowed.

"Aye," was the only answer I could make.

Hastily I rammed home the ball in its greased patch and with trembling fingers spilled a few grains of powder in the priming pan. The action forced me to a sufficient recovery of my composure. I rammed the weapon home once more in my waistband and wiped the back of my hand upon the seat of my breeches, for the blood made my fingers slippery. Then I crossed to him quickly and dropped to one knee beside him, keeping an eye cocked on the opening above. It was my intention to drag him aside, though why I could not say at this point, for obviously it would have been better for him to die where he was. He glanced up at me as I knelt.

"You—you're hurt—too!" he gasped. "That—that's a—nasty gash. Better let—Mc—McKay—d—dress it. My—arm—I—I——"

"You haven't any," I interrupted him bluntly, stupidly, speaking only out of haste and never pausing to think.

As soon as the words were out, I could have bitten my tongue.

He turned his head slowly and with a great effort, just a little, and stared down. Then, mercifully, fainted.

It struck me then that somehow I must stanch the flow of blood from the stump of his arm. Fortunately I was not altogether ignorant of such things. There are no doctors in the north woods, and a man who stays long among the fur hunters soon gains a crude knowledge of emergency medicine. I whipped out my kerchief and tied it tightly about the stump. With the ramrod from one of my pistols I wound it tight, so that after a moment the frightening stream dwindled to a seeping trickle, after which I tucked the end of the ramrod up under the torn remnant of his sleeve and braced it so that it stayed an effective stopper.

I would have turned then to some means of covering up that hideous, almost indecent, quaking brain that showed through his shattered skull, but I was interrupted by a pounding at the bulkhead forward and the sound of voices shouting. Among them I recognized Westlake's. But at the same instant a fish spear whizzed savagely down through the hatchway and thwucked into the deck beside me, to stand quivering and shaking with the force of its passage.

All of this takes minutes in the telling, but I think it could have been no more than fleeting seconds in the event. I stayed no longer in that spot than it took me to leave it! Bending, I snatched Lewis beneath the armpits and, with his heels dragging, pulled him to a place of comparative safety underneath the long table. There, at least, we were not only covered by the thick deal surface, but we were at one side, at an acute angle to the open hatchway, so that any who might come at us from above would have to lean far over and down.

There, I felt, I could hold out indefinitely, and the voices and pounding beyond the bulkhead had aroused my hope. From the other side of the barrier Westlake's voice hailed.

"Ahoy the cabin? Who's there?"

"Westlake?" I called. "There's but two here—Lewis and O'Rourke—and Lewis is beyond fighting. How many are you?"

"Six of us," he replied. "Four jumped safe from the capstan into the forward hold, and two slid down from the rigging in through the midships hatch. There are three yet aloft, as near as I can tell. They got McKay and the captain."

"I saw!" I replied grimly. "Can you get through?"

The *Tonquin*, unlike a man-of-war, was not equipped with demountable bulkheads on her main deck. The officers' country in her was separated by a permanent partition from that of the petty officers forward, and the only passage was secured by a stout door, opened only to allow access to and from the galley, the key to which was kept by the mulatto mess steward.

"Steward's dead and pitched overside," Westlake called. "We'll have to smash down the door. Are you armed?"

I said I was.

"Can you hold them off above?"

"I'll try," I told him. "If you can break in and get to the arms chest, we may be able to clear the decks."

"Aye!" I heard him growl. "Are you ready?"

"I've been ready this ten minutes past," I replied. "If you waste more time in talk, God knows what they'll be about! Break through. Man! Hurry! Mr. Lewis is sore wounded."

I looked at the clerk. He must have had his pistol in the hand that he lost when the blow fell, for it was nowhere upon him now.

Why the savages did not rush us when Westlake and those who were with him began battering at the bulkhead door I will never know. They found a spar lashed amid the supplies below and used it for a ram, and the racket they made must have been heard on shore. Perhaps the Indians were reluctant to be first to show their heads above the coaming, for not more than one could appear at a time in the narrow opening and they knew I was armed. A few spears came whistling at random through the opening, seeking a victim but finding none. One stuck in the table not far from my head, but the rest clattered harmlessly upon the deck.

Nevertheless my heart gave a great bound when I saw the stout timbers splinter. A moment later the door burst inwards, and I could see the group of them huddled in the passageway beyond, Westlake wisely holding them back.

For an instant they stood staring into the topsy-turvy cabin, not seeing me or my companion under the table, but not missing the great splotch of blood upon the deck, under the hatchway. They only saw me, crouched in the shadows, when I spoke.

"Come around the edge," I called. "Stand clear of the hatch. I think they're afraid of the guns."

They came in, one by one, passing left and right, so as to work around the cabin walls, and I swallowed as I watched them. There was Westlake, of course, then the lank, spare figure of James Thorn, the captain's brother, who had been acting as second mate. These were unhurt, so far as I could see. Mike Shea's scalp, however, was matted with blood, and little Charles Roberts had been cut about the neck and shoulders, while George Bell and Peter Verbel, cooper and seaman respectively, showed signs of savage fighting. One of Bell's eyes had been thumbed from its socket, and his face was streaked with blood, while Verbel's ear was all but torn from his head. Were these, I wondered, all that were left?

"You know where the arms are kept," I called to Westlake as he entered. "If you'll serve them out, I'll stand guard."

He nodded, without stopping to speak, and passed into the captain's cabin, returning in a moment with an assortment of pistols and muskets, powder horns and shot pouches. These he doled out quietly, one by one, to the men. Not until this was done did he catch sight of my companion.

"Great God!" he cried.

"Aye!" I replied. "You'd not think it, but he lives!"

I saw him swallow.

"God knows what we can do for him," he said. " 'Twill be little enough until we have cleared the ship."

"What do you intend?" I asked.

" 'Tis the devil and all that we're below hatches," he replied. "Yet we may do it! Fraser's aloft, you know. So's that half-blood, what d'ye call him—Charbonneau?"

I caught my breath.

"Alive?"

"And kicking, last I saw." He nodded. "I don't know how they can help, but at least they'll be two more at the final count. I've a notion Adam Fisher is somewhere in the rigging as well."

"All right," I said. "What do we do?"

"Let me go forward," he told me, "with three of these. You that are left here open fire through the hatchway, to give them the notion you mean to sortie. When we hear the firing start, we'll give time for those that may be covering the forward hatch to turn their attention aft. Then we'll rush the deck there and, if we can make it, get to the fo'c'sle swivels."

" 'Tis worth a try," I told him. "If you can turn the swivels upon them, it should draw their attention from us. When we hear the guns forward, we'll make a break here and try for the after swivels. If we get them between our fire, the ship should be ours. Are you sure the guns are loaded?"

"I saw to them myself only yesterday," he assured me, "and they've not once been fired since."

"Too bad we didn't know that before," I said acidly.

"It would have made no difference." He shrugged. "There was no chance to come at them without guns in our hands."

I realized the sense of that. But now a counterattack with small arms might well disconcert them and allow us the instant we needed to turn the guns on them. I nodded, and Westlake made his choice, picking the soundest—Mike Shea, James Thorn, and Peter Verbel. That was agreeable to me. After all, they would bear the brunt of the action.

Together they slipped through the shattered bulkhead after a whispered good luck, and we in the great cabin waited, each crouching behind some bit of cover, holding our breaths and counting the ticks of the captain's chronometer in its rosewood case upon the table above. One minute, two, I let pass, and then on the third it seemed to me they had ample time to get forward and ready. I gave the signal and we began to fire up through the hatchway, not all at once in a volley, but one after another, singly, in the fashion of Indian fighters, so that each had a chance to reload while the others fired. In this way we kept a steady, even, accelerated stream of lead flying up through the hatchway, tearing splinters off the coaming, and suggesting that we were readying a concerted rush.

Our fire, it seemed to me, had creditable order, and apparently it aroused some confusion on deck. Whether the savages had had the foresight to station any of their number about the foreward hatchway, as Westlake thought they might, I do not know. If so, at our fire they turned and ran aft to meet us. Simultaneously, at the sound of our shots, Westlake and his comrades burst from their hiding place upon their rear, emptying their pistols among the savages with good effect, then swinging round the swivels mounted at the break of the fo'c'sle and blasting them at point-blank range.

We below, in turn, so soon as we heard the bark of the four-pounders, scrambled for the ladder and spewed fighting out upon the deck. Even as we had hoped, the Indians, taken by surprise with the attack upon their rear, had been thrown into confusion, enabling us to scramble in our turn to the after swivels and bring them to bear upon the naked mob. I paused only long enough to point my gun and flash the priming of my pistol at the touchhole. There was a crack and a roar, and I could hear the vicious whine and rattle of the langrage as it slashed across the waist and rattled upon the farther bulwark. Screams, howls of pain and terror answered, but for an instant the smoke was such that I could not see what damage had been done. Then the wind caught and rent the gray, swirling curtain, first lifting a corner, then tearing it abruptly away.

IV. ABANDON SHIP

TO MY amazement, save for a huddle of bodies, the deck was empty. When I looked overside canoes were flying from us in every direction. A few lay overturned close by, but their crews were not troubling to wait and right them. The water was acrawl with the heads of men and women, swimming with might and main for shore and cover. Half-a-dozen bodies were strewn in the water near us, one or two kicking feebly. The rest, both red and white, were ominously still, and there were crimson threads and a spreading stain in the water about each one. Some, especially the whites, who had apparently been thrown over to the waiting women, were mutilated in such a manner as to make my stomach turn over. Cautiously I looked back upon the deck. Westlake and the three seamen were forward, busily reloading their swivels, while across from me Roberts and Bell struggled to bring a six-pounder to bear upon the fleeing canoes. As I watched, Alan Fraser and Charbonneau slipped from the forward rigging and ran to assist Westlake and his crew, and at the same time a voice in my ear startled me near out of my wits.

"Handsome work, Misteh O'Rou'ke, suh!"

I whirled to find Adam Fisher, a Norfolk sailor, tugging at the swivel.

"Where did you drop from?" I demanded in surprise.

He glanced aloft.

"Mizzen riggin'," he replied. "On'iest place the' was. I skinned up the' in a herry, you bet!"

We sent a couple of parting shots after the fleeing canoes, more to show them that we were still capable of fighting than from any hope of doing serious damage at such range. After that we paused long enough to count noses and lick our wounds. Out of thirty-three on board, twenty-one had been killed outright. One, the clerk, James Lewis, had been so desperately wounded that it was a miracle that he still lived; and one, the Indian interpreter, Kasciascall, had simply disappeared. Of the remaining ten I think there were no more than three or four who had escaped entirely unscathed. Charbonneau had had the flesh of his forearm torn by a hurled fish spear, and Fraser had sustained a knife slash from mid-thigh to knee that miraculously had severed no arteries when he leapt for the main shrouds. Only Fisher, apparently, had escaped aloft unseen in the melee.

"Moose and I got three of the fish-eating bastards," Fraser reported. "God sakes! It's a shambles down here!"

"Do you think they'll be back?" I demanded.

"Not so long as they think we've powder and shot," Westlake replied. "Not for a while anyway. But we're in no shape to stay here, and I'd hesitate to take the old hooker to sea in this weather."

He nodded toward the inlet, where we could see the white breakers marching steadily against the jagged rocks.

"She'd not live to gain sea room in that," he said. " 'Tis a wonder she floats at all! There are whole sections of her timbers beaten so soft by that crack she took upon the reefs that I can all but put my fist through them. She ought to be careened, but we've small chance of any such thing now!"

"Not even to save our necks?" I demanded.

"Would you skip from the griddle into the coals?" he asked.

I ran my eye across the deck where the savages lay tumbled in grotesque, bloody heaps, with here and there a white hand thrust out like a trailing claw.

"We might have known 'twould come to this," the younger Thorn growled. "Jon always did think he knew better than anyone else. He got his, and no mistake!"

Westlake shook himself impatiently.

"Come, man!" he cried. "We've no time for that!"

Thorn shrugged.

"There's always the longboat," he said, thinking aloud.

Westlake glanced first at me and then at Fraser.

"She wouldn't carry us all," he said flatly. "Anyway, we've more important things to occupy us! Mr. Thorn, let's clear the decks and see how we stand! Get these red devils overside. You'd best roll our own in canvas—weighted. Make sure 'tis secure. After that have the guns shotted and trained ashore in the best posture to repel attack. If you can, you might see the boarding nets rigged——"

"Shutting the cage when the bird has flown?" Thorn grumbled.

"Attend to orders, Mr. Thorn," Westlake snapped. I wondered if the tendency were congenital among naval officers.

Westlake turned to Fraser.

"Get those sails furled!" He glanced aloft where the canvas hung as it had been left. "They'll do no good like that. When you're done aloft, you and Charbonneau might try to rescue one of those canoes and some of the paddles. You know more about that than any of us. They might come in handy. Fetch 'em in on the seaward side and don't let the savages know what you're up to if you can help it."

I saw Fraser draw back and open his mouth, but fortunately I caught his eye and shook my head. With exaggerated resignation he subsided.

"Aye, *aye*—sir!"

Westlake half-grinned humorlessly.

"For the sake of all our necks," he said, " 'twill be as well to work together."

Fraser nodded briefly. Westlake glanced at Shea and myself.

"Will you look below?" he asked.

"Lead the way," I said.

We followed him into the gloom of the main cabin.

I was as well pleased that the task of cleaning up above decks fell to the others. As it was, working below was not a happy business. Doors banged disconsolately along the passages, forgotten in the general activity, sending hollow claps and rappings through the ship. Sadly, as if she were weary of her earthly lot, the vessel groaned in all her timbers as she rolled gently in the long swell that came drifting in from seaward. And there was Lewis who had, somehow or other, regained consciousness, and who lay now underneath the table, moaning piteously, sucking in his breath between his teeth with a harsh, almost snoring sound; then letting it out in a long, gusty, sibilant sigh. It seemed to me extraordinary that he should live at all with such a wound; that he should remain conscious and capable of understanding all that was said was little less than a miracle. He steadfastly refused to cry out as we lifted him to the table, for all it was plain to see he must be in the most excruciating agony, and it came to me that there were qualities in the man I had never before appreciated. On the table Westlake tenderly turned his head upon its good side and pillowed it upon a cushion from the captain's cabin. Nonetheless Lewis cried out involuntarily against the movement and momentarily fainted. Blood spilled across the table as the stopper on his arm came away. Both Shea and I snatched at the stump, and when I reached it first, he made offer of his belt to replace the kerchief I had used—a far better article for the purpose since it could be buckled tight.

After that we worked more swiftly. I set Shea to heat a bucket of pitch upon the galley stove and then turned to help Westlake complete a makeshift job of trephining; using an inverted wooden bowl as a cap across the gaping hole in the man's skull and fixing it securely in place with straps and bandages from the medicine chest. By the time we had finished, Lewis was conscious once more, and the pitch was ready. So that he could not see what I was about, I stood between his head and shoulder as Shea fetched up the bubbling boiling bucket and held it ready. I steeled myself and plunged the stump of arm in the boiling fluid, at once to stem the bleeding and form a cap upon the wounded place. Lewis uttered a scream that choked off, bubbling horribly, and once more fainted dead away, which may have been a blessing for him but was only a nuisance to me, for I could not tell if the dressing I then applied were comfortable or if it merely added to his pain.

With the most serious of our wounded attended to, we turned our attention to the others. None of these were nearly so serious. Bell's gouged-out eye offered the most grave problem. When it would not slip back easily into place we did what any naval surgeon would have done and snipped the retaining tendons with a pair of the cook's shears, dressing the empty socket with a compress moistened with madeira. Poor man, I think he, too, would have fainted had we not shamed him by telling him how bravely Lewis, so much more terribly injured, had withstood our ministrations.

For the rest, there was nothing that a little clumsy stitching and washing and bandaging would not take care of temporarily. Nevertheless, when we were done, we looked a patchwork crew of ragamuffins. Mike Shea, as I recall, was the last to be tended to, and I was washing the matted blood out of his hair, snipping about the edges of the long gash that had laid open his scalp from temple to ear, when he cocked an eye up at me through the bloody water.

" 'Tis comin' dusk," he said.

Surprised, I glanced up. Sure enough night was coming on. I called Westlake's attention to it, and he swore mildly.

"The devil!" he complained. " 'Tis always so. Whether the fight lasts longer than you think or the cleaning up afterwards is more a chore, the dark comes on too fast. We must see to our defenses; let them know we are still watchful, then make up our minds what we're to do before it comes dark."

He summoned the younger Thorn.

"Leave two men to watch," he ordered. "Fetch the rest below here."

The captain's brother departed with ill grace. It was, I could see, a family trait. Nonetheless he was back in a few moments with the others, leaving Fisher and Verbel to stand the first watch. When we were assembled, Westlake addressed us.

"Well, gentlemen," he said, "we're all in this together. What's to be done? The vessel's not fit for sea. There are ten of us able-bodied and Mr. Lewis too sore hurt to bear a hand. If the ship were sound, I'd not hang back, for I've been to sea with fewer hands. As it is—any suggestions?"

"There's always the longboat," Thorn said darkly once more.

"I heard you before," Westlake retorted. "You heard my answer."

Fraser was rubbing his chin.

"Mr. Fraser?" Westlake demanded.

The red-haired Scot considered the deck planking.

"We fetched in one of those canoes," he said slowly. "Nothing wrong with her that I can see. We got paddles for her too—almost a dozen of 'em. She's built to hold eight or ten, but four could handle her easy enough. We moored her alongside to seaward. I don't think any o' the redskins caught sight of us."

"Thank you, Mr. Fraser," said Westlake curtly. "That may be the answer. If we delay too long here, there's not much doubt they'll come after us in force. Unless I miss my guess they're already gathering, and guns or boarding nets, notwithstanding, they need only put fire aboard to roast us out."

"Aye," growled Thorn. "That's what I mean."

"Then how's it to be done?" asked Westlake.

Fraser hitched at his belt with a characteristic gesture.

"For me," he said, "I'd choose to go in the canoe. 'Tis a craft I'm more familiar with."

"Ouai! An' me—Moose!" put in Charbonneau.

Westlake nodded, scowling.

"That's fair enough. You'll be better than any of us in such craft. You, Thorn. You'd best take most of the seamen, Verbel, Fisher, Roberts, and Bell, in the longboat. I'll take charge of the canoe with Fraser, O'Rourke, Shea, and Carbonneau."

"Charge, is it?" demanded Fraser. "What makes you think you're qualified to handle a canoe?"

Westlake grinned at him. Nonetheless his reply surprised me.

"Maybe you're right," he said. "We'll solve the matter by letting O'Rourke here command—I'll simply navigate."

Thorn's shifty eyes glinted his satisfaction.

"Well, then!" he cried. "Let's be off!"

"One minute!" snapped Westlake. "Let's not forget that so long as we're aboard ship, here, I still command."

"Who's to take Lewis?" I demanded.

I don't think it had occurred to any of us that Lewis himself might be listening. Frankly I doubt if any of us expected him to regain consciousness at all.

"Don't—worry—about me," he said faintly.

We whirled. He was gazing at us out of pain-filled eyes.

"The devil!" cried Westlake. "You go with us in the canoe."

Lewis looked at me.

"D'you think there's room?"

"Plenty." I nodded. "If the craft is as big as Alan says 'tis. If not, we'll make room."

Lewis started to shake his head and winced with pain.

"No!" he gasped, then closed his eyes and was silent for so long that we thought he must have fainted again.

"But——" Westlake began.

Lewis's eyes flew open again.

"No!" he repeated more strongly. "Don't be a fool, Roger! You—you're not a man—to abandon—a shipmate. Th—that I know. But——" He drew a long breath. "I know when the game's up!"

"Nonsense!" scoffed Westlake. "Why——"

Lewis made a feeble gesture with his good hand.

"No use, Roger," he said. "Let's not—delude ourselves. With—a—hole—like this in my—noggin and a—flipper gone—to boot, I'd not last—till you—put me—in the boat, let alone—get clear—to Astoria. That's where—you're going?"

Westlake glanced round at the rest of us.

"I—I guess so," he said. "Unless some of you think Chitka, to the north."

"Too far," said Thorn. "Astoria's the best."

On the table Lewis sighed.

"It doesn't—matter, Chitka—Astoria—I'd never make either!"

"You'd never!" began Westlake.

Lewis smiled slightly.

"Aye!" he said, "I'd never—so—put—it—out of your thoughts. Besides—there's a thing—I'd—yet do!"

"No!" cried Westlake. "What sort of beasts d'you think us? That we'd leave you to the pleasure of those savages? I grant 'tis a long chance. But at least you'll be among friends!"

Lewis raised pale eyebrows and rolled his head again slightly, as if to shake it, and winced.

"No, no! Look—I cannot even move—my head! Let me have—my way, man! Lay me a slow train—to the magazine and put a slow match—in my hand. When—they come aboard—as sure they will—after you've left, I'll be away to glory—but—not—alone!"

We stared at one another, scarcely knowing whether to laugh or cry; to be proud of him or shamed for ourselves; half of a mind to fall in with his proposal, partly because we knew his case hopeless, but mostly for the sake of our own skins, yet at the same time feeling a sense of shame for even thinking of it. It was simple, yet magnificent. It was bold. It held the kind of heroism that leads men to die alone, unsung, even unnoticed for the sake of their fellows. It also had a quality which we dared not admit even to ourselves. It was practical, and I think each of us recognized it. Neither in the longboat nor the canoe could we carry him to safety, and it was an undeniable fact that he must be a desperate hindrance, even an actual danger to the party that assumed responsibility for him. Yet I think that not more than one or two yet harbored the thought. Thorn, I recall, growled.

"For God's sake! He's right! Let him make his own choice!"

But Fraser turned upon him.

"Shut up, you!" he snarled.

Thorn fell back against the ladder.

"Take him in the canoe then, if you're so set on it," he said.

There was a long silence in which we stared at one another, each wondering how we could solve this problem, until abruptly our attention was fetched back to the table by a scrabbling sound. Lewis had wrenched himself upright and dropped his legs over the edge of the board and was standing there, with feet braced wide, leaning, half-sitting, steadying himself with his one hand. His face was livid with pain, his eyes glazed. Sweat stood out on his forehead as if he had lifted it to a drenching rain.

"No!" he cried hoarsely. "No! I will have no—comrade's—blood upon—my—head! If ye will not—— Then 'twill not be—too hard to solve!"

He lurched toward the ladder, at the same time clawing at the bandages that bound his head. Two, three steps he took. I saw a crimson stain appear at the edge of the white binding. Several of us sprang forward to catch him. But Mike Shea was first at his side, and even as he reached him, Lewis's knees buckled under him, and he fell fainting against the bos'n. Shea caught him and eased him gently to the deck; knelt to examine him.

"Sure he's passed out again!" he said.

Westlake shook his head grimly, his face white.

"Poor devil!" he echoed. "Fetch him back!"

When we had done so, we replaced the cushion from the captain's cabin underneath his head and covered him with a blanket. Westlake meantime paced up and down the cabin with his thumbs in his belt, looking in turn at each of us.

"Well?" he demanded.

Only Alan Fraser had the courage to speak.

"There's a deal of truth in what he says."

Thorn snorted darkly.

"I wonder you've the sense to see it at last!"

Fraser merely cocked his fist and moved toward him. I interposed, turning to Thorn.

"Are you so dim-witted you cannot see we recognize the fact?" I demanded. "At the same time we've a reluctance you don't seem to share to abandon a shipmate. 'Tis not in my book of friendship!"

Thorn flushed darkly.

"Nor in mine!" he retorted. "If there were the least chance to save him, I'd be the last to see him left. But the man must die in any case, and to fetch him along might well endanger the lives of all. Are we to sacrifice ten for the sake of one? Do as he says! Give him his match and let him go to glory in his own way. 'Tis kinder so to him and better for the rest!"

"Ah, you foul scut!" raged Fraser.

He lunged, and I could not hold him, but Thorn avoided him, skipping quickly aside, and placed the table with its injured man between him and the angry Scot.

Westlake came to my assistance.

"Hold on!" he cried. "Maybe we have no choice. At least we've other matters to attend to. We'd best be at them."

From the far side of the table Thorn spoke boldly.

"Aye! Settle it among yourselves, for I wash my hands of it! If he goes, 'twill not be in the longboat, and for my part I mean to be far from here by dawn. Bell and Roberts! I'll need your help with the boat. Mr. Westlake, I'll appreciate it if you'll put one of your own people to share the watch. 'Tis hardly fair the whole task should fall to my crew."

I could see Westlake flush, but it seemed to me he kept his temper admirably. The fact that he held himself in check and answered reasonably was indication enough to me that he kept his humanitarian instincts uppermost.

"All right!" he said. "Shea, will you relieve Fisher and tell him to report to Mr. Thorn at once?"

"Aye, aye, sir!" replied Shea smartly. He went up the ladder quickly, and Westlake turned to the rest of us.

"The watch," he said shortly, "will be relieved every two hours until we are ready to abandon ship. At the least sign that the natives are on the move, the watch will give the alarm. In case of alarm each man will go to his station. No one will fire until I give the signal. In case of a concerted attack, unless the ship is actually being boarded, once commenced, you will keep up as rapid a fire as possible with both your guns and your small arms so long as you can see a target. If you can't see a target, don't waste your ammunition! Is that clear?"

Each one of us nodded.

"Good!" said Westlake curtly. "One more point before I assign you to stations: In the event we are boarded, you are to do the best you can to clear the decks with the swivels, small arms, and cutlasses, which I will distribute. I don't need to remind you what our chances will be should that happen. It will be best to see it does not happen. I think you understand me!"

He opened the arms chest and fetched forth belts and cutlasses which he passed out to us. At the same time he assigned us in pairs to the six-pounders, alternating pairs starboard and larboard so that both flanks might be guarded. When he was done, he glanced at Thorn.

"Is that satisfactory, Mr. Thorn?" he asked dryly.

The captain's brother shrugged.

"Very well!" Westlake accepted the gesture as acquiescence. "I suggest that you send Fisher down for arms and instructions. I'll do the same for Shea."

"Suits me!" said Thorn, and set one foot upon the ladder.

"Just a minute, mister!" Westlake barked. "I'm not finished. We've not yet decided on supplies or a course to steer."

Thorn whirled, standing with one hand on the ladder.

"What's to settle about that?" he demanded. "As to supplies, let the commander of each boat see to them. I know what's needed and I'll see to my craft. You look to yours! As for the course, where's the difficulty? We'll probably be separated as soon as we're outside, if not before. Once clear of the inlet I mean to take a course south-southeast a quarter east till I fetch the coast of Oregon. What more's to say, I ask ye?"

Westlake shrugged.

"Please yourself!" he said. "But mind you this, Mr. Thorn, I and the partners at Astoria will hold you responsible for the lives of those entrusted to you!"

"If any of us come there alive," Thorn sneered, "I doubt 'twill be questioned how 'twas done!"

Since it was obvious that there would be neither co-operation nor assistance from him, those of us who were to go in the canoe set to our own preparations. Fraser and myself looked to the canoe, while Westlake and the Moose began the collection of necessary provisions: two breakers of water, a cask of ship's biscuit, and one of salt pork and the like. Because of the construction and size of the craft we were to make our attempt in, it was impossible to take as much as we would have liked, and this handicapped us considerably. Moreover, for the canoe, at least, it was necessary to fashion a mast and stays, a sail and sea anchor. Fortunately we had a good choice of paddles. Still it was thought best to rig thole pins and ship oars in case we needed them. Tarpaulins and lines, a compass, and at Charbonneau's insistence axes and a hatchet, a pair of kettles, and straps for tumplines, in the event we were forced ashore, were added. In addition there was our personal gear, little enough for each of us, for we dared to take with us only what would be most useful besides our fishing gear, arms, and ammunition, trusting to the clothes that covered us to see us to our journey's end. A roll of blankets apiece completed the lading.

As I have pointed out, however, in the case of the canoe in particular, all of this took time. Since it carried no mast of its own, a thwart must be bored for one, and a step and braces must be improvised to hold it steady. Tholes had to be bored and pins hastily whittled out and set; a number of cleats placed along the gunnels to which sheets and braces, sea anchor, and the like might be secured. All this must be done in the dark.

In the case of the longboat, which was kept always equipped with a minimum of gear and supplies against emergency, much less was necessary. As a result Thorn and his companions were ready to leave long before the rest of us, and he took small pains to conceal his impatience. For a long time we ignored him, largely because our own tasks kept us too busy to pay much attention. But matters came to a head toward midnight, when the tide turned and began to ebb.

"By God!" Thorn cried, storming down into the cabin. "Ye'll be all night about this, and I for one have no mind to be here when day breaks."

"No more have I," Westlake told him calmly.

"The tide's turned and is setting out," Thorn ranted. "Even with its help 'twill take an hour or more to reach the inlet. My boat's ready and I mean to go."

Westlake flushed and drew in his breath, I have no doubt to make some sharp retort, but I put out my hand and stopped him.

"Let them go!" I said. "They're ready, and he's right. Those that can escape should lose no time. Besides, matters will be simpler when he's no longer here to make trouble!"

"Very well," he said grimly. "Get your men overside, Mr. Thorn. The rest of us will cover your departure!"

It was a luminous night, moonless, but not dark as we would have preferred it, rather faintly starlit by the brightly studded skies, across the face of which the wispy clouds raced from seaward. So far we had been untroubled by visitors. Our own craft lay moored securely alongside, toward the sea, lying in the ship's shadow and hidden from view ashore by the hull, so that we were reasonably sure its presence was undetected. However, since the booms were to shoreward, it was necessary to lower away the longboat on that side. There was naught we could do but see the blocks well oiled, the tholes muffled, and everything arranged on board to receive her people as silently as possible, then lower away, holding our breaths the while.

So far as I could tell, not a sound escaped her as she settled in the water. Ashore not a dog barked, not a whisper sounded. Only far away, in the hills behind the village, an owl hooted. One by one Thorn and his comrades slipped over the side, each pausing to shake hands with the rest of us as he went. But one of them stumbled over an oar, raising a clatter that woke the echoes and set us all to cursing under our breaths.

For painful seconds we crouched tense, listening for a hint that the Indians suspected what we were about. But no sound came, and after an instant we relaxed.

"Are you ready?" Westlake whispered.

"Aye!" came Thorn's low growl in response.

"All clear, then, so far as we can see. Cast off when you are ready. Good luck."

"Aye!" said Thorn again, and as if in response the dark gap between the black blob of the boat and the shadow of the ship's side widened. We saw the oars thrust out and begin to swing, moving with ghostly silence in the gloom. For a moment we could make out her vague outlines, creeping like a great black bug across the oily waters, and then she was swallowed up in the darkness.

Those of us who remained on board were well aware that we could lose no precious seconds of our time. We were familiar with the brief span of those northern summer nights; and the truth of Thorn's remark about the tide had not been lost upon us. We must leave the *Tonquin* as quickly as we could lest we be caught there, for, reduced in numbers as we now were, such an event would be fatal.

"What about lights?" I whispered. "The ship's dark now. Shouldn't we keep her so?"

"Why?" Westlake asked.

"The boat!" I replied, perhaps a little impatiently. "She's gone. If, by chance, she was seen, they'll not know now that any of us are left on board!"

I could feel him staring at me.

"I see," he said slowly. "So they'll follow her and leave us to slip away unseen. Is that it?"

"That's it!" I assured him eagerly.

"You don't mean that," he said, not unkindly.

I felt myself flush.

"I—I—well, I——" I stammered.

"Don't let it upset you," he told me. "I know. You didn't stop to think. But now you have, you know they're entitled to all the help we can give them. If she wasn't seen and the ship suddenly goes dark, the Indians are not fools. They'll know she's gone. But if we show a light, they might not guess it."

"That's true," I was forced to agree.

"So we'll cover them," he said. "But so far as we are concerned I can think of a better reason."

"What do you mean?" I asked.

"If the ship is dark and the Indians think we were gone, they'll come out to board. Had you thought of that now?"

"No!" I exclaimed, startled. "I hadn't!"

"Aye!" I heard him chuckle. "And the longer it takes them to discover our departure, the further we'll be upon the road!"

Shea hissed from the break of the fo'c'sle.

"Mr. Westlake, sir! Look sharp over forninst the shore!"

We turned back. With eyes by now accustomed to the darkness I searched the shadowy line where the forests came down to the water's edge, but I could see nothing until Westlake jogged my arm and hissed in my ear.

"Look! Broad on the larboard bow! There! See them, slipping along the shore?"

Given a point, I could pick them up quickly enough: the bulk of a half-a-dozen war canoes, which must have been three times the size of the one we planned to leave in. They were moving along silently, swiftly, heading in general down the sound, toward the inlet and the open sea. Each one of them, I thought, must carry thirty or forty warriors.

"They must have seen the boat when she left," Westlake growled. "Else they've set a guard at the entrance and these are bound out to relieve them."

"Well, for God's sake, let's fire then!" I cried. "With luck we should deal them some damage. At least the shots will serve as a warning to the boat!"

I must have spoken louder that I realized, for the words were not out of my mouth before the larboard swivels flashed almost in unison and I could hear the scream of the langrage as it swept across the water.

Not more than the tick of a second after came the roar of a six-pounder forward.

I think we must have caught at least one of the craft, for there was a sudden pandemonium of howling and screaming and we could hear splashing and shouts and groans. But the flash of the guns momentarily blinded us, and by the time we had regained our owl's eyes we could find no sign of them anywhere.

We were not troubled again after that, and we went about our various tasks in comparative peace. Nonetheless we kept one of us always at the lookout and saw to it that the guns were shotted and primed, the lanterns moved frequently, and every now and then we would pause to hail one another from poop to fo'c'sle, or vice versa, or indulge in a flurry of hammering, as if we were engaged in repairs. Ever and anon we would stop, too, to hold our breath and listen.

The tide was close to the turn, however, before we were ready at last. It was yet full dark, but the smell of morning was in the air. Fortunately for us the wind had turned and was drifting in from the sea, fetching with it long streamers of fog to mingle with the mists that rose like gray wraiths from the water. Ashore it crawled amid the forest trees, while on board it twined clammy fingers in the rigging and ever and again grew thick enough to hide the black loom of the land. In general we could not ask better conditions for what we meant to do, unless we were to pray for a few more hours of darkness. But since this was out of the question, we must move swiftly and make the most of what remained to us.

This final moment, for all of that, fetched us at last to the problem we had sought to postpone. Twice in the night Mr. Lewis had regained consciousness, only to struggle to a sitting posture and then lapse off again. Obviously he was growing weaker, and it was actually a grave question whether, if we dared to move him so far, he would live until we fetched him into the canoe. But now we were ready, it was time to face the responsibility squarely. We stationed Charbonneau on deck as the sharpest-eyed of us all; the rest of us dropped into the cabin to fetch him or to leave him, as the decision might be.

Lewis himself endeavored to settle the question. He opened his eyes as we came down the ladder.

"I've been waiting, lads," he said. " 'Tis no use!"

"Nonsense——" growled Westlake.

"No, no!" Lewis interrupted him, almost pleadingly, speaking with a visible effort. "Hear me out! I ask you—as a favor. If you think—on it—as I have, 'twill be clear—I have not long to live. If I go—I must die and—what will ye do? Will ye leave me alone—to be dug up and gnawed by wolves, to wander alone in the outer dark? What choice—would ye have? No, no! You can't! I cannot tell better than yourselves what comes to a man when he goes on beyond—but I like to think he does not walk alone. I see no reason to disbelieve—the savage notion—that a man's soul is waited on—by the souls of the enemies he has slain! I want company on the voyage I've got to take—lads! Since I must go—I've set myself to it. Then let me go my own way! I beg ye! Please! Good friends! If I don't take a hundred of them with me—there'll be none left for the wolves! Come, friends! Ye'd not deny a dying man's last wish?"

We stared at one another. To me it seemed he must be wandering. Yet there was truth in what he said. I saw Fraser swallow.

"He puts it to us fair," he said.

"Aye!" Westlake nodded, and his voice was harsh.

They both looked at me.

"What do you say?"

I glanced at Lewis, and it seemed to me his eyes were smiling.

I squared my shoulders.

"Since you put it up to me," I said, "I cannot help but think he is more reasonable than us all. God forgive me! I say let him have his way!"

So in the end it was I who cast the deciding vote. Had I been in a like case, I believe—indeed, I hope—I would have asked the same, and it was on this I based the decision.

We lost no time setting about our final preparations. Two of us gently moved him to a place amidships where he would be able to see and hear the Indians as they came on board, while at the same time he himself would be hidden, or, at worst, inconspicuous. This was below decks, for we could arrange the powder train only upon the level of the magazine. The train itself we laid carefully, running the grains in a thick ribbon around the bulkheads and along crevices, away from any ordinary track of passage, so that there would be no likelihood they would be scattered by passing feet. Inside the magazine room we made assurance doubly sure by dumping out a whole cask upon the floor and arranging a dozen others in a sort of pyramid over the glistening black pile.

When we were done, we returned where we had left Lewis. He was awake.

"Thank God, good lads!" he said. "God keep you!"

We lit a slow match and stuck it in a seam, close by his hand amid the powder, so that if, by chance, he should faint or die before the savages came on board it would in due time burn its own way down and touch off the train. At the same time, should they discover him, a quick movement of his hand would suffice.

In silence we wrung his hand, one by one, and hurried above. While we had been at work, Shea and Charbonneau had set themselves to hanging lanterns at points of vantage, cleverly, so that they swung to the ship's motion and for a time, at least, would give the impression that there were yet folk aboard and moving about.

It was not light, but there was a faint thinning of the darkness as we slipped down the ropes into the waiting canoe. I cannot describe the feeling of sadness and regret, almost of guilt, with which we left the *Tonquin*, creaking in the slight roll of the sound. For an instant she loomed above us, her masts and spars limned sharp against the scud, her hull half-shrouded in the creeping fingers of the fog. Then we bent to our paddles.

Charbonneau as steersman kept the ship between us and the village for as long as possible. We coasted silently along the shore, hearing only the sigh of the tide amid the rocks, the gentle whisper of the branches of the overhanging trees as they trembled in the wind. Somewhere, far off in the mountains, a wolf howled, and faintly from below came the persistent muffled thunder of the breakers at the entrance. We were a mile from the *Tonquin* and there was a definite hint now of morning in the graying dusk, when we were startled by the sound of voices in the fog ahead. Fraser, in the bow, held up his hand.

"Indians!" he hissed warningly.

We stopped paddling and sat motionless, listening. Over the sound of the occasional voices coming toward us from the direction of the entrance we could hear yet another, a sort of moaning, keening, terrified sobbing that stirred the hackles at the backs of our necks.

Hastily Charbonneau lay back upon his paddle, swinging our bow toward a tiny cove that notched the line of overhanging forest. At the same instant his whisper, urgent, desperate though it was, barely carried to the bow.

"Paddle!" he commanded fiercely.

With one thought we bent to our blades, not lifting them from the water lest the drip betray us.

"Praise God for the fog!" muttered Westlake. " 'Tis thickened!"

"Hisshhh!" warned Charbonneau ominously.

Under the blessed cover we slipped into the little bay, seeking the shore line, frantically nosing for a rock or an overhanging bough with which to hide ourselves. Only at the last instant had we the luck to find the half-dead crown of a great wind-blown cedar lying out at an angle from the bank, thrusting its branches, yet half-covered with green-brown needles, forty feet into the cove. Behind this we slid and crouched low, sitting still as death, only partly screened, it seemed to me, from the outer sound. Indeed, sitting there, squinting seaward through the branches, as still as a deer must stand as the hunter passes, I felt as naked as a babe upon the day of his birth. If they glance our way, I thought, they must surely see us, for they passed within a few rods—two war canoes, slipping along the shore toward the village, each carrying thirty or forty men. And though we could not see them, for they must have been bound and flung like meal sacks in the bottom, yet from the sounds that rose it was clear that they had with them our comrades of the longboat. Surely enough, these were scarcely past when the longboat itself went by, clumsily manned by six laughing savages.

For a long time, perhaps half an hour, we sat still as stone behind our sheltering log. Charbonneau spoke at last, voicing something of what was in all our minds.

"*Deux canôts* an' six hommes in longboat! Dere be deux canôts, maybe t'ree, still at entrance. Dat fog, she's lif'!"

In the bow I heard Fraser swear under his breath.

"You needn't sound so goddamned cheerful about it!"

There was silence for a moment, so complete that I could faintly hear Westlake swallow.

"What d'you think we ought to do?"

"Take to the woods," said Fraser. "What d'ye think, O'Rourke?"

For the second time they had called upon me to decide. Somehow their faith in my judgment bolstered me.

"We certainly can't get to sea," I replied.

They nodded.

"On the other hand," I went on, "close as we are to the village, overland is like to be as bad. We'd best go to ground."

"How?" Westlake asked.

I pointed down the sound.

"There's a little island under the point yonder," I told him. "I noticed it as we came in. It can't be more than an acre, and 'tis rocky and wooded all over. At the same time 'tis so small it might well be overlooked if they should search for us. They'd have to bring dogs from the main, even then, and I doubt they'd think of that, not with all the other islands in the bay. If it comes to that, 'tis small enough for a stout defense. I say let's try to get ashore there. If the fog holds only a bit longer, we should be able to do it. We can hide the canoe in the underbrush and lie out ourselves until night, when we can decide what's next to be done."

The others exchanged approving glances.

"If 'tis me ye're askin'," Shea remarked, "I tell ye 'tis not good! But I see the point. We be beggermen, be Jasus, an' we can't be choosin'!"

"That's right," said Fraser.

Westlake and Charbonneau nodded.

We watched for a thickening of the fog, which was coming in now in patches, and under cover of it slipped out from our hiding place, crossed the cove, and sneaked along the shore and around the point to a tiny bay upon the island I had noticed from the *Tonquin* as we entered.

We were not a moment too soon, for we had no more than hidden our canoe under a heap of windfallen timber and were seeking cover for ourselves, when yet another war canoe swept past, coming in from seaward, filled with savages all in high good humor.

It was broad morning now, and we dropped flat as our ears first caught warning of their approach. They must have passed within fifty feet of our island, but never so much as glanced our way. Yet we lay still long after they had gone. By the time we dared move, the fog had been blown aside, and we could see the ship lying over against the shore, between us and the village. And we could see the smoke of fires plainly, blue-gray, as it rose against the dark green of the forest.

Apparently they were preparing for something, we could not see what. Yet we could guess. And presently our ears confirmed it. Toward midmorning a faint but unmistakable, shuddering scream rose from across the bay, sending the cold prickles chasing goose flesh all up and down our spines.

"I Jesus! I knew we should have attacked the canoe!" Fraser growled.

Westlake shook his head.

" 'Twould not serve," he replied. "We'd have done them no good and only sacrificed ourselves."

"The devil you say!" cried the Cock-of-the-Woods. "We'd have caught 'em by surprise."

"On their very doorstep, with others coming in behind, and the village in hail?" replied the mate. "In the end they'd have had us all for their sport!"

He was answered by another blood-chilling scream, followed by another and yet another. Fraser did not trouble to retort but swung round and squinted across the top of our log, fingering his musket.

"The devils!" he gritted.

Charbonneau stepped quietly across, stooping low, and plucked the gun from his fingers. Fraser stared round in surprise.

"Wha—what the devil?" he demanded. "By God! Give me back——"

Charbonneau held out the weapon to Westlake who laid it beside him. The old half-breed grinned.

"*Alors!*" he said. "*Ca va mieux!* Goddam, you feel lak shoot. *Ouai?* Now you can'! Is better so!"

"Goddammit, give me my gun!" Fraser shouted.

Westlake clapped a hand across his mouth, and for an instant the Scot struggled, then quietly subsided.

"I'm sorry!" he said.

"W'at you do?" Charbonneau demanded. "You lak to be fun for dose dere? *Sacré tetons bleus de la Vierge!*"

After that we only lay and listened through the morning as the screams rose. Then one by one they dwindled away until we could hear them no longer, and only the rising howl of the wind in the trees above our heads sounded sick in our ears.

It was midafternoon before the first canoes put off and cautiously began to circle the *Tonquin,* and I must say that my stomach twitched and jumped with nervousness as the minutes passed, for I knew the slow match must be burning down close to the powder. Nonetheless, no mental urging could persuade the savages to put aside their wariness. For nearly an hour they cruised round and round, doubtless hurling insults at the silent vessel, whipping themselves to a vengeful fury, and watching, always, for an answering movement on deck. At our backs the wind was rising, and we could barely hear their shouts above it.

At length one of the smaller canoes detached itself from the circling line and drove straight toward the vessel, sweeping in under the stern and halting in a place of safety. For an instant it lay there, while its occupants doubtless recovered their audacity. Then cautiously it crept along the ship's flank to where a loose rope trailed idly in the water, and one by one its occupants swarmed up over the side. For an instant we could see them, like ants, scurrying this way and that upon the deck. Then abruptly they appeared at the rail.

At their signal the entire mass of canoes converged upon the vessel, and others began to put off from shore. We could feel the hair along our backs begin to rise, though whether that was due to the rising wind or not I could not say. High over our heads the great pines and firs moaned and whipped, and out upon the bar and the entrance we could hear the great seas crash, more angrily, it seemed to me, than ever we had heard them before. With one half my mind I recall thinking it must be making up to storm. With the other I kept saying, impatiently, over and over to myself: "Hurry! Hurry! Hurry! Get on board!"

Once the great rush to board and loot had begun, however, they needed no mental urging. What they thought when they found her abandoned I could not guess. The lanterns must have been still burning in the rigging and below decks. I wondered if they could have found Lewis. Seconds first, then minutes, and then hours seemed to drag by.

"Why doesn't he touch her off?" Fraser growled.

"I gave him an extra long match," Westlake replied, "but it must be close to finished now!"

It began to rain, a slow, misty drizzle, steady and disheartening. Our gear we managed to stow safely where it would keep comparatively dry beneath the upturned canoe. But for us there was no shelter. Nor did we feel the need of it. All about the ship, now, the water was black with canoes, some empty, but far more of them filled, all waiting their turn to get on board. The decks and rigging swarmed with savages. Instinctively we pressed our elbows into the soft earth beneath us and tensed so that our bellies grew taut and sore with waiting. Near the end of the log I heard Fraser grumble querulously:

"D'ye suppose——?"

He got no further. The world about us seemed suddenly to leap alive and bend inward to the vessel. Just that, for an instant. Nothing more. A sensation as if we were all inside a giant bottle and some invisible hand had suddenly pulled the cork.

I think I could have counted three before, of a sudden, across the bay, the *Tonquin* appeared almost slowly to grow before our eyes; too great to hold within its own planks, I saw the ribs and timbers stand apart as livid fire gleamed through the openings. Then, all at once, the silence burst—was shattered—in the most hideous, rending roar. The *Tonquin* seemed to clap for an instant together, and then amidships she bulged grotesquely. A huge white mushroom spewed skyward. Fore and mizzen toppled away from one another at crazy angles, and spars went spinning slowly, end over end, like toothpicks in the air.

Bits of timber, arms, legs, heads, shreds of human bodies, spurted up amid the cloud of smoke and scattered all about the vessel, raining down upon the water and the massed wreckage of canoes. With a slowness, almost majestic, the white cloud grew and billowed upward, little by little spilling from its incandescent maw the horrid debris it had sucked aloft.

At the end of the log Fraser picked himself out of the ruck of twigs and rotted pine needles, where the force of the blast had flung him, and said, with quiet satisfaction: "Aaahhh!"

V. Escape

~~~~~~

I. SOUTHEAST ARM

AS IT unfolded, with almost what seemed retarded motion, before our eyes, I, for one, was gripped with a feeling of utter impotence. It was as if the world before us were suddenly wrenched into the air and split asunder by some mighty but invisible hand, torn splinter from splinter, and the crumbled remains tossed back again to earth, while we could only lie and watch.

I would not have been too terribly astonished, I believe, had the very island under us been destroyed. Overhead, the trees whipped first toward the blast and then away from it. Bits of bark and twigs showered upon us, and some of the heavier branches came crashing down. Fortunately none landed either on us or upon the canoe. The great mushroom of white smoke and water, yards and planks and bits of battered bodies, rose into the air, and a sort of miniature tidal wave fanned out in a spreading circle from the spot. Those canoes which had crowded closest about the ship seemed to be drawn on end, spilling their human contents like so many toys into the sea, while those behind were tossed and turned over and twisted to splintered wreckage.

Following the clap of dreadful thunder there was a long instant of stricken silence in which there was naught to be heard but the suck of the water against the island shores and the steady drip of the raindrops from the trees above. Then, like an answering roll of thunder, came the echo from the mountains, invisible behind the lowering clouds; and almost with it rose a wailing, keening sound of mourning from the village.

Perhaps we should have had a sense of wonder. But somehow all the feeling that any of us had, once we recovered from the immediate effects, was one of fine elation. We showed it in our glances at one another. We said it in our expressions. I think it was Westlake who voiced the common thought.

"We'll count that one for James Lewis!" he exclaimed.

Throughout that day we lay upon the island, and I truly believe the explosion may have saved our lives. The survivors at the village were themselves too stricken to be troubled with the thought of us, even if they were aware of our escape. By night the new storm was in full blast, roaring through the tops of the pines like a horde of devils and whipping even the surface of the sound to a considerable surf. At the entrance we could hear, above the roar of the wind, the crash of the seas upon the rocks, and before it fell dark we could see the angry breakers roaring across the reefs.

"Ha!" said Westlake mirthlessly, hunching himself against the rain and hugging his elbows. "Much chance have we now. We'd not live five minutes in such seas."

To my surprise Charbonneau spoke in reply.

"Ummmm!" he agreed. *"Petits tetons de ma soeur!* Moose no dam' good for sailor. I don' wan' go out in dat!"

Westlake made no answer. Charbonneau persisted.

"Many tam' I ride in sea bad lak' dese inside. Yes, by goddam! On Lac Superieur. *Ouai!* W'en we comin' in Moose see, *la bas,* wan long arm, *un étroit*—narrow, narrow! W'at she's reach off dese way! Lak' long lac."

"Ouai!" said Fraser. "What of it?"

" 'Ow far you t'ink she's go?" asked the Moose.

We looked inquiringly at Westlake.

"I couldn't just say," he replied. "The charts differ as I recall, but at the best guess I'd say maybe twenty miles. Why?"

Charbonneau scratched his head.

"S'pose we follow dis? Bimeby, goddam, she end. Den maybe we see w'ere's bes' we go from dere, no?"

"And stick ourselves right in the Indians' bloody pocket?" Fraser snorted.

"Dis wan bay in coas' so crooked, she's mak' like snake's back!" The Moose waggled his hand to indicate how the shore line looped in and out. "Maybe we fin' at bottom of dis bay jous' leetle short carry-over to de nex', so we go creepin' 'long till de win' she's stop. W'at you say to dat?"

Fraser stared at him with interest.

"That's true! This isn't the forest about Superior. But, by God, 'tis forest! It can't be much different! What d'ye think, Rory?"

"I think 'tis the first sensible thing I've heard," I replied. "It's evident we can't leave by sea now. Lord knows we can't stay here!"

It was near dark. Carefully we uncovered our canoe, and slipping, sliding with it, we launched it again in the little bay where we came ashore and set out once more, keeping the island between us and the village for as long as we could.

All night we paddled southeast, rarely speaking save in brief monosyllables. For protection we crossed this new arm of the sound, which was perhaps four miles wide, and allowed a bit too much sweep to the wind for comfort. After the easy-paddling, sleek birchbark canoes of the north, I found the high-sided, flare-gunneled dugout a little awkward, yet there was no doubt it was meant for such waters as these. Where a loaded bark canoe would have been quickly swamped in such seas, this craft rode high and dry upon the most vicious waves, bobbing over them like a cork. Nevertheless I was pleased when we came into the shelter of the shore, for I found it as touchy of balance and temperamental as any craft I had ever seen.

Throughout the night we drove, covering, I judged, better than twenty miles, including the stretch from the island into the arm itself. When dawn came, we had not come to the end of the reach, though as near as we could tell we must be approaching it. All about us the country had closed in, running in forested ridges that dropped abruptly to the water's edge, and a dark, crested slope directly ahead seemed to hint either that the bay ended abruptly there or turned at a sharp angle.

In the gray light we crossed the mouth of a small cove where a doe and a fawn were feeding upon the eel grass. They threw up their heads, startled, as we passed within fifty feet, watching us, but they did not turn to flee.

A little longer we paddled in silence, rounding yet another point to a deeper cove. A small stream tumbled from the ridge above to a flat, and came in meandering curves to join the salt water. Ahead, the ridge came down to the water's edge, and the bay itself swept on around to the right; while on the left, perhaps three or four miles away, there seemed to be the mouth of a sizable river. Charbonneau rested upon his paddle.

"No!" he said. "Dat's far enough now! We pitch in cove an' hide canoe. Camp today up creek. By goddam, she's daylight now. Might be we com' 'roun' point an' fin' Injun village right w'ere dose dog set up holler! We have wan hell of tam den! Bimeby, Moose take look see round. Fin' out bes' way we go, eh?"

Even if it had not been sound advice, I doubt the rest of us would have demurred. We were too weary. Charbonneau turned into the inlet, and we worked slowly up the creek, following the channel, avoiding reeds and grass which, pressed down, would reveal our passage. When we came to a bank where the current ran strong enough to undercut a channel and leave us room to fetch alongside, we stepped ashore gingerly and lifted out canoe and gear.

In the course of the night the rain had ceased, though the wind still howled in the tall trees overhead and along the ridges we could hear the crash of falling timber. It was, we were to learn, not extraordinary, even in quiet weather, amid the tremendous forests that clothed the island.

The place where we stopped led up at a sharp angle to a low wooded ridge where, in the midst of a tangled blowdown, we could find shelter against the wind and ever-threatening rain. At the same time, hard by, on the bay side, there was a dense, tangled swampy place, almost impenetrably overgrown with salal and salmonberry, scrub birch and alder and aspen, hummocks of deep moss and swamp cedar. There it was a simple matter to cache canoe and gear. When this was done we withdrew to our blowdown, and, after a ration of ship biscuit and cold pork and a dollop around of rum to warm our bellies, we rolled up in our blankets.

There we spent the day, and I will admit that I, for one, slept from one end of it to the other. Some time during the day Charbonneau left us and worked his way up through the dense undergrowth to the high ridge above us, where he risked a tumble, and climbed a tall tree despite the whipping of the wind. From there he surveyed the countryside around.

It was late in the afternoon when I woke. Charbonneau hunkered on his heels, setting out a row of ship biscuit and salt pork upon a nearby log. In a crude basket of bark by his elbow were several quarts of luscious-looking salmonberries that he had gathered in his return journey from the ridge.

I sat up and yawned and glanced at the sky.

"Great God!" I cried. "Have I slept all this time?"

"Ummm!" Charbonneau responded. "Soon again you get used to life in woods. Not need so much sleep. Bimeby, we start along. By dam', we don' wan' stay here! Mebbeso you wake *les autres*. Tam come now we see w'at's bes' to do."

I followed his suggestion, and we were hungry enough to fall ravenously upon the rations he had set out. As we munched, he told us of his afternoon's explorations.

"What did ye see?" Fraser demanded.

"The other side av the mountain!" grinned Shea. "Aye, and a bloody highway straight to Astoria! What else?"

"Hush!" growled Westlake.

"Ummph!" grunted Charbonneau. "Mebbe you wish for highway 'fore we come home! Beyond dat ridge is long bay. She is mak' sharp turn southwest, mebbe t'ree, four mile. *Au bout*—at end—I'm see big Injun village, fifteen, twenty lodge. By dam' me! Ol' Moose think it goddam hard to get by that!"

The rest of us sobered.

Charbonneau continued.

"Behime village she's wan steep ridge, like this only worse. Beyond, I'm count me two, t'ree others, but no sign of nex' bay. *Sacré tetons!* I'm t'ink she's goddam rough country *la bas!*"

Our hearts sank. After a pause the Moose spoke again.

"Mebbeso we fin' him too long, even if we get pas' village. Goddam! I don' t'ink dat's good way!"

"Well, for th' lovva Jasus!" cried Shea. " 'Twas yer own notion!"

"Quiet!" growled Fraser. "He's got something in mind."

"Yes, by dam!" Charbonneau agreed emphatically.

"What is it, then, will ye be tellin' us!" Shea demanded.

The Moose glanced across at Westlake.

"You say dis islan'?"

The mate nodded.

"How big?"

"I couldn't say for sure." Westlake shook his head. "Fifty, sixty miles across; maybe three hundred long. Right here the coast is not too high. But all down the middle there runs a ridge of mountains seven or eight thousand feet high."

The half-breed grunted.

"*Ouai!* Moose see dese mountain. Big, big, all up along nort'eas'. You t'ink dose mountain she's lie close by oder coas'?"

Westlake nodded again.

"W'at lak' dat water on oder side?" the Moose asked. "Wide? Big? Deep? Rough? Or mebbe wan beeg lac wit' lots of islan' an' not too rough, eh?"

The mate shook his head.

"I've never been there," he said. "But it can't be too bad. There'll

be the Straits of Georgia, lots of islands and high shores, enclosed between this and the main, with high mountains on either side. What are
you driving at, anyway?"

"Suppose we go dat way?" Charbonneau suggested.

"You mean—cross the island?"

"By dam', you smart feller!" Moose grinned. "Where dis bay she's
make turn, I'm see big river come in from nort'eas'. She's big enough
for float canoe I'm t'ink, me. We go long way up him. Dam' long way!
He's valley she's run straight up 'longside dose mountain. We follow
him up to good place an' den we go 'cross divide and fall down oder
side. By dam', dese lazy Injun don't follow dere! Dat safe water!
Maybe she's paddle all de way home!"

"By God!" Westlake cried. "It's never been done, that I know of, but
maybe he has the answer at that!"

"Umm!" grunted Charbonneau. "Sure she's right answer! W'at else
dere we do? By dam', dat's rough country, but we fin' way!"

I remembered something Maquinna had told me.

"These coast Indians don't go deep into the bush," I said. "They're
fisheaters, and when they do feel the need of game, 'tis plentiful along
the beaches. Maquinna himself said he'd no notion what lay beyond
the ridge and implied there was a race of devils lived there."

"I can't imagine any devils worse than those!"

Westlake nodded in the direction we had come.

"I'm for it," I said, "if we can get the canoe across."

"Don' worry 'bout canoe," Moose growled. *"Par les gros tetons blues
de la Vierge!* If he mus', Moose mak' canoe on oder shore, by dam'!"

We looked again at one another; Charbonneau stirred.

"We go now?" he demanded.

We broke camp carefully, taking infinite pains to obliterate all
traces of our presence. The shadows were long when we poked out of
the mouth of the little creek and looked up and down the bay, to make
sure that all was safe. Yet Charbonneau was even more cautious. We
did not drive directly across to the mouth of the river. To do so must
fetch us for a time in view of the village; at a distance, to be sure, but
nonetheless where there was danger that we might be seen. Instead,
therefore, we went directly across to the opposite shore, where, while
the rest of us held the canoe in the shelter of an overhanging branch,
the Moose, with utmost care, stepped ashore, and here and there, in
such a way that the sharpest searcher would hardly suspect them missing, he picked up odds and ends of brush and fallen branches. These
he fetched back, and we draped them along the gunnels upon the

side of the canoe which would lie toward the village. Other branches he stuck upright to form a screen for us.

So disguised, we crept at snail's pace toward the river's mouth, keeping close to shore around the point and into the long cove. Anyone glancing our way from a distance would have taken us for a fallen tree and given us little thought. Naturally, had any come up at a few rods, the disguise would scarcely have served, but at a mile or more our progress could scarcely have been perceptible, even to a careful watcher. From the village at the foot of the bay, between three and four miles distant, I think we could scarcely be distinguished from the background. Only when we had entered the river and passed around the first bend did we nose cautiously into shore once again and scatter our brushwood trimmings carefully amid the tangled woods, so that by morning none would ever know they had not merely fallen where they lay.

The stream in which we found ourselves was a good-sized one for all its short length, which, I think, could scarcely have exceeded fifty or sixty miles. At its mouth it was close to two hundred feet wide, and it narrowed only a little during the first mile or more. We made our way up it fairly swiftly in the dusk, swinging from side to side of a narrow valley in great oxbows.

But the loom of the land ahead, as we could see it barely through the quick-gathering darkness, gave warning that we would not go very far before the current grew swifter and the course less meandering, and it would be necessary to take to the poles or perhaps even get out and drag. On either hand the black hills bulked steeply in mysterious folds: dense-forested, thrusting down steep ridges and hogbacks, gashed by the black shadows of evening. Thrice we saw deer feeding upon the sand bars and in the backwaters as we swept about sharp bends where the current flowed dark and deep against an overhanging bank. But they made no effort to flee at our approach, only standing tense and attentive, curious, as we passed. Everywhere salmon and sea trout dimpled the water as they fed on the mosquitoes that filled the dusk with their singing. Those same mosquitoes hung about our heads in vast clouds, thicker than any I had ever seen upon a northern muskeg, and with greater individual voracity than those amid the marshes beyond Lake Superior, about the Lac des Bois and Lac Winnipic.

They gave us fair warning of what we might expect. Westlake and Shea appeared to be especial targets for their attack, and they slapped and ducked and cursed as we plodded upstream, though Shea made every effort to meet the situation with Irish wit and resignation.

"Begod! If I'd known I was to be ate alive by these winged boogers, sure I might have stopped to think twice!" He slapped at his jaw with a force that all but knocked him out of the canoe. "Got ye, me lovely sweet, be Jasus!"

For my part I seemed to retain yet a certain amount of immunity, as did Fraser, who was certainly more entitled to it than I. As for Charbonneau, there was nothing, so far as I could tell, could pierce his leathery hide.

The darkness of night came upon us with the suddenness of a clap of thunder, so swiftly that in one moment I could see across the river, yet when I turned my head away for an instant and then looked back the other shore was no more than a shadowy line against the darker shadow of the forest. I knew already that it was characteristic of this part of the world. There is no gradual lengthening of the shadows.

We were still paddling at that moment, and I recall that Charbonneau asked if we should go on.

"The farther, the safer," said Westlake.

"Aye!" agreed Fraser.

"Aaarrhh!" growled Shea. " 'Tis not the red devils I'd be thinkin' of now! If only we can be after outdistancin' these winged barstids! Mother av Gawd, were there iver such bugs?"

We were well up the river by now and still able to paddle, though there were signs of swifter water ahead and our progress was now much slower. Indeed in about a mile we came where the reedy pools and wide-sweeping bends ceased and the current came down in a long glide, smooth and sleek and dark as a stream of rushing ink over a bed of skull-sized stones, here and there broken with huge boulders around which it swirled and eddied, not quite exhibiting white fangs, but in the darkness curling a lip a little so that we might know its strength.

"Ah, for the luvva Jasus!" cried Shea at the sight of it. "Sure, here's where we get out an' walk!"

"Not yet!" I laughed.

"No?" he demanded. "How the divil can we make headway forninst such a run as that?"

"Wait now and you'll see!" I retorted.

"Begod, now, and ye are Irish, aren't ye?" he replied.

"No doubt you'll get some exercise to sweat the salt out of you." I chuckled.

"No, by goddam!" said the Moose behind me. "She's not got the hang of dis yet! Sailor no dam' good for dis now! You, me, Coq-des-

Bois, *la bas,* we push'm up! Dese sailor she's sit an' smoke tonight like goddam bourgeois!"

He swung the canoe in along shore and shipped the paddles, while Fraser and I held to a boulder so that we would not lose headway. Three of the small yards we had shipped for booms would do for poles until we could cut better and fit them with iron spikes. Charbonneau dealt them out, and we swung again into the stream.

It was a fumbling business, of necessity. Each in rotation set his pole, or tried to, while the others held and thrust, so that properly it would have been a one-two-three movement. In the dark, however, it was tricky. Often as not the end of the pole slipped on the bottom or caught between stones, almost jerking the holder over the side. The current was strong, and we had to feel our way, frequently dropping back a foot upon the current for every two we gained.

In this way we plodded, going more and more slowly, until we no more than held our own, and the Moose, with a curse, swung us in against a bit of stony shingle and flung himself out to the waist in the water.

In two hours we could scarcely have covered more than a mile. Charbonneau clutched at the gunnel and thrust his pole down alongside the packs.

"Ha!" he cried. *"Ca, c'est trop fort!* Never we come safe, holy ol' dam'! Put down dese pole, an' into de water now! *Coq!* Rory! If she's don' drag, we's don' get now'ere! *Crotte alors! Viens!"*

So for two hours more we slithered and stumbled and fought our way up the swirling current, often plunging into holes up to our armpits, never knowing from one step to the next where we could place our foot. Anyone who has dragged a canoe over a slippery bottom in broad daylight or who has tried to follow a stream alone in the dark will have some notion of what we endured. Yet I think we made better time than we had with the poles, and we might even have made another mile and a half or more by midnight had we not come at length to white water, chuting down in a sweep about the foot of a long, level shelf, crowned with a stand of tall, fragrant firs and cedars, under whose overhanging branches we cached canoe and gear and fell into our blankets in exhausted slumber. As near as I could guess, we had come barely eight miles from the bay. It seemed my eyes had barely closed before the Moose was shaking my shoulder, and I opened my eyes again to find it dawn.

"What is it?" I demanded in alarm. "Are they—coming?"

Charbonneau grinned and shook his head.

"We go now."

"By daylight?" I blinked at him.

"Ol' Moose be down river since before daylight," he said. "By dam', no Injun follow. I'm t'ink she's scared me, or else he's don' know we escape. Don' see even sign of search, no goddam! She's safe for walk by day wit' sharp lookout!"

I got up, stretched, shook the twigs from my blanket bags, and rolled them up. The others sleepily followed suit. So far as I could see, it promised to be a fine day. The storm had blown over. There was clear sky overhead, though it still appeared windy on the ridges.

"Sure, 'twill be good to be movin' by daylight," Shea remarked. " 'Tis but an indifferent owl I'd make."

"Ah!" said Fraser ominously. "Wait!"

Our clothes were still wet from our ducking of the night before and clammily uncomfortable. We ate a breakfast of cold salt pork and biscuit—a repast that was fast growing monotonous to all of us. Yet we dared not light a fire or kill game, close as we were to the coast and our enemies. When we had finished we divided our forces as the Moose directed. He had already looked upstream a considerable distance and found the rapids not so bad by daylight. The canoe could be floated and dragged up over them on the cordelle, or towing rope. Those not so engaged would tote the heavy gear across. To this latter part of the task Fraser and Westlake and myself devoted our efforts, while Charbonneau introduced Shea to the intricacies of canoe travel—outside the canoe! For more than an hour one or the other of them dragged at the rope's end, while the other fended off, either from the rocks ashore or from waist-deep, or sometimes from the craft itself hugging the shore, keeping to the shallows and eddies, wherever there was enough depth to float the craft. In about a mile we came to quieter water and re-embarked. Not, however, before both Charbonneau and I had gone back over the route we had come and carefully obliterated all signs of our having passed that way.

We had easier going after our portage: long, still pools and smooth, swift glides over a deep bottom against steep banks, interspersed with short, quick ripples and chutes, over which the canoe could be poled or dragged with ease. In this stretch Shea and Westlake were initiated into the intricacies of canoemanship upon the river. Charbonneau demonstrated to them the correct way to hold the paddle, to dip and turn it. And what was more important here, it seemed to me, he instructed them in the use of the pole. Both were quick to learn. Shea was catlike, nimble from years of running aloft in the rigging and balancing upon a slatting yard in a heavy sea. Westlake, too, had an instinctive sense of balance, so that we had not poled beyond the second chute before they both had the hang of it. From that point we devised a system whereby four poled at a time while the fifth man rested, and at this we took turns.

By this means I believe we made better than ten miles in the course of the morning. At midday we paused upon a sand bar, the upper edge of which was well covered with scrubby brush that afforded us a view of several hundred yards in either direction, while at the same time it effectually concealed us. There we ate yet another meal of cold salt pork and ship's biscuit, washed down with a ration of rum and water.

As nearly as we could tell, the country round about was uninhabited, for the slopes of the hills ran steep to the river bank and were densely clothed in thick forest in which the undergrowth grew six to ten feet high and was so dense that, without a cutlass or some such blade to hack his way through, a man could scarcely hope to penetrate it. Though we scoured both sides of the river, we could find no sign of a trail, nor did we see any other indication of human beings. Yet one thing seemed to trouble Charbonneau.

"I not like dis, me. Dis river she's don' cut back like she should. We go 'long islan' de wrong way, not 'cross lak we wan'."

It was true. So far the stream paralleled the mountains rather than falling out of them. To be sure a range of hills, or perhaps rather a long ridge, now stood between us and Nootka Sound. It was high enough to cut off the ocean fogs, and in all likelihood it also offered protection against savage inroads across them. Yet, as the crow flew, we could not yet be far distant from the sea.

Accordingly, after a brief rest, we embarked once more and resumed our journey, plodding up against a stream that became more precipitate, leaping and roaring between the high hills, so that more and more frequently it was necessary for us to take to the water, up to our middles, and seize the long craft by the gunnels, to drag it upward against the sweep. After about an hour we came to a quarter mile or so of rugged, foaming, swift, white water, almost enough of a rapid to force a carry. Up this we had as much as we could do, all five together, to struggle with the weight of our canoe and load, only to find, at the upper end, that the river made a sharp bend to the right and came leaping and tumbling down in a roaring series of chutes and cataracts straight out of the mountains.

"Now, by dam'!" Charbonneau cried. "We go to work!"

It was true. For all we would at last be facing the way we wished to go, we had come to the end of the easy water. We must carry—at least about this first series of cataracts. And if we could judge from the configuration of the country above, so we must for some distance.

We had come by now some fifteen miles above the previous night's camp and possibly twenty-three or -four from the sound. For this, at least, we were thankful, for beyond this point there was little hope of effectively concealing our trail. On either hand the mountain slopes rose so steeply as to be all but precipitous. Thorny salmonberry grew in a tangled mass half as high again as the tallest man, and as if this were not enough, ferns and devil's-club grew as high as a man's head, while creepers and tangled salal and lower growth choked the underbrush, matting together to make a veritable jungle. Overhead immense firs and cedars, hemlocks, pines, and spruces pointed dagger fingers to heaven, towering often one hundred and fifty to two hundred feet, sometimes more, in the air. And all about us, like giant jackstraws, their tremendous trunks, some blown down by the storms that raked the island, others merely fallen under the ravages of decay and old age, lay tangled in a disheartening mass. Yet there was no question of turning back. Through this mass, along the steep slope, over immense boulders enormous as houses, over and under and along trunks that frequently were twenty and thirty feet in diameter, across matted windfalls, we must hack our way, and not only cut out a path, but drag the canoe and all our heavy gear as well!

I, however, was actually little enough concerned. For once I discovered an advantage in my size. As the lightest, smallest of our party, I could most easily conceal myself, while at the same time I could carry less. Accordingly I was posted as a guard at the foot of the portage, while the others hacked the path through the thick undergrowth with their cutlasses and, inch by inch and step by step, wormed their way through with the canoe and the packs.

I had both time and opportunity to recoup something of my energy while the others worked. To my vast amusement, Shea and Westlake sweat and swore, for up here, at least, the fog was gone and the day was bright and hot. I fear I did not count my blessings as I should until evening, when Charbonneau and Shea returned from the upper end of the trail for me and the balance of the gear. Apart from holding back a pack that I need not be ashamed of carrying, I was content to lie amid the bushes, basking in the warmth and sunlight and keeping an eye out downstream.

"Ah!" cried the bos'n as they came in sight of me taking my ease. "Sure now we'll be seein' how the O'Rourkes uphold the honor av the

Irish! Ye can get up off yer lazy tail now, me son. The red divils'll not be comin' this day, an' we've come to the ind av th' carry above an' must fetch ye home with us. Begod! If iver a shipmate had told me I'd pick up me boat on me back an' walk with it, sure I'd have beat out his brains with a belayin' pin, that I would!"

Although we had seen no sign of any pursuit, the Moose took no chances. He set both Shea and myself to seeking out brushwood on the higher slopes, up the trail a bit. At the same time he himself spent half an hour searching for a fallen sapling, which he carefully carried down and dropped across the beginning of the track, laying it in so lifelike a fashion that I doubted one Indian in twenty would have noticed anything out of the way about it. Behind this he sprinkled the brushwood that Shea and I had gathered, and amid the brush we set stalks of salal and salmonberry upright in the ground for a distance of twenty or thirty feet, so that from below it gave the impression of unbroken forest.

"That good for wan day," the Moose grunted. "By goddam! But w'en berry leaves wilt, I t'ink me dese trail she's stick out, *comme tetons d'une Vierge,* by dam', to show w'ich way we gone."

I found they had chopped out a trail four or five miles long around the first series of falls by dint of what must have been the most exacting labor. It was like a tunnel through the jungle, always at such an angle that one had to cling actually to the hillside, by such roots and shrubs and projections as came handy, to keep from rolling willy-nilly into the thorny bush below. If this were not enough, great boulders and rock outcroppings barred the way, often with seemingly insurmountable obstacles, but always the trail wormed around and found some niche or crevice, often well-nigh vertical, between immense logs and boulders, up which it wormed and struggled. Sometimes we must walk the length of a fallen giant to slither off at the smaller end and worm our way through the matted top. Or perhaps to drop off at the butt and struggle among tangled roots, only to find another windfall confronting us beyond. How they had managed to work the canoe through such places was a mystery to me. Yet it had been done. And later I had my own turn at it. With a pack on my back that weighed nigh as much as I did, I was ready to drop by the time we reached the upper end of the trail. I wondered how these others must have felt after fighting their way through and opening the track for me. Yet everything had been carried over, even the sails and oars which we thought we might need on the other side.

That night we supped again on cold salt pork and biscuit and rum.

No doubt the fact that all were close to the dropping point put tempers on edge.

"Now where are we?" growled Westlake. "Off in the middle of God-knows-where, dragging a boat through the forests! Where's the sense in it?"

"For God's sake! You were yourself a party to it! Pah! You think we've had hard going today? Wait till you see what's to come," Fraser jibed.

He spoke as a more accurate prophet than he knew, but Westlake was in no mood for concessions.

"Be damned to that!" he cried. "I was sold into it. Aye! And so was Shea here. You know bloody well had we stuck to the coast we'd have no such trouble as this!"

"No!" cried Fraser. "But a damn sight worse I'll guarantee!"

"Ho!" retorted Westlake, with illogic that could only be born of fatigue. "You're a man that thinks he knows it all!"

The Cock-of-the-Woods glowered at him, as unlike the bird that was his namesake as anything I can imagine.

"Well, by God!" he retorted. "I know one thing! An intelligent girl will have naught to say to a pretty clotheshorse that knows naught of anything but the sea!"

"You concede that much?" Westlake demanded coldly.

"Aye!" growled Fraser.

" 'Tis better than a great oaf, smelling of wood smoke and guts of the beasts he has skinned!" the mate taunted. "What have you beyond your mop of hair and the witchery of your trade?"

I might have put in my own oar at that moment had there been opportunity, but they were at each other's throats before the rest of us could say a word. And Fraser, for the moment, was at the bottom of the tangle.

"Give us a hand here! Give us a hand, Shea!" cried Westlake.

I spilled my rum in leaping up. But Charbonneau was before me. Shea spun back across a log, to fall with a crash upon the back of his neck. Westlake doubled up with hands clasped across his belly, while Fraser rolled on the ground and clutched his shins.

So fast was it all that I could see only the result. But that was worth watching.

"*Alors! Petits tetons de ma grosse soeur!* W'at the 'ell? Is Moose to die for such damfool? *Par les balons de l'evêque!* Is dere no sense in anywan?"

Such shamefaced giants I think I never saw, as Charbonneau went

on from there to speak his mind: of the need for us all to hang together
lest we end our days separately. For the time being, he pointed out, we
must do only what could benefit us all, and old hatchets must be buried
for the moment. Let any stand between him and safety, he said, and he
would shoot them down as an enemy, with no more compunction than
he would defend himself against the warriors of Nootka. What's more,
there was no doubt he meant it.

Not to dwell at too great length on matters of small importance,
that night passed quickly without further event. We broke our fast
in the morning with yet another meal of the aglutinous, cold salt pork
and dry ship's biscuit, and after that resumed our struggle on and up.

We were a subdued party that day, and well we might have been.
For one thing, the quarrel and Charbonneau's attendant and certain
fury left three of us, at least, feeling somewhat abashed. Volatile as he
was, the Moose was not one to put aside quickly such anger as he had
felt the night before. While for my part I think I was a little awed by
the apparently cataclysmic results of the whole unimportant affair.

But this alone did not account for the grim silence in which we
labored. Although we had passed the actual cataract, our journey that
day was one of continuous and intense struggle. There was no paddling. Nor was there any poling. Indeed, there was but little dragging
our heavy craft. The river roared white and foaming down a precipitous canyon, leaping from side to side and from pool to pool, raging,
frothing. The only times we rode at all that day were when we came to
some point where it was necessary to cross some deep, swift-running
pool, to pass a cliff upon one side and claw our way across to the other.
Sometimes the stream raced between sheer walls, over which it was
impossible to carry. And here it was necessary to inch along, taking advantage of every crevice and rock outcropping, clinging and forcing
ourselves upstream against the raging current by the very strength of
our fingernails. More than half the time, it seemed to me, was spent in
hacking out a way, halfway up the canyon side above the stream,
while below us the river roared and growled and the flies swarmed
about our heads, getting in our eyes and ears and noses, even in our
mouths, and being sucked down into our windpipes by our breathing.

The stream was actually little wider here than a good-sized creek, yet
it carried an amazing flow of water. And, as the Moose pointed out, it
was possible that after we had struggled up this turbulent stretch we
would come into a reach of quieter water. But we did not find it that
day. I do not think we covered more than four miles between dawn
and dusk, and when at last we dropped into our blankets, we had

little thought of food or, indeed, of anything but sleep. Gone was any notion of hiding our trail. If they followed us this far, there was little we could do about it but turn and fight! The next day we struggled forward again, over country much the same, clawing and fighting our way up, until at last, perhaps an hour or so before dusk, we struggled over a last, wild, desperate pitch and found ourselves faced abruptly by a pretty little lake some six or eight miles long by two wide, from which our small river hastened busily in a frantic spate of froth and foam.

I must say we were heartened and delighted and glad of an opportunity to ride once more. The comparative leisure of paddling was an actual pleasure, and we re-embarked with the best possible humor and traversed the lake to find that at its upper end it split into two arms. One, fed by the main inlet, a temptingly slow, navigable stream, came in at the west on a course that paralleled the coast, while no more than a tiny runnel, not three feet across, straggled down from a low saddle in the mountain ridge to feed the northern arm. We pitched our camp at the mouth of the larger stream—for which way we would go from here was problematical and a flat point of fairly high land offered the best possible place from which to view both the lake below and the mountains before, as well as to watch, so to speak, over our shoulders for savages behind.

II. DISASTER

WE MADE our camp, and our half-breed scratched his head and scanned the sky.

"I'm tired, me, of dis goddam fat!" he growled. "W'at you say, you fellers don' grow tired of dis pork?"

Westlake retched realistically. The Moose grinned at me.

" 'Ow far you t'ink we come?"

"We must be close to forty miles from the bay," I replied.

"I bat you me if we be here five-six days ago," he replied. "Mebbeso, goddam, we hear de *Tonquin* w'en she's blow. I don't t'ink we see smoke. I t'ink she's safe for light wan leetle small fire. Yes, goddam! You bring hook an' line, no?"

"Oho, be Jasus!" cried Shea. "Break out the gear an' let us be havin' a cast at it."

I was not one to object. I unpacked the hooks and lines, and using a ration of our pork for bait we made our best casts. Within twenty minutes we had as much fish as we could eat: three trout of some curious gray variety with black spots and a slash of brilliant red beneath each gill, weighing between two and three pounds apiece, and two salmon that ran seven or eight pounds each. Broiled over a small fire of hot willow coals and basted judiciously with fat pork, eaten with salmonberries and wild strawberries, they seemed to us a feast fit for a king, and a most welcome change from the monotonous diet to which we had become accustomed.

Just before dark three deer, a buck and two does, came down to our lake upon the other side of the creek, and I think for as much as half an hour nosed about and peeked out at us from behind the bushes with the tamest of curiosity. Though we would have relished fresh meat, we dared not shoot yet. Such a light smoke as our fire made might be overlooked. But the sound of a gun might carry, and such a sound could only mean white men!

Doubtless it was sight of the animals that sent Charbonneau into the woods, to return presently with a small sapling cedar, which he spent the evening whittling and carving. Nor would any prying induce him to say what he was making. The shavings he laid carefully by against the morning's fire.

We slept that night comparatively well-filled and comfortable—it seemed to me for the first time since we had left the ship. In itself and so mentioned, it scarcely seems worth the trouble of telling, yet it was so unusual it should be noted! We slept late, not rising from our blankets before sunrise; then, by common consent, made a leisurely breakfast of fish and berries.

No doubt in one form or another the same thought was in all our minds. A council of war was indicated. The river, or, rather, the good-sized creek which was the main inlet, on which we were now camped, seemed to lead almost opposite to the direction we wanted to take. It dropped off the southwestern shoulder of a high, snow-capped peak. But as nearly as we could tell the smaller inlet and the saddle from which it dropped seemed to offer a more likely route. It was Charbonneau's suggestion that he and Fraser scout both possibilities, while the rest of us remained in camp, first to guard our gear and second to obtain fish and berries and the like for supper.

I heard no objection, and in these pursuits Shea and Westlake and I whiled away the day, growing lazier as the sun grew warmer. The wild strawberries and salmonberries we found in considerable quantities; the former, near the end of its season, and the latter just coming ripe. My companions and I caught such fish as I thought we could consume in the next day or two, after which I called a halt, for it did not seem to me there was time to smoke it.

Both of our scouts laid out all day, Charbonneau, I noticed, taking with him the cedar stick he had worked so carefully. Fraser cut up upon the mountain, when he discovered that the main creek he followed lost itself in a huge swamp to the westward. He came back overland about sundown; while at the same time the Moose came over the lake from the north inlet, straddling two logs which he had bound together with his belt and paddling his improvised raft with a long pole. Across the logs before him was draped a young doe which he had shot with the bow and arrow he had made, much to our delight and amazement. He grinned at our praise and surprise, and that evening we forgot our fish and supped on venison.

Both of our scouts were so exhausted, however, that there was no discussion that night of the course we ought to follow. Both fell asleep while they were eating. Again we slept the clock around, beyond doubt benefiting from the rest, and in the morning, as the sun pushed over the tops of the firs, brightly dappling the still surface of the lake, the two explorers blew upon their venison and told us the results of their day.

"That country thick, thick," said the Moose. "You think we been t'rough somet'ings? Oh, goddam! I'm follow up creek mos' tam's walk in de water. I'm tell you goddam little room for dat!"

He nodded toward the canoe.

"Up, up, way up!" he went on, "maybe t'ree, four mile, I'm fin' beaver dam. We go little way on pond. Afterwards no water."

"Well," I replied, "we'd expect the stream to peter out in time. What about the saddle?"

"Ah!" he said. "You t'ink of h'open woods lak between Pigeon Rivaire an' Lac des Bois? I tal you, goddam! *Sacrés tetons bleues!* She's lak walk in sugarbush by dis!"

"Well," I said at length, "we can't go back. If we don't break through to the eastward someway we might as well stay where we are. Did you reach the saddle at all?"

The Moose nodded.

"What did you see?" I demanded.

He glanced ironically at Shea.

"I see the oder side of de mountain!" he said. "By goddam! She ridge! Dat valley! Dese *forêt!* Pigeon! Such as dese you don' see!"

"But beyond, man! Beyond?" I cried. "Was there no sign of any break-through? No glimpse of blue water?"

He shook his head. Fraser spoke.

"He's right," he said wearily. "That's a hell of a stretch! Canyons and forest—I tell you, man, you've no notion of it! I worked up on the mountain, above the trees, where I could get a look off that way. There's some sort of pass between this and the next peak, eastward. But there are a thousand gullies and canyons and ravines and ridges between here and there. It won't be easy!"

"Beyond that," I said, "what did you see?"

"Nothing," he said.

"No water?" I demanded. "No bay?"

"Not in that direction. All I could see was what we've left behind us. To the east 'twas hazy. There could be water between, but I could see naught save, far off in the northeast, some great high peaks—much higher than any of these."

"How far?" I asked.

"As the crow flies," he replied, "a hundred to a hundred and fifty, two hundred miles, perhaps."

I glanced at Westlake, eyebrows raised.

"Those would be on the mainland," he said.

"Did you see no sign," I asked, "of any stream?"

Both Fraser and Charbonneau shook their heads.

"By dam!" said the Moose. "That's rough country, I'm tell you!"

Fraser was more constructive.

"It's hard to tell. There are gaps and passes. It may be that somewhere there's a way through."

"Well," I said, "there's naught for it but to try. The only alternative is to cut back and try to pass around the coast villages."

Charbonneau shook his head violently.

"No, goddam! That not possible. *Sacré tetons!* W'en we pass before, word she's not spread. Now, *par le ventre de la Vierge,* every Injun on dis coas' she's know!"

"All right," I retorted. "What do you advise then?"

"Leave dat canoe——" he began.

"After fetching it so far?" I cried.

"You don' see dat country!" he exclaimed. *"Sacré balons!"*

"I'll grant it might be difficult," I replied, "but I'll not admit 'tis impossible! Isn't it better to go slow and take the boat with us?"

"We steal canoe on other side!" he suggested. *"Sacré* goddam! An' tam Ol' Moose can' fool dese stupid Injun——"

"No!" I cut him short. "We're running away because the Indians here are hostile. We don't want to turn those against us."

"We don't know if she's frien'ly," he pointed out.

"They're not apt to be friendly if we start by stealing canoes from them!" I replied.

"Den Moose mak' canoe!" he growled. "Goddam!"

"How long would that take?" I scoffed.

"Mont', six weeks!" he retorted.

"Yes!" I gibed. "In a month, maybe less, we should be able to drag this one over."

"Dat's goddam rough goin'!" he insisted.

"I think he's right, Moose." Fraser came to my rescue. "We've fetched it this far, 'twould be a shame to leave it. Better to have patience and drag it across. We'll be ahead in the long run!"

"We'll have to have transportation when we come to the other side," Westlake pointed out. "There's no other way home."

"Begod!" cried Shea. "I've not put me skin an' blood along the gunnels av yon blasted craft to be leaving the god-damned thing lay idle in the forest! Take it along, I say!"

"*Eh bien!*" Charbonneau shrugged. "But don' say ol' Moose she's don' speak! Now we go?"

"Sure, the sooner started, the sooner done!" cried Shea.

We struck out that very morning. For perhaps seventy-five or a hundred yards we were able to float the canoe, but after that the forests closed in about us and the going grew more and more rugged, even as Charbonneau had warned it would.

There are no words with which to paint a picture of those mountain forests. Our struggle from the bend of the river as far as the lake had been child's play by comparison. The vines and creepers and tangled blowdowns, the thorns, the huge logs that lay across the way, the swarming, blinding clouds of flies and mosquitoes and gnats, the hellish swamps in which a man would sink to his middle before he could save himself by snatching at the gunnel of the canoe, hanging on while his companions cut poles and thrust them forward for him to straddle; many of these we had experienced below, but never in such degree as we found them now.

It seemed to me that Charbonneau had been unduly optimistic, for in that first week if we covered a mile a day it would very much surprise me. At the end of the first week we were only as far as the beaver dams. And in a day then we were able to pole and paddle and drag the canoe fully as far as we had gone since leaving the lake. But there the stream all but ended. So, too, did our rancid pork and by now stale ship biscuit, the putrid fish and venison we had fetched from the lake. That evening, by dint of much labor, we managed to catch enough fingerling trout to make a meal. Beyond that we had no notion what we should eat other than the berries and wild fruits that we might pick along the way. In these there was but scant nourishment.

I set out snares that night for rats or rabbits or what small deer might come our way. But nothing came to my traps, and in the morning it was necessary to catch our breakfast before we could eat it. Curiously, we had seen no sign of deer or any large game since we left the lake.

At the Moose's suggestion we rested where we were for nearly a week while we worked—the word is literal—at fishing and hunting and trapping to provide ourselves for the road ahead. By retracing our steps unburdened to the beaver ponds, we were able in that time to fetch in, I think, close to a thousand small trout, running in size from four inches to a foot, and a few scrawny beaver. These we partially smoked over a fire of fir and hemlock bark and pounded into shreds, which we mixed with dried salmonberries to make a sort of pemmican. Yet the result was pitifully small; the whole not amounting to a full pack in any man's brigade. One would have thought that the swamps surrounding those upper waters would abound in small game, even deer and elk. But though we managed to find a little old sign, by dint of much hunting, the animals themselves had disappeared, and we had the luck to snare no more than a dozen rabbits and a handful of ptarmigan and grouse.

Such of this game as we did not eat immediately we smoked and added to the pemmican bag. But by the end of a week it was obvious that we consumed nearly as much as we gathered and that, if we insisted upon remaining there until we had an adequate supply for every possible contingency, we would scarcely be likely to leave that summer. Accordingly we packed our gear and set out once more.

We must have looked a comical cavalcade dragging a canoe through those tremendous, dense forests, so thick that had we not had our cutlasses with which to hack a path I think we would never have been able to penetrate them at all. Miles we were from any water before the week was out, and we had reached the top of the saddle which we had seen from the lake below. We had left the last of the runlets behind and had only such water to stay us as we had gathered in the boat's water breakers that we had fetched with us. The rum had long since given out and the cask we had wastefully tossed aside. Fortunately we had had the foresight to refill the water breakers. We wished now that we had done the same with the rum cask. The fish we had smoked and the game we had jerked was half gone by the end of the first week, and though we stopped early and set out snares, we took little to eke it out.

At the crest of the saddle I climbed a tree and felt something of Charbonneau's discouragement as I looked northeastward across the tumbled hills and ridges. How, in God's name, I wondered, could we hope to make it at the rate we went? Yet we struggled on, hacking, dragging, sliding across immense logs, worming our way through windfalls. The footing was treacherous, and more than once we fell. Several times we narrowly escaped being crushed by trees or branches, which always seemed to be falling, wind or no. I suppose they simply came suddenly to old age and just gave up. Or perhaps the worms that constantly bored at them cut through the last shred of fiber that held them erect and, releasing the delicate balance, sent them crashing down.

To make matters worse, July was hot and sultry, bright and blistering as any weather I have ever seen, so that we stripped to the buff in camp and wore only our clothes—or what shreds remained of them—as we struggled through the forests, for we could not pass naked through the thorny scrub without leaving half our skins behind us. The seams of our shoes burst and were patched with bits of fiber and bark in place of sole leather.

It took us a fortnight to fight our way from the last spring on the lake side of the saddle, over that dreadful ridge and down into the next hollow; by which time, it seemed to me, we were as dry as ever we could be, though we persisted in dragging the canoe, as much because it had become an obsession with us as from any idea we had now that we might be able to use it! We found no water, yet the ground sloped southeastward, generally following the trend of the island. If it was not directly the way we wished to go, it was at least toward home, and accordingly, rather than scale the next ridge willy-nilly, we followed it down.

Two days of fighting through the undergrowth, scratched, tattered, and tired, weak from hunger and thirst, brought us to an immense cedar swamp, where we were at least able to fill our casks. But when we cached the canoe and the gear and searched for an outlet, what was our disappointment to find it in a tiny stream that flowed southwest and obviously fell into the very river we had ascended to the lake! We refilled our water breakers once again and drank our fill, then, haggard and desperate, we put it to a vote whether to strike back down toward the coast or to continue to fight our way northeastward. By my calculation we could not have gone, in our zigzag course, much more than ten or a dozen miles as the crow flies. Yet to a man we voted in favor of going on.

Another week, rationing the water sparingly this time, carried us through the next gully, which was dry, and over an intervening ridge and down into the hollow beyond, where the blow fell that came near to breaking the hearts of us all.

It was not as if we were five healthy, well-fed men following a beaten track. For more than a fortnight we had lived upon four small rabbits, a partridge, and three wood rats that we had been lucky enough to catch in the snares. Because of our noisy, lumbering progress, no doubt, we had seen nothing that we might shoot, even if we dared. This diet we had eked out with the leaves of the salal and salmonberries. Except for the water we had found at the outlet to the swamp, we had no drop of moisture, and that we had was getting dangerously near the bottom of the casks.

Such a regimen told upon us. Our eyes were sunk in our heads. Our beards were long and scrawny, and our clothes—what was left of them —hung in flapping tatters upon our gaunt frames. I wondered what Valerie would think if she could see any of us now! Yet we kept on, dropping down the slope, no more than thirty or forty feet at a time, so thick was the growth and so slight our strength. We would clear a stretch, then boost the canoe over it, go back and fetch the gear, and then sit down to rest a moment before we rose listlessly to repeat the attack.

We were sitting so when it came, elbows on knees, heads in our hands, panting against the heat; Westlake and Fraser at the down side of the trail we had cut and Charbonneau and myself and then Shea opposite them. Our tongues were big with the thirst that plagued us, and we had hardly the energy to slap at the flies that swarmed about us.

I heard the crack behind me only vaguely. I seem to remember that I gave it no more than fleeting thought. The day was still and hot and sultry and not so much as a twig stirred. Not until Fraser's look of frozen horror swam into my glance did I realize aught was wrong. I don't suppose it could have actually been more than an instant between the sound and his warning shout.

Instinctively I screwed about in my seat and saw the great fir toppling toward us.

What happened then I am not exactly sure. I remember giving

Shea a shove to the right and shouting at him to run. Charbonneau, I must have assumed, was woodsman enough to take care of himself. Out of the corner of my eye I saw Fraser seize Westlake by the shoulder and send him scrambling before him in the direction opposite to that I had taken. I felt the air shiver as I leapt, and then the very earth beneath me jumped and trembled as the huge trunk crashed across the very spot in which we had been sitting. I remember that both Shea and I fell flat, he on the bottom and I on top of him, in our mad scramble to escape, and even now I can see him lifting his face out of the ruck of fallen needles and forest compost and demanding plaintively:

"Holy mither av Jasus! What was that?"

I looked back where we had been. The air was still full of debris, bits of bark and needles, like a cloud of smoke.

"Dear God, punish me if ivir I breathe a word against men that spind their loives in th' woods again!" Shea cried.

I might have laughed had I not been so frightened.

"Glory be to the Lord Jasus!" he went on, crossing himself. "Where's Mr. Westlake? I'm obliged to ye, Mr. O'Rourke!"

"Don't mention it!" I replied, mechanically ridiculous. His question struck a sudden chill into me. "Westlake! Fraser!"

"Aye!" came a voice faintly.

"Is it you, Fraser?" I cried. "Shea's here and me—O'Rourke. Is Westlake with you? And Moose?"

I heard a frantic curse beyond the twisted branches.

"Here's Westlake!" came the response. "Are you sure the Moose is not with you?"

I looked about me swiftly.

"No!" I called. "Are you?"

There was a long silence; then a desperate voice.

"I—I don't see him!"

We both called simultaneously.

"Moose! Moose! Charbonneau! Where are you?"

There was no answer except the faint, mocking echo of our calls upon the hot summer air.

"Fraser!" I shouted. "Can you see under from your side?"

"Not much," he called. " 'Tis too thick. God, what a crash!"

"Aye!" I said. "Dig in toward where we sat. We've got to find him!"

Shea and I flung ourselves upon the tangled branches. On the other side I could hear Westlake and Fraser crashing amid the brush. It was Westlake who first came upon him. We were abruptly arrested by his voice.

"O'Rourke! O'Rourke! Fraser! Shea! I've found him! Oh God! Come quick, lads! Bear a hand!"

III. L'ORIGNAL

OUR canoe, our packs, our gear, everything, was forgotten for the moment as we clawed frantically through the laced branches, scrambling over the trunk, until we came to his side, to find Charbonneau lying face down, unconscious, a deep gash in his head and pinned by the leg with a branch as big as my thigh.

"Great God!" I cried. "Is he dead?"

Fraser was already before us, kneeling beside him. The other two glanced up as we appeared, white-faced above their scraggly beards, wide-eyed, desperate. The mate shook his head.

"I—I don't think so," he said. "He's hurt. He's hurt bad."

"We've got to get him out," I said.

He looked at me helplessly.

"How?" he demanded. "We can't lift that!"

He nodded toward the immense trunk. It was obviously true. Had any of those jagged branches struck him directly, the Moose must have been speared against the ground as helplessly as a fly on a toothpick. As it was, well-nigh the weight of the tree was on that branch. Fortunately, Charbonneau's knee had been ground between two rocks, so that his leg below was trapped in the V of them, and though it seemed badly mangled, pinned there helplessly, yet the full weight of the forest giant was upon the stone rather than upon him.

"Where are the axes?" I demanded.

Fraser looked helpless.

"Under the tree," he replied.

It was true. Everything we had carried was buried under the tangle.

"Well!" I said desperately, "we've got to get them! Come on!"

All four of us turned to the task, clawing and pulling at the branches, breaking off ends and tips to fight our way into the snarled mass.

It must have been ten minutes before we came on the first of the packs, almost ground into the soft, forest compost by the weight of a smashing branch. Fortunately one of the axes thrust out of it at a crazy angle, and we snatched at it and after some struggle wrenched it free. There was no time to search for the other. I struggled back with it and set to hacking frantically at the branch. Westlake continued his search, while Fraser followed me and wisely set braces to keep the great trunk from rolling or settling.

So thick was the limb, at that, that it needed twenty minutes for me to chop through it. When it finally cracked and gave way, the Moose's eyes were open, his lower lip caught in his teeth, yet never a sound escaped him. Gingerly we lifted off the immense branch to find that miraculously, although the bones appeared broken, the skin had not been burst and no jagged ends of the fracture stuck through. To be sure, skin and flesh had been mashed and bruised. But the injury, though unquestionably serious, was no worse than any of us had seen many times before. Only our present situation made it a matter of extraordinary danger, and that situation was such as to make it very grave indeed!

Westlake, who was by far the most skilled among us, examined it carefully while the Moose spoke through blue lips.

" '*Cré nom—'cré nom!* Must it come off?"

We knew well enough what he meant. To lose a leg in this wilderness would be to die.

Westlake pursed his lips, then shook his head.

" 'Tis worth a try," he replied. "I've set as bad. We may save it. You don't mind a bit of a gimp, do you?"

He attempted a reassuring grin. The Moose leered back.

"Go on, goddam! *Sacré gros teton!* You got all day?"

Westlake set to work. Charbonneau clung to one of the nearby stout branches, while Fraser and I held fast to the thigh and Shea and Westlake pulled at the ankle until the muscles were extended and we could feel the bones come end to end. While I fingered them as nearly as I could into position, Fraser split out two rounds of stiff bark from a nearby cedar and gathered armsful of moss and ferns and whatever would serve as padding. This he placed evenly about the leg and enclosed it in the sections of bark, the while we held the bones in place above and below. Then, with strips torn from the remnants of our shirts, we bound the whole in place, immobilizing the leg from thigh to ankle.

When this was done and Charbonneau lay trussed and sweating, as comfortable as we could make him, Westlake shook his head.

"I hope 'twill serve," he commented.

"You don' leave me!" gasped the Moose.

"Don't worry!" I told him. "You go where we go!"

The Moose grinned painfully. "Wit' dis Moose fix better dan before. By goddam! I show you!"

Westlake, looking on, twisted his mouth in a wry smile.

"What now?"

"We'll have to rescue the gear," Fraser said. "What we can of it."

It occurred to us then to see the total of what damage had been done. It is true we had struggled in as far as the ax, but our main attention had been centered upon our comrade. Now we looked and saw to what pass we had been brought.

Everything that we owned and carried with us had been buried beneath the fallen giant. Our packs, our gear, axes, hatchet, kettles, even our weapons, and—worst of all—the canoe. The latter had been crushed to kindling. Even the shreds of it were not worth saving to build a fire. Daily we had fought the all-but-impenetrable jungle, satisfied to move inch by inch and step by step, just to fetch the craft across with us. Now it was all for nothing! Yet we could not stop!

Little by little, by dint of labor and digging and struggle, one by one, we fetched the rest of our scant belongings to light. Some were bent and dented. One of the kettles was ruined, crushed as near a lump of molten metal as any I have ever seen. One of the tarpaulins had been punched through and through by an immense branch. The shreds were useless as a diaper. The haft of one of the axes had been broken off six inches from the head, and the helve of the hatchet was splintered, though neither the ax nor the hatchet was more than chipped. Miraculously my rifle was unharmed, and my pistols I had carried in my belt. But Shea's musket was bent and smashed to matchwood. The stock of Charbonneau's gun had been split, and Fraser's weapon had been badly scarred and scratched. Westlake's compass and chronometer, perhaps our worst loss apart from the canoe, had been reduced to a handful of wood, wheels, and wire.

Having rescued what we could, we took hasty stock of the damage and decided—such is human optimism—that hurt we might be but destroyed we were not! Westlake voiced the thought.

"We're still alive," he said wryly, and shot a glance at Fraser. "I owe my thanks to you for that."

Fraser scratched at his beard, embarrassed.

"Rot!" he replied gruffly. "A man acts by instinct in his own bailiwick. No need to make much of it."

The mate eyed him strangely.

"Maybe you're right," he said, and shrugged.

We camped that night upon the spot, determined to leave naught that could possibly be rescued. Next morning, having fetched together all we could find, we made a litter of poles and strips cut from the ruined tarpaulin. Upon this we gently laid the now-delirious Charbonneau, strapping him securely to it so that he could not throw himself off.

We took turns carrying our wounded man, two at a time, while the other two went ahead and hacked and slashed a way through for us, step by step. I would have thought that, burdened by the sick man, we would have been forced to a slower pace, but the fact was that, having no longer to struggle with the canoe, we went more rapidly.

Apparently, however, this catastrophe crowned our share of ill fortune. On the second day after the accident I caught five full-grown wood mice, which cooked up into a not-too-unsavory stew when bled into a kettle and then mixed with the leaves of white pigweed and wild peas, for green, and the inner pith of young white cedars, for bulk. And on the third afternoon we struggled feebly to the crest of yet another ridge, to look down at last upon what was unmistakably a broad swamp, spreading all across the upper end of a deep-cut valley, with the glint of water showing ever so faintly through the trees at its lower edge. From where we stood it seemed little more than a rill. Yet it was water! And it seemed to flow off to the east.

Heartened by the sight, we hacked our way toward it, angling down the mountainside to avoid passing through the swamp, and came to the stream, just at nightfall, at the edge of a little meadow, where the wild grasses grew in tufted bunches and a great blue heron rose on ponderously flapping wings at our approach, to go sailing off across the tall trees of the swamp. It was an indication, it seemed to me, that mice or frogs and fish were not far off. The creek, we found, was four or five feet across the runs and a good deal bigger at the pools.

It swung in a curve about a low sandspit where we came upon it, and I think few can blame us that we put down our burden and ran to it, flinging ourselves down and burying our faces in the clear, cold, running depths. For the moment everything was forgotten, ignored, except our tremendous thirst.

Behind us, on his litter, half-askew, the Moose moaned plaintively. *"De l'eau! De l'eau! Pour l'amour de la bonne Vierge!"*.

Yet I think we would have been superhuman had we been able to refrain from drinking our own fill first. His pleading was not enough to distract me. I wonder then what it was that prompted me to raise my head. A crackle of brush, perhaps; the faint thud of a step upon the soft ground; maybe a half-consciously heard whistle of challenging breath caught my ear. I jerked up my head sharply from my ravenous gulping to see standing, not fifty feet away, and staring at us more in indignation than curiosity, a great bull elk.

No thought of savage enemies crossed my mind at that moment. Quickly I raised upon my knees and brought up my rifle. So still was he that I needed no more than a flickering second to aim and send a ball crashing into the point where his pendulous throat joined his neck. For an instant he stood stock-still in astonishment, then opened his mouth to utter a bellow of rage. Instead, a stream of blood gushed out, and at the same time the hole in his chest spurted crimson. Two long bounds he took and then fell, his legs askew and great eyes glazing. My comrades leapt to their feet and capered crazily upon the narrow beach, pounding me upon the back and whooping for joy. Meat! Food! Water! Ours at last, and in abundance! We might stay there, if we wished, the rest of our lives, and we would not be hungry or thirsty again! We had come so far! What lay before us now, we felt, could be no more than child's play!

That night we fed heartily on elk steaks, tough and sinewy to be sure, but none the less meat. We drank our fill of clear, cold water. We slept, heedless of danger, beside a roaring fire. And the next day we rested, fishing a little, hunting some, but mostly sleeping or lolling in the warm sun, slowly regaining our strength.

After a little search we found an excellent camp site at the lower end of the meadow, hard by where the creek began its swift, chuckling descent of a wooded valley. There, in a level wood, perhaps four or five feet above the meadow, so that we could look off across it, sheltered against possible prying eyes, we built a lean-to of bark and poles. Inside the shelter we made a deep-piled bed of fir tips, on which we made Charbonneau comfortable. In front of the shelter we built a log reflector, so that the warmth of the fire was thrown inside of a chill evening, and after that we set ourselves to restock our larder.

The creek abounded in trout, and the huckleberries were thick in the swampy meadow. As suddenly as they had disappeared, game seemed to return to the forest roundabout. Deer came down to drink at the creek. So did elk. And bears clowned in the berry patches. There were rabbits in the swamp above and grouse drummed in the woods. We were not afraid to shoot, for so far as we could see the woods for miles were totally devoid of human habitation.

Little by little we regained our strength, filling out wonderfully. With our knives we trimmed one another's beards and bled the

Moose's leg, so that the swelling went down and by the end of the third or fourth day his head had cleared and he was able to sit propped up in his bed and recognize us when we fetched him meat broth and marrow bones and berries and fish. He was able to sleep, to lie, even to move about a little without the pain he had formerly felt. The leg appeared to be healing as well as could be expected, though it seemed to me there was a twist to the set that indicated the bone was not so thoroughly meshed as it might have been. It would probably, I thought glumly, be crooked and possibly an inch or so shorter than the other. I think there must have been moments when it ached horribly, yet never once did the Moose complain. To occupy himself with useful pursuits when he was able, he asked us to fetch bones from the elk we had shot, and from these he whittled a number of good-sized needles. From the gut he made thread of a coarse sort, and with these and his knife as tools he worked swiftly and cheerfully upon the elk and deer hides that we fetched in. Of the former he made moccasins, after the Ojibway pattern, while of the latter he managed, in the time we were there, to turn out a fringed shirt and a crude pair of hunting breeches for each of us, replacing the tattered rags we had worn since we had left the ship.

We had been there about a fortnight when Fraser and I suggested that it might be well to explore a little downstream in the direction of the coast. The others agreed, and accordingly we two set out the next morning and followed the creek some six or eight miles down to an astoundingly beautiful little lake, set deep in the surrounding mountains, forested all about, and fed not alone by our creek but by half-a-dozen mountain streams which fell into this basin. Two of them were good-sized rivers, such as had fed the lake at the other side of the mountains, and there were four smaller streams, such as the creek down which we had come.

It seemed to us incredible that such a place could be uninhabited, and we circled it cautiously, peeking carefully about each point before we rounded it. Yet, though we stayed several days and scoured the shore thoroughly, we came across no sign to indicate that Indians or other humans had ever set foot in this place.

On the second day of our stay we worked our way to the end of the lake, where we found a stream tumbling out, as big as that up which we had come upon the opposite shore. Though at this point it was rather more gentle in its first descent, the indications were that it became steeper and more rugged a little below. There was every evidence of game, both at the inlets and the outlet, and we scarcely troubled ourselves to question the presence of fish in these waters. On the third day we ascended to the top of the ridge that dominated the lower end of the lake to find it wooded all along its crest. However, I climbed into a tall pine, and peering off through the branches to the north and east, I saw the unmistakable gleam of water between the green forests, widening to south and east to a limitless bay.

It is strange how the road back always seems shorter. What had taken us a full day to cover coming down, took us but a morning going back. We reached the camp to find our companions beginning to grow somewhat apprehensive at our absence. When they heard our report, however, they whooped with delight, and Shea and Westlake, at least, were for moving at once.

"Hold on!" I protested. "What about Moose?"

Westlake, at least, had the grace to seem shamefaced.

"Sure we carried him this far!" cried Shea. "There's no reason why we can't do the same from here on, especially an' him in better shape an' all!"

But the mate glanced at the old half-breed.

"How do you feel?" he demanded.

"By dam', never better! If she's not for dese dam' t'ing, I be dere before de res' of you. Yes, goddam!" retorted Charbonneau.

"D'you feel up to moving?"

"Sure, by dam'!" the Moose replied. "I can' walk yet. She's hurt lak' hell for hang down, but if you wan' carry me, *petits tetons!* By goddam, I'm ready!"

Since he was agreeable, we wasted no time in further discussion but agreed that Shea and I, as the lightest, should go on ahead in the morning with tools and whatever we could carry to begin camp. We were to set to work to clear the ground and perhaps erect a rude shelter for the others who would follow the next day. On the way we were to clean yet further the path that Fraser and I had hacked out, so that the others would have little difficulty carrying the Moose on his litter. A certain amount of inedible gear was to be left cached at the upper camp, to be fetched down later at our leisure.

In accord with this, Mike Shea and I left the meadows at dawn the following morning, and by the time our comrades had followed us we had cleared a sizable patch of level ground upon a tiny point amid the trees, jutting into the lake near where our creek fell into the still waters. We had also erected an open-front shelter, similar to the one we had thrown up at the upper camp, save that it was larger—big enough, indeed, to accommodate all of us. We rolled logs and stones to build a fireplace and fetched in quantities of firewood and fir tips for the beds. We had even found time to shoot a brace of deer and catch a score of trout and salmon.

When they arrived, Fraser and Westlake were amazed to see how much we had accomplished. Indeed, they were even abashed, they said, that we should have been working so strenuously while they, as they put it, loafed along the trail. It was nonsense, to be sure, but we were the last to say so. We made long, dour faces and let them believe that we considered ourselves imposed upon. By this means we induced them to return to the meadows and fetch down the remainder of the cached gear, the while Shea and I smugly loafed and spent the day fishing.

By the end of the week we were snugly settled in our new camp and ready to hold council to decide our next move. That afternoon the Moose made bold to test his leg, pulling himself erect on the poles and clinging to the edge of the shelter for support while he tentatively set his foot upon the ground and slowly, carefully, eased some of his weight on to it. Though his face showed no flicker of pain, yet I could tell by the alacrity with which he sat down again that he was still far from ready to walk upon it. I went into the woods, a little upstream, where there was a stand of hardwood, and there sought out a pair of forked saplings, sturdy enough for the purpose. These I cut down and fetched back to camp, where I whittled and smoothed them, making a rude pair of crutches. When I presented them to him he was delighted, and that night before the camp fire he demonstrated them to us and stumped on them down to the lake shore, where he cast his line for more than an hour, catching three fine salmon for our supper.

After we had eaten, as we loafed about the fire, feeling comfortably full, and wondering that we had ever come close to starving in this land of plenty, the Moose began the discussion.

"*Eh bien!*" he said. "What now? We can' stay here forever."

Each of us, brought to it, considered the question.

"What day of the month d'you make it?" asked Westlake.

There was a silence as each realized he had lost track of time. Shea chuckled.

"Sure now, come to think av it," he said, "what month would ye say 'twas?"

"Hoh!" Fraser snorted. " 'Tis July, of course!"

"It is not!" said Westlake. " 'Tis August!"

"What are you talking about?" demanded Fraser.

The mate, beyond the fire, sighed.

"Look you!" he retorted. "What was the date the *Tonquin* was destroyed? 'Twas June the twenty-fifth, was it not?"

"Aye," Fraser agreed doubtfully.

"Well, then," said Westlake, "count it out!"

Fraser looked unconvinced. I daresay he was about to make some contrary answer, for all it was obvious, when the Moose cut in again.

"W'at difference?" he demanded. "Fact is, dese summer she's half-gone an' we got goddam long way yet to go."

"I had some notion of finding another canoe," I said. "Maybe one of the coast tribes would trade us one."

The Moose snorted derisively. "W'at we trade, eh?"

I was forced to admit that only our guns and gear would tempt an Indian, and if we were ever to reach Astoria, we would need both. Even if we did not, it was a grave question if we could muster enough between us to purchase a canoe—all presupposing we might be so lucky as to find friendly Indians with whom to trade.

Charbonneau's dark eyes glinted, seeing my hesitation.

"You see? Goddam!" he said. "Mebbe ol' Moose's first scheme still bes'. We steal canoe?"

"Too risky." I shook my head emphatically. "There are always dogs in these villages, and we're bound to turn the natives against us if we try it."

"All right," he said. "Den, by goddam, we make one. Moose, I'm make Ojibway dugout many tam. Now I do what I can. W'at I can' do I tell you how. Tomorrow we begin, hé?"

So that was decided. The next day the Moose stumped out upon his crutches, scouring the woods near by. But not until afternoon did he find just the tree that suited him, a tall, straight cedar, with a grain as straight as a ruler. Its taper was slight and it rose eighty or ninety feet before it put out its first branch.

This tree he ordered us to cut down—a task which took four of us the better part of four days to accomplish, for we must first clear a place for it to fall and cushion it with saplings so that it would not shatter. When it had finally been brought down, after a careful inspection by him we cut out a section, which he indicated, some thirty feet long. This, with the help of skids and pry poles and a good deal of sweat and labor, we jockeyed aside to a comparatively level lie, where we rolled it on small skid logs and temporarily braced it in place with stakes.

There Charbonneau himself set to work. I must say, as I looked at it, it seemed to me that it would be an endless, if not impossible, task to shape any kind of craft from that enormous trunk. Yet the Moose himself appeared nowhit dismayed. He had help from us, to be sure, at various points. But in the main, he worked largely by himself, for only he had the experience to give just the right touches to the work.

I will not attempt to describe every step of the undertaking, but, working largely with the hatchet, using a wooden maul and wedges of hardwood and bone and such crude tools as we were able to make from the remnants of the gear destroyed by the tree fall, he first squared off the log, riving perhaps a foot from the top of it and six inches from the bottom and each of the sides. Then with knife and hatchet he set to work to chip and shape the sides and bottom roughly, so that the outline, at least, of what he meant to have when he was finished was there. When this was done, he used a slow fire to hollow out the log itself, charring a section, putting out the fire, and scraping away the charcoal to the solid wood, then moving along to repeat the process in the next section and the next, and so on, until a trough was cut from the heart of the log that was roughly canoe-shaped. This he worked upon with his sheath knife, sitting in it with his crutch beside him, patiently smoothing and scouring the results, with a rough stone first and then with a smooth one, until the inside was as clean and highly polished as if it had been sanded.

After that it was surprising to find out how much lighter the log had become. We were able to roll it over easily and prop it upon its side while he worked and shaped the bow and stern and gunnel, giving flare to the forward and after ends, smoothing the bottom, and allowing a slight tumble home to the sides. The ends were saved until last and were shaped finally into low, curving points, only a little higher than the sides. The gunnels themselves were somewhat higher than normal, so that, save for a very slight rise at bow and stern, the resulting boat was nearly level throughout its length. When we launched it, it rode high and dry as a duck in the water, and I was pleased to see that he had allowed for the possibility of rough weather ahead. It was all of three feet from keel to gunnel in a vertical line, so that even loaded it had a freeboard of eighteen inches or more and as much as a foot above what one would expect of a bark canoe of similar size.

IV. RETURN TO ASTORIA

ALL of this was not accomplished in a week or a day or even a month. Gradually under our eyes it took form, a curious-looking craft, doubtless because of our purpose, not quite like anything I had ever seen before. Over-all, when finished, she was about twenty-six feet long, by four broad, reinforced by cross thwarts, two forward and two aft, with a fifth directly amidships. In addition there were cross braces for the portable mast, which could be stepped immediately abaft the foremost thwart. From start to finish the task must have taken close to two months, perhaps even two months and a half, so that October was nearly past, according to my calculations, and the rains were beginning by the time she was done.

During all that time nature did not stand still. Charbonneau's leg mended slowly but steadily. At first he could only hobble about upon his crutches and sit astride the great log while he worked, but as the craft appeared to grow, so did his shattered limb regain its strength. By the end of the first month he was able to throw away his crutches and move about with the help of a cane. Although he still clung to his stick by the time the canoe was ready for launching, yet I noticed he depended upon it less and less, preferring to hobble, gimping, with it only held in his hand.

At the same time the rest of us were not idle. Indeed there was plenty for all to do. There were paddles and floorboards to make, braces to cut, a mast to finish, and stays and a sail to shape. These Shea and myself, with Westlake's aid, worked upon in every spare moment. The rest of the time there were chores which were both necessary and numerous. If we hoped to make our way to Astoria, we must provide for the journey. Westlake fished. So did Shea. Fraser and I hunted.

As nearly as we could tell, once at salt water, there would lie before us a journey of close to five hundred miles, and it was on the basis of this estimate that we made our preparations. Some of the fish and game taken we consumed, as indeed we must, upon the spot, but most of it we readied to carry with us. The lean meat of elk and deer and bear we cut in strips and smoked or jerked, then made into pemmican and packed in bags made of the animals' hides, approximately the size commonly used by the Northwesters. Roughly each contained ninety pounds of concentrated meat food and was carefully sewed and greased and stored against our need.

This would be our staple diet, although there might be occasional luxuries. Salmon and trout and the tongues of deer and elk were smoked and packed; so were bear's hams and bacon. Breasts of partridge, ducks, geese, and ptarmigan were also smoked; while hearts, livers, kidneys, and the like, which would not keep well, we ate at once.

The bladders and seemingly endless intestines of the larger animals were excellent for keeping fats, oils, and the more delicate sorts of pemmican. The brains we used for tanning, along with the inner bark of some trees, such as red cedar, hemlock, and the like. Sinews and guts made ties and strings and ropes, and the scrotums of large bull elk and buck deer were fine for carrying tobacco and our smaller personal possessions.

Indeed only once during all that interval did we find time for anything else, and this is scarcely to be regarded as pastime. It occurred to us, perhaps a little belatedly, that it might be well to investigate the route to salt water. Accordingly Fraser and I were picked to go and study the situation.

The outlet, we found, was swift, but not nearly so precipitous at the outset as the stream up which we had struggled on the other side of the island. But this comparatively quiet water did not last, and below it plunged into ten miles of writhing, leaping, churning white water that pummeled and gouged the bottom of a steep ravine all the way to a broader valley below. After that it ran with a sort of eager urgency through a series of long glides and chutes over rubbly bottom, another fifteen miles to the Straits of Georgia.

The first pitch, it was evident, would be our most difficult. There were at least three points at which we must carry. Yet we viewed these stretches with almost smug complacence. Had we not fetched a much larger craft over half the island already, through woods as thick and across cliffs as sheer and rocks as rugged as these? Between carries, we thought, the canoe might be let down by means of ropes and poles—no use rushing at matters. But once below that ten-mile stretch we should ride at a swoop, almost without stopping, to tidewater.

Just the same, as a matter of caution, we followed the stream to its mouth, and it was as well we did so, for at the last reedy point we crept through the brush, with the scent of the tide flats and the sea in our faces, to see, not three hundred yards before us, between the open water of the straits and the muddy banks of the winding stream, a considerable village of long huts, built up on poles, after the manner of these northern savages. Out beyond it the channeled arm of the sea seemed narrow indeed to me, for it was no more than three or four miles across. Beyond that we could see the dark, forested shores of the opposite coast backed by the sheer folded slopes of the jagged mountains of the mainland, green below and ending above in a series of sharp-edged peaks and ridges of rock and snow.

But it was the village that held our attention. All along the low beach before it, muddy now at low tide, a variety of canoes, long and short, were drawn up. Naked children wallowed in the mud under the houses, where offal and garbage were incontinently flung; and lean, wolf-like dogs prowled among them with complete indifference. I could see a few older people upon the platforms, but the younger men were evidently away, either hunting along the shore or fishing against the coming winter.

I glanced at Fraser as we lay peering through the reeds.

"Well," I said. "There it is!"

"Aye!" he growled. "Poor Moose! We could snatch one of those easily."

"I'm not so sure," I replied. "I don't care for those beasts prowling about."

"Pooh!" he snorted contemptuously. "Well, let's get back!"

He started to rise to his feet before I could catch at him, and doubtless the movement in the tall grass caught the attention of the dogs, for they were out of the vlliage and racing up the shore of the slough between us almost before we could think what had happened. Yapping and baying and snarling, they were like so many wolves, and worse, I have no doubt, for like most Indian curs they were half-famished and anything that moved in the woods was fair game to them.

"Come away!" I cried. "If those savages once get the notion we are here, it will not be pleasant."

We stooped low and took to our heels, running upstream as lightly as we could, avoiding soft patches that might show telltale tracks for the Indians to follow. Fortunately, just above the first bend the river split and ran deep on either side of a long island. There we were forced to take refuge, cutting across the loop of intervening land to strike the stream above, and plunging into the water up to our chins and floundering across to fling ourselves down in the brush at the upper end. We were scarcely hidden when the pack burst in full cry from the woods along the riverbank, where, losing our scent, they ran up and down, this way and that, sniffing and nosing after it, while the pair of us lay still, scarce daring to breathe, for the beasts might swim if they thought we were there.

I was glad that none of the savages came after their dogs. No doubt they thought them chasing some animal in the nearby woods, as probably they often did. The animals prowled up and down the bank all the rest of the afternoon and only gave up toward dusk to return home to the comfort of the mud. In the meantime Fraser and I lay close in the brush.

"D'ye see what I mean?" I whispered.

"I see!" he replied dryly.

It was only long after dark that we dared to stir. Then we crept out cautiously, keeping to the water, and for as much as a mile we floundered and plowed upstream. We were two days getting back to camp, where we reported what we had found and gave an account of how we had been pursued. As we told it, the others seemed to find it highly amusing. I think, however, that when they came to look at it more soberly, they recognized the danger of discovery, for always after that one or another of us was posted to keep watch upon our camp. Yet the masters must have been as lazy as the hounds, for in the three weeks that we yet remained we were not once discovered.

The day came at last when the canoe was ready. I doubt, I declare, if any boatmaker could have improved upon her, for all she appeared somewhat awkward owing to the purpose for which we intended her. Yet it was with some anxiety that we carried her cautiously to the lakeside and put her to the test.

But we were quickly reassured, and at first by pairs we took turns at showing off her paces so that the others might admire her lines and ease of handling. Then afterward all five of us embarked for a cruise upon the lake. The next morning we loaded her with a weight equivalent to what she would carry upon the journey, and Westlake stepped the mast and rigged the sail and sideboards, and we all went out in her again to see how she might behave in those circumstances. Once again she proved herself seaworthy, for she handled smartly and rode dry as a bone and lightly as a feather, for all she must be carrying nearly a ton and a half.

"By goddam!" cried Charbonneau. "She's work good! Ha? We don' meet no Injun w'at can catch dat! *Tetons de p'tite Vierge!* I'm tal' you, we soon be home in dis! By goddam! Tomorrow we go, hé?"

I heard no dissenting voice, and I daresay it was as well, for that night it poured, the great drops drumming savagely on the roof of our shelter while we lay wakeful and thinking, wondering what might lie ahead for us.

I will not say the journey down the river was easy. Far from it. After the first moderate stretch it was necessary to carry, not three times, as we had calculated, but five times, so that more than half the stretch was covered on land, and it almost seemed to me that we might as well have taken it all in one long portage. Charbonneau's injured leg impeded us seriously for all he was able to move along now without the help of either stick or crutch. His gait was slow, limping, and I judged yet rather painful. He was strictly forbidden to carry anything but himself, and one of us was always near by to accompany him and give him a hand, while the others, as a rule, cut trail or tended to their assigned chores. We were five days covering that first ten miles. But on the sixth day we raced down through the swooping runs and rapids, in that single day covering all the distance that remained.

At the island on which Fraser and myself had hidden we landed and drew our craft up out of sight. It lacked but a little of dusk, and since we felt it might be wise to scout ahead, we sought concealment and huddled close in a brief council of war.

I was glad that the wind was from the northeast, gentle as it might be, for it prevented the curs at the mouth of the river from obtaining our scent. Logically either Fraser or myself should go forward, and I, as the lightest, was chosen, while the others remained in hiding. I stripped to my moccasins and, crossing to the main shore, crept through the brush to a point where I could watch the settlement, while at the same time I remained well hidden in the undergrowth.

What I saw appeared to me reassuring. There was nothing to indicate any suspicion. Blue smoke rose from the holes in the bark roofs or seeped through cracks purposely left open between the planks. The dogs had evidently retired for the night. The light breeze that blew from the strait beyond carried with it the odor of salt flats at low tide, mingled but faintly now with the stench of the offal that lay between. Even the grotesquely carved poles upon which the clan had immortalized their totems leaned at rakish angles before the row of sorry huts, as if sickened by the smell. The tide was out, just beginning to set in, and I could mark the channel easily, winding in loops between the ready point and the salt water beyond.

A wispy fog obscured the farther shore, hanging low against the ghostly line of firs and cedars, and the snow-capped mountains I had seen beyond were hidden now underneath a blanket of clouds. There was a smell of rain in the air. The tide was coming in faster now. I could see the water creeping over the mud flats before the village and filling the small depressions and hollows on either side.

I crept cautiously back through the brush to a place opposite the island where I took to the water, which now felt positively warm, and finding my friends resting comfortably where I had left them, I drew on my clothes and told them what I had seen. When I had finished, they peered through the murk at Westlake, who took charge of navigation from this point. He glanced at me.

"What do you think?" he demanded.

"The tide should set out about two in the morning," I said. "By that time both dogs and savages should be deep asleep. We should be able to slide by on the current then unseen."

There were no objections, and I, having done my duty, rolled into my blankets and fell almost instantly asleep, while the others drew straws for the watch.

I was roused in the wet dark by one of my companions shaking my shoulder, and I rolled from my blankets with a sort of subdued excitement. Some time in the course of the night it had begun to rain, not heavily, but a steady, misty drizzle such as soaks through whatever it may touch. Cautiously we repacked the canoe, covering the amidships cargo with the tarpaulin, and took our places with Charbonneau serving as bowman and Westlake to steer, a compromise between the fresh- and salt-water arrangements. I took the place just in front of Westlake to act as pilot.

At the upper end of the island the water was still fresh, untouched by the tide, the current moderately strong. But by the time we had reached the reedy lower and we were come into tidewater end, I saw that the ebb had begun. There was no moon or stars, and to my surprise, where in the evening there had been no water at all, now there was often as much as two or three feet. Only a vague shadow against the lighter darkness of the fogbound sky marked the loom of the forested shore on either hand, and the black outlines of the village against the deeper darkness of the woods were so faint as to be all but indistinguishable. It was scarcely necessary even to paddle, for the sweep of the tide and the current carried us out, not swiftly, but steadily. Quietly the village slipped past. Neither man nor dog woke so far as we could see. Within a quarter of an hour we were clear of the points in salt water, with the set of the tide tugging us toward the north and west along the shore, in the opposite direction to that in which we wanted to go.

Westlake leaned forward and touched me on the shoulder.

"We've left the river," he whispered. "Tide and current set north-west through the channel. So does the wind. We'll have to paddle hard to buck them. Pass the word. We'll cross to the other shore and run close to it. With luck, by morning we may gain sailing water and a different set of current."

I passed that forward in a low tone, and one by one paddles came up and out. We bent our backs in the darkness, scarcely able to see as far as the man ahead of us, yet Westlake seemed to know by some sea-man's instinct the way to steer.

We cut across diagonally until the whisper of the current among the rocks ashore told us that we were close to the other side. There we turned and made our way south and east along the shore. It seemed to me interminable, though it could not have been more than three hours before the blackness began to thin and little by little we could see the shores and the dripping forests, looming through the ghostly fog. To-ward dawn we put ashore long enough to break our fast, then pushed on through a maze of tangled channels and islands in which no human being stirred. By midmorning the fog began to lift, and we passed out of the narrow channel and the myriad islands into broader waters. A breeze sprang up. Clouds parted, showing us, first, patches of blue sky and then the sun. We shipped our paddles and set over our sideboards and raised our sail, picking up speed as we went skipping merrily over the water. By noon we had left the tugging tide behind and were in the broad straits, the land looming blue in the distance on either hand. To our left tremendous snow-capped mountains towered. On our right lower peaks, not less spectacular, raised their craggy heads. For the time being, at least, we felt safe from pursuit, for it was doubtful if our dark sail and our tiny craft could be seen so far from shore. Our only danger lay from the considerable seas which ran before the stiff wind, forcing us to tack diagonally across them, every now and again throw-ing spray across us and forcing us to bail frantically.

However, we took turns steering, following the course set by West-lake, while Shea improved matters by rigging a canvas "dodger," as he called it, cut from the remnants of the damaged tarpaulin, to keep the spray off, increasing our freeboard some eighteen inches. At the same time he took a piece to form an awning, beneath which those of us not engaged in navigation might rest and sleep.

We covered nearly three hundred miles in that canoe and could have gone a thousand more if need be. We sailed day and night where it was possible. Later, when we came into the maze of islands that pep-

pered the southern end of the strait and Puget Sound itself, we often
slept by day, first because of the danger of meeting hostile Indians in
these narrow waters, and second because of the unpredictable winds
and currents that made it necessary frequently to unship the sail and
mast and take to the paddles. As we pushed farther and farther south,
we encountered more and more wet and foul weather. Often the rains
sluiced down upon us endlessly for twenty-four hours at a stretch, without the slightest abatement. Especially about the entrance to the sound
and the end of the straits we met fog—thick, clammy, impenetrable.
When rain and murk threatened to engulf us to such an extent that we
could not tell which way we were going, then we would go to ground
and lie close, waiting for the weather to pass, and though toward the
end of the journey it was all bad and wet and soggy, at least there were
brief intervals when it was better and it was possible to go forward
slowly, feeling our way from point to point.

Three times we were pursued by savages, yet each time we managed
to outdistance them by raising our sail and bending to our paddles.
Perhaps they were not hostile but merely curious. But we dared not risk
encounter here. Twice we lay through the day within sight and sound
and smell of native villages; hidden in the undergrowth and quaking
lest the dogs discover us, waiting for darkness to slip past. Whenever it
was possible we put ashore at some secluded spot to refill our water
breakers or to take on fish and small game; to cook a hot meal or snatch
a few hours' sleep ashore.

As we drew near the end of Puget Sound, the points, shrouded in
immense forests, grew longer, reaching out to intercept us, while
hundreds of green, rocky-shored islands spattered the surface of the
water. Between them the tides and currents swirled and jostled, forming mysterious whirlpools, often setting unpredictably against us so
strongly that we barely crept along by dint of the utmost labor. On
either hand the towering mountain ranges seemed to be closing in upon
us. Though none of us mentioned it, I think we were all of the same
thought: when we came to the end of navigation, what then?
Obviously Westlake's hint of a possible passage to the Columbia was
no more than a pious hope.

The day came at last when we poked cautiously around a low point
to find before us no further navigable water but only a curving stretch
of reedy shore backed by the dark, dripping forest and broken midway
by a small, meandering stream, upon the far bank of which sprawled
a considerable Indian village. So abruptly did we come upon it that
there was no time to draw back. Among the long huts the dogs set up

a clamor, and almost before we were aware of it the natives were troop-
ing to the water's edge, slipping their long canoes into the water.

"That's it," said Fraser. "Shall we run for it?"

Charbonneau answered him.

"Better take chance."

We rested our paddles across the gunnels and waited while several
of the long Indian craft put out from shore and came tentatively toward us. When they were within hailing distance they, too, laid their
paddles across the gunnels before them and drifted, watching us alertly.
The Moose held up his hand in the Indian sign of peace. Quietly we
all followed his example, and, to our delight, the savages in the foremost canoe returned the greeting. After that they came alongside us
and clucked at us in a tongue that was reminiscent of the Chinook we
had heard at the Columbia. Charbonneau, whose Indian background
made it easier for him to learn their speech, cackled back at some
length, talking mainly with a stocky copper-hued man who wore a
robe of dogskins across his shoulders. Presently the Moose turned back.

"Dese Injun," he said, "she's call himself Nisqually. Dis chief, she's
name Mitsukwik. Dey cousin wit' Chehalis. He's friendly. Dat's good!
Dat's very good, oh yes, goddam! Long tam' now he say dey hear 'bout
white man in south dat's build fort an' trade furs. Firs' tam' she's tol'
white man he's enemy to hes people an' won' trade only wit' Chinook.
But dese Chinook, he's say, she's robber, an' wan' keep all trade for
himself. Now he's hear dese white man wan's be frien' an' trade wit'
all Injun. Long tam' he's t'ink mebbe she's goin' to go see white man.
Now he's say mebbe he don' need to."

"How far is it?" I interrupted him.

He turned and spoke to the smiling chief.

"He say 'bout one half moon," he told me presently. "Twelve,
maybe fourteen sleep. Mebbe we comin' home quick from here, eh?"

I thought quickly.

"Tell him," I said, "that we're not here for trade now. We are here
to explore the country. But we have presents to give to him, and that
if he will come with some of his young men to Astoria with us and hold
powwow with our chief, we will have other presents for them all and
give them good prices for their furs."

Once again Charbonneau chattered at considerable length, and all
around us the hitherto stolid, somewhat dour savage faces burst into
smiles of anticipation and excitement.

"What did you offer 'em presents for?" Fraser growled.

"Keep your hair on!" I retorted. "How else would we interest them? Let each cling to his weapons, powder, and ball, but we'll have to pool stuff like blankets and kettles and knives and fishhooks and the like. 'Twill be worth parting with if it will induce them to guide us to the Columbia."

The others nodded. Fraser shrugged.

"Perhaps you're right," he admitted.

"You talk sense." I grinned.

But for all our impatience, we were not to be allowed to move swiftly. We feasted that night and the next and the next upon roast dog and smoked clams, well-aged, fine, ripened salmon and sturgeon and boiled camass root; a diet, I must say, that appealed to me but little. Yet I thought it worth it to retain the friendship of Mitsukwik and his people.

Had we wished, we could have stayed among them all winter, for they were hospitable and obviously flattered to have white men as their guests. But, naturally, we were impatient to be off.

Mitsukwik and his fellow chiefs produced a number of furs for our inspection: marten, beaver, sable, fisher, and the like. These they offered as presents, and in return we presented them with some of our gear, the hatchet, one of the axes, a kettle, some blankets, and various other odds and ends as we could part with. These, we made it clear, were merely a token of our friendship. If they would come with us to Astoria, where we had ample supplies, we could be far more lavish. But it was not until we told them the prices we would pay for their furs that they became genuinely enthusiastic. Hitherto, they had followed the usual practice of trading their skins to the Chinooks, and the prices in trade goods that we mentioned were astoundingly lavish to them, though they were actually no more than we offered the Chinooks themselves for the same furs! The canoe, with her sails and paddles, we presented to Mitsukwik, who was delighted with her.

We left the village about a fortnight after our arrival, accompanied by the chief and a score of warriors, who led us almost at a trot up along the small stream on which the village was located, until we had reached higher ground. There we swung, by a well-defined path, generally southward, through dense, dripping woods, up over a low ridge to a much larger stream. This we followed up several days, twisting and winding through the incessant rain, deep into the ridgy hills, until at length we swung off sharply, a day to the right, then another to the left, and climbed up over a well-defined ridge, to drop down upon the other side directly into Concomly's Chinook village on the north shore of the Columbia estuary.

The distance, I guessed, must have been something like a hundred and twenty miles altogether, though I admit I lost all track of time in the crossing. The rain fell constantly, cold and soaking, and the forests through which we passed were almost as dense as those through which we had struggled across the island to the northward.

The old one-eyed chief of the Chinooks greeted us with an enthusiasm not less genuine because we were survivors of the *Tonquin* or because he smelled a generous reward for such assistance as he might be able to afford us. I think he was rather less delighted to welcome our companions, in whom I believe he scented possible business rivals. With a show of hospitality he proposed a great feast in our honor—a somewhat ticklish matter, for now that we were almost in sight of our destination we were in no mood to dally. Fortunately Charbonneau was able to make him understand our impatience, and after extracting from us a promise to return and allow him to welcome us properly, he placed three canoes at our disposal and even accompanied us himself in his barge of state—in order, I more than suspect, that our Nisqually comrades might not, in his absence, obtain any greater advantage with us than he himself enjoyed.

I find it hard to describe, even today, the feeling of mingled joy and relief and sadness with which we saw those forested shores. As we drew near, we could see that our companions had not been idle in our absence. The roofs of the cabins and warehouses showed now above a stout stockade of logs set vertically in the ground, and a flag waved from a tall pole above them. Blue smoke rose against the thick forest, telling us that inside was warmth and cheer; a battery of six-pounders, overlooking the anchorage before the point, bespoke security such as we had not known since the loss of the *Tonquin*. To seaward no ship rode at anchor, but a small schooner, beyond doubt that which we had carried out with us, lay moored alongside the landing in the cove, and long before we reached the dock beside it we could see the figures of men moving about, coming and going between the water and the fort itself.

At first, apparently, they paid little heed to us, no doubt thinking us no more than the neighboring tribesmen come over for a visit. Yet as we came closer, evidently Fraser's red hair and our scrawny beards, our buckskin dress, caught their attention, and first one, then another, and another stopped to watch our approach. In the bow of the first canoe Westlake waved, and after an instant the men on shore waved tentatively back. Then some turned and ran toward the fort, while the rest hastened toward the wharf. Swiftly we drove in, yet by the time we came to shore the gate was open, and all except those actively on duty and unable to leave their posts were either gathered at the dock or streaming down toward it.

We slid with a flourish alongside, and I caught the planking and leapt out, turning quickly to catch the craft by the gunnel and steady it for the others.

"Fetch her down this way," said a voice vaguely familiar—a voice that came a long way down through the years past; an unpleasant voice; a hateful voice. "Make room for the others to come in alongside."

I turned about and stared and stood up slowly, forgetting the canoe I had just left, forgetting the journey I had just made and the comrades who had made it with me; conscious of a sudden chill of suspicion. There was no mistaking that scowling, barrel-chested, black-browed, and black-bearded speaker.

It was Dirk MacPherson!

VI. Astoria

~~~~~~

I. OREGON OUTPOST

EVEN now I can sometimes feel the sharp wrench of surprise and shock that seemed to block the breath in my throat and made my face feel pinched.

"You!" I cried. "What the devil are you doing here?"

"What matter is that to you?" he growled.

"I mean to make it matter to me!" I snarled.

I think we might have been at each other's throats in another instant, but there was no opportunity for quarreling, for at that moment MacDougal and the younger Stuart came elbowing through the crowd.

"O'Rourke! Fraser! By all that's holy!" cried Stuart.

"Aye!" rumbled MacDougal, grinning. "An' Westlake, an' yon girt rum-pot Moose, tae say naethin' o' Shea!"

He clapped us on the back and wrung our hands. The others closed about us—dancing, capering, pummeling, reaching out to touch us, calling our names in welcome, though for the moment we had small chance to make any coherent answer; Franchere, De Montigny, McGillis, Wallace, Bouvier, Koaster, Lafantaisie, the younger McKay, all were there. It was MacDougal who reminded us.

"Whur's th' ship?" he asked, squinting and peering out toward the entrance, no doubt expecting to see the *Tonquin* riding at anchor just inside. "Aye! An' whur air th' ithers?"

He turned toward me with a look of dawning apprehension, for the first time seeming to see our tatters and beards. The others fell silent and looked toward us. I felt a tightening of the throat that was hard to speak around, and salt tears stung my eyes and made me blink. In all that time we had been so driven by the need to save ourselves that we had been unable to give more than passing thought to the fact that the rest were gone.

Something of the same thought must have been in the minds of the others. They looked toward me. I opened my mouth to speak and found I could not. I swallowed and tried again, and this time fetched out something like a croak.

"They're gone," I blurted. "Gone! All of them! Murdered by savages at Nootka. The ship's blown up!"

There was a long moment of silence in which they all stared at me. We could hear the water lapping gently at the dock beneath our feet; patter of rain all about. Tom McKay was first to speak.

"My—my uncle——?" he half-whispered.

"Aye!" I nodded glumly. "Among the first. We—we're all that got away."

MacDougal sighed windily, as if the words had robbed him of the power of thought and action. But Rob Stuart put his hand upon my shoulder, and I was grateful for the friendly pressure.

"That's—dreadful hearing," he said. "Aye! And sore for you as well. But at least we may be glad that some escaped. Come up yon to the fort, and let us see you warmed and fed. When you're refreshed, you can tell us about it. 'Tis not right to ask now!"

"Aye!" grumbled MacDougal, reminded of his duty. "Come get ye'rsel's cleaned up before ye tell us aboot it. At least ye've pickit a fine day tae coom hame tae us!"

"Day?" I looked at him blankly. "What day?"

"Dinna ye ken?" He looked startled, amazed. " 'Tis Christmas Eve!"

Abruptly he fell to laughing. My lack of response must have disconcerted him, for he stopped as shortly as he had begun and glanced about him. For the first time he caught sight of Mitsukwik and his warriors.

"Who'er yon sovages?"

I explained quickly. Both Stuart and MacDougal shook hands with the Indian ceremoniously and bade him welcome. Whatever else one might think of him, the round little Scot was experienced with red men. He knew the proper gesture.

I cannot describe the sense of unreality with which I stepped back into this world of comparative civilization. So long had we lived upon the country, using our wits for survival, that all this luxury, crude as it might be, seemed to me to be utterly unreal. Hot water and a warm bath, soft blankets, clean clothes, the pampering luxury of a shave, feeling my face clean again and hairless to the touch, civilized food, plain but hot, aye, and belly-warming drink, and all about us the faces of friends—these were all part of it. So, too, was the somber realization of other friends now gone forever.

That night, over what seemed to us an immense banquet table, we must tell our story over and over and over again: of fighting our way through thickets, battling cold and wet and hunger and insect pests, misery and starvation and injury, rain that drenched and sun that burned, thirst and deadly fatigue; how we had fled from savages and found our own food; how Charbonneau had made the canoe, hobbling about first on crutches and then a cane; how we had run the river; the falling tree; the long carries; the homeward voyage. Incident by incident, step by step, we had to tell time and again. The treachery of the Indians, the self-sacrifice of James Lewis, the costly stupidity of Captain Thorn, and the tragic foreboding of Alec McKay; we reviewed it all to the point of exhaustion. Yet in the intervals we managed to learn some of what had taken place in our absence.

The elder Stuart had gone with Ross and Pillot and McLennan far up the river to Oakanagan to establish a post to serve as a foil to the Northwesters, who had already pushed their way from Kootenay to Kullyspell and Spokane House. Of the overland party not a sign had been seen or rumor heard. MacDougal was serious when we asked for them, and he shook his head.

"Na, na!" he growled. "They maun ha' been here th' noo. I fear they met wi' disaster somewhur i' th' way."

"Aye," agreed De Montigny gloomily, "nor have we seen aught of the relief vessel Mr. Astor promised us."

MacDougal looked even more grim.

"Dinna ye remind me o't," he grumbled, "now yon *Tonquin's* gaed wi' mair than half o' ouwer supplaes!"

"You're short then?" I asked.

"Aye!" he replied emphatically. "Th' nicht we've killed th' fatted calf!"

His words fetched a silence all about that great board as the rest of us considered their implication. Outside the rain drummed upon the roof and the sweet stench of the Indians rose in the heat of the sputtering candlefish. Stuart sought to inject a note of greater cheer into our welcome.

"Come now!" he cried. "The moment is not one for gloom! They'll both be here before long. At least we've proof the journey overland can be done, and we'd not be here ourselves if ships could not sail!"

"Proof?" I looked at him. "Oh, you mean Lewis and Clark?"

"Oh, more recent than that." He laughed. "You were not out of the river mouth before we had visitors—Northwesters from upstream."

"The devil you say!" I cried.

"Aye!" said MacDougal. "An' who d'ye think fetched 'em?"

"Am I supposed to know?" I demanded.

" 'Twas an auld acquentance o' ye'r ain," he assured me. "Davie Thompson nae less!"

"You don't say so!" I stared at the pair of them in amazement.

"No need to take our word for it," Stuart chuckled. "The proof of it sits yonder." He nodded at MacPherson.

"So that's——?" I began.

"He'd a nasty gash in his foot that he'd done with an ax," Stuart explained. "Thompson left him with us to convalesce."

MacPherson said nothing. I thought he was ill at ease.

"Did he, now?" I growled.

"Oh, aye," said Stuart airily, "and two voyagers had a mind to stay with us. We sent two of our own back with him in place of them. And there was an Indian lad that had served him. Kalikash, or Kashkishum, or some such they called him. He ran away the day after they got here."

Over the board my eyes met Fraser's, startled. I took refuge in small talk.

"Was Davy here long?" I asked.

"Almost two months," he replied. "They did not start back until the end of July, when Uncle David and his party went upriver. We thought at first of sending overland for you. We could have intercepted you easily at Gray's Harbor."

"You knew we were there?"

"Of course!" he replied. "All the Indians on the coast knew it and passed the word. We heard it almost before your anchor had found holding!"

"I'd forgotten news traveled so fast," I said.

Again my eyes met Fraser's across the table, and it seemed to me that he looked strained. I shook my head, and he looked down at his plate. Later, in the privacy of our room, he turned upon me.

"Why?" he demanded. "Why would he do it?"

"You're pretty well convinced he did, aren't you?" I said.

"There's no doubt about it!" he exclaimed hotly.

"The man's the devil himself," I interrupted him, "and more slippery than an eel! I'm not protecting him. He hates me——"

"So that's it!" he cried.

" 'Twas me he wanted," I said. "He arranged for Kas to run away and join us at Gray's Harbor."

"That's evident," he retorted. "That's——"

"That's why I didn't trust the dog," I went on, giving him no chance to say what it was he had in mind. "I sensed he was waiting for something, watching for a chance at me. But the Indians at Nootka struck before him! Do you see? Do you sense the irony of it? They got everyone, or nearly everyone, except the one he wanted!"

"That's what I say!" he cried. "He set them on——"

"I don't think he had anything to do with that," I broke in. "MacPherson hired Kas to do for me, but what happened was outside their ken. They were not counting on it, and it wrecked everything so far as they were concerned!"

He stared at me in disbelief.

"You mean to say they weren't responsible?"

"I'm afraid that this can't be blamed upon him!" I replied. "I know well enough he'd be only too happy. But much as I hate to admit it, I am afraid he had no hand in what really happened."

He sat down upon his log bunk, utterly nonplused.

"Now you know the answer," I said, "I hope you'll keep an eye upon him. MacPherson and I are not done with each other yet!"

"I will!" he promised grimly.

We fed our Nisquallies well that night and the next day again, and gave them presents, to the infinite disgust of Concomly and his people. MacDougal agreed with Mitsukwik to deal with him, and then on Christmas night we all went in a body across the river again to the Chinook village, where once more we ate smoked rancid salmon and sturgeon and dog stew and wapatoo roots by way of proving to the one-eyed chief that we had no favorites. The next morning we bade our Nisqually friends farewell.

There followed, then, for those of us, at least, who had survived the *Tonquin*, an interval of lazy recovery. Strange how quickly the human animal can grow accustomed to his surroundings! One month I was feeding myself upon cold pemmican gone slightly sour and counting myself lucky to have that or jerked biche. Next I found myself critical of the sauce and complaining that the steward had cooked the roast venison until it was overdone; complaining that we were served salmon or trout four days out of seven!

It did not take as long to find out just how hard the loss of the *Tonquin* had served our little community. Half the year's trade goods and supplies had been lost. As a result there was little actual difference

in the ordinary daily fare at Astoria and that which we had found in
the forests by dint of our own foraging. Salmon, which the Indians
fetched to us in great quantities, and sturgeon were the staples of
our diet. A few soggy potatoes and similar root vegetables had been
rescued from the kitchen garden planted in the spring; as had some
corn meal from the field beyond the creek. There was a little flour
left and some boxes of dried fruits. But such luxuries were so scarce
as to be brought forward only upon Sundays and special occasions.

In the nearby forests the elk, which had abounded hereabout on our
arrival, seemed to have withdrawn, no doubt to higher ground to
escape some of the wetness of the rainy season, so that even jerked
biche was a comparative luxury. Now and again one of our hunters
or the Indians would fetch in a deer, a brace of geese, or a number
of duck or partridge. But in the main we lived upon fish, for when
game was scarce, it was difficult to get enough of it to feed so many.

Otherwise, however, and in spite of this, we slept in bunks, in ample
blankets, and listened to the drumming of the rain outside. We were
dry. We were warm. We were snug. We had no reason to complain,
and in general we did not. Indeed I might say that during that period,
for me at least, the only flaw was the presence of MacPherson.

Fortunately for me I believe there were enough others who shared my
mistrust, so that it was not necessary for me to sleep with my eyes open,
as you might say. Both Fraser and the Moose were as positive as
myself. I believe Franchere and De Montigny, both of whom knew
the background of our feud, suspected. Shea and Westlake, knowing
naught of what had gone before, naturally saw nothing out of the
ordinary, except that MacPherson and myself lost little love between
us. But after what we had been through together, they were ready
to take my side of it.

So, in a way, I made allies of Fraser and Westlake. Indeed it is
scarcely wonderful that our experience had forged a bond between us
all. We had learned respect for one another. Even the rivalry that
had existed between those two seemed largely forgotten, or, if it was
remembered at all, was thought of rather with humor that with any
bitterness. They seemed to have conceived a kind of wry liking for
each other that was reflected in the friendship between Shea and
Charbonneau; as if now, at least, they were forced to recognize each
other's worth in his own field. The woodsman was prepared to admit
that there were points of skill in navigation and ship handling that he
could not approach. The sailor recognized that every individual was
not, ipso facto, born a good woodsman. Come to think of it, save for

that one outburst as we approached the lake, Valerie was never mentioned either by inference or by name. For myself, strangely enough, I rarely seemed to think of her now, and when I did, it was only as a creature remote, ephemeral as a phantom. She did not even appear more in my dreams, though several times I seemed to hear her younger sister taunting me for having made a botch of things.

The time passed quickly enough. The rain, which they told me had been falling here almost without intermission since the beginning of October, suddenly ceased. The year 1812 dawned bright and mild and warmly springlike. We welcomed the new year with a salute from the battery and dealt out some of our precious store of rum to all hands for an appropriate regale in which we five survivors from the *Tonquin* took part with a feeling of especial thanks.

After that matters settled into rather dull routine. I, for one, felt myself growing fat and lazy and sluggish with luxury, until an evening, toward the end of January, I was at the dock with Charbonneau gutting a score or more of good-sized trout when I heard Charbonneau beside me grunt.

"Canoes comin'!"

"Concomly, more than likely," I growled facetiously, "come to sell us some fish!"

"No Injun dose!" Moose grunted again.

I looked up then. Beyond the point I could see two canoes driving in toward us, coming from upstream. But how Charbonneau could tell at that distance that they were not Indians is more than I knew. He must have had much better eyes than I. I watched them draw near, puzzled, curious, until they were close enough for me to see that he had not been mistaken.

There were five men in the foremost craft, six in the second—bearded, emaciated scarecrows, whose clothes hung upon them in rags and tatters. I nudged the Moose.

"Run to the fort," I told him, "and fetch Stuart and MacDougal."

He turned away and went loping up the pathway, limping, as his bad leg made him do. In the dusk I watched the canoes approach. For some reason my first thought was that they must be survivors from Oakanagan. The post probably had been attacked. But as I waited, squatting again to my task of cleaning fish, absently, almost automatically, I did not recognize any of them. So far as I could tell they were all strangers, until one in the first canoe spoke, not to me but to the others, without turning round.

"This is it all right! It is for sure! Yonder's O'Rourke on the dock!"

I gaped at him. Hearing my name from that gaunt, bearded figure gave me something of a turn. The man swung back and waved his paddle.

"Hola! O'Rourke!"

I stuck my knife in the puncheons beside me and stood up.

"Hallo!" I called back. "Come in and welcome, whoever you are. I can't make you out from here."

The man grinned with a flash of teeth in the midst of a scrawny tangle of beard.

"Ye don't know me then?" he cried. "D'ye not recognize Donald Mackenzie?"

He laughed as I stared at him. Mackenzie! But Mackenzie had been a rugged man—a big man, tall and powerful in the shoulders, heavy-set for all his height, and thick enough in the body to earn the nick-name "Fats." This man was little more than a walking skeleton, bearded like a southland oak, so heavily, indeed, that I almost wondered if, once we cut the hair away, there would be anything left but skull and bones for it to grow upon. The clothes he wore, as I saw them nearer now, were mere rags, so patched and tattered and thin as to be all but transparent. Here and there they were pieced out with bits of bark and the skins of small animals. The eyes that stared at me across the intervening water that was rapidly narrowing between us were like bright coals thrust deep in some tangled cavern. Abruptly I saw how my four companions and myself must have appeared to those watchers who had waited for us upon this self-same dock not much more than a month ago.

"Mackenzie! In God's name, man! Come in! We've been all on the watch for you!" I cried.

"We're comin' fast as we can," he assured me.

II. UNVARNISHED YARN

I WOULD like to set out here all the tale that they told us that night —the story of their adventures in coming to us, yet to do so would force me off the path of my story, which, after all, is scarcely concerned with their troubles save in the large view, and would be to a great extent but a repetition of our own experiences.

These two canoe loads, eleven men in all, were not all the party that had left the Missouri. Sixty-five people had set out together from the Aricara villages on the eastern slope, yet only four of them had been lost, by death or illness, up to the time these folk had left the main body. To be sure, they had left behind one or two parties of hunters, and one man had deserted them. They had gone through tremendous hardships. But all, at least so far as Mackenzie knew, were alive at last accounts.

They had crossed the eastern plains and struck up into the mountains, crossing the Wind River Range well up among the heights, and dropped down into the valley of the Spanish River. Thence they had wormed over into the valley of the Snake, where they had abandoned their horses in favor of canoes and attempted to ride the river down. That had been a mistake. They saw it now.

As far as the Caldron Linn they had clung together, only to find their way blocked there by impassable rapids. They had retraced their steps a little distance then, half in hope of returning for their mounts. But this had proved impracticable, and Hunt had cached the bulk of their supplies and trade goods in a series of holes near the river, and there they had broken up into smaller groups to find their way overland afoot to the Columbia as best they could. Not a post had been planted. Not a site had been picked. Mackenzie had struck northwest, away from the stream, but had eventually been forced back to it. Dark, surly McClellan had taken one bank and followed it, while the lean, wiry Irish clerk, Reed, had clung to the opposite. Where the Snake plunged into its last tremendous gorge, before it joined the Columbia, the three of them had come together, and, joining forces with eight voyageurs, they had fought their way through the mountains to the Big River, and so had found their way down to us. Behind them, somewhere in that vast stretch of country, weakened by starvation and disease, beset by hostile savages, with winter sweeping down upon them—yet still alive so far as he knew, Mackenzie told us—were Wilson Hunt and Ramsay Crooks, in at least two parties, with the rest of those with whom they had started.

"If we see them at all," Mackenzie predicted direly, " 'twill not be before next summer, for yon Hunt is of a vacillating nature, and there was snow in the mountains when we reached them!"

But in this he was mistaken evidently, for we had scarcely begun to fatten up Mackenzie and his crew when, in the middle of February, Hunt arrived at Astoria in a very like condition, fetching with him some thirty-three of their party. Neither John Day nor Ramsay Crooks was with him. Some of the men had grown too weak with hunger and privation to be able to continue, and they had been left behind at one of the Snake villages. Crooks and Day had stayed to fetch them on, if it were possible, but surely such a pair must well have known how slight their chances were. It seemed unlikely we would see them again.

Somehow or other that news appeared to be the straw which cracked the camel's back. I, for one, was distinctly conscious of a sense of failure about the entire undertaking. After all that these men had been through it was not strange, it seemed to me, that they should be discouraged. But the impression went deeper than that. The feeling was everywhere, on all hands, and I, who had been sent out precisely to observe such reactions, undoubtedly felt it as strongly as the rest. I could not escape a feeling of vast depression at the terrible mortality and ill luck which seemed to beset us. Nor was there any lack of signs of disagreement and discouragement on every hand.

It should be remembered, even by myself, of course, that I saw this thing at firsthand. I could not view it then from the retrospect of years. I was not gifted with a reliable crystal ball in which to gaze and foretell the future. I could not know then that we might fail in what we had undertaken, yet succeed in what would be of far more lasting value to the nation. We were establishing a claim to the area which one day would not be denied. But at the moment it only seemed to me that Mr. Astor must somehow be told how things were going. He must be informed of the slow and deadly disintegration of all he had schemed. To be sure the Northwesters had been sent back disappointed whence they came. But here at the mouth of the river we were only a handful of traders, wondering and a little doubtful if what we had undertaken would be profitable! We were not a part of the United States. As for being an independent nation, self-supporting, self-sufficient, as I more than half-suspected Mr. Astor dreamed, the idea was a joke.

Nothing seemed to work out as it had been planned. For one thing, the goods and provisions destined for Astoria should have been put ashore before ever the *Tonquin* started north, and Captain Thorn should have had positive orders to that effect. As a result of this one oversight the entire undertaking had been seriously jeopardized. By her loss we had already been left hard-pressed for provisions; yet we had managed to eke out a somewhat precarious existence by means of fishing and hunting ourselves and by using our trade goods for the purchase of food rather than furs from the Indians. Now, with the sudden addition of nearly fifty half-starved mouths, the seriousness of the situation can well be imagined. A small party may find it possible to live upon country through which they pass, even if game is scarce. But the quantity of food necessary for close to one hundred hungry men is quite something else again. It became necessary to take a hitch in our belts and put ourselves on rations until the promised supply ship arrived, for we could expect no increase in our supplies except what we ourselves might shoot or catch. As a parallel, even a corollary problem, what trade goods had been left ashore by the *Tonquin* were now well-nigh exhausted, and even smoked salmon, sturgeon, and Uthlecans must be bought with beads and blankets, knives and kettles, files, axes, and the like.

I think it is scarcely surprising that we worried, even that a number of disgruntled voyageurs sought to desert to the Spanish colonies to the southward. But these were fetched back captives by our red neighbors, whom it was necessary then to reward from our scanty stocks. MacDougal, no doubt obsessed with worry, took a leaf from Captain Thorn's book, which it seemed to me he should have had the vision to throw away, making example of the runaways by having them triced up and flogged at the whipping post.

It was at least an occasion which served to fetch matters to a head. The truth, of course, was that now that Hunt had arrived, MacDougal was no longer actually in command. To be sure, Hunt had felt overpowered by the same lassitude that had beset me and my companions upon our arrival from the north. After his ordeal, who could blame him? He had been content to rest, permitting MacDougal to act as his executive in the thousand-and-one matters that daily called for the commander's attention. His mistake was that he had come to no formal agreement with the Scot upon this but had simply allowed it to come about, doubtless through sheer fatigue.

As a result, MacDougal had grown, if anything, more pompous and self-important; no doubt leaping to the conclusion that Hunt was too vacillating to dispute his authority and that he might do as he pleased. More, I truly believe he actually envisioned the entire command as being centered in him. But for this once he appeared to have overreached himself and, temporarily, at least, have stirred Hunt to replace him. That very evening Hunt called a meeting inviting the men to sit in but take no part in the discussion. A stormy session followed.

Almost immediately the meeting was broken into two camps.

Among those who supported MacDougal I was not greatly surprised to see Donald Mackenzie; while Hunt and the letter of the agreement were upheld by Robert Stuart. I had no doubt but that David Stuart, had he been there, would have taken a like position. But there could be no arguing Hunt's right. He took charge and MacDougal retired to a corner at the back to sulk.

It was possible then to turn to the consideration of business, and since the most imperative need of the moment was obviously to relieve the dreadful drain upon the post's larder, it was decided to send out several parties. The first and largest of these was to go up-river to Oakanagan, under command of Mr. Stuart; to learn the state of affairs at that post, to relieve those who were scheduled to return, and to fetch back such furs as had been gathered in the course of the winter. The second party, composed of Farnham and McGillis and six or eight voyageurs, was to search for Crooks and Day and the remainder of the Hunt-Mackenzie party and were to fetch back the goods cached by Hunt. These were to accompany, as far as the cache, yet a third party, headed by Reed. Beyond the cache this last group was to strike back overland with despatches for Mr. Astor at New York.

Reed's was to be a small party, traveling fast and light, and to this I determined, if it were possible, to attach myself. For it seemed to me that the situation here had become such that a report from me would be expected. As a result, as soon as the meeting was ended, I looked in upon Hunt in his quarters and, since it seemed to me necessary, explained something of my purpose in being there.

He heard me out without comment, only eying me with his dark, rather sad-seeming eyes, never once smiling.

"I wondered why you came," he remarked when I had done.

I remembered, abruptly, that he knew nothing of the circumstances that had pitched me into all this.

"I'm sorry," I said. "I should have explained——"

"I need no explanations from a man that has been set to spy on me," he replied.

"Don't be a fool!" I retorted hotly. "In the first place, I did not ask for such a task, and, in the second, if you are the man I think you are, I'm sure you know well enough there's nothing I could or would say against you! Surely some such person is needed to give Mr. Astor a true and complete picture of the state of matters here."

"I am quite capable of doing that by letter."

"I have no doubt of it," I said. "But my account will mean more to him. Great God, man! 'Tis the very reason he sent me!"

I must say I cared not a bit for the way the wind appeared to be blowing.

" 'Tis more cogent," he replied, "that we can spare no more than a few at this moment."

"What do you mean?" I cried. "You have more people here than you can feed now. We both know it!"

"I think we can feed everyone," he retorted stiffly. "I can't spare you at this moment. If you care to write out a confidential despatch for Mr. Astor, I'll see it goes with the party."

I own I should not have lost my temper.

"Does your conscience trouble you?" I demanded.

His face froze.

"I'll tend to my conscience," he replied. "You look to your own! I'll repeat my offer. A confidential despatch——"

"Thank you," I said stiffly. "I have Mr. Astor's orders. I will wait until I can carry them out myself."

"Very well!" he snapped with equal sharpness, and I left him, clumping back to the quarters I shared with Fraser, looking like a thundercloud, I daresay, and not at all pleased with the equivocal position in which I found myself.

Some of it must have shown in my face, for Fraser grinned as I came slamming in.

"Tick you off?" he demanded.

"I daresay you'll have a taste of him yourself before we're through!" I retorted.

"Hoity-toity!" he cried. "What's the trouble?"

I could not explain to him my entire position. I took refuge in half-truth.

"I was of a mind to go upriver," I replied.

"And he refused you?" he demanded.

"Aye," I said.

He lifted his eyebrows, as if he found that hard to believe.

"I see naught to fly into a pet about," he remarked.

"I haven't flown into a pet," I retorted.

That was the situation when, toward the end of March, Mr. Stuart left us with seventeen men, all three parties intending to travel together as far as the Walla-Walla, above the falls of the Columbia, where they were to separate. Ben Jones, who had come overland with Hunt, had been designated to accompany Reed, and I took no consolation in the fact that at the last moment McClellan, in a fit of disgust with the whole business, resigned his shares and demanded to be allowed to return to St. Louis with them. It seemed to me strange, to say the least, that he could be spared if I could not. But there was obviously no point in talking about it.

I noticed, too, that MacPherson made no move to rejoin his own people but stayed on eating our provisions and sleeping in our blankets, enjoying our hospitality exactly as if he were one of us, and no one denied him the privilege.

The greatest precautions had been taken. The despatches for Mr. Astor had been sealed in a bright tin box which Reed carried slung upon his shoulder, proposing not to set it aside, day or night, for any reason until he had delivered it at New York.

I will not deny that I watched them go with a twinge of jealousy. Yet in the final analysis it is true it made no difference. A few days after they were gone Matthews and I accompanied Mackenzie and six of the men up the Wallamat, a river falling into the Columbia from the south no very great distance above Astoria. Our purpose was both to explore, seeking fresh sources of furs, and to refill our food lockers, for we had had reports of game in plenty upon its upper waters. In this, at least, we were successful, for we followed it nearly two hundred miles, finding plentiful signs of beaver and other fur-bearing animals near the upper end, as well as abundance of elk and black-tailed deer, so that we were able to return in a month's time with several tons of fresh meat to eke out our, by now, desperately scanty supplies.

So far as I could see there was little change, unless it was for the worse. Mr. Stuart had not yet returned from Oakanagan, but there was nothing extraordinary in that, for he was not yet expected. Nor had any word been received of any relief vessel, although it was now May. It began to appear that we must count her lost if she did not arrive soon.

To add to the situation, nothing was improved by the fact that Fraser had challanged Hunt to carry out those parts of his contract that promised him a partnership as soon as any vacancy should occur. McKay, he pointed out, was no longer with us. McClellan had resigned his shares. Surely such a vacancy was now available!

But for some reason Hunt would not consent to any such solution, and as a result he had merely added Fraser's dislike to the rising wave of hostility creeping up all about him.

But it was only a few days after our return from the Wallamat that the fort was suddenly galvanized into erupting life by the cry of the lookout in the high tower: "Sail ho!"

Immediately as many of us as might crowd up, either to the platform above or onto the shaky ladder, did so, and looking off to where he pointed, saw her, a tall ship, picking her way in carefully. MacDougal was at once sent off to meet her in the longboat.

All day we crowded the fort's palisades or the dock, or paused as we went about our routine chores to stare down toward the inlet where the ship seemed to be taking her good time about coming in. Indeed she was not over the bar and safe anchored inside, in the shelter of the point, until midafternoon, and it was early evening before we spied MacDougal returning. With him were several strangers.

"Why!" I cried. "This must be our relief vessel. That's George Ehninger. He's a cousin of Mr. Astor!"

Hunt glanced at me.

"Which one?"

"The one on the second thwart aft," I said, "the young lad with the moonface and the pearl-gray beaver."

"D'you know the others?"

I shook my head.

Our excitement and anticipation were boundless. At such a remote post any indication of an outer world was to be received with delight, and the thought that the all-but-despaired-of relief ship was at last arrived was enough to turn us all light-headed. I am surprised that some one of our jubilant crowd did not fall off the wharf into the river, as one or another of the voyageurs usually managed to do.

We waited with what patience we could muster, and the bearded, smoke-stained, rough-seeming crowd that swarmed upon the dock presented a sharp contrast to the three gentlemen in the boat. The older man wore neat gray trousers and a sober, dark blue coat topped with a good, but not extreme, well-cared-for brown beaver. But the two younger men were dressed in the epitome of the latest fashion, with bright fawn-colored trousers and high polished boots and flowered waistcoats. One wore a wine-colored broadcloth coat. The other was in bottle-green. But both were cut high in front and low behind, with mother-of-pearl buttons, and each youth sported a pearl-gray beaver with the biggest crown and most curling brim I had ever seen.

The boat swept to the dock and the newcomers stepped out, while the rotund MacDougal, obviously well-mellowed, scrambled up and did the honors.

"Mr. Clarke, Mr. Ehninger, Mr. Seton!" he hiccuped, "I'll acquent ye wi' th' only partners we ha' remainin' wi' us th' noo. Mr. Hunt, whae commonds th' pust! An' Mr. Rubairt Mockenzie——"

"Donald," Mackenzie corrected him sourly.

"Eh?" MacDougal blinked.

"The name's Donald, ye old sot!" said Mackenzie.

"Is it?" MacDougal asked. "Ah, ye're two mony f'r me, ye Mocken-zies! 'Tis Donal' Mockenzie I gi'e ye, Mister Clarke! T'ithers're but folk! Ge'lemun! I gi'e ye Mister Clarke, new win'erin' pairtner, an' Mister George Ehninger an' Mister Alfred Seton, yoong gen—ge'lms wh've c'me oot tae lairn th' tred—— Hup! 'Scuse 'm! Bit regale aboord!"

"Hello, George," I said.

Astor's young cousin blinked while MacDougal looked shocked. But Ehninger recognized me, smiled, and held out his hand.

"Mr. O'Rourke!" he cried. "I wondered if we'd find you here. 'Tis good to see you! I—didn't recognize you for a moment. You—you've changed!"

His eyes flicked over me, and it seemed to me he had scarcely said as much as he was thinking. I grinned.

"I daresay I do look different."

" 'Tis not that altogether," he blurted boyishly. "I—I mean, you do look different in those clothes, but you've changed too."

"Maybe I do," I said. "Come on up to the fort. We'll find you quarters, and you can tell us all the news. I'm glad—we're all glad to have you here!"

The ship proved to be Mr. Astor's *Beaver;* the same, indeed, that had carried our "Mandarin" to Canton a few years since. She had aboard a full cargo of supplies and trade goods, as well as letters from friends and relatives for most of us; instructions for Mr. Hunt and the rest of the partners, and orders for Captain Thorn, who was obviously expected to be present. Under the command of Captain Sowles—a cautious, droop-nosed man if ever I saw one—she had left New York on October 10, 1811; and I could not help thinking to myself that at the time those of us that had survived the *Tonquin* must have been about readying ourselves for the escape downriver in our dugout canoe. The letters she carried were from nearly everyone we could think of, save that I heard from neither Valerie nor Deborah. Mr. Astor wrote a kindly note, hoping that matters went well and that I would have nothing untoward to report when opportunity arose. I reflected a little bitterly upon that. He added news of the business world and of politics in some measure, but told nothing of what had happened or what might be happening in New York. Will Sanders wrote, too, reporting that we retained the old quarters and that he had the latchstring out awaiting my return. My investments, he reported, were prospering. Some of my acquaintances were married and others had drifted away, but there was still a nucleus of the old club left. "Jonathan" Irving was making a name for himself with his writing. It looked as if Mr. Madison would be re-elected. Just that and no more— no word of Valerie; nothing about Deborah. It was curious how I coupled them! Doubtless, I told myself, it was because they were sisters.

At the table I sought information from George Ehninger, which may have been the wrong place, though it was he who prompted me, after all!

He had done well by our rum, and he fixed me with an accusing eye.

"There's a young lady," he said, "in New York that's eating her heart out for a sight of you! I believe she thinks you may starve or drown or be murdered before you come back to her!"

I grinned at him, elated though I tried not to show it.

"Indeed?" I said, shooting a glance at MacPherson. "She could be right on at least one of those counts! How *is* Mistress Valerie?"

It seemed to me he gave me the most curious look.

"Mistress Valerie?" he demanded.

"Aye," I assured him, quite pot-valiant at the moment.

"Oh—ah! Mistress Valerie!" he said, and then grinned. "Why, never better! She's still the toast of New York!"

And that was as far as that went.

Scarcely had we managed to accustom ourselves to the fact of the vessel's arrival when the river once more spewed up a surprise. The two Stuarts returned from Oakanagen—and with them came both parties that had been sent to the eastward. It was scarcely necessary to press for an explanation, for they were only too eager to tell us. On their northward journey, at the falls of the Columbia, the whole group had been set upon by Indians, and each of them acknowledged he owed his life to McClellan, whose quickness and agility had so disconcerted the savages that the party had found time to re-embark.

Unfortunately, however, in the melee the bright tin box in which the despatches for Mr. Astor had been carried had disappeared. And since Reed himself had been wounded seriously, it had been decided that there was no point in pressing the expedition. Accordingly all hands had accompanied Stuart to Oakanagan and then retraced their steps with him.

This was welcome enough news to me, for it meant yet another chance for me, I felt. But better yet they fetched with them Ramsay Crooks and John Day. In their journey from Oakanagan they had heard faint voices hailing from the river's edge and, going ashore to investigate, had come upon the two survivors of Hunt's party, naked and destitute, starved and emaciated, but alive.

There is no need to outline the hoorah which these events occasioned. In so far as the overland expedition was concerned, I think Wilson Hunt may have been secretly relieved, for the arrival of the *Beaver* considerably changed the look of things. Also, for the first time since Hunt's arrival, except for Astor himself, all the living partners were present. Accordingly a new meeting was called to decide matters of future policy. Fraser boldly and without bowing to other matters restated his claim.

"I have a contract," he said, taking the floor. "It guarantees me a partner's place when there shall be an opening. That opening now occurs——"

Hunt rapped on the long table before him.

"I've heard your request before, Mr. Fraser," he said.

"What d'you mean——?"

"Mr. McKay's vacancy has been filled by Mr. Clarke."

"Who joined the Company after myself!" stormed Fraser.

"But was appointed by Mr. Astor, may I remind you!" snapped Hunt.

Fraser sank down, bitter-faced and angry. For the moment he would hold his tongue, but if I knew the man, he would have more thoughts and further uncomfortable things to say.

Hunt went on, looking about the room:

"Captain Sowles will confirm me," he said. "The *Beaver* is to go north to the Russian outpost at Chitka. From there she will drop down to the Sandwich Islands. After that she returns here for cargo and then will go back to New York by way of Canton."

We looked at one another. Surely, it seemed to me, the least voyageur must realize the length of such a voyage. To go north to Chitka and thence to the Sandwich Islands and back to Astoria would take the better part of a year. After that to return to New York by way of China would call for nearly another. If he depended upon the *Beaver,* it must be at least a year and a half, possibly two, before Mr. Astor could receive news. Since we had already been out for two years, that would mean that four of the original five years' existence of the Company would be passed before he had so much as a report of its success or failure.

No doubt he believed the *Tonquin* to be, if not already upon her homeward voyage, at least ready to depart upon it. It seemed to me, and I said as much, that altered circumstances altered plans. But in this I was supported only by the newly arrived Mr. Clarke, who would not go so far as to say that the *Beaver* should not make her northward voyage, but who did believe that she should sail directly homeward from there.

Unfortunately Hunt had instructions to visit Chitka and the islands but none to return, or to go on to China. I knew the workings of his mind. These were his orders, and these must be done.

"Mr. Astor's instructions are explicit," he said. "It is not for me to set them aside."

MacDougal smiled slightly, if one could call his expression by such a name. Certainly he showed his satisfaction.

"As you say!" Clarke shrugged.

"But surely," I put in, "you mean to send some word to Mr. Astor of the situation here. It seems to me more than ever necessary that some report should go to him in the light of events!"

"I intend to send word to him," Hunt replied grimly. "Our first effort failed, possibly because it was not properly prepared. This time we will be more careful, and the party will be equipped to travel swiftly. I'll call for volunteers."

I held up my hand, but though he looked directly at me, it seemed to me he deliberately ignored me. His glance swept on to Rob Stuart, who rose to his feet.

"I'll be pleased to carry the dispatches," he said.

"Very good, Mr. Stuart!" Hunt nodded. MacDougal's expression of satisfaction grew more pronounced. "If you will select——"

"I have not changed my mind. If anyone goes east, I mean to accompany him," McClellan interrupted him.

Hunt raised his eyebrows.

"That will be quite satisfactory," he replied. "Mr. Stuart, I suggest you take Jones as hunter, and the voyageurs, Vallee and Le Clerc, in addition to Mr. McClellan."

"They suits me," Stuart replied. "I'll be happy to have any others."

Both he and Clarke looked at me curiously, almost expectantly, but before I could speak Fraser leapt up.

"Who's to fill McClellan's place?" he demanded.

Hunt could not escape the challenge in his tone. I saw his jaw set.

"I believe the agreement with Mr. Ross predates your own," he retorted, "and Ross is at Oakanagan."

Fraser flushed.

"All right, then!" he flared. "That's as much as I wanted to hear. To hell with you, Hunt! And to hell with the whole crew! I found you men in Montreal, when you could find none for yourself, and I came out at the risk of my life on the strength of a promise that you have broken."

"Just a minute, Mr. Fraser!" protested Hunt.

"You've had as many minutes of mine as I propose to give you," retorted Fraser. "I tell you I'm fed to the teeth! You may take your bloody partnership and do what you like with it for all of me. I go East with Mr. Stuart!"

From far back in the dark recesses of the room came a voice that could only be Charbonneau's.

"Dat's for me too! W'ere goes Le-Coq-des-Bois, you fin' also L'Orignal!"

There was a chuckle at the breach of formality.

"Very well!" Hunt snapped. "I don't——"

Westlake interrupted him.

"Pardon me! I'm not strictly a part of this. I am only a naval officer on leave to serve in the *Tonquin*. That ship is now lost, and my leave is near its expiration. I must return as promptly as possible. I'll ask your indulgence to accompany Mr. Stuart."

Hunt's face was growing redder.

"Very well!" he snapped. "We want no malcontents!"

Westlake flushed angrily and half rose to his feet.

"Sir——" he began.

From the back of the room Shea shouted.

"By Jasus! Malcontents, is it? Sure an' I stand wid Mr. Westlake! Where he goes——"

Somebody pulled him down, and I daresay it was the Moose, while Mr. Clarke interposed between Westlake and Hunt.

"Gentlemen! Gentlemen!" he cried. "I think Mr. Hunt spoke with more haste than heat!"

Westlake sank down, eying the senior partner expectantly. Hunt returned his look grimly.

"Sorry!" he growled. "I'll see to it!"

His glance swept belligerently about the room.

"Any others?" he barked.

I grinned to myself. Fraser may well have spoken in anger, but I knew without asking that other calculations had prompted Westlake. Neither one nor the other could let the man he looked upon as rival arrive at New York before him. In the very nature of things they must travel together.

As I turned the thought over in my mind, other voices spoke. To my surprise Ramsay Crooks was dry.

"If you don't mind, Will," he growled, "I must tell you I feel much with Mr. Fraser. If 'tis the same to you, I'll turn in my shares and go back with Mr. Stuart!"

"You may say the same for me!" rumbled John Day.

Hunt swallowed. It seemed to me that if ever I was to speak for myself I must do so now.

"Mr. Hunt!" I put in, "I have already volunteered, for reasons that you know, to go East with Mr. Reed. You saw fit to reject my offer. I daresay that any similar offer to volunteer for this party would meet with a similar rejection. However, since you seem to be accepting resignations, let me give you mine! As of today I consider myself no longer in the employ of the Company. I demand to be sent East. If Mr. Stuart will not have me, then I will undertake to make the journey alone!"

Perhaps I spoke more sharply than I intended. Stuart seemed startled.

"Of course I'll have you!" he cried. "That is if——"

He glanced at Hunt, who nodded.

"I will hold no man against his will." He gave me a venomous look.

Before I could reply, yet one other voice spoke.

"Forgive me, gentlemen! I must also remind you that I am not one of you. I think no blame will be attached to me if I take the occasion of Mr. Stuart's party to rejoin my own people at Montreal."

At the head of the table Hunt nodded, glad, no doubt, that for once he could read no criticism in the request.

"Of course, Mr. MacPherson!" he said. "It is for us to allow you every facility."

I think only Hunt himself, and perhaps those who were but new arrived, misunderstood the silence that followed.

VII. Oregon Trail

~~~~~~

I. THE COLUMBIA

THAT was the way of it. Robin Stuart's party was become a consider-able one, counting in all thirteen members. In addition to Stuart there were Crooks, McClellan, Ben Jones the hunter, John Day, the voy-ageurs André Vallee and François Le Clerc, Fraser, Westlake, the Moose, Charbonneau, Mike Shea, the sailor, Dirk MacPherson, and myself. I would have been happier had MacPherson chosen some other means of rejoining his people, but I could not well object; nor was I seriously surprised that he had elected to come with us. At least, I reflected, so formidable a party should offer a measure of protection through its very size.

There were yet other matters, however, to be taken under consider-ation at this meeting. Now that the relief ship was arrived, with sup-plies of both trade goods and provisions, matters did look a bit brighter, and it was possible to start the work of setting up interior posts; both to serve as a bulwark against the encroachments of the Northwesters and as trading depots. In addition there were matters of policy to be laid down and a general course of action to be decided upon.

I see no need to repeat all the argument and deliberation which consumed near half the night, but the results are worthy of notice. Clarke was designated to establish a post upon the Spokane, while Mackenzie was directed to undertake the foundation of another upon the Snake, probably at its junction with the Big Woody. The elder Stuart was to return to Oakanagan, while Reed was to carry a flying column across the northern bend of the Snake to the caches above the Caldron Linn, for the purpose of recovering the goods left the pre-vious season by Mr. Hunt. In addition he was to search for and rescue, if possible, those hunters and stragglers from the westbound expedition that had been dropped at various points along the way.

This accounted for the bulk of the year's activity. But it was the end of June before everything was ready. Since the expeditions for the interior were to travel in company as far as possible, when the day came at last, the boats and canoes were loaded in the morning and sent forward to Tongue Point, whence, it was felt, we might be able to make an earlier start. With them went all of the men, for the moment under the command of the clerks and hunters, to prepare a camp and commence the inevitable regale without which no brigade could possibly set out for anywhere. Late in the afternoon the partners designated to command the various parties, together with all passengers and non-company people, of whom I must be now counted as one, embarked upon the schooner for the short sail to camp, and thither we were accompanied by Hunt and MacDougal, Ehninger and Captain Sowles, who, I must say, viewed all this with a round and wonder-stricken eye.

I confess I felt a twinge of sadness at the farewell. Familiar faces lined the landing as we cast off, and those on shore watched, I think, with some wistfulness as the sleek, dark waters widened between us. Behind them the neat stockade of the fort, the weathered roofs, the tall flagpole with its lightly flapping colors, all blended together and loomed in stark contrast to the dark forest behind. We waved, then looked ahead. The next time I glanced back, the watchers on the dock had turned away and by ones and twos were moving off.

At Tongue Point we found the regale in full swing. There was all the customary dancing: jigs and clogs and reeling round the fire, like so many children playing ring-around-the-rosy, by the men who were made hilarious with rum. There were the usual brawls and ribald jokes. But by midnight it was over and we were able to take to our blankets. As I lay down in them, it occurred to me that this would be the last night I would spend upon the Pacific, but I had little time to reflect upon the thought, for in the midst of it I fell asleep.

With the coming of gray dawn we were out upon the bank with the boats loaded and the canoes packed, heavy of eye and furry of tongue, but ready to start. There was a quick handclasp with those who had accompanied us thus far, and then, as day broke, stabbing through the wispy mists that drifted smokily through the trees, we were off, sixty-two of us altogether, counting our Clatsop interpreter, in two boats and fourteen canoes, all under the command of Mr. Clarke for so long as our parties would remain together.

That first stretch of the river was familiar to me. Yet it was one I had never ceased to marvel at, for it was broad as a lake, with here, at least, a gently rolling current, sometimes whipped to a nasty cross-chop by the wind that never seemed to stop blowing. On either hand the forested hills ran down to rocky, cove-indented shores. In the late spring and early summer, as now, the melting snows of half a continent combine in this one outlet, to drive down through the narrow mountain passes and swell the stream above its banks, so that the neighboring bottom lands and low-lying forests often give an appearance of swampy, flooded jungles, and it is necessary to paddle from hill to hill and highland to highland to find land sufficiently elevated for a camp fire; dry enough for a night's rest.

But, as a matter of fact, until we had gone well upriver, our troubles, in the main, were of a superficial sort. One, however, was to me, at least, both depressing and foreboding. It concerned the hunter John Day, who was number two in my canoe.

It seemed to me that he was scarcely well even before our departure from Astoria. The moodiness which had been so marked in him of late grew more pronounced. He seemed little interested in his food, picky, irritable. He complained much of the cold, although it seemed to most of us a trifle more than moderately warm, and he was troubled with fierce blinding headaches. On the first day of our journey scarcely a word could be drawn from him, and that night he retired early to his blankets, grumbling and cursing, so that I believe no blame could be attached to us if in our own preoccupation we failed to observe that he was behaving strangely.

The next morning, the second after our departure from Astoria, the first outburst occurred which we undoubtedly should have noticed more seriously than we did. The Company provided each man, at least at the outset of the journey, with a pewter plate and mug. Other utensils he might provide for himself, according to his tastes, but these were given to him. As a rule, they did not last long but were like to be melted down into bullets, lost, misplaced, or traded to an Indian wench for what she had to offer. Thereafter they were replaced by the usual tools of the woods: a bit of bark or a chip of wood, a flat stone, or the like. This early, however, we all were yet so supplied; and of course each man was expected to look after his own. Needless to say such things were often interchanged through carelessness. So it was this morning, when Charbonneau banged his ladle upon the edge of the kettle.

"Venez manger! Soupe!"

There was the usual scramble for the nearest cup and plate, and devil take those who had set theirs down out of reach!

It happened that I was at the riverside washing my face at that moment. I had set my gear out upon a log beside my blankets, and I daresay MacPherson, on the lookout for just such an opportunity, helped himself to them at the first outcry and was already on his way to join the line by the fire when truculent John Day stepped in front of him.

"Goddamn you, you black thief!" he snarled. "Give me that plate and cup!"

"They're mine," protested MacPherson, blandly innocent, though anyone could yet see the wet spot where they had been.

"The hell they be!" retorted Day tartly, and presented the muzzle of his rifle gun at the Scotsman's breast.

"Put 'em on the ground," he commanded. "God damn you! Get your own before I blow your bloody guts out!"

Eyes swung in their direction, and silence settled on the camp. There was no question that the hunter meant it.

Slowly and with infinite caution MacPherson bent his knees, never taking his eyes from the rock-still muzzle of that gun, and set the things down upon the log whence he had taken them. When he had done so he stepped back one, two, three paces.

"There they are," he said.

Day jerked his head to one side and the muzzle of his rifle never wavered until MacPherson had turned to his own blankets and fell to fumbling in his sack. Then the hunter dropped the butt of his piece to the ground and, stooping, still staring belligerently after the black-bearded man, picked up the cup and plate and turned away to take his own place in the line.

My own eyes slid sidewise. I looked where Day had kicked off his own blankets, and not three feet from them, in the lee of his *sac à commis*, I saw his plate and cup where he had tucked them the night before.

Unobtrusively I cut across that way and scooped them up and fell in behind him. There was no need, it seemed to me, to call attention to the fact that both of them had been mistaken—if indeed they had. John Day was welcome to use my gear so long as I might have the use of his.

For the moment, at least, the incident was forgotten in the serious business of breakfast and embarking gear. Yet apparently John Day did not forget. He kept mumbling and grumbling about it all through the interval.

The rest of the morning passed quietly enough as we nosed our way up the green stream. It was not until late afternoon that anything further occurred. But Day evidently brooded, for once, as our canoe veered close to the other, the hunter glowered balefully at MacPherson.

"God damn you!" he growled. "I'll shoot you dead! By God I will!"

"Hush, John!" I told him shortly, and purposely steered off beyond earshot of the other canoe.

Jones looked at me over his shoulder, frowning.

"I don't like that!" he whispered.

I nodded my head in agreement but said nothing. After that we tried to avoid the other craft as much as possible. Yet this could not always be done, and to some extent I am afraid MacPherson provoked matters. Out of sheer contrariness he persisted in weaving back and forth ahead of us, so that there were bound to be moments when we passed within speaking distance. When he did so, it was to meet with black looks from Day, and once the latter flared out at him.

"You black-bearded bastard!" he called. "I know you! Keep away from my gear, hear? Aye! An' keep away from O'Rourke! Everybody knows you got your evil eye on him. You keep away from him, God damn you!"

The jibe, for all he sought in his muddled way to take my part, I must confess, was more than a man could bear. MacPherson was not noted for his patience. I scarcely blame him for flinging down his paddle in a sheer, blind rage and reaching for the musket at his side. In our craft Day snatched at his rifle. That we were not overset, both of us, is a wonder to me, for in his canoe Stuart, with his paddle, knocked up the muzzle of MacPherson's gun, while Jones before me reached up and grappled with Day.

"I'll take those guns—both of them!" Stuart said. "You, Day! Keep a still tongue in your mouth! Sheer over this way, O'Rourke, and let me have that piece."

I fetched our canoe easily alongside Stuart's, careful that Day and MacPherson did not pass within reach of each other. Jones passed over the rifle. After that I kept well off, while Stuart, beyond doubt, saw to it that MacPherson stayed well out of our way. Day, perhaps feeling himself unappreciated, had nothing further to say, and indeed for the rest of that afternoon fell into a fit of black sulks.

A good supper appeared to calm Day somewhat, and for a moment, at least, when we all relaxed with our pipes before the fire after the day's labors, it seemed as if we had seen an end of his vagaries. But apparently he was not yet done, for most unexpectedly he began to talk again, speaking now of the country that lay ahead.

" 'Tis hell!" he mumbled, so that at first we scarce could hear him, but in a voice that rose quickly till he was all but shouting like a drunken man. " 'Tis sheer, plain hell, I tell you! You don't know what you're comin' into! There're mountains, mountains all around you! God! You never see such mountains! Terrible black mountains, full o' snow, an' rocks as big as churches, I God! An' beyond them lies desert, an' Injun savages! Ah, those red bastards! Thieves, murderers! I don't hanker to cross 'em agin! Not me! Not much! I'm here, I am! I ain't goin' over there!"

"What's the matter, John?" asked Crooks. "Are you getting jumpy?"

"Jumpy?" cried Day, staring at him without recognition. "By God, you'd be jumpy, mister, if you'd been through what I have!"

"I went through it, John," Crooks reminded him. "Don't you remember?"

The hunter looked about him wildly.

"A man's better off dead," he cried, "that's what! I'll shoot the top off my head before I go back, that's what!"

"No, you won't," said Crooks quietly. " 'Tis bad, but not so bad as that. And 'tis never so bad the second time over. Besides, we're well supplied now and in good company. Look at O'Rourke there and Mr. Stuart, John. They're not friends to let a man down! You know that!"

Stuart leaned over and tapped me on the shoulder.

"Get him into his blankets," he told me. "Has he got a bottle cached away in his gear?"

"I haven't seen him take a drink since we left Astoria," I told him. "He wouldn't even take his ration."

"The man's not well then," he replied. "See if you can get him off to bed!"

I stood up and stretched and yawned.

" 'Tis past cock-shut time. I'm for bed!"

But though we talked with him, pleaded and cajoled, we could not seem to persuade him to it, and at length it was only Stuart's direct command that roused him surlily and sent him to his blankets.

The next morning there was another brief flare-up at MacPherson, the cause of which I did not learn but in which Stuart himself bore a hand.

"If I have any more from either of you," I heard him say as I came up, "I'll send you both back to Astoria. That's especially for you, MacPherson! You know well enough what you're about!"

MacPherson did not like it, yet he complied as he had no choice but to do. But Day took it with poor grace. All morning he sulked. At midday, when we stopped for our nooning, he went, unnoticed by any of us, to the canoe, where he rooted in his sack returning at length with a pistol in either hand. Only then were we warned by Jones, who yelped:

"Look out! He's got a brace of guns!"

At the sound of the cry we leapt up, startled, and Day whirled and backed against a great tree, facing us, presenting the pistols so that no one dared move toward him.

"Disarm that man!" cried Clarke, who thought him drunk.

"Why don't ye disarm him yourself?" said a voice from somewhere in the brush, and I could not help but grin.

But there were no volunteers. Day glowered about, and I could almost hear each man he looked at swallow convulsively. But apparently he had no aims against any except himself.

"Now!" he growled. "I'll show you if I mean it!"

Before we could move to prevent him, he lifted the gun in his left hand to his temple and pulled the trigger. But evidently he had neglected to prime the weapon or the powder was wet. The hammer merely fell into the pan with a dead click.

With a snarl he flung the piece away from him savagely and quick as a flash turned the other upon himself. But this, too, refused to fire, and in the next instant those nearest had swarmed over him. He struggled and wept, blubbering like a scared child, but in the end, at Stuart's direction, he was bound as gently as might be, until we could decide what must be done with him.

We finished that day in darkest gloom, for I think there was not a man among us, unless it might be MacPherson, but had a full-hearted affection for him. Still, it was clear that he was unbalanced. To take him back would be dangerous, both to himself, for he could never withstand the rigors of such an undertaking, and to the rest of the party. Accordingly, it was decided to commit him to the friendly Cathlapootle Indians, to return to Astoria. To insure his safety and make certain that they would care for him as tenderly as their own, we made lavish presents to the chief and saw that each man of the canoe that was to carry him was well rewarded, though his own condition and the awe in which the savages regarded such should in itself have been enough.

Poor Day! We bade him farewell with more than a little distress. Long afterward I learned he never reached Astoria alive but, growing violent on the way down, overset the canoe in which he had been traveling and drowned before he could be rescued.

For two days after that we were yet able to hold to comparatively quiet water. The course of the river was generally southeast, tending to the east, and finally somewhat north of east. It was narrower than formerly but yet rolling majestically, deep and silent, between high-wooded hills, almost large enough to be called mountains had it not been for those higher snow-clad summits in the background. Mount Hood loomed always in the south and appeared to be drawing nearer, while to the north we could catch occasional glimpses of the other symmetrical cones. During the second day we passed a rocky promontory that was called Cape Horn and beyond this we saw a number of high, wispy cascades, tumbling from the rocky, wooded height to southward with a great fanfare of mist and spray. On both sides the walls closed in; the banks of the river grew steep and rugged, just short of precipitous, indeed, though yet heavily timbered. Both at our nooning and again at night we saw considerable sign of elk and bear, though being well provisioned we did not bother to hunt. On the following day it threatened rain, and our leaders deemed it wise to move forward only as far as the foot of the first carry. That night we slept with the vast, bull-throated bellow of the rapids in our ears.

Now I had my first glimpse of the force with which this stream had battered its way through the mountains. Such tremendous power is a thing that must be seen to be believed, for we were confronted by a deep, narrow valley, not yet a canyon, but a sort of gorge, through which the green waters roared and thundered, beating white-fanged upon rocks, enormous as cathedrals, that seemed to shudder and tremble under the buffeting.

All that day and the next and even yet the next we portaged, for the water was moderately high at this season, and this first chute, which was known as the Grande Rapide, was one long sault from start to finish. We had been warned against the Indians here, and accordingly we moved carefully and systematically, setting out guard parties at both upper and lower ends, while the rest of us plodded back and forth between, carrying over bales and bundles and canoes, never out of sight of a man with a gun.

Thus, shuttling back and forth between guarded points, we passed over without any loss, though we were not so fortunate where we had to drag the canoes on the cordelle. Below the start of the portage, David Stuart's canoe got foul of the rocks and was overset, spilling its contents into the river. At the upper end of the carry two of Mr. Clarke's canoes filled, but without loss or damage to the goods or craft.

Above we turned to paddle and sail once more, driving upstream against a smooth, sullen current. In the course of two days more we came to the mouth of the Klikitat, where we paused again to refurbish

our arms and put all in readiness for the carries about the Dalles, the
Long Narrows, and the Falls above, for it was here that Mr. Stuart
and his party had been set upon.

We approached this stretch with some misgiving, for we had heard
a great deal about it, and I must say that if the rapids below had
appeared vicious, these made them look like the meek ripples of a little
brook. Mile after mile the waters of half a continent were brought together in a narrow compass, squeezed together at a tiny opening in the
mountains, and hurled fighting, struggling, surging, roaring, pushing,
leaping toward the sea. There were occasional stretches of comparatively quiet water; a few yards here, fifteen or twenty rods there. But in
the main the force and spate of the torrent were such that navigation
was out of the question, even with the cordelle, and we were forced
to transport ourselves, the canoes, and the goods over at what
amounted to snail's pace.

Easy seems to do it often, however; and no doubt because we were
cautious, we passed over and around them without event other than a
momentary false alarm, occasioned by the accidental firing of one of
our islander's guns, whose ball lodged rather painfully in the calf of
Mr. Pillet's leg. Above the Lower Falls we were able to travel by water
only a short distance before we came to the Upper set. There we had
it all to do over again.

Since we had passed the Grande Rapide, the forests had been thinning, growing first scattered and dry, then actually sparse and rocky.
Now, as we passed the Upper Falls, we came into what seemed to me
the most barren, dreary, desolate country it had ever been my mis-
fortune to behold. Here we left the forests behind us and for the first
time I looked upon a land virtually without trees—a wild and tumbled
country of high-piled knobs and buttes and stratified bluffs, covered,
where growth was possible at all, with sagebrush and greasewood.
Only here and there along the river bottom could we find actual green;
a little patch of grass or clump of willows or cottonwoods, often not
more than ten or fifteen feet high. I would become accustomed to such
country in time, for indeed it was as much as I was destined to see for
almost a year. But at the moment I must say I was stricken with its
desolation, for all there was a sort of wild beauty in the varicolored
rocks and dusty grays and greens of the countryside. There was a sort
of limitless vastness to it all that was frightening, awe-inspring. For a
moment it almost seemed to me that I could understand John Day's
crazy reluctance to throw himself once more into it.

Above the falls we embarked again upon the river for occasional stretches of navigation, interspersed with roaring, growling, brush-grown rapids. It turned hot; blistering and dry, so that we grew thirsty even with water all around us, and the river flowed like a molten blue ribbon between tremendous bluffs and crags of multicolored rocks, through the yellow heart of a barren, sun-parched land. Passing, it seemed to me impossible that any people could be so witless as to dwell in such a desert. Yet they did. Some Indians lived by the river and subsisted mainly upon fish and roots; while others even appeared to live back in the high, barren, dusty plains and supported themselves like nomads, by hunting. The river Indians, in the main, seemed a poor lot, save where the hinterland people came down to spend the hot months in the comparatively cool proximity of water. For the most the regular river dwellers were crafty, treacherous, and were called by our own as well as their people, Fish Indians. They seemed to be a mixture of tribes east and west of the Falls, with those dwelling closest to that place being the most worthless, no doubt because of the ease with which comparative luxuries and a wealth of food were available. Those higher up kept horses upon which they traveled to and fro, and these were undoubtedly of a superior sort.

It took us nearly a month to reach the mouth of the Umatilla, where Stuart had entertained some hopes of finding a village of Horse Indians. But in this we were disappointed, for they seemed to have moved on up the Columbia, and it was not until the following day that we came upon an encampment of Walla-Wallas, where we spent the night and managed to procure a number of the animals we needed. These folk were friendly, quite different, indeed, from the dirty, surly, insolent savages below. They were proud men with regular, weather-beaten features; superb horsemen, who seemed anxious to make peace. We stayed a day among them and by patience and friendliness succeeded in procuring a number of mounts. These, Jones and McClellan, both plainsmen and therefore riders rather than canoemen, were happy enough to drive along the riverbank as we continued our way upstream. A little beyond the Walla-Walla River we came upon yet another, much larger village. There again we smoked the calumet with our hosts, while the squaws and young braves danced for us about the camp fires, a sort of pounding, hallooing shuffle, much enjoyed, amid the thump of drums and the swish of rattles.

By a judicious distribution of gifts and presents we were able to get as many more small, wiry nags, packsaddles, riding saddles, and bridles as we would need, so that at this point we set all our goods ashore and turned over our canoes to our comrades. There we said yet another farewell to those who had journeyed so far with us and turned southeastward, away from the river upon what seemed to me to be actually the first lap of our homeward journey.

II. THE CACHES

I HAVE often wondered if any of my companions, or the dog, for that matter, which Stuart had bought from the Indians for a blanket and a handful of beads, had any notion of what was in store for us that first day. By nine o'clock we had crossed the Walla-Walla, scaled the sandy bluffs beyond, and entered a barren, miserable waste, threading between the desolate, bone-dry hills in a general southerly direction. Even then it was pantingly obvious to me that this day would be scarcely comfortable. There were no trees, and the country was baked, parched, and dry. Even the sagebrush seemed to shrivel in the sun's glare. The wind that blew was hot, stifling, and just strong enough to raise the dust upon the ridges, so that we must bury our noses in our kerchiefs and ride with heads and eyes bent. There was no water. We seemed to walk a treadmill in an endless sea of sand. The brassy sky covered our heads like a hot metal bowl, and we had not gone a dozen miles before our tongues grew thick and swollen, and in our hearts we wished ourselves back beyond the mountains where a clear day was unusual and weeping skies were better than the rule. It seemed to me that day I sniffed the breath of hell, while the saddle I sat was like a rack to my aching backside. I could cheerfully have given all I owned for a quarter of an hour in which to loll in the coolness of the river we had left behind.

Like greenhorns everywhere we fell into the same trap. For some reason we did not think that this might be but a momentary phase. We did not trouble to load ourselves with water. Consequently we made a dry nooning. By midafternoon we were parched and drooping, and nowhere in all the vast desert that surrounded us was there the least sign of relief. Everywhere the low, bare hills rolled off to the horizon with never a spot of green to show anywhere that, even underground, there might be moisture. I have no doubt it was unusually severe. I cannot recall anywhere later encountering like conditions as these, and there was proof of the fact in that the little dog we had fetched from the Indian camp gave up before the afternoon was done and died in the trail before our eyes for want of water!

As night came on, none felt like stopping, yet it became apparent that for the sake of the nags, if for no other reason, we must ultimately do so. We were seeking a possible spot when our horses suddenly pricked up their ears and sniffed the wind, then started forward at a shambling trot. A moment later we came to the edge of a bluff, look-ing down into the broad, tree-lined bottom of the dancing Umatilla.

It is a wonder to me that one of us, in that mad scramble down the precipitous, rocky slopes below, did not fall and break his neck. Yet none did. Within ten minutes we were knee-deep in the wide, twilit stream, men and beasts together, sucking immoderately at the clear, cool water that rippled over the stony bottom. When we had satisfied our thirst, we pressed on, fording by a gravelly bar, and camped on a sandy spit on the far side, underneath a bank of willows. There we ate a frugal supper beside an infinitesimal camp fire and made ourselves ready for the night.

We spent that night curled up on the hard bed of the sandy bar, and such was our weariness and soreness there was not one of us that noticed the discomfort. The sun was already high when we woke and we were off to a late start.

That day we struck east-southeastward over the plain toward the mountains that piled in tumbled heaps across our path. There in a few miles we came upon a fork of the river, well shaded with cottonwood and willows and evidently the haunt of beaver, but carrying water only in a few small pools. Here we camped for the night, and in the morn-ing we were away again, with the dawn following up the fork and over the low divide, to a branch of the Glaise flowing southeast.

I see no need for day-to-day account of that month's journeyings. We found ourselves in the mountains now, wild, rugged, rocky, though not nearly so grand or awful as those behind through which the Colum-bia poured. Having climbed from the plains, we were in a region of pines and scattered timber that grew upon rocky slopes. We followed streams that poured through tortuous ravines and canyons, twisting sinuous ways across lush green mountain meadows, banked with alder and willows and cottonwoods, while the valley floors were carpeted with needles of pine and spruce and fir and an amazing variety of daz-zling wild flowers. This was the haunt of elk, bear, deer, and beaver, and there were salmon in the streams.

By comparison with the first day's march and with much of what was to come, this portion of the journey was a stroll through Elysian fields, for all the mosquitoes swarmed about us in clouds and the warning buzz of the rattlesnake was not unusual. Though in many places the going was rough, rugged, or swampy, yet we were well fed and well equipped, our mounts were strong, and the forage was good. Our spirits rose, and we wondered why Hunt and his people had made such hard going of it all—until we recalled that we threaded these rocky canyons and dizzying precipices in the midst of summer, while they, weak and starving, carrying everything on their own backs, had made the journey in the dead of winter, when snow piled deep in the passes and the way must have been hard indeed. I was to remember later how we marveled at it then and were glad, so smugly, that we were not in such a case!

Slowly we crossed the hills, following the streams down into the Big Flat, then pushed over the divide, slipping down the other side by tortuous bends and turns, to leave the big timber behind us once again and come out into the sagebrush and greasewood, upon streams bordered by the inevitable cottonwood and willow. About the middle of the month we burst out at last upon the banks of the Snake at a point nearly opposite the mouth of the Big Woody, not far from the place at which McClellan had fallen in with Mackenzie the year before, and almost at the spot where Hunt and his people had turned away from the river and struck up through the mountains, the way we had just come, toward the Columbia.

Where we struck it, the Snake was about four hundred yards across, running swiftly between high, sandy banks with little or no willow or cottonwood on either side. Looking at it, I must say I felt almost disappointed. Some of the feeling must have communicated itself to McClellan.

"She don't look the same, does she, Ram?" he said grimly.

Crooks shook his head.

"No, she don't," he agreed. "She ain't the same stream she is in winter. I'll guarantee that!"

I daresay that was true enough. Even now, with the sunlight warm and bright upon it, there was no question that the stream was deep, sleek, powerful, and, for all its openness immediately about us, the country appeared far from hospitable. McClellan looked at it and then turned his glance downstream.

"There's where she gets rough!" he commented.

That was easy to believe, for, looking down toward the gorge below, mountain seemed piled upon mountain, and it was obvious that any stream which must cut its way through must be sorely racked and tortured in the process.

From here we turned southeast, following up along the river's course, riding endlessly, it seemed to me, across barren, brushy country, now and again dipping into coulees and canyons, the dry bottoms of tributary streams, but in the main holding to the high ground, skirting the turgid flood. It seemed to me a poor country, a sad country, by far less desirable for human habitation than that we had just left in the mountains behind us. Yet curiously enough in the hills we had seen no sign of man, while here, from time to time, we encountered wandering bands and occasional villages of destitute, half-starved, poverty-stricken Snake Indians; Shoshones whose only apparent sources of sustenance were the fish they caught in the river or the roots they dug. So far as I could see, the plain above produced nothing but occasional antelope, and these were so wild that it was impossible to get near them. Even rabbits, ordinarily so plentiful upon the plains, seemed to be scarce.

As foot by foot and mile by mile we worked slowly up the southern bank, we heard, not once, but several times, rumors of white hunters in the neighborhood. These, no doubt, were some of those left behind the previous year. But though we were diligent in our inquiries, we could not seem to come upon them. One day we would be told that they were at a village on the other side of the river and we could wait, while, for a trifling present, one of the local braves crossed upon a curious reed raft to inform them of our presence. But always these messengers came back to report the white men were not to be found. Then we would be told that at a village farther on we might obtain information, for there, it would be said, there was a man who had fetched them furs or given them food or received presents from them.

Going thus from lodge to lodge and village to village, we came at last upon an Indian who claimed to have been the very one who had guided Hunt and his party through the Mad River Mountains the year before. He declared to us flatly that not ten nights since he had parted from three of our hunters, who, he said, had caught a great many beaver during the winter and had started east with them, but had been set upon and robbed of both their packs and their horses by the Absorokas—the Crows—who had come southwestward into the Spanish River Valley to hunt buffalo. These men had been forced to flee westward and were now somewhere on the Snake above us. He also told us of a better pass to the southward of the one that Hunt had followed in crossing the Wind River Mountains the summer before. The Indians, he said, knew of this pass and often used it. Indeed an Indian trace ran through it, and if we would take it, we would find it a far easier route than the other.

It was Rob Stuart's idea to engage him to guide us, and to this he readily agreed—in return for a pistol, a blanket, a blue cloth, an ax, an awl, a fathom of blue beads, a looking glass, a little powder and ball, and a knife. In addition, he assured us, he would help us find the white hunters of whom he spoke, and he added indifferently that he did so only because "*la vache*"—by which he meant the buffalo—was far better meat than salmon; implying that but for that he would not dream of serving us for such a paltry consideration!

His hauteur, considering his own raggedness and that of his people, made us laugh. But our amusement was short-lived. We set out that day crossing a small tributary river and striking up through sandy hills were both ourselves and our horses were well-nigh consumed by flies and mosquitoes. On the advice of our guide we slogged some nine miles to the eastward through this desolate country, after which he calmly told us that there was a better road that we might have taken a little distance across the hills to the southward!

However, since it would take us all of a day to reach it, we stopped where we were for the night, making a dry camp. When we rose in the dawn both our guide and Robin Stuart's horse had disappeared!

Though we followed his tracks in an effort to overtake him, they circled around toward the river above and finally disappeared in a direction nearly opposite to that we meant to take. Rather than lose valuable time for naught—for we knew his own people would never surrender him—we gave up and continued our journey, dividing one of our packs, by now grown considerably leaner, among the several pack animals, so that one of these might be turned over to Mr. Stuart to mount.

From this we learned a costly lesson. The fact that the pack had been so easily distributed among the other pack horses fetched the realization that we were already growing low of supplies and trade goods, upon which last we had depended primarily for the fish and similar provisions we had purchased from the Indians along the way. As a result, we made up our minds we would have no more to do with these treacherous folk than necessary and that we would post a guard at every halt upon both horses and gear.

We pressed on from there, turning a deaf ear to all rumor and blandishments. The country remained much the same: up and down, hilly, rocky, rugged, now desert, now swamp, now a maze of willow and alder thicket, rank with thick growth and acrawl with every winged pest the insect world contained: midges, gnats, flies, fleas, mosquitoes, deerflies, blows, wasps, hornets, bees. Fortunately, as we struck into the higher hills we found some relief, for though the days remained hot and parching, the nights cooled noticeably and the legion of mosquitoes, at least, dwindled away to only an occasional stout-armed, wandering warbler.

On the whole we seemed to be going reasonably well. We had grown accustomed to the saddle, having developed calluses at the most strategic places, and in the course of less than a month's time after leaving the Columbia we had gone at least half the distance to the mountains that divided the waters of the Pacific from those that flowed to the east. Once we reached the caches, we felt, we could replenish our stocks of trade goods and replace our, by now nauseous, fish diet with some of the jerked buffalo stored there by Mr. Hunt. After that we could press on more rapidly, perhaps even gaining the Missouri before snow fell. It might even be possible to reach St. Louis by Christmas.

It was a little after the middle of August when we made a short cut overland, passing two sweeping bends of the river, and struck the stream again at the mouth of a small creek, not much more than a runnel, where we stopped for nooning, unsaddling and hobbling our horses, and turning them into the bottom, while we sought out a shady place, well up on the bank, from which we might keep an eye upon them while we rested.

While Charbonneau built a small fire upon which to brew the tea and broil the inevitable fish, I, for the sake of doing something helpful, picked up our canvas bucket and scrambled down the bank to the river's edge, where a sort of deer track led down between thick willows on either hand to a narrow opening. There I was leaning down to scoop up the water when I heard a grunt and the snap of a twig in the brush behind me. Startled, I whirled to find myself staring directly into a gaping mouth surmounted by a pair of bulging, astonished eyes of agate blue, both half-hidden in a tangle of scrawny, matted, sandy beard.

I scarcely know which of us was the more startled. The cracked mouth formed an "O" for an instant and then drew back over yellowed teeth into something that apparently was supposed to resemble a grin.

"Hey!" it said.

I blinked, and the pale blue eyes blinked back at me.

"You—you're white!" I exclaimed foolishly.

The eyes blinked again and then widened.

"I ain't no Christ-bit Injun!" came the reply. "Who're you? Where'd you come from? Hey? Jumpin' Jesus! Ketch your bucket! Th' god-damn thing's adriftin' away!"

I looked around quickly, just in time. The bucket was caught in an eddy and was being sucked out toward the tips of the willows. I leapt after it, floundering in water deeper that I had anticipated, caught it, and came back, scrambling up the bank soaked thoroughly from the waist down.

The stranger came out of the willows as I did so and was standing in the opening when I regained the bank. He was a lean man, indeed, almost emaciated, ruddy, weather-beaten, somewhere, I judged, in his late thirties or early forties. I would scarcely say he was starved, but he was hungry-looking. He was dressed in ragged, smoke-stained, tattered buckskins, and in his hand he carried an improvised willow fishpole and a couple of foot-long chub, establishing his occupation at the moment of my arrival. He grinned and held out a helping hand.

"Sorry I give ye a start," he said. " 'Fore Jesus, I didn't mean to. Name's Hoback—John Hoback. Whut's yours?"

The name twanged a chord of memory.

"You'll be one of the hunters left at Henry's Fort last fall by Mr. Hunt!" I cried.

He spat and wiped his mouth on the back of his forearm.

"That's right. How'd you know?"

"I've come from Astoria—the mouth of the Columbia," I told him. "Mr. Hunt came in this spring and said he'd left you—my name's O'Rourke, by the way!"

I held out my hand and he took it in a solid grap.

"Do tell!" he exclaimed. "I Jesus! So they finally got thar, hey?"

"Are there any more of you?" I asked.

"Shorely!" he replied, almost as if he was surprised that I would raise the question. "Joe Miller and Ed Robinson and Jake Reznor are yereabouts. We four hung together right along. But Cass, he lit out. Pore bastid. I hear he got jumped by redskins."

He raised his voice.

"Ed—Joe—Jake! Come on along yere! We got comp'ny!"

He glanced back at me and spoke a little apologetically.

"We were fixin' to ketch us a mite to eat, but fishin' ain't ben so good th' last day or two," he said. "You et lately?"

"Oh, yes," I told him. "As a matter of fact, we were about putting the kettle on for nooning when I came down. You'll come up and join us?"

I didn't think how foolish the words must sound until they were out. He grinned.

"Oh, yes!" he assured me. "We'll do that, you betcha! I Jesus! I declare, I ain't put tongue to honest grub since Christ fust grew whiskers!"

There was a crackling and scrabbling in the willows and I made out the loom of the others through the brush. They came up one by one. Miller first, a dark, dour man, about middle height and I judged once rather heavy-set, but now lean as a half-starved alder sprout. Behind him was Jacob Reznor, a tow-headed, red-faced man. Because he was normally a round-faced person, he showed his hunger more than the others. His eyes were sunk and his temples stood out prominently. His cheeks were hollow and his lips drawn taut above his even teeth. His eyes were light blue, lighter even than Hoback's, so that they seemed almost to have a dusty overcast, and I judged that according to circumstances they could be merry or they could be hard.

Robinson came in from upriver and proved to be an older man, close to seventy, I judged, spare of frame, a little stooped, but not much, rugged, tough as nails. His face was craggy, jutting, even more so than usual, I judged now, and like the others hollow-cheeked. His eyes were a mild brown but shrewd, and his beard was a spattered, juice-stained gray. Over his head he wore a blue cotton bandanna, such as we used to trade with the Indians; to keep the flies off, I thought, though it was a long time before I saw him without it even momentarily.

All of them were in rags and tatters, patched and worn, darned and repaired in half-a-hundred different places—rags that hung upon their frames like sacks and ribbons. Hoback must have noticed that I stared, for he explained a little apologetically:

"We got cotched by the Arapahay headin' east last spring," he said. "They run off our hosses an' stole our skins. Fact is we didn't manage to come off with much more'n what you see us in right now—them an' our weapons!"

He slapped the lock of his rifle.

"Yup!" said Robinson. "Ain't had much chance to visit a tailor sence, I God!"

He laughed, cackling. Robinson, Hoback, and Reznor were clearly Kaintucs. Miller I took to be a gentler background, perhaps a shade more sensitive to the niceties, but somewhat decayed. Of the four I preferred the three woodsmen, for there was a surly sort of an air about him that led me to believe that he might be thoroughly unpleasant if the occasion arose. Later I learned that he had sprung from good stock, in Baltimore, and it may be that he went back to it for all I know.

I led all four of them up the bank to the camp, where my companions clustered about them and pumped them for their stories, while Charbonneau and I set out to ready for them the best we had among our own scanty store of luxuries.

Not to dwell at too great length upon it, they could add but little flesh to the bare bones of the story they had already told me, and after we had regaled them to the best of our ability, we pushed on with them about three miles farther up the river, until we came to a good fishing place with pasture close at hand. There we pitched our camp.

This addition to our party was scarcely calculated to ease matters. Our horses already were jaded and in poor condition, having come far through a land but ill supplied with forage, and our own supplies were growing embarrassingly low. With four additional hungry mouths to feed they dwindled even more rapidly, not that we grudged them, but it was a fact that could not be blinked. However, we expected all of this would be remedied when once we reached the caches. There we would be able to replenish our stocks and, at the same time, we could turn the nags out to proper pasture and perhaps a week's rest. God was still in His heaven and, so far as we knew, all was yet right with the world!

Continuing through the barren, desolate country, we pushed our way on up the river, clinging to the bottoms where possible, struggling up the bluffs where it was not, cutting out long stretches of the stream by crossing the tablelands that lay between the great bends. From time to time in the river bottoms we passed sorry, dilapidated lodges full of half-starved Indians who seemed content to take their living by picking up the dead and wounded salmon that drifted down the current from the falls above. Here, it seemed to me, the river might have been navigable for canoes, and so both Crooks and McClellan assured me it was, but cited the vast stretches not far ahead of wild white water and tumbling cascades and rapids, in which no craft could possibly hope to live, and flowing through country over which no band of struggling, half-starved men might hope to drag them.

We were close to the end of our own supplies when we came out at the Salmon Falls. There we found Indians all busily occupied in killing and drying fish as they swarmed to pass upstream. In great numbers the savages with their spears swam in close to the rocks of the lower pools and speared the fish as they struggled over one another at the foot of the churning chute. Thousands, I estimated, were thus slaughtered in a single day and pitched ashore to the squaws to clean and split and lay upon the drying racks of willow withes. But our stomachs rebelled at the sight and smell of them, and we could scarcely bring ourselves to trade for sufficient of them to carry us as far as the caches. Had we had a modicum of sense, we would have taken all we could carry, but it is always easier to know what should have been done than it is to guess which way to turn tomorrow.

Beyond the Falls we began to come into the country which Crooks and McClellan had described, where the river roared over a jagged, ragged bottom composed of boulders, in the main, great as houses, that had tumbled from the adjacent cliffs, compressed within narrow, often perpendicular, walls. Here it was impossible to keep close to the water's edge, and it was necessary to struggle up the crumbling cliffs to the tableland above, over which we passed amid seas of sagebrush, rarely in sight of the river below, but always within sound of its grumbling roar.

A few days farther journey fetched us to the Caldron Linn, where we saw from the cliffs above—it being totally impossible to get down to it—why the place had been so named, for here the river, low as it was, was dashed into one vast whirlpool, then compressed at its only outlet between walls of perpendicular rock, not forty feet apart, so that literally the stream seemed hurled on edge and driven through the opening. Below, there was a forty- or fifty-foot fall, and from this it went bounding and raging away in a series of seething, twisting, grinding cataracts. Above, for a distance of fifteen or twenty miles, falls and rapids and cataracts formed a practically continuous sheet between sheer walls, a plunge so violent that it seemed to me impossible that anything that walked the earth could possibly pass along it. Yet it is true that Hunt and his companions had passed their canoes some distance down before they found it necessary to retrace their steps. In spots the stream expanded to perhaps a hundred yards, but in general it flowed for close to fifty miles through the narrowest of canyons, and I think the name our hunters gave it, "The Devil's Scuttle Hole," was far more descriptive than any other that had been applied.

It was at the top of all this, some miles above the Caldron itself, that we looked for the canoes and caches left by Hunt and his companions the year before, this being the first point at which we were able to descend to the river. Fortunately, according to the map which Hunt had given us, the caches were located upon the south bank, for without a craft of any kind to take us across we could not possibly have gained the other side. We reached the place shortly after midday, and not a moment too soon in our own estimation, for that very morning we had eaten the last of our fish and had between us only a small bag of rice, perhaps fifteen pounds in all.

As soon as we had made our camp, we shouldered axes and rifles and set out at Robin Stuart's heels. For an hour and a half—till long past midafternoon—we fought our way through thick-clumped willows, approaching the spot. As we drew near it, we came upon a veritable network of animal runways, mostly the trails of wolves, who seemed to abound in the vicinity, and at last we broke through to the place.

Stuart was in the lead. Ordinarily he was a mild, even-tempered sort of a man who rarely swore, save on occasion. Yet as we crowded in behind him, he flung his ax savagely upon the ground before him and broke into a fit of the most violent swearing I have ever heard.

"What's wrong? What's the matter?" cried Fraser, still shrouded in brush behind me.

"Oh, Jesus God!" cried Stuart in an anguished voice, the sound of which came tumbling back to us through a filter of sunlight and green willow brush. "Ah, Christ! The cursed holes have been opened! The cache is rifled!"

Frantically the rest of us struggled through the intervening brush to the open space beside him. All along one side the canoes had been ranged, stacked in neat rows, and these now lay smashed and broken—man's work beyond a doubt! Across the middle of the clearing was a series of holes, opened, gaping, empty save for a few books and papers that lay open about the edges, their pages fluttering in the light breeze. The wolves may have been the first to come, drawn, no doubt, by the scent of the furs and the buffalo meat the holes had held. But two-legged wolves, red wolves, had undoubtedly followed, perhaps shown the way by their four-footed brothers, for not a thing remained but what animals or Indians found worthless. By the same token what was left was worthless to us!

Hoback began to swear softly, evenly, steadily, but none the less bitterly.

III. ABSOROKA

"WHAT now?" I asked.

The question evidently roused Rob Stuart. He shook himself, then looked at me dully.

"How many holes d'you count?" he demanded.

I looked, peeking under the brushwood, counting.

"Five," I said. "No! Wait! Six."

"Are you sure?"

"That's all I see."

"Well, then, they've not got all," he said. "Hunt's map shows nine holes. There should be three left!"

We set to work then, all of us, even MacPherson, who was not known for his eagerness for such labor, to clear away the undergrowth and find the three unopened caches. But this proved more difficult than we anticipated, and it was already growing dark before we came across them. If we were to fill our stomachs, or even partly fill them that night, we must abandon the task till the morrow. It seemed hardly likely, now that we stopped to think about it, that any food was left in these remaining holes, for by the paths and runways which made a network through the brush leading to the open holes it seemed quite probable that wolves had first discovered the hiding place, drawn by the scent of meat. If there had been food in these other holes, they would have found them too.

That night we dined on willow bark, a handful of wapatoo roots, and three small fishes, which were all we could catch. The hollows of our stomachs we filled with tobacco smoke by the light of the camp fire afterwards. The fire, at least, was cheerful.

For a long time we were silent. At length it was Hoback who spoke, addressing Stuart.

"What d'you reckon is in them three holes?"

Stuart shrugged.

"Traps, likely, some ammunition, dry goods, trade stuff."

Hoback stared across the fire at his companions, then glanced down at his own rags.

"I dunno about you fellers," he said. "But me, I'd ruther a heap stay out an' try an' make a little stake before I'd go back in this shape. If 'twas any way possible——"

I gaped at him in astonishment. The man had been bound down the Missouri with Robinson and Reznor, bound out for Kentucky and home, after several years in the wilderness, when he fell in with Hunt. Since then he had been out near two years more; he had been attacked and robbed by Indians and close to death by starvation. Yet here he was more than half-hinting, even begging for a chance to take a grubstake and strike out again to make his fortune! Across the fire from him the elderly Robinson nodded so violently that the kerchief he habitually wore, and which I had never seen him remove waking or sleeping, slipped aside, revealing a skull stripped of flesh, livid, horrible in the firelight. I must have gasped, for Reznor grinned.

"Skelped he was when he was a younker," he explained. "Thet's why he wears thet goddam thing, to cover up his nekkidness!"

The elder man flushed with embarrassment and replaced the cloth over the spot gingerly.

"Sorry ye see it," he mumbled. " 'Tain't purty!"

He glanced at Hoback, turning the subject.

"If'n ye're lookin' fer a pardner——" he said.

"Aye, an' me!" put in Reznor.

All three looked at Miller, but the latter shook his head.

"I know when I've had enough!" he growled.

Their eyes swung to Stuart, and I think he must have had somewhat the same feeling that I had.

"You mean," he asked, "you'd rather stay out?"

"If it's anyway possible," Hoback repeated.

He might have said more if Robinson had not interrupted him.

"Lookee, Mr. Stuart," the older man said, "you ain't none too well set up yourself. That's plain to see! If we go along with ye, there's that many more for ye to feed. If we stay here, we're old hands at it. We kin feed ourselves. We had some bad luck back there a piece, but it don't foller it's got to happen again. One o' these days we'll come out lucky. I say, if we can get anywhere's near a decent stake out o' those holes, let's tie to it! You fellers go on ahead, an' we'll stay here."

The others nodded their agreement.

For a long moment Stuart stared into the camp fire without speaking. Then he looked up.

"I'd not ask it of any man that didn't want to," he replied. "But since you tell me you're a mind to, I'll say 'tis fair enough."

"Done!" said Hoback.

We looked to our traps in the morning, finding them, as we had half-expected, empty. As a result we went breakfastless to work. Miller and McClellan we exempted and set them to fishing on the river, while Jones and Reznor we sent upstream some distance, to a point that we could not yet have disturbed, there to hunt and set out traps. The rest of us dug, opening the caches, only to find in them, much as Mr. Stuart had predicted, a few dry goods, some traps and ammunition, a little trade goods, and some hardware, out of which we were to furnish the three hunters with most things necessary to a two years' hunt—apart from provisions. During the day our fishermen caught a respectable mess of good-sized trout, a species that here replaced the chub and lampers of the lower river and made a welcome change, I must say. On these and a handful of rice we made our meager feast that evening. The next day all hands turned to to mend the saddles and prepare new packs, and in the evening we closed the caches again, having taken out only what was necessary for our hunters and ourselves, and to some extent replacing these articles with various items which could only burden us beyond this point.

I, for one, said good-by to our brief companions of our trail, Hoback and Robinson, with more regret than I think I showed. As traveling companions they seemed to me far more desirable than some with whom I journeyed onward. In about six miles we came up with Jones and Reznor, who had taken only two beaver in the course of their hunt. Jones mounted his horse and Reznor struck back along the trail to rejoin his comrades below, while we went on our way. The riverbanks drew farther apart so that frequently it was a mile to two miles between the low hills at either hand, and from the top of these the dreary sagebrush plain stretched off in every direction as far as the eye could reach, level as the flat of a man's hand and even more extensive than the deserts of the upper Columbia.

Beyond the caches we continued up the river several days, until we came at last to the Portage Falls, where the country, being overgrown with willow and alder and cottonwood, lent itself more readily to the support of game. There we killed a small beaver and caught several fine trout and found excellent green pasture for our nags, so that that night, at least, all hands and hoofs fed well for once.

As the course of the river now seemed to be generally tending northward—an indication, it seemed to us, that we were drawing toward the Pilot Knobs—Stuart called a council of war to remind us of the better pass that had been mentioned by our treacherous guide.

"From all I hear," he told us, "it lies a little to the south of east from the great bend of the Snake, rather than to northward. If we go farther on our present track, we may miss it."

"Would you take the word of a renegade Shoshone and a thief at that?" MacPherson growled.

"I have more than that to go by," Stuart assured him. "Hoback has confirmed him, and Mr. Miller here has passed over a good deal of the country between here and there. He assures me 'tis a fact."

He glanced at Miller for confirmation. The latter nodded.

"It seems to me 'tis worth a try," Stuart went on. "If we find our way through, by that means we should avoid the Blackfeet and we might even that much sooner fall in with the buffalo!"

"Do as you please," MacPherson grunted, "but it seems to me we'd do well to stick to the way we have some knowledge of."

Miller gave him a venomous glance, and it occurred to me then that the man had an unhappy knack of alienating even those that were inclined to be friendliest.

"Are ye calling me a liar?"

"Make what you will of it!" MacPherson shrugged.

"Gentlemen!" rapped Stuart. "We're all of one party. We will abide by the will of the majority!"

"That's fair enough!" grunted McClellan. I was to recall his remark not very much later.

The vote. when it was finally taken, supported Stuart almost unanimously, with only MacPherson's own voice dissenting. Perhaps it would have been better if we had followed his advice, but who could know that?

We set out the next day across the flat bottoms above the Falls, weaving through the willows, keeping well to the southeast side of the huge flat, until in the evening we came near what seemed to be a channel of the river. Next day, however, the stream we were following bent sharply and flowed out of the southeast, and it was only then that we discovered we were no longer upon the main Snake. Still, since this new stream flowed from the direction we wished to go, we determined to follow it, although I must say it struck me as odd that Miller, who claimed to be familiar with the country roundabout, should fail to recognize it.

Doubtless he felt some of our unspoken criticism, for I was not alone in my feeling, and it may have been this as much as anything that prompted him to declare, more and more positively as we ascended it, that this was the very stream he had followed with Hoback, Robinson, and Reznor that spring. Since we had no reason to doubt him, we accepted his statement and continued on that route until we reached a fork, at which point we took to the more southerly branch and by evening found ourselves cutting back again in a southwesterly direction, not at all the way in which we wished to go. What was worse, the man we had depended upon to guide us now appeared quite obviously confused.

"I'd swear," he said, "that was the fork we came down last June. But, sure, it can't be! The crick we were on never followed that course!"

We made a quiet camp some time before sundown, while Ben Jones scouted in a half circle ahead and to the southward. He returned with the report that the creek tended even more toward the west, and as a result we cut east the next day, over into the valley of the other fork, and followed it for two days more, climbing across a series of lava steps and at length striking southeast across a saddle in the low, brush-clad hills, trusting rather to our sense of direction than to either the flow of the water or Miller's guidance. Beyond the gap we dropped down until we came upon a considerable stream flowing almost due southward, along whose bank an Indian trace meandered, marked by the trailing lodgepoles. Here again Miller declared himself on familiar ground, and at his insistence we turned and followed up the river, bending in the course of the traverse, first to northeast, then almost directly east, and, at length, once more to the south. Here we found a fork coming in from the southeast, and this once more, since it came from the direction in which we generally wished to go, we followed some distance to a bottom that was comparatively well timbered with scrub willows and young cottonwoods—almost the only timber we had seen in all the course of that week's journey. There we camped.

In all this way the best game we had seen were a few antelope, so wild that we could not come within reach of them. About the only sustenance we had was what we were able to catch in the rivers—poor trout, in these waters, and wormy suckers—and what roots we could scratch from the ground. We saw considerable sign of buffalo, but all of it was months old, and once we had the luck to fetch down a number of geese that stopped for the night, in their southward flight, upon the river.

At our camp in the cottonwoods, on the banks of the little river, we followed our usual procedure and, leaving two to guard the gear and horses, took our fishing tackle and set out to catch our supper. We had but indifferent luck and returned in the twilight with visions of yet another meager meal of fish, unsalted and unsauced, to find, as if sprung from nowhere, half-a-dozen or so Absorokas, who told us they were camped upon the other side of the timber and, having seen our smoke, had come over to investigate.

I must say we were suspicious, for the Crows, as these Indians were sometimes called, were noted thieves. Yet they seemed civil and behaved themselves properly, smoking the calumet with us and grunting pleasantly, and two of them even went back to their own camp to fetch us a supply of buffalo meat, for which alone, I must say, we were abjectly grateful. Yet for all their friendliness, our suspicions were not lulled entirely. They had come across the mountains, so they told us, to hunt for buffalo; which could easily be true, for, by all the signs, the animals had lately been plentiful here but had been driven from the range. At the same time we bore their reputation in mind, and knew them especially covetous of horses. I, for one, noticed that their eyes swung more than once in the direction of our little herd, as if calculating the strength of the animals and the number of them. Accordingly we set a double guard that night on both our camp and our nags, while the rest of us took turns at sleep, a precaution by no means uncalled for, since by midnight nearly a score of braves had come across to make themselves free of our fire, to sit and smoke and while away the night.

As dawn approached and we began to make ready for our journey, they grew more and more insolent and demanding, calling for presents of powder and trade goods, which at first Stuart stoutly refused to give them. But finally, deeming it better to consent than to antagonize them, he did so only on the condition that they would present to us in return commensurate supplies of meat. Apparently we parted friends. Yet as we pushed on through still another gap in another sagebrush and scrub timber-covered range of hills, we noted that a number of smokes rose thin against the sky in a circle nearly all about us; signals, advertising our presence, we were sure, and summoning reinforcements with which to raid us.

It was as a result of this and of what they had told us—that a much larger party of their nation were traveling in a parallel course some distance to the southward—that, so soon as we had left the gap behind us and descended into the next well-wooded valley, we turned north and put what distance we could between us. Thus we left the smokes behind. We passed one night in a state of apprehension. Yet nothing happened, and on the next day we breathed somewhat easier when we came upon a river flowing northward.

For three days we descended this stream until, at length, it fell into a river, issuing from the high mountains to eastward. This, we agreed, must be the south fork of the Snake, and if this were the case, to turn and follow it eastward could only fetch us to an impassable canyon. The pass by which Hunt had come lay somewhere to the northward, and to reach it we must cross this barrier stream, even though such a course must fetch us closer to the territory of the Blackfeet. Indeed, even here we were upon the fringes of their range, and the choice of Scylla or Charybdis, Absorokas or Blackfeet, struck us at that moment as being little different.

However, it was not possible to cross the river here, for it flowed too swift and deep to ford. Accordingly we turned westward, following the stream down, camping once at a level meadow, where we shot a young buck antelope, and again fighting our way through a swampy region of alder thickets and beaver ponds until we believed we must surely be safe from any possible attack from the southward. After all, we told ourselves, the Crows we had encountered had been on their way homeward and would scarcely be inclined to follow us so far. That evening we made camp in a little swale where there was a fairly clear piece of level table upon which to set our camp, with close beneath it a pretty stretch of good forage, interspersed with willows for our horses, while the brushy banks of the river offered several excellent places from which to fish. As soon as we had unsaddled and turned our horses out to pasture under hobbles, we set one of our number to guard the camp. The rest of us slid down the riverbank to try our luck.

Apparently we had picked a good spot, for the fishing was excellent, and that night we ate well. Nothing, so far as we could tell, appeared amiss. The horses grazed contentedly, while we above ate the trout we had caught and rolled in our blankets. Several times in the course of the night I woke to hear the howling of wolves mingled with the ululating yelp of coyotes at various points among the hills around us, and I remember now, thinking somewhat sleepily, that it was strange. It was not often that we heard the two together. But it did not occur to me to call attention to it. A little before dawn Rob Stuart roused us with the reminder that if we cared to breakfast we must be on the stream at daybreak, and with some growls and grumbling we rose, leaving only a single guard at the camp, and made our way to the river.

But angling that day was no sport! It seemed to me we had barely baited our hooks and cast them into the stream when the savage whoop rose from the hill behind our camp and we could hear Vallee's frantic cry: *"Aux armes! Aux armes! Les sauvages!"*

Close behind was McClellan's bellow.

"Injuns! God damn their red souls! Head the bastards! Head the red sons of bitches off!"

IV. HUNGER

I DROPPED my gear where I stood and scrambled up the bank, legging it toward camp, cocking my rifle as I ran. All about me in the bushes I could hear the others doing the same. Yet we were not within two hundred yards of the pasture when the red devils came swooping off the hill, fifteen or twenty of them, riding their ponies like painted fiends, clinging like burrs to their bare backs, whooping and yelling and driving our horses, hobbled though they were, away from them at a full-stampede gallop.

Though we emptied our guns after them, they were beyond our range, and for all the noise we made, the shots were little more than a gesture of our rage and despair and defiance. Nor did we dare to run in pursuit, for there was no doubt in our minds but that this was exactly what they wanted. Others, beyond doubt, were yet lurking in the hills, and once they saw us drawn off, they would swoop down and fall upon our gear. Accordingly we fell back upon our base and took up the best positions of defense we could find.

For an hour or more they whooped and hallooed upon the heights above. Then after a time they withdrew, doubtless judging us too strong to attack and satisfied with what they had stolen. Evidently they were part of the same band we had encountered and they were primarily after our horses. But Jones and Le Clerc, descending to the river some time later for the fishing gear that we had dropped there, reported having seen two of them skulking in the neighborhood, without doubt hoping to see where we might cache what we could not carry. As a result of that we determined we would do anything to prevent the red dogs from taking any further profit of us.

It is true, indeed, that for a time we were stunned, dazed by the blow. We were stripped and destitute in the midst of a hostile continent. Without horses, it seemed to us we were all but helpless. Winter was approaching, and winter in this region was as fierce and bitter as anything we dared imagine. But for the clothes we stood in, our arms, and a few odds and ends of assorted gear, much of which we could not possibly carry, we had nothing. There was no food. There was no shelter. The nearest habitation of civilized man lay we knew not how many hundreds, even thousands, of miles away, and close beside us, to northward, lay the country of the dreaded Blackfeet, the cruelest, most savage, and relentless enemies that white men had.

In the circumstances I think it rather more wonderful that we should recover as promptly as we did, than that we should lie ground down by despair for a matter of a few hours. It was when our bellies began to gnaw at the rest of our vitals that we came gradually to a sensible view of the situation. Desperate as we might be, we were yet alive. It was Stuart who began the impromptu council. He turned his back to the log behind which he had been lying, sharply watching toward the woods behind us and the pasture down below.

"We can't stay here," he said flatly.

"What do you suggest?" Miller demanded almost derisively.

"Walk!" replied Stuart. "Unless you'd rather lie down here and die."

The other glanced significantly at the pile of baggage, the pack-saddles and other horse gear, now worse than useless to us. Stuart shook his head.

"I know," he said. "We can't carry that. We'll just have to take what's most needed and throw the rest away. If they're still watching, there's no sense hiding it. We'll burn what we can and the rest throw in the river."

"I'll second ye on that!" growled Jones approvingly.

"Is everybody in favor then?" Stuart demanded.

Some growled their acquiescence. Others were content with a mere nod of the head, but all agreed, apparently, save Ramsay Crooks, who neither spoke nor moved.

"How about it, Ram?" McClellan prodded.

Crooks looked up slowly, and it seemed to me that I had never seen such blank despair upon a man's face. It curled my stomach to look at it. Yet, at the same time, my heart went out to him, for I had suspected for some time that he was not well, though he had been careful to say nothing to any of us. For a long time their eyes met, then Crooks merely shrugged slightly and looked down again at the ground before him. Stuart frowned, but he made no comment.

"All right!" he said briskly. "That's agreed. Now then, have you any suggestions what course to follow?"

"There's naught the matter with me," sneered MacPherson, glancing disgustedly at Crooks and spitting on the ground. "So long as I've two feet to stand on and a gun in my hands to shoot I'll get along. I say try to cross yon river and cut northwest. Henry's Fort is over that way. We'll have shelter there, at least, and, with luck, game——"

"Aye, and Blackfeet before spring, sure as you're a foot high," interrupted Jones. "Why d'ye think the place was abandoned?"

"Who asked you?" snarled the Scot.

"Nobody!" retorted Jones. "I'm telling ye! If ye want to make somethin' of it, ye're welcome to!"

He shifted the gun in his lap savagely.

"That's enough, gentlemen!" said Stuart sharply—more sharply, indeed, that I had thought he could. "There's no need to quarrel about this. Thank you, Mr. MacPherson. I have your suggestion—that we head for Henry's Fort. Are there any others?"

"Aye!" growled McClellan. "I daresay there'll be as many as there are men in the party. We're afoot now. I say go upstream. Follow the river east. 'Twill fetch us through the mountains—at least to the mouth of Hoback's—and we can follow that up and over to the headwaters of the Spanish——"

Crooks looked up wearily.

"You'll never make it that way, Bob!" he said hopelessly. "We looked at the canyon above there when we came down—remember? You can't get through that way!"

"Then hit for the pass!" cried McClellan. "Hit for the nighest pass through the mountains that'll lead us over onto Hoback's. Like as not 'tis the same we crossed by last year."

"I'm for that," commented Jones laconically.

"*Quai!*" agreed Charbonneau. "On dis Hoback or dat Spanish, de game she's can' be less dan w'ere we bin. Maybe we get over dere we can winter, eh? *Sacré nom!*"

"It seems to me," said Stuart, "that may be the best course—ultimately. But you forget one other possibility, gentlemen. The main valley of the Snake lies not far below, and down there we may find Shoshones with horses. If we can get some animals from them, we should easily get through the mountains and possibly even be able to winter on the Cheyenne, in the buffalo country."

He looked at me.

"It's worth a try," I said.

He nodded and glanced at Fraser.

"I'd gamble on that," said the red-haired Scot.

Westlake shrugged.

"Don't look at me," he said. "I'm only a poor sailor!"

"Aye, an' God pity poor sailors at a time like this!" put in Shea.

The rest of us laughed, and it seemed to me the tension was broken for the first time since the Indians had attacked. I nodded at the little Irishman, who grinned back.

"All right," chuckled Stuart, "suppose we put it to a vote?"

That we did forthwith, and the result was that Stuart's suggestion won by a small margin, with McClellan's suggestion that we seek the high passes without delay trailing it a close second. Only MacPherson, it seemed, was in favor of Henry's Fort and the Blackfeet, and I wondered if he had had it in mind to pass by that route to his own people at Kootenay or the Cœur d'Alene.

We went to work then sorting out our gear, setting out only such as we could carry upon our backs to take with us and committing to the flames everything else that would burn. What would not, we flung into the river. Our weapons we kept and our knives and axes, and what powder and shot we were able to carry, a few odds and ends of clothing, a single beaver trap, and such supplies as we had in the way of food. The rest we eked out with trade goods and rolled in our blankets, so that each man's burden was not more than fifty pounds, yet even this we found abominably heavy before we had gone five miles, such was the state to which we had become dependent upon our beasts. Our fishing gear, of course, we kept beside us, and, indeed, it seemed to me we might have carried more trade goods and ammunition and rather less personal clothing, but in this I was overruled, and, bearing Mr. Stuart's admonition in mind, I was not insistent.

That night we lay where we were, keeping guard against the possibility of surprise, and in the morning, after a breakfast of trout, pushed on downstream some distance, fighting our way across logs and through swamps, over benchlands and sagebrush flats, always within sound of the river, until we had made sure we were in safer country. There we camped again and fished, catching forty trout to stay our appetites.

Yet another day we continued this struggle, watching always for a good crossing place, for it seemed to us that the sooner we put the river between us and the Absorokas, the sooner our scalps would cease to tingle. That night, finding that the timber was thinning and promised soon to disappear almost entirely, we determined to build rafts and cross next day. Again we caught forty trout and supped on those and a beaver we had been lucky to take in our trap; and in the morning we cut our trees and made our rafts and, losing no time about it, got ourselves on board with poles and pushed out into the river.

At this point the stream was swift and rugged, yet we had stout hopes of gaining the opposite shore. But the current caught us and swept us down upon a wild ride, in the course of which we were agreeably surprised by the seaworthiness of the craft we had created. We were neither swamped nor overset, though I will admit it was a hairraising experience, and since the water appeared to be generally calmer by the time we gained the opposite shore, we decided to scrap our first plan to continue overland in favor of continuing downstream as far as possible on the rafts. As a result, that day we made as much distance upon the river as we might have done upon our horses, and encamped upon the north shore, for the first time with a sense of security from the Absorokas, though by no means positive that there were no Blackfeet about!

We had good luck from this point for a few days, for Jones, going to set our trap, managed to kill a fallow deer and a wolverine, by which we had a good supply of meat which could the more easily be carried on the rafts. A little farther we had the luck to kill an elk, which also added to our larder, but which, skinning out, we found to have been lately wounded by a musket bullet and an arrow, so that we deduced that the Blackfeet had been not long before us in the neighborhood. However, we could not regret what we could not help, for in addition to meat, the beast provided us with leather for moccasins, of which we were in sore need. Nevertheless we decided then that for a time at least, unless it should be absolutely necessary, there must be no more shooting, lest it fetch our enemies down upon us and cost us our hair.

We continued thus until, at last, from the shape of the land, we decided that we must be drawing near the river's junction with Henry's Fork. Accordingly we abandoned our rafts and set out overland, each man carrying approximately twenty pounds of meat in addition to his pack. This we ate dry and raw, not daring to kindle a fire for fear the smoke of it might reveal our presence.

Alas for hopes, however! We found no sign of Shoshones. Day after day, it seemed to me, we struggled northward, paralleling the course of the main river. In all that time we saw no trace of any living being, and coming, at length, to the fork that fell from the pass by which Hunt and his party had crossed the mountains the year before, we turned up it, by common consent striking eastward and abandoning all thought of finding horses, placing our dependence now upon shanks' mare to carry us through the mountains that loomed grim and forbidding and snow-capped above us.

MacPherson grumbled when the purpose became evident.

"We've come this far," he said. "I'd think we ought to head for Henry's Fort."

Jones cocked an eye at him.

"Ye have a purty head of hair," he growled. "I'd hate to see it decorate a Blackfoot lodgepole!"

"Be damned!" cried McClellan. "Are we to do now only what I suggested in the first place?"

Stuart looked at him.

" 'Twas second choice," he reminded him. "We've tried my plan and failed. Now why do you object if we follow yours?"

McClellan had no answer to that but apparently he was brooding upon it, for the very next day, as I remember, we had our falling out with him. All day we had struggled up a spur of the mountain, cutting out a great bend of the river, and it was his turn to carry the beaver trap. We were perhaps a third of the way up the steep slope when he flung the trap down.

"There!" he cried petulantly. "Anyone who wants it can have it! I'll carry the goddam thing no further!"

" 'Tis your turn," Stuart protested.

"Turn or no, be damned to it, I say," cried McClellan. "Let one of the Canadians carry it, if they think they must have it."

"You know damned well we must have it!" Stuart flared. "We'd be half-dead of starvation now but for that. Every man here must bear his share! Pick it up! Fetch it along!"

"I say to hell with it!" cried McClellan. "I'll not carry the goddamned thing another inch!"

"All right, then," said Stuart. "I'll take it, but you'll carry its equivalent in meat!"

"That I'll not do either!" cried McClellan. "I'll carry myself, and that's as much as I will carry. I must consult the condition of my poor, sore, damned feet!"

"You'll carry what's for the good of the party so long as you're one of it," flared Stuart.

"To hell with you!" McClellan snarled. "Since you feel so, I'll be as glad not to be one of your goddam party! Here's your goddam trap and here's your goddam meat! I've got my rifle and my own eye for game, and I daresay I can fend for myself better than I can fend for the lot of you! I'll find my own way east, and to hell with all of you!"

"Don't be a fool," argued Stuart.

"Am I a fool to know 'tis plain stupid to climb over this mountain when we could as easily go around?" demanded McClellan. "If that's being a fool, then I'm glad to be numbered such, for that's the way I'm going."

"You'll go alone then," said Stuart.

"That suits me!" McClellan retorted.

He glanced about at the others, but even MacPherson did not move to join him.

"That goddam well suits me!" McClellan repeated, and he snatched up his pack and turned away, striding off diagonally through the brushwood that covered the hillside.

"McClellan!" Stuart called after him. "Mac!"

But he did not look back.

Stuart shrugged.

"Very well!" he said. "If he feels so, let him go! Would any stop him?"

No one replied.

"Are there any others that feel so?" he demanded.

There was still no answer.

"All right!" he snarled. "I'll take the trap today and the rest will take their turn at it, share and share alike. You've all had your chance, and I'll shoot the first man with my own hand that balks the party now. Is that understood?"

"'Tis not only understood," I growled. "I'll second you!"

"So will I," said Westlake.

Fraser merely held up his hand and nodded. As for the rest, they said nothing. Stuart nodded and turned.

"Let's go then!" he said.

The events of those next few days, I must confess, are by no means clear in my memory. Brief flashes of them stand out in my mind like pictures viewed in leafing through a book. I remember Crooks was ill and Stuart insisted on dosing him with castor oil, until it seemed to me the man was scarcely strong enough to stand, and I took it on myself to protest, after which Stuart held his hand and, slowly, at the cost of lying a day in the snow, our patient began to mend. There was a brief council to decide if those of us who could should go ahead, leaving our sick man to his fate. Stuart and I were alone in that we would not leave him, and one by one, Fraser first, then Westlake, and finally the others, all except MacPherson, came round to our viewpoint. The latter stayed perforce; whatever one might think of MacPherson, he had the courage of his convictions.

After that we waited, while Crooks sucked on raw meat and chewed lethargically at the stuff that gave him strength. We saw game in that

time, but yet we dared not shoot, until Jones, one evening, going out to
set the trap, encountered a white bear. He fired in self-defense but had
not the luck to kill the beast. If that shot did not reveal our presence
to the Blackfeet, so we decided, then others would not, and the next
day we let Jones go forward of the party, with the result that he killed
five elk and we ate meat, raw to be sure, but nonetheless good red meat,
until we scarce could stand. But we could carry only a little of it with
us, so that was the last full meal we were to have for some time.

From there we plodded onward. Once we saw McClellan far below,
stalking forward, some miles in advance, but none cared to sprint
ahead and try to catch him, so we followed mainly in his tracks and
let him lead us, coming now and then on the cold ashes of his fires, but
never seeing where he had eaten.

Beyond that, I recall days and nights of struggle over rocky, sometimes barren, sometimes heavily wooded, ground, where we were as-
sailed by rain and sleet and snow and always the wind that bit viciously
through the tattered rags that were all that remained to us as clothing.
I remember waking in my thin blankets at night, shivering, and laughing aloud that once I had thought it a hardship to walk across Vancouver Island!

In the course of time we fought our way up through the Teton Pass,
often slogging waist-deep in snow and ice, now and again coming upon
McClellan's tracks before us and wondering among ourselves how he
was faring. On the far side we dropped down abruptly, with the snow-
capped pilot knobs looming now to north and westward over our
shoulders, into the dry, grassy bottom of the South Fork of the Snake.
There we rested for a day in the hope of finding game.

But though there was a quantity of old sign, we found but little game
to put in our bellies, and we pushed on. Crooks, who remembered the
country, for all he was yet weak, marked down the canyon of Hoback's
River for us, and we plunged into it, fighting our weary way through
it. Vaguely I recall the roaring of that lusty little stream, the great
cliffs that overhung it. Once, I remember, we came upon a camp where
McClellan had stopped and feasted upon the carcase of a poor wolf,
the only meat, so far as we could see, that he had shot since leaving us.
We cracked the bones with our teeth and cooked what he had left of
the mangy hide, boiling it thoroughly and then cutting it into strips that
we could gulp down, and so preserved a little of our meager store.

That night we lay cold while it snowed, and the next day, as I recall,
we passed on across the rim to see, spread before us, bare and desolate
with ne'er a sign of life, the valley of the Spanish River. I seem to

remember weeping for sheer joy, for somewhere in those folded bottoms, we all felt sure, we were certain to come upon buffalo.

But for all our certainty, it seemed we were mistaken. Leisurely at first, and then swiftly and more frantically, we descended; looking, searching, always on the watch for some sign of the animals we sought. But only the tracks of a few old bulls could we discover, and those were well above a month old. Some antelope we sighted in the distance, far off, but so shy were they that not by any stratagem could they be lured within gunshot. Nor was there any hope of stalking them. Sage hens, prairie chickens, seemed to have abandoned the countryside, and even the fish in the streams stopped biting. I knew then what it was to starve, for all I had been hungry in Vancouver. Here we cut strips from our shirts and moccasins, until the latter were mere slippers, and but shreds of those at that! An old hide boiled and boiled and then cut into thin strips that might yet be slimy, but could possibly be swallowed, offered constipation but a degree of nourishment, and an eelskin that Stuart had sewed into his cap for a hatband gave not just one but actually three meals for us all!

Only once did Vallee find a beaver in the trap, and this we carefully apportioned among us and lived together upon it for nearly a week; meat, guts, lights, brains, and even the skin we chewed. So we lived!

How long we were upon this stretch I am not sure. I do know that my feet were blistered and raw, my moccasins, what was left of them, in tatters, so that, even had I stopped to boil the last of them, I doubt I could have cooked off enough life and sustenance to keep me going more than a day or two. How I must have looked there is no telling. We carried no such luxuries as looking glasses, even for trade. But I can speak for my companions. A wilder, more hollow-eyed, ragged, sunken-cheeked pack of walking skeletons I never hope to see again. Our rib cages stuck out like immense chests, and our bellies sunk almost to our backbones, and so reduced were we in strength that we could scarcely, even in this open country, going downhill with the wind behind us, cover more than a few miles a day.

I recall once that I asked Stuart if he knew the time of year. He replied that it was the eleventh.

"The eleventh of what?" I said.

"The eleventh of October," he told me.

That night we set the trap again as usual, upon a creek that fed the river. But it was empty in the morning, and for breakfast we had little more than enough to fill a hollow tooth between us.

When I say that we were hungry that morning, which would have been the twelfth, I hope none will accuse me of exaggeration. At dawn we pushed on, going two miles or so to the base of a mountain, and there we found the ascent steep and difficult. Nonetheless we struggled across, bearing to the east, and beyond, going fairly rapidly because of the pitch of the land, down to the Spanish River. Even the antelope did not come within view this day. We followed the river, east-southeast, down as far as we were able to walk, to a place where there was some faint indication that beaver had been in the neighborhood.

There we camped, not long before dusk, and seeing a sizable smoke to the southeast, in the direction we expected to go, we fed Le Clerc what little food we had and sent him off to learn the cause of it. After that we stripped willows, until we had a pot of the stuff and ate what we could of it, the while the sun sank and we chewed and eyed one another speculatively. In our bellies we felt the gnawing pinch of starvation; and the rasping, acid sharpness of regurgitant gastric juices was bitter in our throats. We swallowed these, thankful that we had something to swallow, and I noticed that Stuart's face was little better than that of a skeleton and caught myself wondering wildly if he would miss his skin if we were to strip it off and boil it. I thrust the foolish notion from me and remember wondering how long we could be satisfied thus swallowing our own bile. I, for one, could not much longer struggle onward, weak as I was, without sustenance. Tomorrow or the next day, or perhaps the next at the latest, I knew, I would pitch upon my face with only my knees, bony and slack-skinned, to break my fall, and there I would lie, too weak, no doubt, to crawl or care what happened to me or my companions, until the coyotes came down off the hills and started gnawing on me. I did not know about these others, but for me, at least, I felt the end of the road was near.

What prompted me to look up I do not know. MacPherson was staring at me across the flames of the little greasewood fire. It seemed to me I heard the wings of death aflutter all about me in the darkness.

Abruptly he stood up and looked from me to Stuart.

"We can't go on like this much longer," he said.

The others lifted their eyes slowly, but Stuart's glance remained fixed somberly on the fire. He nodded almost imperceptibly.

"I know," he said.

"A bone a man will carry us through until we reach the eastern ranges of the buffalo!" said MacPherson.

"A bone a man!" said Stuart. "Where are we to find that?"

"We could draw straws for it," replied MacPherson.

I stared up at him. He was looking directly down at me, and to me, at least, there was no question what was in his mind.

"You ought to know, MacPherson," I said. "Human flesh is as good as any when it comes to keeping folk alive, eh? You ought to know!"

He scowled at me furiously.

"Why not?" he demanded. "Why not? None of us will get through unless we do. And if each of us eats, who'll talk about the rest? Come to think of it, O'Rourke, I don't know why there's any need for straws!"

The whole circle was staring up at him now, fascinated by his intensity, the bitter fury with which he spoke, and it seemed to me that all this was happening at a great distance; this ragged scarecrow, standing over across the fire, accusing, threatening, fetching up his musket in slow, retarded action, the while my own fingers groped toward the butt of the pistol in my waistband.

"Why talk to me?" I demanded, and I could feel the sweat break out on my forehead, and my arms felt slimy underneath, not so much with fear as with the tension. "You ought to know that human flesh will keep a man alive. Why don't you admit it? Why don't you say so?"

He leered at me wolfishly, hollow cheeks sunk deep and lips stretched taut across his animal teeth, while his mouth stretched wide in the midst of his matted beard in a horrible grimace.

"All right!" he snarled. "Why not? What difference will it make? I killed MacBean—and ate him. He would have died anyway. We'd all have died if I hadn't. We beat him on the head until he died, and then we divided his body—half to Hamel and half to me. And we lived on him until the ice went out and we were able to get back!"

He laughed horribly, and I saw Stuart staring at him in a kind of horrified fascination. I saw his finger slide into the trigger guard and the black-nailed thumb move up and swing the hammer back.

"That's true!" I said, trying to delay him as long as I might in the hope the others might recover. They were all so tired and so slow. "That's what Hamel said! And then you would have done for me, the way you finished him if you could!"

"You have it all figured out, haven't you?" he sneered. "Well, you're right! I fixed him so he couldn't talk, and I'd have done the same for you if I could have caught you. But you were back at Fort William before I could come up with you. That would have saved a lot of trouble! How do you like it, now I say it? Eh, O'Rourke? You're going to die, you know that, don't you? Sit still, the rest of you! Sit still, now!"

He didn't look to right or left, yet he gave the feeling of having done so. I could almost sense the others stiffening. I saw his finger begin to tighten on the trigger in the firelight, and the muzzle of his musket poked across the fire almost in my face. Yet I could not look down that round hole. Instead, half-fascinated, I watched the knuckle of that finger as it drew slowly, tightening, whitening.

"Mr. Stuart——!" I cried.

"MacPherson!" said Stuart, whispering as if his throat were tight inside his collar. "MacPherson! You can't——"

"Shut up, you!" growled MacPherson. "I've listened enough to your preaching! Shut up!"

I flung myself sidewise, rolling over and over. Above me the gun roared and there was a flash of powder and smoke all but in my face. With my knees under me, I tugged at the pistol in my belt and jerked it free, flinging it up and firing point-blank upward at the place where I had seen him last. My eyes were blinded by the flash of his gun, and I could make out nothing. Almost instantly, when I had shot, there came the roaring echo of a musket to the right. I blinked the flash of fire from my eyes and stared, even as I tugged, kneeling, at the other pistol I had carried.

But across the fire MacPherson was staring at me—staring in a way I had never seen him look before, with a sort of puzzled, open-mouthed expression, as if he couldn't believe he saw me. Drunkenly his bearded chin dropped upon his chest and his eyes flew wide, with an almost comically surprised look. His curling fingers straightened, and the musket he had held dropped unheeded to the fire, knocking the sticks and sparks in all directions. Then, all at once, his knees gave way beneath him, slowly at first, and then more rapidly, so that he sank like a settling tree trunk, slightly twisting. His mouth opened wide, in a final, desperate gagging gesture, and blood fountained from it. He pitched forward suddenly upon his face, lying half across the fire, and the stink of his singeing beard and flesh spread quickly across the sharp night air.

For an instant no one spoke. Then Charbonneau rose, holding his musket ready before him as if he might shoot again, although a thin wisp of smoke curled slowly from its muzzle. Tentatively he stretched out a broad, moccasined toe and unceremoniously pushed the dead man over on his back. Fascinated, I saw the sparks race through his beard and saw the burnt place in his tunic widen unevenly. Nobody made a move to beat it out.

"Goddam! Long tam he's got dat comin'!" growled Charbonneau. "Now w'at you say, eh? *Sacre tetons!* Is someone t'ink she's like to eat?"

VIII. Home Again

~~~~~~

I. WINTER QUARTERS

I SEE no reason to pretend otherwise. My feeling then, my feeling now, was that the death of Dirk MacPherson was of benefit to us all. For a long moment after Charbonneau had spoken there was a stunned silence about the fire. It was Miller then who croaked:

"You've killed him!"

The Moose looked directly at him, puzzled.

"Ouai!" he said.

"That's murder!" Miller half-whispered.

Shea was on his feet at once.

"Who calls that murder?" he demanded. "It is murder then to be standin' up in the definse av others?"

"Hold your tongue, Shea!" rapped Westlake, the naval officer in him perhaps coming out instinctively. "This is not for you to decide. A man has been killed——"

"And who asked you?" demanded Fraser hotly.

It seemed to me incongruous that it would be he who came to the defense of the sailor. But instantly argument broke out all about the fire, and some were close to blows about it. It was all so swift that I was still resting on my knees, with the smoking pistol clutched in my fist, while Charbonneau stood half-straddling the dead man. But quickly as it flared, Rob Stuart was as swift to snatch control once more and fetch us all to order.

"Gentlemen!" he cried. "We prove nothing but bad temper if we fall out among ourselves. If we are to disagree, let us at least do it like civilized beings! The thing has happened. So much we must accept as fact. Let us go on properly from there!"

The others looked up at him in surprised silence, though it seemed

to me that Ramsay Crooks lifted one eyebrow and smiled a shade
cynically.

"Shall we call a constable?" he demanded.

Someone chuckled, and it seemed to me the tension eased.

Stuart shook his head mildly. "Something not far from it."

The fitful light of the fire flickered hollowly upon his gaunt face.

"It has always seemed to me," he said, "that the power of law
depends upon the consent of those governed by it. We are a long way
from any regular court, but I daresay we represent a majority of white
men between the mountains and the Pacific settlements."

"I'd say we were about as many as there are right hereabouts anyway," agreed Jones. "What you gettin' at?"

"We're all the law there is on this side of the mountains and for a
long way to the east," Stuart replied. "It seems to me that whatever
orderly course we choose, according to the will of the majority, will be
the right one, and nobody could quarrel with it."

The hunter nodded and spat into the flames.

"I suggest, then," Stuart went on, "that we name one of us to sit as
judge. Let him hear the arguments and give us his decision; then abide
by it. What do you say?"

"Hear, hear!" I growled.

Jones nodded again.

"That's fair enough," said Fraser.

It was so agreed. Stuart, having put forward the suggestion, preferred not to be appointed, and in the end the choice fell upon Ramsay
Crooks, who accepted it, glancing left and right and all about the ring
of solemn faces.

"All right," he said at length. "It looks like I'm elected."

He looked at me.

"I don't know as I like it much, though," he said soberly. "If you've
got any objections———?"

I shook my head.

"Go ahead, Ram," I told him.

He glanced at Charbonneau.

"You, Frenchy?"

The Moose shrugged.

"She's look lik' goddam foolishness to me," he replied. "But w'at
you say, *tant pis!* She's wan to me!"

"All right," Crooks nodded. "Then suppose you stand over yonder
with O'Rourke and let's get on with it. I reckon you'd say court's in
session, eh?"

He glanced about once more, encountering no dissenting looks.

"Fair enough!" he growled. "First thing is to agree what happened. How many shots were there?"

"Three," said Jones promptly.

"I don't see——" Miller began.

"You'll get your chance," Crooks growled at him sourly. "Let's get this first. Anybody don't agree to that—three shots, I mean?"

No one appeared to disagree.

"That's what I made it," said Crooks. "Three shots. MacPherson shot first?"

"I don't think anybody will dispute that," cried Miller petulantly. "It's plain enough! MacPherson shot first. Then O'Rourke fired in self-defense from the ground with his pistol. And finally Charbonneau shot from the side and killed him!"

Crooks glared at him.

"As to that," he retorted, "you run a mite ahead of the rest of us. Still, maybe you've cut it shorter. Is there any argument about that order of shots?"

"That was the way of it," said Westlake.

"Thank you!" Crooks nodded. "Now then, suppose we find out just how many of those shots took hold."

I looked at him abruptly. Until that moment it had not occurred to me that I might have hit the man. I had fired wildly. Yet it was possible. The range had been all but point-blank.

"Oh, for Christ's sake!" protested Miller. "What the devil does this prove——"

Crooks turned on him savagely.

"You sit down and bide your time!" he snapped. "You'll find out what this will prove when I'm ready to show you. Till then, I've been picked for this. I'll do it my way!"

Miller shrugged and subsided, and I saw Shea grin.

"All right," said Crooks, resuming. "Stuart, Fraser, Jones; look at the dead man and see if you can tell how many times he was hit and where."

The fire was poked up and all three squatted down beside the staring corpse, two on one side and one on the other. The ruddy firelight flickered on Fraser's gleaming beard, made dark pockets of Stuart's eyes, and cast Jones's sunken cheeks in shadow. Their three heads bent together and for a long moment they whispered among themselves. Then they rolled the body over and looked at both sides. Stuart pointed at something, then wiped his hand on the tatters of the dead man's shirt. All three stood up, and Stuart turned to Crooks.

"We find," he said, speaking for the group, "that he was hit by two bullets."

There was a slight stir about the fire. Some faces turned toward Miller. Crooks looked almost satisfied.

"At that range," Stuart went on, "it could scarcely be otherwise. O'Rourke should consider himself lucky indeed that MacPherson's shot missed."

"Aye!" growled Crooks in agreement. "If he hadn't been quick as a cat—— What about these bullets?"

"One," Stuart said, "struck him in the chest, low just under the V of the ribs, and traveled upward at an angle to lodge behind the shoulderblade, which it shattered. Charbonneau could not have fired that. So it must have been O'Rourke. The other seems to have struck him squarely in the left side, about midrib, and smashed all the way through and out upon the right."

"Ah!" Crooks spat. "Did they hit the heart, either of 'em?"

"They both did." Stuart half-smiled. " 'Tis well smashed, but from their course neither one could miss it."

Crooks grinned, breaking through his heavy solemnity.

"There's your answer, Mr. Miller," he said. " 'Twas yourself said Mr. O'Rourke fired in self-defense."

Miller scowled.

"You'll not deny, I reckon," Crooks went on, "a man has a right to defend himself?"

"Of course not," retorted Miller petulantly. "That's clear enough so far as O'Rourke's concerned. But Charbonneau——"

"Look you!" cried Crooks impatiently. "If O'Rourke's shot killed him, MacPherson was already dead when Charbonneau fired. I never heard there was any law agin shooting at a dead man!"

Miller flung up his hands.

"All right!" he cried. "All right. I have no more to say."

"You can't deny it?" Crooks demanded suspiciously.

"No, I can't deny it," Miller replied.

"Good, then." Crooks nodded, satisfied. "It seems to me the only crime that's been committed here is waste of ammunition. If there's no further argument about it, I'll so decide."

He glanced about the ring of faces, gaunt in the firelight. But there were no dissenting voices. He turned to Charbonneau and myself.

"You've been tried," he growled, "and acquitted. You can't be tried on the same score again. Now suppose you clean up this mess you've made. Get that thing out of here and bury it where the wolves won't find it. If we got a chance to eat a wolf, I'd hate to think we might be eating him!"

In our weakened state it was a far more difficult thing to do than the mere shooting, for we had neither tools to dig with nor the strength to wield them if we had. Fortunately, however, not far from where we were camped we discovered a shallow wash, meandering through the sagebrush. To this we dragged the already stiffening body, through the darkness of the night, and rolling it in unceremoniously, kicked away the bank about it, so that when we were done he was buried as deep and snug as if he were in a proper grave.

I have not hesitated to say that I felt no shadow of regret at the passing of MacPherson. Perhaps I ought to add that it even seemed to me his death marked a turning point in our fortunes. It was as if some sort of curse had been lifted from the undertaking. Matters seemed to improve generally for all of us; not all at one fell swoop, to be sure, nor even swiftly. Yet it remains a fact that without him things appeared to go better.

We would scarcely have been aware of it the following morning when we dragged ourselves alive once more. When we visited the trap, it was empty except for the paw of a large beaver. And as Le Clerc had not yet returned from investigating the smoke we had seen the previous evening, we set out on his track, by no means sure of what we would find.

A few miles along the way we met him returning, and he told us that he had spent the night at McClellan's camp and that the smoke we had seen had been occasioned by the place catching on fire while our erstwhile comrade was at some little distance fishing for his supper. Only with great difficulty had he been able to stumble back to fight the flames, and but for Le Clerc's opportune arrival, not only his gear but he himself might well have been consumed.

He had, he told Le Clerc, been much indisposed and had lived on little or nothing ever since he had parted from us. He was happy, he said, to know that we were near—as well he might be, considering the circumstances in which he had left us—and that he would wait where he was in hope that we would have something to eat. Without it, he said, he could not go on much farther.

Our feelings at this may well be imagined. Nevertheless we pushed on, stumbling over the rough ground, forgetting even to give an account of what had happened to us in Le Clerc's absence. And evidently he himself was so bemused with starving that he did not even notice MacPherson's absence.

We found McClellan lying on a bed of river grass and reeds, worn and emaciated, little more, it seemed to me, than a living skeleton clothed in flabby folds of skin, with cheeks so hollow and eyes so sunk in his head that every outline of his skull was clearly apparent. His lips drew back over his teeth in a horrible grin like that of death itself, and there was a bluish cast to his skin. His arms and legs seemed little more than pipestems, and the bones of his feet showed sharp through the dirt against the blisters and calluses. He had eaten his moccasins long since, he told us, and for nearly a week had been traveling barefoot.

His exertions in attempting to put out the fire had apparently sapped the last of his strength, and he was scarcely able to speak or raise his hand, such was his extreme weakness, while his disappointment at our lack of food brought tears to his eyes and plunged him into despair.

Stuart talked to him, and so did Crooks, while we built a fire and set a kettle on to boil. As soon as it was bubbling, we added a few hair-thin strips of rawhide, and an hour's steady boiling softened them so that, if they were not palatable, at least they could be bolted and so fill a corner of the empty stomach. I might add here, incidentally, that any animal's hide or leather is better eating if it has been cooked slowly overnight. But there was no time for that now.

He was reluctant at first to go on with us, saying that he might as well die there as anywhere, but after he had chewed for a time on the rawhide, he seemed to gather some strength, and at length, despite his grumbling and complaining, he agreed to it.

That day we divided his gear among us and took turns carrying the heavier portions of it, stumbling on over nearly seventeen miles of sandy, stony, barren ground, finally camping at an early hour on a small tributary of the Spanish River, because we saw some antelope in the neighborhood and hoped we might be lucky enough to kill one.

As soon as we had laid out our camp, those who could, crept out upon the stalk, but though we tried every trick and stratagem, they would not allow us within gunshot. As soon as any of us, however cautiously he crept, came within half a mile, up went their tails and away they would go, sailing in long, fantastic leaps over the sage and across the nearest ridge, and we would have all our work to do over again. As a result we returned to camp long after nightfall, fetching with us only heavy hearts and light stomachs.

From this it would scarcely seem that any great good fortune attended us immediately. But I have said it was not instantly apparent. The next morning we dragged ourselves out before daylight, finding great difficulty doing so, but that was the best and coolest time to travel and it was clear that we must keep going, for we would find nothing here to live on. In the gray dawn we struggled across a long plain and by sunup had come to some low hills, up which we struggled, keeping in a general southeasterly direction, with the ragged, tumbled mountains on our left and the valley of the Spanish River on our right.

It was as much as we could do, I will not hesitate to say, to drag ourselves up over the crest of that low ridge, but when we gained the top, we looked down upon the southeastern slope, across the ever-present sage, to a thin line of cottonwoods, which we took to indicate that there was at least water there. Accordingly we began a stumbling descent toward it, to come, within a distance of two miles, into a little pocketed swale, invisible from above. There, to our immense delight and excitement, we came upon a very old, much broken-down bull buffalo.

He was alone, and I do not doubt he had come there to die in peace. For my part, I believe I would have rushed forward, gun in hand, but wiser heads and hands deterred me. McClellan, being too feeble for the undertaking, Jones organized the hunt, pointing out that this was an opportunity we could not afford to let slip. Under his guidance we crept forward, each man so posting himself that should the beast escape the first shot he could not leave the swale without passing within gunshot of another of us. It was a proceeding we would ordinarily have disdained, but this was more than sport to us. It might be a matter of life or death. By this means we finally succeeded in pocketing the animal in a little gully, where we blasted the life from him, and so ravenous were we that we did not wait to skin him out, but fell upon him immediately with our knives, cutting out whatever meat we could reach, and wolfed it ravenously, raw, and dripping blood.

Our manners, I daresay, left something to be desired. But surely starving men may be forgiven!

When we had in some measure dulled the edge of our hunger, Mr. Stuart called a halt upon our guzzling, and we cut up the rest of what was edible and carried it between us, down to the little creek that we had seen from above. There we made camp for the night and our Frenchmen fell to preparing a blazing fire and a well-cooked meal. While they were about it, the rest of us returned to the spot where we had slain the animal and gathered up the hide and the bones and the entrails, for which, it occurred to us, we might find a use.

This was our first and, I truly believe, our greatest stroke of fortune, for had we not killed that bull that day, we never could have found the strength to go on to the next. At Stuart's insistence the bones were used for broth and the marrow extracted from them and set floating in the stew, and I think perhaps it was due to this precaution that we felt no ill effects from our gorging, for it is the truth we sat up half the night, barbecuing steaks and eating.

For all our greediness, however, there was a considerable quantity of meat left when the next morning came. Long after sunup we rolled from our blankets, much recruited and considerably refreshed. According to rule we made a bundle for each of as much as we could carry and resumed our journey.

In a few miles we came upon a large Indian trace, perhaps fifteen days old, leading northeasterly, which we judged to have been made by Crows on their way homeward from their hunt, for in every direction the landscape was dotted with the whitening skeletons of buffalo. This day we saw only a few antelope, which were exceedingly wild, so that we made no attempt to pursue them, being for once tolerably well satisfied. That night again we ate buffalo, and the next day set off to skirt the mountains on our left, over a level plain, passing during the day the remains of a large Indian camp and yet another trace bearing in the same direction, and everywhere signs that the buffalo had not long since been plenty in these parts. By that we judged the remnants of the herd itself could not be far away.

We kept on so a matter of several days, as I recall, just to the point where what remained of our poor old bull was beginning to stench, when our second stroke of luck befell us. We fell in with a wandering band of Snake Indians, who had been hunting in this direction and who had been attacked by the Absorokas. Despite their misfortunes they were kind to us, and we assured them that it would not be long before the whites would take vengeance upon their enemies, after which our friends, the Snakes, would be plentifully rewarded. We smoked the calumet, finding them possessed of a sort of wild tobacco much better than our own kinnikinnick, and, thereafter, in return for a pistol, a breechclout, an ax, a knife, a tin cup, two awls, and a few beads, they traded us the only horse remaining to them, and for a few additional trinkets supplied us with as much buffalo meat as we could carry and leather for moccasins—an article of which we were all, by now, in dire need.

We felt wealthy, indeed, when we went on our way, rested and with lighter hearts, and I truly think even beginning to fill out a little from our recent bout with hunger. And there was added cheer in the Indians' assurance that the mountains, which had been marching in great, high-piled ranks to the east of us, turned at a little distance to the southward and ran in a diminishing chain north and east, separating the waters of the Big Horn and the Cheyenne, on the north, from those other rivers to the southward that fell into the Missouri below the Sioux country. They confirmed their rascally compatriots' rumor of an easy pass, and toward this, following their directions and keeping a little aside and to the southward in our approach, to avoid the possibility of encountering wandering bands of Crows, we made our way. We came to it, or to the flatter region just below it, at last, after several dry days, for we were above the sources of the drains that run down into the Spanish River.

Uncertain yet whether or not we had found what we sought, we pushed across the low divide, everywhere clothed with rank sagebrush and the home of biting winds. Once or twice we came upon stinking pools of stagnant water, ringed with white rime and the skeletons of animals that had tasted it. But at last we stumbled upon a good-sized stream flowing northward, and, following this downward for nearly a day, we came at length to a brawling little river, chuckling across a rugged bed of stone and gravel on a course that was almost directly east; waters, we were certain now, that rolled on down the eastern slope of the continent and would fetch us finally to the Missouri.

The shouts of excited delight with which we made the discovery can be imagined. To us, after our months of struggle over the barren land behind us, it truly seemed as if now, at last, we were all but home. We took a new grip on life and started eastward with a lighter step. Even our patient nags, I think, felt the better for it, and the truth was that we were not a day too soon, for already we had experienced a number of swirling, howling, biting flurries of snow and sleet and, indeed, all the night before had lain huddled in our blankets, clutching our ribs against a whistling northeaster. A week, two weeks at most, we might allow, and after that the route would have been closed by winter.

As if this were not luck enough, it appeared we had come abruptly out of pinch-belly land and into the smiling plains of plenty. We had not got five miles down our new river when we came to the edge of a low bench, down which we must drop to a lower level, and under it we saw the buffalo, hundreds and thousands of them, I daresay, scattered across the plain in little knots of five and six and seven, bulls and cows and half-grown calves, visible in all directions as far as the eye could reach.

We had learned by now to take advantage of Fortune's favor when she was of a mind to show it to us, and we lost no time in killing all that we could use and, I daresay, a little more besides; and immediately we treated ourselves to a grand feast of buffalo tongues and hump steaks, confident, at last, that nothing short of sickness or savages themselves could stop us now!

That evening, when we came to camp, Stuart called yet another council, at which we took stock of the situation and reached the general conclusion that we were probably upon a branch of the Cheyenne. If this were true, it would not be wise to go too far down. To do so might well fetch us to a village of those Indians, and although they themselves were friendly, they were blood cousins to the savage Sioux, who must surely learn our presence there. Obviously we could not possibly reach St. Louis that winter, and our only alternative, in such an event, would be to winter among the Cheyennes. Should that happen, there was little doubt in any of our minds but that in continuing downstream in the spring we would be ambushed by the Sioux. On the other hand, if we were to winter farther up and without the knowledge of the Cheyennes, there was every likelihood that we might be able to slip through quickly and unnoticed when the time came and so gain the lower reaches of the Missouri in safety.

As a result we decided among us that the best course would be to continue downstream only until we came to the first likely spot where we might find timber and game and fodder for our animals and there remain, as much in hiding as we might, through the snowy months of the year. If it was not now the first of November, it must be very nearly so. Indeed there was some difference of opinion as to the date, Crooks maintaining that it was the second of the month, while Stuart pointed to the journal he had kept all the way from Astoria as proof that actually it was no later than the twenty-ninth of October. Whatever the date, it was cold enough in all conscience, and it seemed to me that if we ever were to build shelter for ourselves and find meat to carry us through the winter we had best be about it.

Accordingly we pushed on over as rugged going as any we had yet encountered, down through a narrow gap in which we almost literally had to hack our way, until the stream we were following joined another coming in from the south. The two combined to flow off toward the northeast, following a rugged canyon for some distance, so that we were forced to country above, but at length we were again able to drop down into the river bed, where we found no scarcity of game. Following the stream several days, until we found a creek that came in upon the north, we decided that there could no longer be any doubt but that we were either upon the Cheyenne or one of its tributaries, and since there was both food and water, good timber, and the promise of solitude, we made up our minds to winter at this place.

The next day some of us set about cutting logs with which to build our hut, while others hunted, for time was growing short now and winter's snows would soon be on us. It was imperative to fill our larder while we might. By nightfall one of the hunters came to report that five of them had already accounted for a dozen buffalo and that our help and that of the nag was needed to transport the carcasses to camp. In the course of the night a further evidence of our new good fortune appeared in the shape of a solid freeze, which formed a hard bridge across the river not far above our cabin site and greatly eased the labor of bringing the kill across the river. While some of us were about this, our hunters fetched down six more of the great beasts, and since it was now unnecessary to leave any part behind, we began to feel a little more secure.

Having covered the ground we had since leaving Astoria, we were nothing if not adaptable. The hut we built, while certainly no palace, was snug. Eighteen feet long by eight wide, it was large enough to accommodate all of us, yet not so large as to require a great amount of heat. The roof was made of poles, covered with buffalo hides, and the fire was placed in the center, Indian fashion, with a hole and flap directly above to serve as a smoke vent. At the eaves it was three feet high and nearly sufficient at the ridgepole for the average man among us to stand erect; though of course it was far from high enough for such giants as Fraser and Westlake. At a glance it might seem cramped, yet it was snug. The floor was of trampled earth, covered with buffalo skins, which, I must admit, grew in time to be somewhat overpowering, but which certainly afforded better couches than the bare ground. The meat we stored in an adjacent shed, upon one side of the hut, with the only access through the cabin itself, while on the other side, somewhat sheltered from the wind, we built another shed for the accommodation of our faithful nag.

In this comparative luxury, then, we settled down to face the winter, feeling reasonably secure from prying eyes because of the remoteness of our situation and the fact that we had been at some pains to hide our little hovel well back in a small bosky ravine through which a tiny creek flowed. All around us were steep, well-wooded slopes, which were the haunt of such game as elk and deer and bear and ibex, to say nothing of little bands of wintering buffalo, so that we had little

fear of starving, and on the fourth day after we had completed our
shelter our Frenchmen went out for hides wherewith to make new shirts
and breeches and moccasins, which, next to food, were our greatest
need. Since quality skins rather than meat were what they sought, they
passed by the elk and buffalo—later we could hunt for them if we felt
the need of heavier boots—and within three days they had each
fetched in a half-a-score of ibex and black-tailed deer, the skins of
which the rest of us turned into rawhide as rapidly as they were forth-
coming. By the end of a week we had enough to make us each a new
suit of clothing with a little more left over besides. And during the next
week six of us fetched in twenty more, so that it was quickly evident
we would not want. Three bears, two white and one black, provided
bacon and grease with which to cook and supple our new clothes and
make tallow dips of a crude sort, and taken all in all we counted ourselves quite comfortably settled by the time we had been a month or so
in our new quarters.

So we lived a lazy life for a little time. The hollows in our ribs and
cheeks filled out and the life came back into our eyes and hearts. Our
nag grew sleek and fat on the winter hay we cut in the river bottom.
For once we found time for plenty of sleep, and the knowledge that we
would be there tomorrow and the day after and the day after fetched
with it a sort of peaceful lethargy that I truly believe was as beneficial
to us as the food and warmth and fancied security.

Do you wonder I say fancied? The question answers itself. So sure
of ourselves were we that we did not even trouble to post a guard, and
so it happened that one trembling dawn we were rudely aroused from
our lazy slumbers by the dread Indian yelp, ringing from the hills
above, not a hundred yards away from our hideaway. Half-naked, in
flapping shirttails, we seized our arms and poured out of our hovel's
door, prepared to fight for our lives, to find ourselves confronted by a
grinning, painted party of twenty-three or -four stark-naked Arapaho
braves, who quickly made the sign of peace, so that fortunately we were
able to catch ourselves in the nick of time and withhold our fire.

Their grins, it appeared, were to be accounted for by the fact that
they had caught us napping, though I dare believe, had we napped a
few moments longer, the habit might well have become permanent.
After the first sharp shock of surprise we made them welcome, and they
told us that they were a war party northbound to take vengeance upon
the Absorokas for some slight or other that had been done them. Like
all savages they were at first affable and friendly, smoking with us about
our fire, joking and eating the choicest bits of our provisions freely.

That night they stayed by us, the braves sleeping outside in their own camp, despite the bitter cold. The two chiefs that led them, we insisted, beneath the guise of hospitality, must share the cabin with us, by which means we had them as hostages for the good behavior of their people. Before they left us the following morning they were insistent in their demands for powder, and when we would not give it to them, pretended to make it a great joke that they had asked. Nevertheless, they were not backward this day either, about helping themselves to the best of our larder. Nor dared we deny them.

They had not much more than disappeared beyond the rim of the plain when Rob Stuart summoned us all to hasty council.

"That does it!" he growled. "We'll have to move!"

Westlake stared at him.

"Why? They seemed friendly enough to me."

"They behaved better than most sailors I could tell ye about!" Shea put in.

Crooks grinned at him.

"So they did," he agreed, "this time! They were outbound and in no mood to be burdened with the loot they might have of us. But they'll be back within a fortnight hankering for a fight."

"And if they don't," added Stuart, "we could not be worse placed, now they have discovered us. We've Arapaho on one side, but a day's journey, and Absoroka upon the other, five days' march. If there's to be war between them, we're in the middle of it."

The rest of us nodded agreement, and both Westlake and the bos'n looked downcast.

"I see what you mean," the mate said.

II. A WORLD AT WAR

HAD it not been so late in the season, we might have got together a greater supply of meat and tried to raft it, at least for a distance down the river, but cold as it was now, with the stream as often as not frozen solid from bank to bank, that was out of the question. We fought through deep drifts and across prairies that the wind swept bare, sometimes wondering if it might not be better worth our time to turn and stand and fight, if need be, rather than drive ourselves to all this trouble. But common sense supplied the answer to that and we kept on.

At first the river flowed north and east, and we were more than ever sure we were upon the Cheyenne. But after two days' dreadful journey, in which we all came nigh to freezing, it turned for a distance and ran due east, then little by little began to swing toward the southward around a spur of a distant range of mountains. At the same time either the weather moderated or the climate of the country changed imperceptibly, for it grew somewhat warmer and the snow that appeared either blew or melted away. At the same time the stream itself changed and grew wide and meandering, running over many sandy channels, weaving and interweaving, which, though often nearly a mile across, not one of them was deep enough to float a good-sized canoe. As this was utterly foreign to the character we had heard of the Cheyenne, we decided first that we must be upon the Niobrara, and then gradually it dawned upon us that we were upon neither, but that, quite by accident, we had either fallen upon the Platte itself or its principal tributary.

This, when it dawned upon us, fetched broad grins, for by following this stream, which we had never dreamed we might have the good fortune to strike, we would come to the Missouri through a territory far to the southward of the land of the terrible Sioux. Accordingly we felt that if we could but survive the winter there was reason to believe that we should have little trouble beyond this point.

But this, apparently, was our problem. Long since we had left the hills and with them the heavy timber. One or two creeks that we had passed had showed a respectable growth of cottonwood in patches. But in the main now even the sage was giving way to sere brown grass and our only fuel was driftwood and buffalo chips. Across these open prairies the wind whipped with a vicious bite, and game quite prudently disappeared entirely.

It seemed evident that the farther we went in this direction, the more bitter must the cold become. Moreover, despite the shallowness of the stream, we still entertained notions of building canoes in the spring and floating down to civilization. Consequently yet another council, prompted by a fireless night on the prairie beneath the bitter lash of a northerly blizzard, decided us to turn back, at least as far as the last point at which we had seen sizable trees. Accordingly we did an about-face, slogging back a distance of several days, until we came to the mouth of a creek issuing from the hills to southward, where there appeared to be at least a respectable stand of timber and some sign, at least, of game. We sent Le Clerc to investigate, and he returned with the report that he had located a half-dozen trees fit for canoes. So we turned away from the main river, and after struggling a few miles into the hills, until we were as sure as we could be that we would be hid from prying eyes, we went into our new winter quarters upon a willow bottom, not quite so secure and comfortable, perhaps as those we had just left, but at least livable and enjoying the advantage of being, for the moment, undiscovered by any of our red neighbors.

To the best of our reckoning, our arrival at this point fell on the last day of the year, and on the following, in celebration of the New Year, we broke out the best for all hands, consuming, I think, as many as a dozen buffalo tongues and puddings of bear's suet and the best of the meat. Cold creek water was our only tipple, but we made pretense that it was the best of rum or sack or ale—according to our tastes—and in it pledged one another's health by proxy, agreeing that as soon as we reached civilization we would take a binding draft for each so offered. To cap the climax, since our tobacco had long since been consumed and even the foul kinnikinnick that we had been smoking, made of willow bark and odd sorts of dried leaves, was gone, we chopped up Miller's tobacco pouch, as merry as if we had been half-tipsy, and smoked that as welcome to the New Year. All the rest of the world might be at war for all we knew, this year of 1813, but we, at least, were prepared to spend that day in friendship and in ignorance.

We spent the winter in that place, I daresay as snug as we might have been in the earlier quarters we had occupied. But human nature is such that a man must be forever looking back. We grumbled and compared, for all that the game, if not quite as abundant, was inclined to be fatter and the weather was a touch milder. As for our actual accommodations, I doubt whether there was a great deal of difference in them.

As soon as we had built our hut and lodged our nag, we sought out the canoe trees that Le Clerc had reported and found them all hollow and consequently worthless for our purpose. A careful search, however, located two good logs, and out of these we made a pair of twenty-foot craft, not capable of carrying our party, but each at least large enough to carry one man and a quantity of supplies, so that by the time the ice in the streams before us broke up and the snows in the hills melted we were ready to get on downriver. We put our baggage in them, and while the rest of us took to the bank and walked, one in each craft took a turn at navigation.

Unfortunately we discovered that that was the stuff that dreams are made of. The river was shallow and the canoes, despite the fact that they carried only one of us at a time, were heavy. They stuck on the bars and called for the efforts of all of us and the horse to dislodge them. We wrestled with quicksand, and time and time again chose the wrong channel, so that by the time we had gone four days' journey we were happy to use the craft for firewood. What we could not eat we loaded on our patient nag, and the rest of the lading we took upon our backs and started the long walk homeward.

We left the hut about the middle of March, and before a month had passed we had put half our journey behind us. Early in April, as nearly as we could tell, we came upon a hut in which we found three squaws, who seemed at first very much terrified at sight of us. We gave them meat and other presents, and restrained our Canadians, so that they might see we made no plan against them, but even so they remained shy. Nevertheless they told us that they had been ill during the winter and had been left there to die by their people. With the food we had given them, they said, they would have strength to rejoin them. They were Pawnees—Pawnee Loup, or Panimaha, they called themselves, whose country lay not far off on the banks of the Loup Fork, to which they assured us we could come in a few days' journey. We offered to take them with us as far as that river, but to that they would not consent, saying they could make their way better alone and assuring us that not far below we would find the Otoes, among whom they had heard there were white traders.

Within a day or two we passed the mouth of the Loup and not many miles below came upon an encampment of Otoes, who assured us that the rumors were true. With their help we covered the last miles to their main village, not far above the mouth of the river and the Missouri. There we found, trading out of St. Louis, François Dourouin and Baptiste Roi, who had reached this point on their north-ward journey only a little before, after a voyage of six weeks.

Only a man who had been nearly a year beyond the bounds of civilization could understand with what joy and good fellowship we looked upon these two somewhat seedy Frenchmen. We hugged them as if they had been long-lost brothers, and I will say for them that they showed us every hospitality. From them we had our first news of the world outside. I daresay they told us many things, but only one word of all they said stood out in the memories of all that heard it, and that was WAR—war between the United States and Great Britain; war declared late in June the year before, so that it must have begun just about the time we left Astoria.

I must say the thought gave us a start. Nearly half of us were Canadians—British subjects—and consequently, by technical inter-

pretation, enemies. Yet our mutual sufferings had given us a comradeship that was not lightly to be broken. There had been no differences
of nationality then. It seemed to us that there could be none now.
Even Fraser and Westlake, for all their rivalry, I realized abruptly,
had grown to be friends. I remembered how Shea had leapt to Charbonneau's defense when MacPherson had fallen. Miles of hardship and
a year of suffering had knit us all together in a group with but a single
heart.

But there would be time enough to think of that. More than six
hundred miles of river lay yet before us, and to put this as swiftly
as possible behind us we traded our nag and such of our gear as we
no longer needed to Dourouin and his companion for two stout skin
canoes and some meat and corn meal.

Running sixty or seventy miles a day now, we came at last to one
of those posts which Captain Clark had told me it was the intent of
the government to build; Fort Osage, at the mouth of the river of the
same name. Here we learned the melancholy truth of the traders'
rumor. There was war between us, but since no one saw fit to ask, we
saw no sense in admitting that all of us were not Americans, and after
giving some account of our long and tedious journey, we set out again
upon our way.

Yet three days more we passed upon the yellow flood, riding between
green bluffs here, with now and then a settler's farm, a snug and trim
reminder that we were approaching civilization. Yet somehow as we
drove along our hearts were not so gay as they should have been.
We talked but little and we laughed less, and it was only when we swept
around the last long bend to see the dappled roofs of the town nestling
amid the trees along the riverbank, dominated by the spires of the
great church, that went by courtesy as a cathedral, that we raised even
a thin cheer and grinned about at one another. For this was St. Louis,
not very large and more sprawled out than I had imagined it, but
journey's end for some of us and civilization at last for all.

Our arrival in St. Louis created more than a little stir, but I, for
one, did not stay to savor it. Nor were certain of my companions
inclined to delay. Robin Stuart had a task to finish, a report to make,
and after all we had been through to carry it this far, a little thing
like a difference of nationality, or nations at war, was scarcely likely
to stop him. Westlake and Fraser and myself had our own reasons, or
perhaps I should say reason—after all, it was one and the same to each
of us—for wanting to come as quickly as we might to New York; and

wherever those two went, Shea and Charbonneau were not likely to be far behind. A shave and a hot tub, some clean, decent clothes, and a well-cooked meal, a bow to the governor, and we were on our way.

Our companions of the trail came down to the ferry to bid us Godspeed. There we shook hands solemnly around once more, then slowly led our horses down the bank and on to the waiting scow. A moment later we were swaying off across the muddy stream under the cable that stretched from bank to bank. When we looked back toward the little village sprawled against the green of the bluffs behind, we could see our friends still watching. We waved, and they waved back, and after that we saw them turn and pick their way up along the dusty pathway toward the town. I could not help wondering then if ever we would see any of them again.

Because of the war the usual route through Vincennes to Louisville was considered hardly safe, especially since there were Canadians traveling with us. Accordingly we took to the more southerly route, through Kaskaskia and Murphysboro to Shawneetown and so on across into Kentucky. Thence we took an inner road a good part of the way. Yet even here we were not without indications of what was happening. At Murphysboro we learned that only a few days before the Indians, set on by the British, had made a raid at the very fort in which we lodged, and killed one man and wounded another; though what both astounded and disgusted all of us was the fact that the people in the blockhouse, at least twelve fighting men so far as we could tell, had watched them kill and scalp their victim within a hundred yards and made no move to help him!

So far as we ourselves were concerned, we experienced no hostile demonstrations, unless it was from fleas and vermin at the crude hostels that we found on the way. The road was miserable now, hot and dusty and choking, or again up to our horses' bellies in mud, and always beset with clouds of flies and fleas and gnats and mosquitoes. We complained, as all good travelers do, yet we laughed at ourselves, too, when we considered the luxury of all of this compared with what we had been enduring but a few months since. At least we now had stout nags between our knees and plenty to eat, even if it was not always so well cooked or so savory as some of the buffalo steaks that we ourselves had prepared over the open camp fire. The fleas we found in our beds at least bit no worse than the lice we had gathered on the plains, and we did have beds to sleep on and blankets to cover us, though often as not there were three of us to share them.

For all our growls and grumbles we moved rapidly, passing through

Lexington and Marietta to reach Pittsburgh in something under a month's time. There we paused while we procured proper mounts to carry us over the Alleghenies, and there at last my own secret was forced from me; not so much because I willed it, but in the interests of our common comradeship. To keep Fraser and Westlake from each other's throats, I felt forced to speak.

From the moment of our departure from St. Louis the rivalry between them, there reborn, had been growing like a lusty, brawling brat. At the beginning, at least, it seemed to me it lacked much of the old animosity. Even by the time we had come so far, they were yet able to grin about it; taunting, jibing each other on their prospects, and grinning like a pair of triumphant cats, each claiming victory already well within his reach, yet now content, by the friendship that had grown up between them, to let the other win if he could—which of course each one was sure he could not.

So long as it remained on such a basis I felt content to hold my tongue and let matters take their course. Indeed, I truly think I rather savored the situation. For there was no doubt in my mind, either, as to the outcome. Our two cavaliers were riding to a thumping fall.

I must admit that I myself had, perhaps from habit induced by the pressure of the fight for survival in the wilderness, scarcely thought of Valerie. Her name had come to me but seldom, and I think the same was true of them. But now, as we drew nearer and nearer to our journey's end, my thoughts as well as theirs swung more and more frequently to the prize that each of us hoped to win.

It was nearly three years since we had seen each other. I had to grant that that was a long time. Had she changed? If so, I did not doubt, it could only be for the better. Such as she, as steadiness and stability were added to the giddyness of girlhood, I thought, could only become more sweet and lovely. And my deliberate flouting must have chastened her. I was egotistical enough to be certain of that. Once she had told me that she loved me, and love was not a thing that died or could be lightly tossed about. What if she had amused herself with a few small, innocent coquetries, such as she had practiced on my unfortunate companions? At the time she had been little more than a child, and by now she would have learned her lesson. She would be ready to receive me with the open, loving arms I knew I longed for; contrite, and with chastened, welcoming smile. Indeed I could even find it in my heart to feel a little sorry for the two eager swains. They were so sure of themselves!

All the time I hugged to myself the secret which neither of them could know. In the end each must watch the hopes, in which he had such confidence, vanish into thin air, and see Valerie herself go, not to the other at all, but rather to one whom they had never so much as considered a rival possibility.

Perhaps a little meanly I savored that. It lent a certain piquancy to the sympathy I felt for each of them.

Yet, curiously, it is a fact I cannot properly ignore, often as I tossed beneath my blankets, listening to the gentle snores of my companions, I felt in myself a certain strange reluctance, almost as if I hoped in my heart that I was mistaken. For all I was sure I could not be. Sometimes I almost wished it might be otherwise. At times I did not much seem to care if we ever reached New York, and when I tried to analyze the feeling, I told myself that this was due to a sense of guilt because I knew that I must, even for their own good, step out in front of these two stout friends with whom I had shared so much and offer myself in preference.

It was strange, too, even, I may say, a little irritating that, now that we were on the home stretch and I turned my mind to her often, I had difficulty fetching a picture of her to my mind. Try as I would I could not be sure of the color of her eyes or the shape of her mouth. Her face and form appeared to me, even in the most vivid dreams, misty, nebulous as that of a half-imagined sprite. Yet when I would close my eyes and steel myself against the gnawing of the tavern bedbugs I might see plainly enough a mass of coppery hair and a pair of gay, amused brown eyes, a freckled nose, and cheeks as bright as apples in the sun. A tomboy seemed to taunt me in my dreams.

"Oh, you!" she would say. "Rory O'Rourke, if you were half a man——"

I would never find out what it was I might do if I were half a man. But the thing remains a fact; I never had the least trouble painting in my mind a picture of Deborah. I found it almost irritating.

It was like that when we got to Pittsburgh, where we lodged at Mr. Sullivan's. Our host, I must say, did us proud. He was a short, copper-haired man with a sharp face and wisely twinkling eyes that held an unexpected glint of humor. He made us welcome and set before us the best his house had to offer. His Monongahela whisky was smooth and strong and his Sherris-Sack of the best; though he himself would partake of neither—a most intelligent host!

I daresay it was the strength of his whisky and the quality of his tobacco that set my companions' tongues to wagging and bragging. Before any of us were aware of it, the argument had flared up and the whole thing was out there in the open where each of us could see it.

It was Stuart himself, who, quite unwittingly, precipitated it.

"Well, gentlemen," he said, "we're almost home. I daresay you've each your own plans."

Westlake looked sardonically at Fraser.

"I don't know about the rest," he said, "but I know what I intend to do."

"Ho! And don't you now?" jibed Fraser. "Why don't you give it up, Westlake, and admit you've never a chance? Make yourself another set of plans. You're not in the running!"

"Am I not?" cried Westlake almost belligerently. "You flatter yourself, my friend."

Stuart grinned from one to the other.

"Oho, so that's the way of it!" He chuckled.

But neither of the others heeded him.

"What makes you think," demanded Westlake, "that she'd have aught to do with you—in a serious way, I mean? She knows the difference between a carroty-topped backwoodsman and a true gentleman!"

"Applying the word to yourself, I suppose?" demanded Fraser, lumbering to his feet and planting his fists on the table before him. "I recall a time when you were grateful enough for a backwoodman's push!"

"Aye!" retorted Westlake, rising, scowling, to meet him. "So I was, I'll admit. And so were you for a hand from me that kept you from being washed over the rail. But this is a different matter. It involves the heart of a lady."

"And mine," gritted Fraser.

"And my own," said Westlake coldly.

It was obvious to me that if this was allowed to go on, in another moment they would be at each other's throats, and for what reason? I counted them both my friends, and I could not see them quarrel needlessly.

"Gentlemen! Gentlemen!" I cried. "Have done with it. You are both mistaken, and there is no need for you to fight about it! Mistress Drake will have neither of you, so you might as well sit down!"

It needed a bombshell of some sort to burst through the tension, and apparently I picked the right one. They both turned and stared at me, and even Stuart looked interested.

"What?" said Fraser.

Westlake merely glared.

"I have kept a lock on my tongue," I said coldly, "for I have been of no mind to upset you, but rather than let you quarrel over such a foolish matter I'll let you pry it off. The truth of it all is that Mistress Drake is betrothed to me."

They both blinked at me in utter amazement, and it seemed to me even Stuart looked unbelieving, as if he thought I had fetched the idea forth only to stop the row.

"I'm not joking!" I said quickly, lest the same thought occur to them. "You may ask the lady herself when we come to New York, if you've the patience to wait until then!"

"Be—— Well, for God's sake!" Fraser exclaimed, and began to laugh.

"I don't see anything funny," I said stiffly.

"What are you telling us?" Westlake scoffed. "Why would such as she look——"

He caught himself abruptly, but we were all aware of what he had been about to say.

"Why would she look twice at me?" I finished for him. "I'll tell you why. Because I can offer her what she wants: a settled life, position, and security! I've earned all those, and she knows it. What's more, she loves me, as she told me herself long ere she met either of you. That's why I tell you you have deceived yourselves. Now have done!"

"Well, I'm damned!" said Fraser.

"Just a minute," put in Westlake. "Just a minute!"

Fraser stopped laughing and looked at him.

"Do you say it was long before ever she met either of us that she pledged herself to you?" Westlake went on.

I nodded emphatically, not seeing the trap he laid for me.

"Curious," he grinned. "I didn't notice you much in one another's company before we sailed. As a matter of fact, it seemed to me there was a coolness between you. How would you explain that now?"

I shrugged and put the best face I could on it.

"We'd a small bit of a tiff before I left," I said. "As a matter of fact, it was largely on that account I joined the expedition. But there's no sense in arguing about it. I've told you the facts. You can make what you like of them!"

"Ah!" said Fraser skeptically.

"Certainly!" I retorted fatuously. "A man can't let a woman get the upper hand of him!"

"Ha!" said Fraser this time, grinning.

Westlake grinned back at him.

"Look here, O'Rourke," he said. "This is interesting. Here's three of us, each bound that he knows the right answer. I'll tell you what, let's make it a proper race. What d'you say? I'll post a hundred dollars on the outcome."

I blinked at him, not knowing whether to be outraged or amused.

"I'd never bet on such a thing!" I said stiffly.

He made a gesture of impatience.

"I'm not suggesting a bet," he retorted. "Each one of us will post a similar amount, the sum to buy a wedding present for the bride, chosen by whichever two may be the losers. What d'you say to that?"

I hesitated, and I daresay I might have refused had not Stuart comment to offer. He looked amused.

"Of course!" he said. "The lady might have something to say in the matter. She might not have any of you!"

"In that case," said Westlake quickly, "the whole amount will be turned over to some worthy cause—the hospital, say, or the almshouse."

Such skepticism galled me beyond prudence.

"All right!" I said, perhaps growing a little angry myself. "I'll just meet you at that! We'll let Mr. Stuart hold the articles!"

We both looked at Fraser.

"Done!" said the Scot promptly, grinning, and we called upon Mr. Sullivan to fetch pen and paper so that we might reduce the agreement to writing. When we had each signed, we put the paper in Mr. Stuart's care, and for the moment, at least, I counted that crisis past.

III. NEW YORK AGAIN

I WILL admit that the fortnight it needed for us to push on to New York was colored with rather more anticipation than the journey so far. In a way it seemed to me it would never end. One after another the green ridges of the Alleghenies rose before us and dropped behind, like the petrified waves of a vast sea, and I began to count the miles as we covered them. Shippensburg, Lancaster, York, Philadelphia, in turn were reached and passed, and we came at length to the rolling green fields and the hot summer sun of the Jerseys. Then, at last, we were looking across the sparkling water of the Hudson to the green trees and clustered roofs and towering spires and gleaming windows of the city at the tip of Manhattan Island.

We wasted no time waiting for the ferry itself, but hired a boat and were set promptly across, and immediately upon landing we went directly to Mr. Astor's counting rooms. I believe Shea and Charbonneau would cheerfully have left us to attend to our official duties, while they sought out the most likely bar. But we insisted they accompany us.

I was not surprised to find Will Sanders still bent on his high stool across a desk, strewn with musty ledgers and accounts. He glanced up as we entered, not at first recognizing us in the dim light, then all at once spotting me and leaping down to greet us.

"Rory! Rory! Rory, boy! By all that's holy!" he cried.

He burst out through the barrier to embrace me, and then I held him off and looked at him. He was the same Sanders, though a little leaner, a little grayer.

"Will!" I cried. "Will, by God! I hoped you'd be here!"

"Where else would I be?" he demanded. "Lord! Who'd have thought this would be such a day? And Mr. Stuart and Fraser and Westlake."

He shook hands with us all around again. I had never seen him so excited.

"Where have you dropped from?" he demanded. "Is the *Beaver* back?"

"No such luck," I told him.

"The *Tonquin* then?" he asked.

I shook my head.

"We've come from Astoria—overland."

"Astoria?" he said blankly. "Where's that?"

"The Columbia," I said a little impatiently.

"Oh," he said. Then: "Ooooh, I see. You've named it. That was dull of me! I should have caught that. D'you know you've brought us the first word we've had? Was all well when you left?"

"Well enough," I replied noncommittally, "though we've a good deal to report. Mr. Stuart carried the despatches."

"Well, come in then!" he cried. "Come in, all of you. The Old Man will be anxious to see you!"

He herded us through the gate and toward the back office. As we went, I seized the opportunity to question him a little.

"Is all well here?" I asked.

"As well as could be expected in the circumstances," he replied, not committing himself.

"What do you mean?" I demanded.

"Oh, the war and one thing and another," he answered.

I decided he'd little to say at this time, at least on the one matter that interested me. I switched the topic.

"We've the same quarters?" I asked.

"I wouldn't dare let 'em go." He grinned.

We were at the door then, and he flung it open.

"Here's company, Mr. Astor!" he cried.

The heavy-set man behind the desk looked up as we filed in, and I think it was a moment before he recognized any of us. Then in an instant he was on his feet. He had put on a good deal of weight and had aged considerably since I had last seen him. But the same square-faced, beaming German smile of welcome lighted his eyes. He held out his hands to us.

"Ach, gentlemen, gentlemen. Welcome to home!" he cried. "Come in! Come in! And, Will, do close the door. *Gott sei danke,* I see you again! Worried have I been that no word comes! How good is it to see you! Good news you have I hope to tell?"

I glanced at Stuart. He merely nodded.

"Not all of the best, sir, I am afraid," I replied. "Though things seemed better when we left."

"So?" he said. "So? Sit down! Sit down, then, all of you, and you, Rory, *ach,* and, Robert, tell me all it is you have to say!"

There is no need to dwell at length on the details of that interview. Since I appeared to have been tacitly elected spokesman, I told him as briefly as I could all that had happened from the time we had left New York; of our rounding the Horn, of our differences with Captain Thorn, of our arrival at the mouth of the Columbia, the loss of the *Tonquin,* our struggle overland to safety and of our winter on the river, of Thompson's visit and the arrival of the *Beaver,* of the expeditions to establish posts at Spokane and the Big Woody, and of the post at Oakanagan, of our terrible journey eastward from the Columbia.

He listened to me without interruption, and I paused only occasionally for confirmation from Stuart or the others, yet it was late when I had finished. When I had fallen silent, he sat drumming thoughtfully upon his desk, his lips pursed, his eyes thoughtful.

"Ach!" he said finally, and his face was somber. "Much you have passed through, ya! And much there has happened! Of the war you did not know, more is the pity, until it was a year gone! You have not heard then, gentlemen, that even now an expedition goes from London, in a ship of war, to seize the colony."

He sighed and shook himself almost hopelessly.

"Yet what can I do? I have appealed to the government for aid, for forces, but these they have not seen fit to give me. What of the money I have spent? Of the lives I have wasted? Are all of these for nothings? I do not like to think so! I will not think so. Once a dream I had of separate nations on that coast, with Astor, maybe, king! Now I do not want that. All that now I hope for is that one day, when the world regains its sanity, that what we have done—the money we have spent and the blood and sweat and sorrow that into this we have put— will bear its peaceful, proper fruit. One day, I hope it, this America of ours will be one land from sea to sea."

"You don't have to worry about that, sir," I said soberly. "It is so now, and what nature has put together no man or group of men can tear apart!"

He shook himself again and brought his eyes back to me, focusing as from a great distance.

"True what you say," he said. "I anyway would know it, the German butcher's boy!"

Once more he shook his head, and then looked up abruptly, seeming to realize that it was growing late.

"But this is not the time! You have not been yet home?"

"Not yet, sir," I replied. "We came directly here."

"Ach," he exclaimed. "And I have kept you! Then go. Go! And let these others quarters find. Eat and rest and play a little! Then tomorrow we meet, eh? You, Rory, and Robert, you too! In the morning, eh, and everything we discuss!"

I rose, and the others rose with me. Stuart fetched out the rawhide pouch he carried and put it on the desk.

"You'll find letters and despatches in there from the other partners," he said. "O'Rourke has given a thorough account, but you might like to study those between now and morning."

Mr. Astor nodded.

"Ya!" he said. "Ya! These I read tonight."

On the street outside it seemed to me that Stuart flushed a little.

"If you don't mind," he said, "I think the folks I stayed with when I was here before would want me to stay with them again. They—ah—live in Brooklyn."

"That's a long way off," I said. "You're welcome to stay with us."

"No, no!" he said hastily. "I think I'll go over, if you don't mind. I have my reasons!"

I had no idea then why he was so anxious to be off, for it was only later that I met the lady, but I did not urge him, since apparently his mind was made up. I looked at Sanders.

" 'Twas in my mind to offer the hospitality of the house," I said. "These others have no quarters of their own as yet."

My roommate nodded.

"Fine, fine!" he assured me. "Suppose you take 'em there, and I'll see you all later. Jonathan's out of town."

"You're not coming?" I cried.

"Why—uh, no," he replied. "You see, I didn't know you'd be here. I have an appointment."

"Tut, tut!" I grinned. *"Et tu Brute?"*

I could see him flush.

"I'll see you all later," he said again hastily, and pelted off.

"You'd think we were lepers or something." I grinned. "Well, come along At least our latchstring is out."

I led the way to the rooms There the old, familiar musty smell greeted my nostrils and I knew that I was fairly home at last.

"Make yourselves at home, gentlemen," I said. "There's room enough here for all!"

I found a bottle of brandy and poured a drink around, which I noticed that Shea and Charbonneau downed quickly and rose to stand first on one foot and then the other, not quite knowing how to leave us, but obviously anxious to do so. Since it was evident that they had made their own plans, we admonished them to caution and sent them on their way, clattering down the stairs like a pair of schoolboys released for the summer.

When they were gone and only the three of us remained, Westlake glanced at me and Fraser.

"Well, gentlemen," he said, "there's no time like the present."

"Oh!" said Fraser, grinning into his glass. "I'd scarcely say it was necessary. If you gentlemen are ready to call it quits, I'm willing enough to save us all embarrassment. But if you insist on all the agony, I can do no more. I'll be as easy with you as I can."

"Be damned to you, Fraser!" Westlake retorted. "How about it, Rory?"

I stared at the pair of them, a little startled.

"What's this?" I demanded. "Do you mean to call upon her in a body and give her her choice?"

"How else would we do it?" demanded Fraser. "Is one of us to have first chance and perhaps walk off with the prize? Not for me! We all go together or we don't go at all!"

"Well, if you insist upon it then," I retorted doubtfully. "But I must say 'twill give me pain to see you both humiliated."

At that they both laughed, and after a brief brush and a look in the mirror we set out, all three together, for the big house in Greenwich Street.

It was only a little after sundown as we approached, and the shadows of the shrubs and trees upon the lawn and across the white pathways were dark already. Inside we could see the warm glow of lights. As we mounted the steps it seemed to me that my two companions had a slight attack of diffidence.

"You knock," said Westlake. "You're better acquainted."

"Is that an admission?" I grinned, yet I admit to a sense of reluctance as I turned and lifted the polished knocker and beat a tattoo upon the door. Inside the great hallway we could hear echoes ring hollowly, and then presently there came the sound of light, quick footsteps. In the next instant the door swung open, letting the light inside stream out upon us, and a girl stood before us—a slim girl, well-proportioned, slender of thigh, if the way the dress clung meant anything, and full of breast under the stuff of her bodice. I saw level brown eyes that flew wide at sight of us, and coppery brown hair; a bridge of freckles across the nose above a curving mouth that was quick to smile.

At sight of us she gasped and caught at the doorframe, but it was to me she spoke and to me she came.

"Rory!" she cried. "Oh, Rory! Oh, my dear! You're back. You've come back!"

Before I could answer she was in my arms, and all at once I knew that all along it was this I had wanted. I knew now why I had been reluctant; why I had had such trouble calling up the one and forgetting the other. I hadn't known it before, but all the time she had been there, close-locked in my heart.

"Deborah." I cried. And then again: "Deborah."

Without further thought for my companions I kissed her.

It was an instant before I realized that we were not alone. Indeed it was Westlake then who cleared his throat and reminded me that they were present. We broke apart, blushing violently, and I caught her hand in mine as I turned.

"Deborah, sweet!" I said. "I think you know these gentlemen. Mr.

Westlake, Mr. Fraser. They've come with me all the way from the Columbia. 'Twas only this afternoon we arrived."

She smiled, I think as bewildered as I at the suddenness of it all, but yet never once losing her graciousness.

"Of course," she responded, holding out her hand. "Welcome back, gentlemen! And thank you for bringing Rory home to me safe and sound, even if he is a little thin."

My companions bowed and seemed amused at something; naturally I knew well enough what, and a panic seized me lest this new love that had come upon me so suddenly be spoiled. Yet there was nothing I could say or do to send them away. Deborah was already inviting them in and they were accepting. She stood a little aside to let them enter, at the same time holding tightly to my arm.

In the familiar hallway we turned aside into the vast drawing room with its graceful fireplace, decorously laid now with white birch logs that would not feel the touch of flame until the summer was ended.

"Won't you sit down, gentlemen?" Deborah asked. "Why didn't you let us know you were coming? We could have planned for it. If you meant it for a surprise, it is a wonderful one—the most wonderful one, in fact."

She smiled at me as she said that.

"We came straight here," I explained. "There wasn't time to send word ahead."

Westlake turned about in front of the fireplace and smiled at her, then glanced at me.

"Ahem!" He cleared his throat. "Excuse me, Rory, is this—is this Mistress Drake?"

I think I must have turned a fiery red.

"Forgive me," I cried, snatching at the first excuse I could imagine. "Of course! You have forgotten! Gentlemen, Mr. Westlake, Mr. Fraser—'tis my honor to present Mistress Drake."

Fraser put his hand over his mouth and bowed low, but I could see from his eyes that he was all but bursting with laughter, while Westlake, in his turn, inclined his head gravely.

"Mistress Drake!" he said quite properly, then turned and leaned his forehead on his arm upon the mantelpiece.

Deborah looked suspicious. She would be far quicker, I knew, to suspect what might be wrong.

"What's the matter?" she asked.

"He has an old wound," I explained shortly. "He was gored by a buffalo bull on the plains and sometimes it pains him."

"Oh, poor man!" she said, and I was not sure but what there was a certain dryness in her tone.

Westlake turned and bowed again, and at the expression in his eyes I scarcely knew whether to laugh or be sorry.

"Ma'am," he said, "I hope you will forgive us. We've come a long way—a long, long way."

Deborah looked at him.

"Of course," she said again. "I—I think I understand."

She looked from him to Fraser and then up at me again.

"I think I understand," she repeated solemnly, and I had a dreadful feeling that she really did.

But she gave no further hint of it. Nor did she give me time to be embarrassed.

"Sit down, do, please," she said. "I'll go tell Cassius to fetch us tea, and you can tell me all about it."

Apparently it occurred to her that she might do better than ring. She excused herself and left us momentarily to confer with the Negro in the pantry, and all the while she was gone my two companions grimaced at me wisely. Indeed I wondered that she did not catch them at it when she returned.

We had our visit and our tea while I squirmed upon the couch beside her and wondered how long these two would prolong my agony. Heartily I wished them gone, and that I had never seen either of them before. But the amenities must be observed, and each of them told long-winded tales of our adventures—tales, I might add, that did not put me in the best light possible. It was only when at last they had drained the cold tea from their cups and she herself was apparently becoming impatient that Westlake ventured to approach the point. With apparent nonchalance he made inquiry.

"And your sister, ma'am?" he said. "Mistress Valerie. I trust she is well."

"Oh, yes indeed, thank you," Deborah assured him. "In fact she was never better."

"I'm sorry we don't see her about," Fraser put in. "Is she away visiting, perhaps?"

"Oh, no." Deborah smiled sweetly. "No, as a matter of fact she's upstairs now, but she is indisposed."

Westlake looked up, sharply suspicious.

"I thought you said——"

"Oh, I did," she interrupted.

"But if she's indisposed," Fraser put in.

"Perhaps there is something we can do—something we can get," Westlake suggested. "An ice, perhaps? A bottle of smelling salts? Fraser, suppose you run out——"

"Oh, no," Deborah interrupted him. "That isn't necessary, Mr. Fraser. There's really nothing."

She shot a mischievous glance at me.

"You see," she said, "she's just been brought to bed with her third. He arrived this morning, a fine boy!"

"Uh?" gulped Fraser.

"Her third?" said Westlake foolishly.

I could only choke.

For just the right space of an instant Deborah let me savor her triumph. Then she went on to the explanation.

"Yes," she said. "This is her third. You see Valerie married Dick Goodwin within a month after the *Tonquin* was gone. Last year she had twin girls, and now she has a boy!"

I was not sure, but it seemed to me there was an almost triumphant note in the way she said it. But I must say I scarcely cared.

At the expressions on their faces I all but burst out laughing in my own turn.

"Ah!" said Fraser at length. "I—uh—I guess congratulations are in order. I hope you'll convey 'em for me."

"Uh, yes, and for me," added Westlake brightly.

"You may be sure I will, gentlemen." She smiled.

I rose to my feet.

"I think, perhaps, we have disturbed the household enough for one evening," I said.

The other two were on their feet before the words were out of my mouth.

"Oh, yes!" said Westlake. "Oh, yes, I must report in at the Navy Yard."

IV. DEBORAH

WE TOOK up our hats and said good-by, passing out into the warm summer darkness, and turned down Greenwich toward the Bull's Head Tavern. None of us spoke until we had reached a table in the back corner and the waiter had set three mugs of good cold ale before us.

Fraser heaved a sigh.

"Well!" he said, and stared at me almost belligerently.

"Come off it!" said Westlake disconsolately. "He's better off than we are."

"Aye," I agreed, for I most certainly did not share their mood. "I'd be better off than either of you, even had things turned out differently for you!"

Neither of them had any answer to make to that, but both sat staring glumly at their ale pots.

"Come, come, gentlemen!" I said. "The fact of the matter is we don't any of us seem to know when we're well off. Ever since I came to New York I have watched Deborah growing, never knowing, never appreciating that there was the real prize! I could accept your money on a technicality, for after all I think you will agree that I have won a Mistress Drake! But that would be a quibble we all know! Let's think no more of it! I give you Mr. and Mrs. Goodwin!"

To that we drank and said no more of the matter. I took upon me the role of host and stood them a stout dinner of roast beef and potatoes, nicely browned, lobsters, and ale, so that I think they were already beginning to feel better when we drifted out into the street once more. All the while I was burning with impatience.

"Well, gentlemen?" I said.

Fraser shrugged. Westlake smiled.

"I was not exactly lying," he said, "when I told Mistress Deborah I must report to the Navy Yard. My time's no longer my own, and in the circumstances, I suppose, the sooner it is done the better. If 'tis the same with you, Rory, I think I'll take the opportunity."

I glanced at Fraser.

"There's naught to keep me here now." He grinned a little ruefully. "I'm for Montreal in the morning. I don't know if they'll be of a mind to use me, but I must make the offer."

"How will you get there?" I asked.

He chuckled in the darkness.

"I'll find a way," he assured me. "And I can't be burdened with a drunken Indian. I've a notion you've something on your own mind, so we'll just go along our way and you go yours. We'll see you at your own quarters in the morning before we say good-by."

They thumped me cheerfully on the shoulder, and I was glad to see that they were themselves again.

"Good night!" they said, and went off arm in arm to locate Shea and Charbonneau.

For my part I turned about and all but ran back in the direction of Greenwich Street.

In the warm, sweet-scented summer dark I came again to the wide, white gravel walk that wound up between the darkened lawns to the great white house that now loomed silent and bulky in the moonlight. There were yellow lights in the windows, and it seemed to me my heart raced faster than my feet as my heels crunched on the pathway. As I hurried up them, the steps were wide and white and welcoming, and the knocker seemed to gleam invitingly in the mellow beams. I reached out my hand to grasp it and to knock once more, when a movement in the shadow to my left caught my eye. A slim figure in white detached itself from one of the tall pillars and moved toward me.

"Rory?" a voice whispered. "Rory! You did come back!"

In the next instant she was in my arms with her head on my breast and her hair sweet and fragrant in my nostrils.

"Oh, Rory, I've been waiting such a long, long time!"

"You'll have to wait no more," I said. "For I've come home to stay! My Deborah! My own!"

ACKNOWLEDGMENTS

"What a devil of a profession! But it has its charms."
                                                    Voltaire.

I have told my tale, and I would have a brief word of all that it involved and of those that helped me. Of the reams of paper and the quarts of ink, of the miles of typewriter ribbon and the quantities of carbon, of secretaries worn out and midnight oil burned, of the three hundred thousand words discarded, let us say no more. No man writes a book alone. He has a hundred, a thousand collaborators, from the anonymous diarist from whom he obtains his impressions of a certain scene to the boy who pushes the library cart that carries away the books he has used. Each one of these plays his part in the making of the story, however small a part it may be. And to each I owe my heartfelt thanks.

Many, of course, whose services were anonymous or whose names I did not know, will remain unknown. Yet their assistance is not to be belittled. They have my grateful appreciation and thanks. Specifically to be mentioned are my wife, Virginia L. Jennings, for her constant help and collaboration; Howard Rowe and the staff of the Santa Barbara Public Library, not only for their assistance in finding material in their own collection, but in obtaining material from other sources; Mrs. E. Bancroft and Mr. Brezee, particularly, and all the staff of the Bancroft Library, of the University of California, in general, for their generous and unstinting aid in locating worth-while matter in the Bancroft Collections and for having microfilmed material which would not otherwise have been available except at the library; Sylvester Vigilante of the New York Public Library and his assistants for like services, and all my anonymous friends at the Library of Congress. I wish to thank likewise all the booksellers and dealers who have helped me in my search for material; Roger and Zella Boutell, of the Tecolote Bookshop, in Santa Barbara, California; Mr. Parke P. Jones, of Lowdermilk & Co., of Washington—incidentally one of the best of the rare book-dealers, in case you are interested; the staffs of Dawson's, in Los Angeles, and the Book Den, in Santa Barbara, to say nothing of various other bookdealers and retailers elsewhere in the country who have helped. Certainly not to be omitted in any such catalogue of gratitude are those who have done the colossal task of preparing the final manuscript.

To each and every one I am truly grateful.

JOHN JENNINGS